STAIRWAY TO AN EMPTY ROOM

Monica Marshall's sister Biddy has been murdered by
her husband. Biddy has a daughter, Winifred, and with
the husband on death row, Monica agrees to take charge
of her. Winifred is anxious to leave the house where she
has been living with Biddy. The house and the woman
who runs it seem so unpleasant to Monica. But nothing
prepares her for Stevens. He is managing a mountain
retreat where Monica takes her new charge for a
getaway—she hates him immediately. Strangely enough,
Winifred recognizes the couple in another cabin. Soon
Monica realizes that there is something very strange
going on here. Her brakes fail… later she almost drowns
in the lake. And Stevens is becoming very protective of
young Winifred. What do all these people have to do with
Biddy's death, and what is *really* going on here?...

TERROR LURKS IN DARKNESS

Kitty has the fright of her life one night when she takes
what she is told is a short cut and ends up on a dead end
street in the rain. And to make matters worse, there is a
savage dog outside her car, causing her to wreck the front
end trying to avoid it. Fortunately, the owner of the dog
appears and calms the dog, then drives her home. But
imagine Kitty's shock when she finds out that Sunny, the
woman who told her about the short cut, is found dead
later that night on the same road, her throat savaged. Of
course, everyone hated Sunny, but that doesn't explain
her strange death. And now Kitty's roommate, Ardis, has
gone missing … and two of her friends are asking her to
lie about what she knows. No wonder inspector Doyle
doesn't believe her story—she has no idea what to believe
herself!

Stairway to an Empty Room
Terror Lurks in Darkness

Two Novels by
Dolores Hitchens

Introduction by Nicholas Litchfield

WITHDRAWN

STARK
HOUSE

Stark House Press • Eureka California

STAIRWAY TO AN EMPTY ROOM / TERROR LURKS IN DARKNESS

Published by Stark House Press
1315 H Street
Eureka, CA 95501, USA
griffinskye3@sbcglobal.net
www.starkhousepress.com

STAIRWAY TO AN EMPTY ROOM
Originally published by Doubleday & Company, Inc., New York, and
copyright © 1951 by Dolores B. Hitchens. Reprinted in paperback by Dell
Books, New York, 1953.

TERROR LURKS IN DARKNESS
Originally published by Doubleday and Company, Inc., New York, and
copyright © 1953 by Dolores B. Hitchens. Reprinted in digest paperback
by Mercury Publications Inc., New York, 1955.

Reprinted by permission of the Dolores Hitchens estate. All rights
reserved under International and Pan-American Copyright Conventions.

"Dolores Hitchens's Stunning Excursions into Terror"
copyright © 2019 by Nicholas Litchfield.

ISBN-13: 978-1-944520-79-3

Book design by Mark Shepard, shepgraphics.com
Cover art by JT Lindroos
Proofreading by Bill Kelly

First Stark House Press Edition: October 2019

Dolores Hitchens's Stunning Excursions into Terror
by Nicholas Litchfield

Throughout the 1950s and 60s, prolific American novelist and playwright Dolores Hitchens was ranked as one of the nation's leading mystery writers. The noted book critic Anthony Boucher often sang her praises in his long-running column in *The New York Times*, admiring her strong emphasis on human character and motivation. Respected crime writer and editor Bill Pronzini singled out her novel *Sleep With Slander* as "one of the best private eye novels written by a woman—and one of the best written by anybody." Marcel Berlins of *The Times* (London) wrote that she has "a way with words that puts her near the top of the genre" and believes she is as good a hard-boiled storyteller as any man in the Forties and Fifties.

Born Julia Clara Catherine Dolores Robbins in San Antonio, Texas, in 1907, she took her stepfather's surname after relocating to California as a teenager and then changed her surname a couple more times due to marriage. She began her career as a hospital nurse, and then a teacher, before becoming a successful professional writer, and from 1938 until her death in 1973, she published forty books, utilizing three pseudonyms (D. B. Olsen, Dolan Birkley and Noel Burke) as well as her own name.

Among her most successful novels were *The Watcher*, which was adapted for the television series *Thriller* in 1960, and *Fool's Gold*, which Jean-Luc Godard made into the influential French New Wave classic film *Band of Outsiders* in 1964. Other notable successes included her five-book series featuring the special agents of a railroad's Los Angeles division, which she collaborated on with her second husband, Hubert Allen "Bert" Hitchens, who was a railroad investigating officer. The first book in the series, *F.O.B. Murder*, published by Doubleday in 1955, won many mentions among lists of the year's best, including the *New*

York Times' "Best Ten." Lauding it as a uniquely fascinating story of railroad detection, Boucher remarked: "On every level this is as good as one can possibly ask."

Last year, Stark House Press reprinted the third book in that series, *End of the Line*, as a mass-market Black Gat Books edition, and here, contained in this two-in-one volume, is a pair of standalone, solo efforts that earned Hitchens high praise when they were first published as Crime Club selections by Doubleday in the early Fifties.

The first, *Stairway to an Empty Room*, is a tautly written suspense novel that *The Los Angeles Times*, the *Boston Globe*, the *San Francisco Chronicle*, and numerous other national newspapers regarded as an especially gripping yarn. First published in 1951, it is about an independent, 29-year-old New York career woman, Monica Marshall, who goes to Los Angeles to take custody of her murdered sister's troubled nine-year-old daughter, Winifred. The child's father, Jerry, is facing the death penalty for the murder of his wife, but Winifred keeps protesting, "Daddy didn't do it."

During a short vacation to a secluded Californian mountain resort, before their move to New York, Winifred claims to recognize some shady-looking characters, but Monica, who is increasingly displeased by the girl's disposition, dismisses these observations as a further instance of Winifred "inventing scarecrows, ghosts, spies." Then, a series of suspicious "accidents," in which Monica is injured and the girl almost drowns, leads Monica to suspect that the child is not making things up and they are both in imminent danger. Along with her changing attitude toward Winifred comes the conviction that her brother-in-law may not be guilty, after all.

One of Hitchens's chief strengths as a writer is her particular focus on character development. Through realistic dialogue, abundant character observations, and an orderly progression of natural interactions between Monica, the fastidious, judgmental, "inexperienced old maid aunt" who struggles to adjust to being a suitable guardian, and Winifred, the solemn, unfriendly, ill-mannered, "sassy" child, Hitchens adds layers of sincerity to the main characters and a believability to their situation. Much like in the second tale in this collection, it is a very tense, unsettling story, full of drama and excitement and atmospheric writing.

In fact, one of the great joys of Hitchens's prose is her keen, visual flair. The *St. Louis Post-Dispatch* referred to *Stairway to an Empty Room* as "slick as celluloid" and "destined for Hollywood." While the novel may not have gotten the expected Hollywood treatment, clearly there is a wonderful cinematic quality to the writing, and the interesting settings and cleverly constructed plot would have ensured it translated well to the big screen. The same could be said of *Terror Lurks in Darkness,* another dark, creepy tale with intense, vivid scenes that linger in the memory.

The opening pages of that story, which feel like something out of a horror movie, dispatch the reader to an out-of-the-way, rutted road in the West Los Angeles hills on a grim, wet night. There, motorist Kitty Quist, who has taken a wrong turn, suddenly witnesses a savage, territorial brute of a dog materialize out of the night like "a yellow phantom filling the middle of the road." After she stops to avoid running it over, the dog proceeds to attack the car, snapping at the windows and climbing onto the hood, and eventually causing the shaken driver to reverse into a boulder, smashing the radiator and twisting the rear axle. Thus, Kitty finds herself cowering in fright in the wrecked vehicle in the rainy dark, her car metaphorically "bleeding to death" and "with a ferocious animal waiting for her to emerge from the shelter of the car."

Similarly, there is a thrilling, out-of-control car scene in *Stairway to an Empty Room*, in which the brakes on Monica's Buick stop working and she finds herself hurtling, perilously, down the winding mountain road in helpless terror. It is one of those breathtaking, dramatic moments that highlight Hitchens's expertise in nimbly setting up a genuinely frightening scenario and then suddenly plunging the reader straight into adrenaline-charged fear.

In *Terror Lurks in Darkness*, Hitchens builds tension from the onset with her depiction of the eerie, haunting landscape, and the introduction of the savage beast that panics Kitty into making a reckless mistake. Then the author escalates the drama, creating an "odd chill under your skin," by introducing a second fierce dog to the scene while the female protagonist is trying to calm down and fathom a way out of her predicament. The creepy, stylishly written opening intrigues and unnerves and lets the reader know early on they are in for a menacing ride.

What follows is a murky tale about the murder of Sunny Walling, the woman who had recommended to Kitty an alternate, quicker route home along this secluded, potholed lane and whose mangled body was discovered in the bushes the following day, at almost the exact same spot where Kitty had crashed her car. Regarded by her close female acquaintances as a loose, mischievous person with an "emptiness of soul" who "enraged a lot of women" because of the way she flaunted her power over men, we learn that Sunny is the type to attract enemies. Evidently, dangerous ones. The brutality behind her death and her familiarity with the murder site indicate that this was the work of "a violent and brutal killer" whom Sunny must have arranged to meet. The comprehension that the discovery of Sunny's body on this sinister stretch of road is no coincidence leads Kitty to wonder if perhaps Sunny had an ulterior motive in recommending this short-cut to her.

It is a testament to Hitchens's capacity for meticulous plotting and her ability to conceive suspenseful situations and realistic characters and backdrops that *Terror Lurks in Darkness* continually holds the reader's attention. Unpredictable and unnerving, this stunning excursion into terror, enlivened by forbidding landscapes and killer hounds, never runs out of steam or takes a wrong turn. As with her edge-of-the-chair thriller, *Stairway to an Empty Room*, she ably demonstrates why she earned her place as one of the nation's most admired mystery writers.

—June 2019
Rochester, NY

Nicholas Litchfield is the founding editor of the literary magazine *Lowestoft Chronicle*, author of the suspense novel *Swampjack Virus*, and editor of nine literary anthologies. He has worked in various countries as a tabloid journalist, librarian, and media researcher. He writes regularly for the *Colorado Review*, and his weekly book reviews for the *Lancashire Post* are syndicated to twenty newspapers across the UK.

Stairway to an Empty Room
by Dolores Hitchens

1

The street had a peculiar arrested quietness, as though everyone on it had suddenly died. The old-fashioned houses behind their palm trees and thatches of lantana looked gray, dusty, and remote under the dull twilight. The porch toward which Monica Marshall walked held a cavernous silence in which her steps echoed; she stopped abruptly by the door and looked at the black button on the wall. "If I touch that button," she told herself, "it means that I am taking over the responsibility of the child. I won't be free any more. I'll have Biddy's little girl." And because the sudden memory of Biddy and the manner of Biddy's dying were unendurable and terrifying, she touched the button quickly, without further thought.

A woman opened the inner door and looked out through the screen. She was middle-aged, with fine black eyes that in her youth must have been soft and lovely but were now as hard as jet. "Yes? What do you want?"

"Mrs. Lannon? I'm Monica Marshall. I've come for the child."

The woman made an animal-like sound of indecision deep in her throat. Then she touched the latch of the screen grudgingly. "I guess you better come in. She's asleep. You'll have to wait."

"I haven't time to wait," Monica said. "I'll take her now."

The hard black eyes flickered. "I didn't have no notice nor nothing. Her clothes ain't packed. They ain't even clean."

"Very well, I'll take them just as they are."

The woman frowned, grumbling: "I don't see why she can't stay here."

Monica didn't answer. She was looking at the room: big, high-ceilinged, full of oak furniture with a lot of claw feet and dusty red velvet. The mantel held a row of framed portraits. There was an overgrown potted fern, mottled by some sort of plant disease, in the bay window that faced the street. The lace curtains hung moveless in the humid warmth. There was no breath of fresh air in this room at the end of a summer's day; no open windows, not even a fan. The place was somehow like a prison.

"You got the court order?" Mrs. Lannon asked cunningly.

Monica opened her purse and took out the papers signed by the judge.

"Yeah, but she's familiar here," the woman argued. "You oughtn't to take her away, leastways not till after the—the—" She stopped there; the black eyes smirked and grew knowing, studying Monica's face. "The *thing*."

"I'll take her today. Now. At once." Monica kept her tone firm, though it was hard not to show the inward confusion, the grief, and the near fear of this obnoxious woman with the flint-like stare.

The woman shrugged and turned to lead the way down a hall. She stopped before a door, opened it to peep in, then threw it wide. "Well, she ain't asleep after all! Bright as a daisy! You got a smile for Mama Ida?"

The little girl was sitting very straight in the middle of the bed. She wore a white cotton slip which was too tight and too short and a pair of blue socks which were dirty. Her face was round, solemn, unsmiling; she did not smile at the black-eyed woman. "I'm not asleep because it's too hot," she said.

"You're going to get dressed and go away, and Mama Ida will cry."

"I don't care," said the child matter-of-factly.

In spite of her own feeling of distaste for the woman, Monica was disturbed. The child's manner was cold and dismissing; and she'd planned the meeting quite differently. Tears, perhaps. Emotion of some sort.

The little girl said, "Shall I scrape the egg off my dress, or can I have a clean one like you said?"

Monica stepped forward. "Winifred— "

The solemn face turned toward her; after a moment the little girl said, "Yes?"

"Aren't you going to say hello?"

The child seemed to study the remark; then she said carefully, "Hello, Aunt Monica."

Monica looked about for some way to open the friendship: a favor she might do. "Shall I help you put on your shoes?"

The little girl tucked her toes under her buttocks. "No, thank you."

"I could brush your hair."

Winifred fingered the fuzzy, unkempt pigtails. "Would you?" She crawled toward the edge of the bed, her big eyes wary. "I'd like it. My head itches."

Monica picked up the brush off the dresser. She rolled the rubber bands from the ends and loosened the braids—Winifred's hair was fine and soft, the color Biddy's had been, a light canary-yellow. When the braids were well brushed out, Mrs. Lannon interrupted her packing to suggest that Winifred should wash up a bit.

The bathroom door slammed across the hall. Monica asked, "Does she know what's going to happen to her father?"

"No, no, of course she don't!" Mrs. Lannon answered—too quickly, too smoothly. The black eyes were opaque as a lizard's.

"You haven't told her?" Monica insisted.

"I wouldn't do that! It was bad enough, the thing that was done to her mother, and going to the funeral and all—"

Monica made an impatient gesture. "You took Winifred to the funeral?"

Mrs. Lannon's mouth became pinched and defensive. "It was fittin'. Of course we didn't get to look in on the body, on account of the face. You know. It was a ball-point hammer he used."

Monica turned away. She knew the sickness must show. She put out a hand, touched the iron bedstead—it was soiled with some kind of grease that came off on her palm. "I wish she hadn't gone."

"They found the body on the stairs," Mrs. Lannon went on, relishing her words. "All beaten in. The skull like jelly and the brains—you know."

"Please stop," said Monica from a stiff throat.

"Of course. I forgot. She was your sister. Younger than you?"

"Three years."

"They roomed here with me when they first came to Los Angeles. Did you know that? I got well acquainted with both of them. He wasn't educated as good as her. You could see that. And from the South—poor white trash. And he had a temper."

"Did you ever know him to—to strike her?" Monica asked, hating to ask it.

"No, can't say I did. He cussed bad when he got riled. She was a cute little thing. Did she marry him in the East?"

"Yes," said Monica. "In New York. In my apartment there."

"Oh, you saw it, then."

The memory was unexpectedly vivid: Biddy in the short wartime white dress, her silver-yellow hair like a cloud under the thin white veil. With eyes like stars. And Jerry—he hadn't shown the temper then; he'd seemed gentle and considerate, indulging the silly whims of his silly little wife. "I was there. I remember my sister—the way I want to remember her."

"Sure," said Mrs. Lannon with the suggestion of a smirk.

"She had a beautiful bouquet of orchids and white carnations. I found it, after a week, in the back of a closet." Into Monica's mind swept the remembered odor of the dead flowers. Funny, that Biddy hadn't left them out to be put into water....

Winifred came back from the bathroom, had her hair braided and pinned up, was helped into a silk dress, blue, with two stains that looked like coffee just above the belt. Mrs. Lannon buckled on the patent-leather shoes. Then a coat was brought out. It needed brushing, but no brush seemed available. "You want the hat?" Mrs. Lannon asked.

"I put the hat in the trash," Winifred said coldly.

"It was an old one, anyway," Mrs. Lannon apologized to Monica. Her eyes communicated the thought: She's a brat. *You'll be sorry.* "Good-by, chick. Come back and see me. I'll miss you." She bent and kissed the child; Winifred turned a cheek.

On the walk outside Winifred rubbed the cheek hard with the back of her hand. Monica pretended not to notice; it seemed ingratitude toward the woman who had taken the child in and sheltered her during the trial and conviction of Jerry Huffman.

But Winifred was looking at Monica, a sidewise glance. "I don't like her. She *knows* things."

Monica reminded herself: she must not seem to be concealing a secret. Her manner must be easy and natural. When the certain day, the certain hour came, there must be no sign. It should be a day like any other day, with things to keep Winifred occupied and happy, and there must be no cloud, no incident, for Winifred to look back on in years to come, and say: *That* was when my father died. *That* day they took his life because he killed my mother. It was at this moment that the idea came back to Monica, that it would be better if they were to get out of the city.

Winifred's picture had been in the papers. There must be people who would recognize her, a little girl with a solemn, unfriendly face, tight pigtails, defiant eyes. Well, fortunately there was the money: not much, but some. She'd sold the furniture in New York, subleased the apartment, drawn out her bank account. "First of all," she told herself, "in the morning I'll get her some different clothes."

The bus left them off near the small Wilshire Boulevard Hotel, and they took the elevator to Monica's room.

Monica put the cheap suitcase on a chair and opened it. The packed clothes gave off an odor. From the bed where she sat watching, Winifred said suddenly, "She made me wear the hat the day we went to see a trial. They took pictures."

Monica, half bent over, felt shock run through her, unbelief; she was frozen, her voice gone.

"That's why I threw the hat away," said Winifred. "There was a picture in the paper, and it wasn't pretty. It was awful."

Monica found herself turning, straightening. Something hot was beating in her throat. "Who took you there?"

"Mrs. Lannon. She told me not to blink when the lights went off in my face. It was just going to be like the Fourth of July," she said.

"Did you see—anyone—there?"

"I saw Daddy. She said it wasn't, but it was. He was at a table with some other men. There were papers on the table. Up in front was a man in a big box. He had whiskers. Daddy didn't look at me."

The judge, behind his podium. Monica found her wits returning; she wanted to believe, still, in Mrs. Lannon. "Well, perhaps your daddy was busy. He was busy with the other men about some business."

There was silence in the room. She stole a glance at Winifred, found the child regarding her with a curiously reflective stare. "Shall we go to dinner? What would you like?"

"Chicken salad with toast," said Winifred promptly.

Monica went to the small stand in the corner of the room to wash her hands. "What did you have mostly at home?" she asked, making conversation. "What did your mama like to fix?"

There was a curious stillness from the child on the bed.

"Don't you remember?" Monica asked, half-joking.

Winifred's glance roved the room. In a way somehow more definite than words would have been, she implied that they were not to talk about her mother. Monica felt oddly at a loss and rebuffed.

She dried her hands on a towel. "Put your coat back on, Winifred."

"It stinks."

"I'll get you a new coat when the stores open in the morning."

Winifred, reprovingly speechless, put the coat on slowly. They went downstairs and into the small café next door. The place was clean and quiet. Winifred ate with a good appetite, not choosily, but with an obvious lack of manners.

Watching her, studying the pale head bent above the plate, Monica thought: There's so much to do, and it has to be done slowly and carefully. The child needs sympathy, training; needs time spent on her. And I'm an old maid. I'm picky about the smelly clothes, I don't like the way she eats, I think she's sassy. I'm twenty-nine, a commercial artist wrapped up in her work, long given over to the single life, the cool narrow bed, the solitary chop shared with the cat.... In the midst of wondering if Winifred might not, after all, have better been left with Mrs. Lannon, Monica was reminded of her old tom, Boozer, whom she had left in the care of the garage attendant.

"When we've finished eating," she told the little girl, "we'll go get my kitty. I brought him all the way from New York. I left him with a man in the garage."

Winifred appeared to think about the cat. "What color is he? Does he scratch? Does he have fleas?"

"He's yellow, he won't scratch unless you torment him, and he doesn't have fleas—usually."

Winifred looked interested. "Can I take him some chicken salad?"

"He won't eat lettuce."

"Oh well, I'll just give him chicken." With no self-consciousness, Winifred dug into the pockets of the coat until she produced a wrinkled sheet of paper. This she spread out beside her salad bowl, and proceeded to spear bits of chicken out upon it.

They found Boozer asleep in the lap of the light-colored Negro in coveralls. The Negro grinned when he saw Monica. "You know what, Miss Marshall?" He stole a cautious glance behind him, as if careful of being overheard. "I was having a bite to eat, and I opened a can of beer. Just going to wet my whistle. You know what your cat done?"

"Yes, I know. That's how he got his name—Boozer."

"He just went kind of crazy. He drank up most of that beer. I put it in a saucer for him. I never saw a cat drink beer like this one."

"He'll drink anything with alcohol in it till he bursts, if you let him." Monica tipped the Negro fifty cents, took Boozer, and went back up to the lobby. Here she picked up a number of resort bulletins from the rack beside the elevator. Then they rode up to the room.

Winifred put the paper down, spread it, and waited for the cat to eat. Boozer, being full of beer, gave it a slightly jaundiced look and jumped up on the bed. Winifred said slowly, "He isn't going to eat it."

Monica was in the single easy chair by the window, glancing through the resort folders under the light of a reading lamp. "Give him time. He's not hungry yet."

"He doesn't like it 'cause it's me—it's my salad," Winifred said with a sudden touch of hysteria. She picked the paper up and flung it at the wall. The greasy chicken clung for a moment to the pale-green plaster, making a splotch, then dropped to the floor. Winifred kicked the lump of stuff, scattering it, then jumped here and there, grinding the food into the rug.

Monica stood up. She felt stunned, baffled, helpless in the face of the child's rage. "Don't do that, Winifred!"

"He didn't eat it!" Winifred shrieked, kicking the bedpost.

"He isn't hungry!" Monica cried in exasperation, her own voice rising. "Leave him alone! He'll eat after a while!"

Winifred ran toward the bed, flung herself on it, and dug her toes into the mattress; with her hands she tore at the pillows and coverlet. This was more than a tantrum. Even Monica, who had been around children but seldom, recognized the excess, the frightful hysteria, the compelling grief. She went to the bed and tried to soothe the Winifred's heaving shoulders. "Don't be angry with poor Boozer. He'll make friends when he's not sleepy."

The child jerked up her head and looked back at Monica, a glance full of fury. "You think he did, but he didn't! He didn't do it!"

From his place of concealment under the chair, Boozer let out an indignant howl. "I know he didn't eat it," Monica said angrily. "Look, I want you to sit up and be quiet. I'll wash your face with a wet towel. I'll—I'll show you a picture of the place we're going tomorrow."

Winifred hiccuped in the middle of a sob. "We're—going away?"

"Yes. We'll go where there are places to swim, where you can be out of doors."

The sobs gradually subsided. Winifred allowed Monica to wash her, to brush the tangled hair out of her face, even to put a cheek against hers briefly. "What kind of place?"

"A resort. A place where people go to rest and have fun."

"Where? The beach?"

"No. Beaches are crowded now. The mountains will be nice and cool. We'll find a place beside a lake."

While Winifred, red-eyed but quiet, watched from the bed, Monica went to the chair and picked up the assorted folders. They went through them one by one. "There!" said Winifred suddenly. The folder cover had a picture of quiet water, a row of cabins under some tall pines, a spindling pier to which rowboats were tied. "Will we take Boozer? Will he go in a boat?"

Apparently no grudge was to be held against the cat for his lack of appetite. "He might. But cats are afraid of water, you know." Monica went to the telephone and called the lobby, and inquired as to the manner reservations were made. The clerk took her name and the name of the resort, Raboldi's, and promised to call back when he had information from the travel bureau.

In fifteen minutes he rang, and told Monica that the reservations were made. She could leave tomorrow. There would be a cabin at Raboldi's for her when she arrived. Yes, he understood that it was quiet: a small, out-of-the-way resort which catered mostly to fishermen. Fishermen, Monica thought—they'll be out in boats all day, their eyes glued to the water. They won't have time to stare at Winifred, even if the new clothes and a new way of doing her hair aren't enough concealment.

She got Winifred's pajamas from the suitcase. They were patched, and they had the unwashed smell, but Winifred put them on without complaint. Her mind seemed taken up with the idea of the trip. The storm over the cat's refusal of the food offering seemed safely past—a small tempest born of frayed nerves and a sense of neglect. I'll learn, Monica told herself, and so will Winifred. We'll get along; we'll be friends.

In the middle of the night Boozer awakened her by walking across her feet. She lay, half-asleep, listening to the faint traffic noises from Wilshire Boulevard, until another sound more close at hand caught her attention. Steps—very light ones—receded softly to silence.

Someone passed in the hall, she thought.

Only—it's funny I didn't hear them come; I just heard them go away. As if someone had been standing by the door....

Some altering in the even breathing, or some small movement, told her that Winifred was no longer asleep—that, like herself, the child lay awake listening to the sound in the hall.

2

When Boozer slept, he had a very Chinese look, Monica thought. His eyes took on an exceptional slant; the yellow face was enigmatic and menacing in repose. Like Fu Manchu, she decided. In the mirror, as she brushed her hair, she could see the bed, the sleeping child, the big cat. My family. People will think that Winifred belongs to me. Well, why not? It will stop questions. I can call myself Mrs. Marshall. I can call Winifred—I can call her Biddy. Biddy Marshall. I'll tell her it's a game.

The morning was crisp and sunny; not yet hot. Today she would buy a car and some clothes for the child, and she and Winifred would start for the mountains. It would be nice—as nice as things can very well be for an inexperienced old-maid aunt and a child whose father was due to be executed for the murder of his wife.

She cut off the bitter thought. Justice had been done. The man would get what was coming to him. It was time to forget.

Winifred yawned, rolled over, sat up. She looked pink and puzzled. She rubbed her face with the palms of her hands, then reached down to scratch inside the bosom of the pajamas. She surveyed the room as if taking it in for the first time. Then she looked at the door. "They listened to us," she said.

Monica had forgotten the incident in the middle of the night. "Who?" she asked blankly.

"Mrs. Lannon, I bet," said Winifred.

"Oh, nuts," Monica said; then she stopped. There mustn't be any more upsets like the one of yesterday. Better to humor the child, to pretend to agree. "Perhaps she was, at that. She didn't want you to go."

"She *knows* things," Winifred said darkly. The remark repeated itself from Monica's memory; Winifred had said the same thing before.

Monica decided to change the subject. "What would you like for breakfast? Oatmeal? French toast?"

"I want a waffle with bacon and eggs. And syrup. When I was home—" Winifred cut the speech off short, as if to think over what she meant to say. Her solemn face was full of concentration. "At home we had waffles—lots."

"Did Biddy make them?" Monica asked, thinking of the day ahead, of the things to be done.

Winifred's glance was sharp with suspicion. "Who's Biddy?"

"I forgot you wouldn't know. I always called your mother Biddy, even though her name was really Barbara. When we were small together, I used to think that her hair felt like little hen's feathers."

"Oh," said Winifred blankly. Obviously the idea that Monica and her mother had been children together was new and needed considering. She sat bent over, her arms hugging her knees, the patched pajamas straining across the narrow back, showing the ridge of her spine. Then she said, "Mama didn't make the waffles. She was always too sleepy. D— Daddy made them." With a movement that was almost surreptitious, she dropped her head lower; in a whisper that Monica could barely catch she said, "He didn't do it."

Something prickled up the back of Monica's scalp, a sensation as if an insect with a lot of legs were walking in her hair. A whole new meaning for the scene last night, the hysterics, the helpless fury, opened for her. Winifred had not been weeping because the cat wouldn't eat. She had been weeping for Jerry Huffman. She knew what had happened to her father. Mrs. Lannon had lied.

She went to the bed and sat down on its edge and touched Winifred's shoulder gently. "Tell me. Tell Monica."

Winifred shuddered a little; her stare was blank and glassy. "Is it till Christmas?"

Rage that she hadn't known she could feel shook Monica to the bones. "Who told you?"

The defiant eyes were weary and adult. "I just know. I just heard— things. Will he—will he—"

Monica sensed the straining control, the effort that cost so much, the tears put down, the sobs repressed. The room grew very still. She thought, almost hating herself: I don't even know what to say, or how to comfort her. Shall I try to explain? Haltingly she began, "Winifred, when someone does something very wicked—"

The reply was quick as a whip stroke. "He didn't do it."

They looked at each other, enmity growing between them. Monica was remembering the sunny day in New York, the brilliant morning when she had been working at the drawing board, and the Western Union boy had rung the bell. She remembered the self-accusing anger, the shame, that she had let Biddy marry the man about whom she had known nothing, that Biddy had gone away West to live in fear, to be murdered. Now she felt her nails stabbing the heels of her clenched hands. "He did it! He did!"

The attack was too sudden for Monica to think of defending herself. When the flailing fists hit her, she put up an arm and scrambled backward off the bed, and leaned on the dresser, incredulous, in shock too deep for words.

Boozer had gone back to the underside of the chair. That's where we both belong, Monica thought. We can't endure her. She's not soft and sweet like Biddy. She's—savage.

Winifred crouched at the edge of the bed. Her face was distorted, a mask of hatred; her breath was a hiss.

"I—I'll have to take you back to Mrs. Lannon, after all," Monica said stumblingly.

The change was instant. "No!" Winifred sank back, huddling among the piled bedclothes. "I'll be good! I'll be a good girl, Aunt Monica!"

Monica went to the chair and sat down in it and held her head, and Winifred crept toward her. There was a whipped, cringing subservience about the child that Monica could suddenly not endure. She got up and began to pack the suitcases, not carefully but swiftly, her eyes stinging with unshed tears. "Wash yourself and dress," she snapped at Winifred. "We won't mention your father again."

"I'll be very good," Winifred repeated, standing a slight distance away, as though aware of Monica's temper. "I won't get mad—ever. Please don't send me back to Mrs. Lannon's!"

"I'm not," Monica promised, "but if you ever strike me again, I'm going to whale the daylights out of you."

Winifred, for no reason at all, seemed to cheer up all at once. "Shall I wash with soap, or just with water?"

"I don't give a damn," said Monica—and this, too, ridiculously, seemed to reassure the little girl. Winifred went skipping off into the bathroom. There were prolonged splashings, the thump of the soap, the gurgle when the plug was pulled. Boozer emerged cautiously from under the chair, and Monica grabbed him and thrust him without preamble into his traveling cage. He let out a single brokenhearted yowl.

Winifred came out of the bath, still half-wet, and knelt on the floor to peer in at Boozer through the wire netting. "I'll buy you some beer, darling," she promised in an oddly adult way. "Don't cry! Don't cry!"

When they went out into the hall, Monica found herself examining the carpet before the door as if there might be a trace there of the person who had passed in the middle of the night. She didn't know quite what she had expected—a collection of cigarette butts, a dropped handkerchief, some kind of baffling, mysterious clue. It was all too silly, and of course there was nothing. She noticed then that Winifred was, just as she, staring at the rug with wary interest.

"I'm getting as nutty as she is," Monica said to herself.

The mountain air smelled clean and piney. They came down through a windy pass to the small valley that contained the lake, and Monica swung into the graveled parking space under the trees. There were two other cars there, a blue Cadillac and a Ford truck, both very dusty. The lake had a single boat in it, and a solitary fisherman, humped and patient.

When she had braked to a stop, the door of the nearest cabin opened and a man came out, down the steps, and began to walk toward them. Under the freckled light she saw that he was tall, lean, and tanned, with a close-mouthed look about him as though he had been much alone and didn't talk much. A little more than thirty, she decided. The outdoor type. Not bad-looking. His eyes came up, and the glance was steely and measuring. I don't like him, Monica decided.

He leaned on the car door with an air of leisurely tiredness. "You're Miss Marshall?"

"Mrs. Marshall," she corrected, glancing at Winifred. The little girl had accepted the idea of changing her name as she did everything that didn't concern her private belief about her father: with philosophical calm and indifference. "This is my daughter, Biddy, Mr. Raboldi."

He glanced in curiously at the child. "Hiya, kid."

"Hello," said Winifred politely.

He continued: "But I'm not Raboldi. He was taken sick suddenly last night and had to go to the hospital at Bishop. I'm Stevens. I'll be in charge until Raboldi gets back."

"I see," said Monica. She thought: It's not important. I wonder why he made such a point of telling me who he is? I don't care for him much.

His voice had a lazy reserve. "Would you care for a cabin close to the lake? The two at the end are empty. You can take your pick of them."

She counted mentally: there were seven cabins all told; two were vacant and one was the manager's. That left four to be occupied, to have people in them who might recognize Winifred, might stare at her.

Perhaps Stevens had seen her gaze, the glance she flicked toward the solitary man on the lake. "Most of the gang right now are deer hunters. They're off in the mountains running down bucks."

"The end cabin will be fine," Monica said. She got out from behind the wheel, opened a rear door, and took Boozer in his cage from the floor. The cat put his nose against the wire, sniffing the new smells, then made a lonely noise.

"You brought a cat up here?" Stevens said disapprovingly. "He'll eat birds, you know."

"He doesn't care for birds," Monica replied.

"He likes beer!" Winifred put a finger through the wire for Boozer to smell.

"Besides, considering the slaughter worked by the hunters—" Monica continued, with some heat; but Stevens wasn't bothering to listen. He loaded himself up with suitcases and walked off, leading the way to the end cabin. The sunlight turned his light brown hair to a deep gold—in a kind of loathsome way, Monica thought. Winifred skipped and hopped along the path, staring at the trees and the water. She looked quite different in the red gingham pinafore with the white puffed sleeves, her hair cut to shoulder length and curled, the shabby coat replaced by a neat sailor's jacket which she carried on her arm. The clothes Mrs. Lannon had packed had been left in Los Angeles to be cleaned. "I don't think anyone would know her," Monica said to herself; and then— almost unwillingly—"She's kind of cute."

The cabin was small but clean and well-aired, the inner door standing open with a screen to keep out insects. The front room contained two cots with innerspring mattresses, a table, and two wicker chairs. In a back cubicle was a shower and toilet, with a closet next to it. A shelf in the big room held a cooking plate, and there was a small row of pots on nails driven into the wall.

"If you go swimming, watch for holes in the bottom of the lake," Stevens told Monica. "And don't try it much before noon. The water's pretty cold—comes straight off the ice-pack, you know."

"We'll be careful," Monica said stiffly. She wondered if he expected a tip.

"I'm hungry," said Winifred.

"About meals." Stevens stood in the doorway, hitched up his faded jeans, and leaned against the lintel. "We keep a small stock of groceries if you want to do any cooking here in the cabin. No fresh milk, or butter, or meats. Just canned stuff. Beer on ice. If somebody gets a buck, you'll probably have plenty of venison. Don't depend on the fish; they aren't biting good right now. If you want to eat a meal out, you can drive on over the ridge—there's a big lodge there and they bring their stuff in from the other side and the food's pretty good. It's high too."

"I brought a few groceries with me. Thanks, anyway," Monica said.

He tossed a key into the air, caught it, laid it on the table by the door. "That's yours. Use it. We get drunks coming through here sometimes on their way from the lodge."

"Thanks." She picked up her purse. He must be waiting for something.

His eyes studied the movements of her hands and something flickered in his face—amusement, she thought, and felt herself flushing. She put the purse on the table and just stood waiting for him to leave.

"Let me know if there's anything you don't understand," he said enigmatically, pushing away from the lintel and opening the screen.

"Thank you, I will."

When he had gone, she untied the small box of groceries, opened a can of soup, some crackers, and a tin of sardines, and she and Winifred had a small lunch. Then, while Winifred fed Boozer, Monica unpacked the clothes and hung them in the closet. She tried to remember how long you were supposed to wait before going to swim after eating. Was it an hour? Two? Three? Finally she decided it didn't matter; it hadn't been a big meal. She got out the bathing suits.

Winifred surveyed herself in the mirror that hung over the table. "I like mine. Yours is cute too. You look nice."

Perhaps it was the influence of the obnoxious Stevens; at any rate, Monica took a longer look than usual. Her figure was pretty good; she had enough bust without falsies and her stomach was flat and firm. The face—well, it was still the same face; she'd had it a long time and it was hard to see it objectively. The cheekbones were high, the eyes slanted a little. "Boozer's not the only one who looks like Fu Manchu," she jeered at herself. She tied her black hair up in a scarf, took Winifred's hand, and went out to walk the piney carpet down to the beach. The cat followed, yowling now and then because the place was strange to him.

The water was cold, as Stevens had said it would be. The sun made a flat, metallic glare on the water. The fisherman was in closer than he had been; Monica swam out until she was almost under the stern of the rowboat. Then she found the man looking down at her. She couldn't make out much about his appearance; he wore a hat with the brim turned down against the glare, dark glasses, a muffler around his throat. But he wasn't a big man. She thought he smiled at her.

"It's too cold!" she cried, turning in the water.

He nodded in agreement, then took a pipe from his pocket, stuck it into his mouth, and began to search his clothes, apparently for matches.

Monica swam away. An hour later she had all but forgotten him. She and Winifred were lying on the beach, half-covered with towels, and she was almost asleep, lulled by the sunny silence. Then Winifred spoke. "I know him," she whispered.

Monica opened her eyes. The man who had been fishing had tied his boat to the little pier and was standing, his hat pushed back and the glasses off, silhouetted against the bright water. He was arranging his fishing gear. "He came to Mrs. Lannon's," Winifred went on. The conviction, the honesty in her voice was so compelling that Monica raised herself on an elbow to have a better look. "Only," Winifred said, "he was taller then."

Monica shook her head to clear it. They were off again. "You mean he's shrunk?"

"Yes," Winifred said, "he's littler and he isn't as old."

"I wish I could do that," Monica commented, half-bitter and half-amused. "Get younger and smaller, I mean. It must be nice."

"I don't like him. He has wolf's eyes."

Humor her. Monica felt lazy, too lazy for real anger. The altitude, perhaps. "Does he growl like a wolf too?"

"Oh no. He talks nice. He gave me a dollar, a real silver dollar, only I let it roll down a hole under the hollyhocks. Mrs. Lannon found it, I bet."

Monica sighed. It was a story she'd made up, then, to give herself a new grudge against the woman she so disliked. "Let's forget Mrs. Lannon for a while, Biddy. You do run the subject into the ground."

"You don't have to call me Biddy when no one's listening."

"I like to call you Biddy." Monica reached out to ruffle the yellow hair. "Like little hen's feathers—just like feathers." She rolled over, cradling her face on her arms, wanting to hide the sudden tears. Oh, Biddy, if I hadn't been so wrapped up in my work, if I'd studied your letters, read between the lines, sensed your fear ... For Biddy must have been frightened for a long time. Murder—such horrible murder—doesn't come without sending its shadow ahead—violence, hatred, terror.

"I know her too," said Winifred.

Monica lifted her head and looked up. A woman had come out upon the little porch of the middle cabin. She was a big plump woman, a cherry blonde. She wore a sun suit of purple-and-white striped cotton, white sandals, a short purple jacket dangling from one hand. She looked out at the water and stretched, a lazy, rippling motion that reminded Monica of Boozer.

"Oh, for the love of Pete," Monica said, taking out on Winifred the impatience she felt for herself. "You can't know *everybody*, Biddy."

"I know her."

"From Mrs. Lannon's place?"

"No. From on the street. We were waiting for a bus."

The blonde woman began to put on the purple jacket, as though the breeze felt chilly.

"A lot of times," Winifred went on.

"Oh, be still," Monica commanded sharply.

The woman on the porch finished putting on the jacket, buttoning it down the front. Then she stretched again, and opened her mouth to yawn.

"She's going to click her teeth," Winifred said. "She always does."

The blonde woman shut her mouth with a snap, and the loud click her teeth made in coming together floated down the still air and into Monica's unbelieving ears.

"See. I told you, I told you." Winifred was grinning.

Monica sat up. There was the sudden feeling of having wakened from a nightmare, to find the nightmare real and staring you in the face.

3

The illusion lasted for an instant longer; then things swung into focus and the tenseness flowed out of Monica; she sank back, relaxing. She
was, after all, simply lying on a beach beside a lake; a very ordinary little man stood folding his equipment at the end of the pier, and an ordinary fat woman had just shut her mouth after a yawn. How insensitive, how uncomprehending I am, she thought, not to realize that to
Winifred the world in which she has lost her mother, the world that
means to take away her father, must seem filled with enemies. Of
course, without knowing precisely how her misfortunes came about, she
sees people everywhere whom she suspects of evil.

It all goes back to Mrs. Lannon—the woman had been a bad choice for
Winifred. Or perhaps, rather, anyone who had kept the child during the
difficult time would have come in for an unearned share of blame.

Monica sat up and pulled Winifred against her and hugged the child.
Winifred's response was not what she had expected, the usual indifference, but an answering hug that all but cut off Monica's breath.

"Don't be afraid," Monica said. "I'm here, you know."

Winifred's clutch grew tighter.

"I'll tell you. We'll plan something nice, something different." Monica
remembered Stevens's words, the remarks about the lodge. "We'll drive
over the ridge to a big place and have dinner. Chicken, if you want it."
She tried to loosen the frantic grip, but Winifred burrowed closer. "You
can wear the blue dress, the new one with the ribbons in the sleeves.
And the white shoes."

"Something will get us," Winifred whispered.

"Nothing will get us." Monica laughed. "Look, we've lain in the sun until we're almost roasted. Let's go to the cabin, have a shower, and oil ourselves so we won't burn."

"She'll see us!"

"The woman in the sun suit? What if she does?" Monica glanced up
at the cabins. The woman had an easy, rolling gait, much like a man's,
and she was crossing the space between the next cabin and her own.
At the steps she paused, looking about idly; then she walked on toward
the end of the path, where the sign that said *Manager* hung above the
door. "She's going to flirt with Mr. Stevens," Monica decided. "She's the
coy type. I'll bet he likes her."

Winifred looked up from a spot just below Monica's chin. "What's coy?"

"Bashful and tittery."

"You mean laughing? No, she isn't."

"What is she, then?" Monica felt no real interest in Winifred's prattle, but the idea had come to her that perhaps it would be best to get it all out in the open—the fear, the suspicion—and have it done with.

"When Mrs. Lannon wasn't looking, she pinched me once."

"Oh, Biddy!" Monica stroked the fair hair, looked into the blue eyes that seemed frank and guileless. Then she realized that a shadow lay across Winifred's face, a shadow that had inched up from nowhere to stand between them and the sun. Monica raised her glance. Stevens stood there, very brown and lean in a pair of swimming trunks, a towel thrown over his shoulder.

He didn't smile, but the tone had a friendly sound. "How's the water?"

"Cold," said Monica. Winifred added, "My teeth jittered."

Stevens appeared to study the lake, the pier, the figure of the small man just bending down to pick up the last of his gear. "Did Veach speak to you?"

"Veach? Oh. I—I can't remember whether he did or not. I think I yelled something to him about the water."

"He didn't get any fish," Stevens said, "but, then, he could hardly have expected to. He didn't bring the right kind of equipment for these waters. I wonder why he stayed with it?" Stevens's eyes seemed speculative between narrowed lids, studying the small man as though some detail puzzled him.

"Has he been here long?" Monica asked, making conversation.

"He came last night, late." Stevens's glance slid around to settle on her. There was something in his expression she didn't like, couldn't grasp.

"After Mr. Raboldi was taken sick?" she wondered.

"No, a little before."

"What happened to Mr. Raboldi so suddenly?"

"Just an old stomach disorder which keeps repeating on him. Nothing serious." Stevens squatted on his heels, picked up a twig and doodled in the sand with it. Winifred had crawled off to investigate what Boozer had found among the pine needles. A cricket. When the bug jumped, the cat fell over himself getting away, then looked embarrassed and offended. "I didn't mind taking over. I like it here."

"Are you here the year around?" Monica wondered idly.

"We aren't open all year. This is deep snow country in the winter. Nothing up here but bears, and they're hibernating." He looked her over in the suit, starting at her shoulders.

"I believe you have someone waiting for you in your cabin," she said hastily. "A blonde woman."

He looked up quickly. "When did she go in?"

"Just before you stopped here."

"Thanks." He rose and started away with long, springy steps, then slowed and turned and came back. "You going anywhere tonight?"

After the appraisal of her figure, Monica was not quite sure how to take the question. She raised her eyebrows a little to let him know she thought he was verging on impudence. "I thought I might take Biddy and go to the lodge for dinner. You said they had good food."

He chewed his lip for a moment, then got out a package of cigarettes and a book of matches from the pocket of the trunks. All the time his eyes were on the water in a blank, thoughtful stare. "Okay. Check your gas first. It's not a very good road. How are your brakes?"

"They're fine. The car was guaranteed when I bought it in Los Angeles yesterday."

"You didn't make it from L.A. in one day," he said, as if thinking aloud. "Where did you spend last night?"

"In a motel. I don't drive fast." She looked at him levelly, thinking: It's none of his business. I don't like him. If anyone's acting suspicious, it's not the people Winifred has her eye on. It's this character.

"I'll see you later," he tossed at her, walking away.

Winifred came back from examining the cricket. "If she pinches me again, I'm going to holler."

Monica turned to look. The woman was back on the path again, swinging along, her beefy thighs shaking inside the wide legs of the sun suit. No, she wasn't the coy type, Monica decided, though most fat blondes tended to be—coy and babyish. This woman wore her fat like an armor, and she'd probably acquired as much of it from drink as from food. She stopped when she saw Stevens coming; they held some kind of conversation, a brief one, and then she went with him back to the cabin. For beer, Monica thought. I'll bet she puts away beer like—like Boozer. I might buy *him* a bottle. It'll keep him quiet while we're gone.

They gathered the towels and called the cat.

"I'm not interested in that man, not a bit," Monica told herself under the shower.

Twilight was beginning by the time they were ready to start for the lodge. The rim of the valley rose high, blue, and distant against a pale lemon-glow sky; the trees loomed taller, darker; the air smelled of mountain sage. There was a light in the middle cabin as they walked past—the man called Veach and the plump blonde must be together, Monica decided—and in Stevens's place a radio played a nostalgic waltz with a lot of flutes. The rest of the place appeared empty; outside of Stevens's music there was only the queer ringing emptiness of high mountain air. The lake shimmered in a blue dusk.

Monica started the car, switched on the lights, swerved out of the graveled space into the road that led on past the lake and into the upper valley and the pass. The car was a 1942 Buick and seemed to have had good care. It took the slow grade easily. They began to climb, and the road turned, so that they overlooked the resort. Far away and very small seemed the houses, almost lost in the gloom. It was a lonely feeling, Monica thought, being high and looking down on the little places where people lived.

Winifred was looking too. The pale light shone in her hair. She said softly, "How long will it be?"

Monica was absent-minded or she would have caught herself before she asked, "How long will *what* be?"

"How long has my Daddy got?"

"Oh." Monica gripped the wheel, felt sweat start out across her face. But it was a time for honesty, for truth. "Not very long," she said.

"Is it till Christmas?"

Monica knew suddenly what this question meant: the being together, the shared days, the fun that Christmas brought—that Christmas wouldn't bring again. "No. Not till then. It's—just a short while."

Winifred turned from the window, panic in her eyes. "Is it tomorrow?"

"No. It's a week or so. I don't know just what day." This was true. She'd lost count in the city, what with buying clothes, planning the trip, getting the car. Or, rather, she'd wanted to lose count; now she didn't want to start counting again.

Winifred leaned toward her. "He didn't do it!"

Oh, for Pete's sake! "Biddy, I can't argue with you. I have to keep my mind on my driving. This road's getting steep."

"The room was empty," Winifred insisted. "Daddy wasn't in it. They said he was, but he wasn't."

"Be still!"

"He didn't do it!"

Monica jerked the gear lever into second; she'd lost her momentum in the middle of the grade. "Winifred, if you start any excitement here, I'm going to stop the car and give you a good paddling. Do you hear?"

"Yes," said Winifred unhappily, withdrawing.

The lodge was what Monica had expected: a big place, sprawling, full of lights, set so as to get the benefit of the view.

Far away in the black valley that led downward lights pricked the dark. She could make out that the exterior of the place was finished roughly. She took Winifred's hand and walked toward the porch. The parking lot was dark and the ground was rough. Once Monica turned her ankle and almost fell, and the hurt brought back the helpless anger Winifred had aroused. Why couldn't the kid keep still about her father? He was going to die, he deserved to, and there was nothing she could or would do to save him. He'd murdered her sister.

Just for a moment another thought floated to the surface of her consciousness: suppose he *hadn't* murdered Biddy. Suppose he *weren't* guilty?

I won't start thinking about that, she told herself.

They went into the lobby. There were fans going, a few people standing around, a pleasant air of leisure and ease. Through the open door of the cocktail lounge Monica could see the bar, not very full, and the people sitting at it, unhurried, placid. Well, this was what came of taking up with a kid, she thought. I can't even have a drink before dinner.

Winifred touched her hand. "I can wait out here. I'll be quiet."

"What do you mean?" said Monica.

"I used to—for Mama."

Monica's face grew stiff. "Biddy never drank."

They went into the dining room, and Monica only half-saw the place: the clean white tables, the potted palms, the boughs of mountain greenery, the friendly waiters. Her mind was boiling with a new confusion. Was Winifred simply a congenital liar? Had the dread and the lost aloneness so upset her that she felt compelled to lie about everything, no matter how trivial? Biddy had never drunk anything intoxicating. Even at the end, the last few letters, there had been no sign of a change in that attitude.

She looked at Winifred above the menu. The child's face seemed solemn and searching, a little lonely, a little wistful. If there was anything wrong here, anything askew, it was deep. It was, Monica thought in terror, permanent.

"Chicken for the little girl," she said mechanically to the waiter.

"She's watching us," said Winifred.

Her eyes were fixed on one of the big windows that faced the dark. Both Monica and the waiter glanced immediately at the spot; Winifred's tone had been urgent, convincing. And there was nothing, of course. Monica felt herself flushing. "Chicken, as I said. For myself, trout."

"Would Madame care for a cocktail?" the waiter murmured.

Brother, would I! "A martini. Make it a double," she decided.

The waiter went away. Monica fixed a stern look on Winifred. "Why did you say that?"

The obvious open disapproval had its effect. Winifred let her eyes sink to the tablecloth, where she made doodling motions with her fingernail. In the pale throat a pulse beat visibly. "It was her," the child said, but softly and without emphasis.

"Mrs. Lannon? Up here?"

Winifred shook her head. For a moment Monica thought the child was going to cry, and helpless anger returned. It had been like this almost from the first, she realized: the child inventing scarecrows, ghosts, spies. Have I got the will, the intelligence, the understanding to go on?

Or should Winifred be with people who could help her? Not a—a bitch like Mrs. Lannon. I'm already starting to cuss.

The cocktail arrived. It was very cold, very dry; Monica sipped it gratefully. The dinner that followed took away some of the irritable confusion. The trout crackled with butter, the little crisp rolls were very hot inside their covered dish, the vegetables were fresh and tangy. Winifred ate the chicken with a good appetite; but then she always ate well; she always gave the surface appearance of a perfectly normal and well-behaved child. It was only on the one subject that she was—say it—a little cracked.

After the meal was over they went out into the lobby and lingered there, looking at the magazines in the racks, the souvenirs, post cards. Later, Monica was to remember this time, to wonder what would have happened had she gone directly to the car. Some half-hour must have gone by. A group of people gathered by the main entrance, preparing to leave, and, for no reason, this made up Monica's mind for her. "Come on, Biddy. We'd better be starting back."

They went out into the cool dark, the strangers following, laughing and talking together. The car started smoothly, in low gear, inching forward on the slight rise that led on to the road, to the gradual, uninterrupted climb to the summit. There was no need to pause, to bring the car to a stop or even to slow down. The headlights picked out trees, fence posts, boulders, the yellow eyes of a roosting owl; the motor purred evenly; they were safe. The only odd note was Winifred's behavior. She sat close to Monica and she was very still.

At the summit the wind hit them, blowing against the car as they emerged from the trees. Here they were on top of the ridge; behind lay the lights of the lodge, and ahead was the swift incline into Raboldi's valley. Monica thought, It's going to be steeper than I remembered. It was then, involuntarily, that she touched the brake pedal.

The car ground forward with a curious lurch. She let her pedal out and pushed it again. There was no response, but there was a strange loss of control. She jammed the pedal to the floor, pulled the hand lever. Behind her she sensed the inert weight of the car, gathering momentum, pushing them into the beginning of the downward plunge. With frantic swiftness she forestalled a runaway by shifting back into second. Still the car gathered speed. And the turns were sharp and spaced dangerously close together.

"Is something the matter?" Winifred asked in a small voice.

"Very much so. Damn all car salesmen," Monica gritted. Ahead, she suddenly made out a low embankment over which heavy brush hung. "Get down on the floor. Quick." Winifred didn't respond; Monica pushed her roughly. The car plowed into the brush with a tearing of branches.

The frame of the car took the shock of the solid earth and Monica was flung against the wheel. Pinwheels went off inside her head, all breath was gone, she felt the caving of ribs, the tearing of ligaments, the bursting pain that filled her brain.

The tinkle of glass all but covered Winifred's stubborn whisper: "She did it, I bet."

It was almost a relief, after that, to drift into sleep. She was aware, at intervals, of the things that went on: of Winifred's hopeful ministrations, head-strokings, huggings; of the grinding approach of another car, coming from the direction of Raboldi's; of a light playing on her face.

The voice of Stevens, the obnoxious man, said, "Here. Easy, now. I'm trying not to hurt you. Where did you learn to drive? And when, for God's sake? After you bought the car?"

"Shut your damned mouth," Monica replied through set teeth.

"That's the spirit." He was carrying her through the dark; she made out the shape of the Ford truck. Then she was lying on the platform on what felt like a spread-out overcoat. The truck smelled of hay and machine oil. The sky overhead was big and dark, and the stars seemed enormous.

"Where's Winifred?"

"She's right here," he said.

"I mean Biddy," she corrected.

He didn't say anything; he began to feel of her here and there.

"Quit that."

"I guess you're all right. I don't feel any bones sticking through your skin, and you can breathe well enough to curse. What happened to the Buick?"

"The brakes quit, right at the top of the grade." Then she stopped, and in the middle of the pain and the tiredness the pain seemed to have brought she considered. She didn't really know when the brakes had failed. "I don't know what happened. The damned thing just wouldn't stop, so I rammed the bank, and I hit the wheel, and something broke—the windshield, I think. Just so—just so Winifred's okay." She closed her eyes. She thought, without any reason probably except that she'd bumped her head, I'm not going to call her Biddy any more. I don't like that name as well as I used to.

4

The doctor had a large and ridiculous fuzzy mustache that fascinated Monica; the bristles grew in all directions; it looked as though he used it to dust the furniture. But his eyes were intelligent and kind. He went over her with dry, antiseptic-smelling hands, and then bound her with tape to the stiffness of a mummy. "Just keep quiet for a few days. I don't think you're damaged seriously anywhere. You took the steering wheel in the ribs—you'll be sore there for a while."

She tried to express her gratitude to him—stumblingly, because of the hypo he'd given her to ease the pain. The interior of the cabin was inclined to wobble, the lights to dance. At the same time, in the back of her mind a kind of numb indignation raged. How could she lie quietly with a kid and a cat to feed and look after?

"Lucky for you that I was already up this way," the doctor said, from the door. "There's a baby due up at Sampson's Flat, one of the camp caretakers. I'll stop here on my way back, sometime tomorrow, if things go as they should."

Well, the wrenched ribs weren't so bad as having a baby, Monica thought ruefully. She tried lifting her head; the room revolved. "Goodby," she said from the pillow.

The doctor, who had on hunting clothes as though he might bag a deer if the baby took too long, answered her cheerfully. "Just keep yourself in bed and relax."

"Oh, I will, I will," she said, wanting to gnash her teeth at him.

"I'll let you go to the bathroom. No bedpans here anyway, probably."

"Thank God," Monica yelped.

When the doctor went out into the dark, Winifred and Stevens peeped in at her as though she were a freak, or dead. "The wake is over," she announced. "And I'm going to live. He says."

Stevens pushed Winifred in ahead of him. "That's good." He looked around the room, then addressed the child. "Time for you to hop into bed. You got a nightgown, kiddo?"

Winifred nodded. She was still staring at Monica, as if something must be wrong with her.

Stevens asked, "Think you can make it alone?"

"Sure." Winifred's chin went up. "You think I'm a baby or something?"

"Don't sass me." He gave her a sharp look that shut her up. "Mrs. Marshall, I'll go up the grade tomorrow with the truck and see what I can do about bringing your car down. I judge you wouldn't like to pay the bill for a tow car from Bishop."

"No, I wouldn't."

Stevens nodded in a way that included them both. "See you at breakfast." He shut the door behind him, then rapped and said through the panel to Winifred, "Lock up now."

The night passed, long and wearisome. A couple of owls who must have been hunting along the edges of the lake made spooky noises; Monica woke when the effect of the hypo wore off and lay listening, and turning over in her mind the puzzle of what had gone wrong with the car. Boozer was restless; he got up and curled himself into a new spot every half-hour or so. The tape that bound Monica's ribs was hot, tight, and unyielding. She waited, reasonlessly, for footsteps to haunt the dark outside, but nothing happened.

Nerves, she told herself sternly; just nerves, and you can't start having them—unmarried female artists are notorious for vapors and temperament, and you've resisted the pattern until now.

She drifted back to sleep, to rouse again when dawn was gray. Something was making a noise, a soft noise—Winifred, weeping into her pillow. No need to ask why, no use starting the argument over again. Monica willed herself to sleep again, and when she woke at last it was broad daylight, Winifred was up and dressed and Stevens was working at the little electric stove, getting breakfast.

She was surprised and not very well pleased. It seemed as if he were taking advantage of the situation to move in on her, to become much too friendly too soon. She recalled, with sudden suspicion, that Stevens had inquired about the condition of the car long before she had started for the lodge.

She crawled to a somewhat sitting position and straightened her gown. The tape pulled and itched. Winifred, under Stevens's instructions, brought her a clean washcloth, wrung out of cool water. After using that, she felt better. But it had been Stevens's idea, and she was keeping a guard up for him.

The food he brought when he was finished was surprisingly good. The coffee was hot and fragrant, the bacon crisp and dry, the eggs done without being leathery. "You're a pretty good cook," she said to Stevens, looking at him over a slice of toast.

"I'm good at a lot of things," he said dryly.

Probably she was supposed to read something into that, she thought with irritation. I'm a good man—a good lover—you'd like me. She turned her attention to Winifred, who sat at the table in a patch of early sunlight, munching steadily. There was no sign of the nighttime tears, but through Monica's mind flashed the illuminating knowledge, a sudden insight into the long hours Winifred must spend in thinking about her father, the grief put down and hidden, the tears never shed by day. Now that I'm flat on my back, Monica thought with a touch of panic, she'll be alone to mope with no one to keep her busy.

"What are you trying to do?" Stevens demanded crossly. "If you want anything, speak up."

Monica lay back, but a stubborn determination had been born. When Stevens and Winifred had cleared away the dishes, and Stevens had gone, Monica dragged herself out of the bed by sheer will and put on a robe over her gown. "Get into your suit," she told Winifred, who watched bug-eyed. "We'll go to the beach. You can swim a bit even if I can't."

"Mr. Stevens won't like it," Winifred decided.

"To hell with Mr. Stevens," Monica ground out. The ribs hurt frightfully when she tried to walk, and her head swam. She made it to the little porch and the steps; where she had to rest. Winifred stood in her swimming suit, waiting; there was gooseflesh along her skinny arms, as though she were thoroughly afraid.

Out on the lake the man named Veach sat in his little rowboat as he had yesterday, dark glasses covering his eyes, his hat brim down. "Smaller and younger," Monica found herself saying aloud; she had a hysterical desire to giggle. She sat down on the top step, jarring the ribs, bent her head to her knees, and shook with a mingling of laughter and crying.

"He used to be all gray and bald," said Winifred seriously, looking at the lake.

"He couldn't be both," Monica retorted between spasms. "And how about the shrinking business? How did he do that?"

"Mrs. Lannon helped him, I bet," said Winifred.

Oh no. Suddenly Monica looked up; there had been footsteps. Stevens was looking at her from a short distance, his expression distinctly disapproving. Well, she had to show him. Monica stood up, walked down the other two steps, then stumbled, and started to fall flat on her face.

Stevens caught her—the final indignity. He carried her in and deposited her with an air of authority on the bed. "Now," he said, "what is it?"

How awful to cry, and she was, and Stevens looking!

He must have some sort of understanding, some intelligence. After a few moments he said slowly, "You want the little girl to have a good time, and you think she won't. Is that it?"

Boozer walked up the bed and looked into Monica's face anxiously.

"And you think your cat might not get his quota of beer," Stevens added.

"I don't let him drink every day."

"He clawed his way out of the back window screen after you'd gone last night," Stevens said. "He came to my place. I was having a limburger sandwich and a bottle of lager. I could smell beer on him, the beer you'd bought before you left. He was all but groggy, too, but he downed the lager like a man."

"He's an awful drunk," Monica admitted.

Stevens paused as if to think. "Would you mind if the kid and I did some fishing?"

"Mind? No, of course I wouldn't." Then her eyes flew wide and her breath caught. She had remembered Winifred's inclination to tell yarns. "If she—she makes some sort of funny remarks, you'll overlook them, won't you?"

"You bet I will." He didn't ask any questions. He was, Monica decided, too self-centered and egotistic to be curious about other people. Even too self-centered, she suspected, to be curious about a man who'd grown smaller and younger and a fat woman who always clicked her teeth after a yawn.

Monica rested until lunch, while Stevens took Winifred out in a boat. The fish were good, after Stevens cooked them. He could cook, even though he did it with an air of not caring whether the stuff pleased anyone or not. While the lunch dishes were being washed, Monica asked from the bed, "Who is Mr. Veach?"

She thought Stevens hesitated over his answer, as if choosing words. "I don't know who he is," Stevens said finally, "except that he isn't much of a fisherman. No—not much."

"Is he from L.A.?"

"My guess is that he is."

Stevens was working at the table with his back to her, his hands in the pan of soapy water. Winifred, drying with the dishcloth, almost visibly popped with something she wanted to say about Veach; behind Stevens's back Monica shook her head at her. She asked Stevens, "Is that fat blonde his wife?"

"So he says." Very cryptic; it wasn't any of Monica's business, his tone implied, whether the pair were married or not. You had to be broad-minded in the resort business.

"You think I'm nosy," Monica said stiffly.

Stevens shot her a look over his shoulder, the same unreadable masked look he'd given her down by the lake. It made her uncomfortable; it made her feel stupid and unknowing, a dunce. "You just lie still for a few days, the way the doc told you, and get well so that you can take care of the kid. I can't say I'm crazy about being a nursemaid."

Monica felt as though he had somehow put her in the wrong, and disliked him more than ever.

Stevens dried his hands on a towel. "I'm going up the grade now. See you later." He balled a fist and tapped Winifred on the jaw, and she bridled at him, grinning. Well, a child was easy to impress, and saw little of a person's character—especially a lonely, mixed-up little girl like Winifred.

The truck pulled away with a roar of its heavy-duty motor. The camp grew very quiet. Winifred played with Boozer for a while, then took a nap. There were westerly shadows on the floor, the sun shining through the trees, by the time the truck returned. Stevens didn't come directly to the cabin. When he did, it seemed he had been on the phone, for he had news.

"The doctor won't be back this way unless you especially need him. A hunter shot himself in the leg up by Clover Lake, and he's going there, and from there home. He wanted to know if you were getting along all right, and I said I thought you were."

Monica brushed it aside. "What about my car?"

"I'm getting the mechanic at the lodge to look it over before I try to drive it down."

"What do you think went wrong?"

Stevens lit a cigarette carefully. "I would say you drove it into a bank, miss." Infuriatingly he looked the match over before tossing it out the door. "What would you and the kid like for dinner? Some venison?"

"Has a hunter come in? I haven't heard anyone."

"I met them at the lodge, having a drink to celebrate their luck. The two in the second cabin from this. If they keep you awake tonight, send the kid to tell me."

"If they give me a venison steak, I won't complain at anything," Monica said reprovingly.

"Check," he said, out of an obviously limited vocabulary. He rubbed his blonde head in a gesture that was a little tired. "The windshield shattered. I guess you know that."

"I have two stitches in my shoulder to remind me."

"I didn't get hurt," Winifred piped up. "She shoved me. She pushed me right onto the floor."

Boozer went to stand in front of Stevens and yowl, his begging yowl that began low and supplicating and ended on a question.

Stevens looked at Monica. "You want him to have a beer?"

"I don't care." Monica's mind was somewhere else. She had suddenly been struck, a sort of mental double-take, by something Stevens had said. He had called her *miss*. Of course he'd been inside her car, he'd seen the papers concerning the transfer of ownership which she had left there instead of putting them sensibly into her purse. The keys must still hang in the lock from the time of the accident last night; one of them opened the glove compartment where she had stuffed the papers.

Stevens, with Boozer and Winifred following like two willing lackeys, paused in the open doorway. Stevens said, "About your car—do you carry insurance on it?"

"Limited liability," she said bitterly. "I have to pay the first fifty. It was cheaper." She bit it off to correct herself. "I mean, I thought—not anticipating any wrecks—that it was going to be cheaper."

"I'll try to get the guy from the lodge to be reasonable."

They all went out, and Monica thought: He knew what kind of insurance I have, if he's read those papers. He knows a lot of things: he knows I'm not married—so he probably thinks I bore Winifred out of wedlock. He knows what I do for a living, where I was born, how old I am, what I weigh, what color eyes I have— She squirmed angrily inside the tape binding. The only thing Stevens doesn't know, she told herself, is what political party I belong to. When he comes back I'll clear that up. I'll confess to being a Democrat.

But Stevens didn't return soon. Winifred came in eating an apple, and Boozer jumped up on the bed and let her get a whiff of his breath.

"Go away!" said Monica to the cat; to Winifred: "Did you see anyone about outside?"

"Nuh huh." Winifred shook her head.

"Not Mr. Veach?" This was madness, but it had been a long day, lying in bed almost without moving; sheer boredom was guiding her tongue.

"He's inside with his wig off, I bet," said Winifred, munching.

"And his wife?"

"That fat lady? No, she isn't. Her name is Wanda. Wanda like I wanda ice cream cone," Winifred explained gravely. "She smells like violets sometimes, only too much, so you can't hardly breathe. Her fingernails scratch."

Monica lifted her head off the pillow. For a moment that seemed an eternity she looked into Winifred's eyes—wide, guileless, and blue under the thatch of yellow hair which was wind-blown and uncurled from being on the lake with Stevens—eyes as unshadowed as the sunny sky itself.

Monica found her throat dry, her voice husky. "Who did you think looked in the window of the lodge at us last night?"

Winifred inspected the unbitten part of the apple. "Wanda."

"Wanda Veach," said Monica mechanically.

"No. Just Wanda."

"She must have another name, a last name." How crazy can you get? Here I am even arguing a point in this fantastic mummery. Wanda should have two heads, then I could really object. Monica laughed at herself—or tried to. "Where did you get the apple?"

Winifred stopped chewing to say, "I found it."

In another second Monica was out of the bed, snatching the apple from Winifred's hand, digging the unchewed portion from the stubborn mouth. The child gagged on her fingers and tried to back away. Monica pried the last bits from between Winifred's teeth. "Where did you find it? *Where?*"

Winifred retched and whimpered.

"Oh, God," Monica groaned, and started running around the cabin, looking for the box of groceries. There was mustard in it, and mustard and water would bring up the apple Winifred had eaten.

"I found it in Mr. Stevens' house, and he said I could have it," Winifred got out.

Monica stood still for a moment. She was near the shelf that held the little electric cooking plate, and she put a hand on the shelf to steady herself. She found that she was shaking from some emotion she was unable to analyze. I must be going crazy, she thought—really crazy; and it's true what I read somewhere in some book on abnormal psychology: if you stay around someone long enough who's off the beam, you get a little off the beam too. Only, I haven't been around Winifred very long. She's a fast little worker. She shot a glance behind her at the child. Winifred had picked up the apple core and was looking it over hopefully.

"Drop it," said Monica hoarsely.

Winifred looked up.

"Drop it, I said!"

"Why?" asked Winifred.

"Because—because I said to." Monica staggered to the bed and sat down on its edge. There was a hot thudding core of pain under the ribs; she'd wrenched them in jumping out of bed to get that apple. Don't worry over ribs, my girl, she told herself—you've got something wrong with your noggin. Worry over that.

Winifred went to the door, opened the screen, and dropped the apple out upon the dirt. Then she came back. She looked perplexed and uneasy for several minutes; suddenly her face cleared. "I know, I bet."

"You know what?" said Monica, rubbing her temples.

"Remember, in *Snow White*, the poisoned apple?" Winifred sat beside her companionably on the bed. "You thought I'd go to sleep and you'd have to put me in a glass coffin."

Monica nodded dumbly. She shivered; her whole body shuddered, as though a cold wind blew through her flesh to touch her bones.

5

Next morning Stevens took the truck again and went up to see about the car. The mechanic from the lodge was supposed to have fixed it so that it could at least be driven safely down the grade. For a while Winifred played with the cat, hunted beetles to make them jump, made little men out of pins and pine cones. But by ten o'clock she was bored; she came in, flushed and perspiring, to prop herself against the bed. "I'm so hot. Can I swim?"

It was hot. Inside the binding of tape Monica stung and sweltered. "I can't watch you. You'll have to be very careful. Stay close to shore and watch where you're going."

"I will," Winifred promised. She began getting into her suit. She was noticeably tanned; the mane of yellow curls had no resemblance to the long, fuzzy pigtails. If anyone saw her now, Monica thought, they'd never guess she was Jerry Huffman's little girl. Jerry Huffman—

There was a calendar on the wall; she found her eyes drawn to it.

"When I'm grown up," Winifred said, squeezing herself into the suit, "I want to be fat like you."

"You think I'm fat?" Monica wondered.

"Only in places. You look nice," Winifred said. She went out, banging the door; the sound of her running steps died into silence.

The calendar showed the days of March. This was July. Monica inched out of bed and pulled herself across the room and tore off four sheets.

And why look and study and be troubled, she thought. There's nothing whatever you can do or would wish to do. Jerry Huffman married your sister. She was young and inexperienced; your parents had left enough to keep her in good schools, to shelter her, to keep her away from violence and ugliness and dirt. Till Jerry Huffman came along, and you let him—

She left the calendar, feeling sick and lightheaded.

It was hard now, even remembering what Jerry Huffman looked like. His image confused itself with those of other men whom she'd met recently—with Stevens, for instance. Jerry had been blond and tall; she recalled that he had stood at the wedding, much taller than Biddy in her white satin and veil, with the strong light from her big north window reflected in his hair. He had a scar on his nose, right across the bridge; she remembered thinking that it gave him the look of a young reformed pug. A circus accident, he'd told Biddy; it had happened when he was a kid. His voice had seemed pleasant. There had been a touch of southern drawl. His eyes, she recalled, had struck her as honest and likable. Underneath, of course, he'd been rotten.

The only complaint she could remember Biddy making in any of the letters had been about money. During the years right after the war they'd moved up and down the West Coast—from Portland to Seattle, then to San Francisco, where Winifred had been born, then south to Los Angeles. To live in Mrs. Lannon's house, if the woman was to be believed.

And all the time things must have been wretched for Biddy. There must have been dreary days and nights full of fear. No one beats in your head without giving a frightening hint of what's to come. Why hadn't Biddy left him, returned to New York? The money left by their parents was gone, the trust dissolved (Biddy's share, Monica suspected, had gone into an unsuccessful garage business for Jerry), but Biddy would have known that Monica would take her and the child in, given them food and shelter, until Biddy could get on her feet.

Jerry had cursed a lot, Mrs. Lannon had said. Yes, he had a temper, cooler now, no doubt, inside stone walls and steel bars. A temper that had burst all bounds at last, that drove him to wield an iron tool on Biddy's small, frail skull under the hair that had been like little hen's feathers.

Monica rubbed sweat from her face. Now that she was up the thought of returning to the hot bed was distasteful. She decided that, taking it slowly, she might be able to get into her swimming suit and limp down somehow to sit on the rim of the water. There was, also, a vague uneasiness in her mind about the child. There were holes in the lake bottom. Stevens had warned them.

Monica went to a window and drew aside the flimsy curtain. Down through a scattering of pines she saw the glare on the water, Winifred's figure black against it like a cricket, her voice caroling something to Boozer about the owl and the pussycat going to sea.

With hands that shook Monica stripped off the sticky gown and pulled on the tight-fitting elasticized suit. She fluffed her hair, too tired to brush it out, then bound it back with a scarf. She wouldn't go in; wet tape was the wretchedest thing she knew. But just sitting by the water would be nice. Better than the close cabin, the warm, untidy bed, the calendar staring at her from the wall....

She paused. Winifred's voice no longer piped its squeaky song. She went back to the window. The lake looked empty, the flat water silky and dimpling. Then she saw Veach's boat, and Veach crouched in it.

The shivering started, the same shivering she'd had last night. She rubbed her temples. There's nothing, she told herself. A man in a boat. A man who wants to fish. Winifred makes up stories about everyone— about Mrs. Lannon, Veach, the blonde. She sees spooks everywhere. I can't start believing—I don't dare even believe a little part of any of it. Then I'd have to believe it all, and that would be—horrible.

She steadied herself by holding the wall, then the doorframe, then the banister of the little porch. The nearest tree was perhaps ten yards. She gathered herself, then made it in a rush and hung against the resinous bark.

She listened. There was no sound at all. She glanced to her right, to the row of cabins. There was no sign of the hunters who had come in last night with the deer, who had given Stevens the steaks that he had fried so expertly. No sign of the blonde, either; the middle cabin had a shuttered, fast-asleep look. Siesta, Monica thought. With a cold bottle.

She pulled away from the tree and wobbled on to the next. The dazzle on the water distorted things, but she thought that Veach lifted his head a little to look at her through the dark glasses. Hateful man, she sneered, watching me bumble my way along. I loathe him. Even if his hair is his own, I loathe him. And if it isn't— She was at the last tree now. She turned her head to survey the lake through the watery glare. Her heart lurched.

There was flat brilliance everywhere, light that smacked your eyes so hard it made your skull ache. But the peaceful lake seemed swept empty even of mud hens and terns. "Winifred!"

Veach's boat turned a little, rather slowly, as though it drifted with a current. She couldn't see that he used the oars, or even that he moved. He held a pole and a line. The motion of the boat, smooth and gliding, brought his back toward her.

Then something erupted from the water. Not near Veach, not anywhere near the boat, but yards away in another direction. There was an up-jet of foam, arms that threshed and churned, streaming yellow hair, a strangled yip.

Veach had his back to it all. He made no move to look around. He seemed intent on something he was drawing from the water, a sodden bit of weed which had clogged his line.

All this Monica saw as she saw things in nightmares: with a hideous, lightning-like illumination in which faces, bodies, and background seemed picked out with a hellish clarity and distinctness. She was running; she felt the hard, rather gritty sand underfoot. She hit the water clumsily and began to swim. Four or five desperate long-reaching strokes; then pain gripped and doubled her, and she rolled in the water and went down.

She was strangling. A pulse beat behind her eyes; her throat seemed bursting. Her mind said coldly, "You damned fool, you're drowning yourself instead of saving the kid. How dumb can you get?" With an effort like the cutting of a knife she forced her arms from her sides and made them reach out, to pull her through the water. The pain was fiery, the water like ice. She sucked water into her lungs and coughed. It seemed forever until she felt the sudden clutch of Winifred's whipping hands. They settled on her, the arms followed, wrapping her neck, and the two of them went down into the green depths together.

Monica fought clear, minnowed to the surface, then grabbed a handful of yellow hair and rolled on her side. She saw Winifred's face break water. She bit her lips and began to pull for shore.

The rowboat danced on the watery horizon. She couldn't tell if Veach was on his way; she couldn't wait; he might not be. Far off she heard the roar of a motor, a screech of brakes, then yells, then splashings. Her arms melted, her face went under. She found herself staring tiredly at the deep, shadowy bottom of the lake.

She flung up her head, forced herself higher in the water. Stevens was in the water, not far off, coming fast. His wet face looked white in the glare. White and furious, as though she'd done something very wicked. He reached out, roaring in Monica's ear: "Give me the kid! Can you make it?"

"Yes." She gargled the word; it didn't get past her lips.

He pulled away, leaving her and not looking back. Winifred lay on her back; she was like some dead thing he towed through the water. Monica swam after, but couldn't keep up. The stabbing pain returned, and she doubled again, put out her hands, and went down retching. I'm gone, she thought. There was no panic and no fear. She let the water take her. Her feet went down slowly, and then she found that she could stand. She could stand, and her head was out of water.

After that came a period of confusion when things happened in a sort of void, without reason or connection. There was giddy timelessness while she lay on her face on the beach, and the world spun. There was a hollow silence, a vacuum, in which all sounds were so loud that they hurt. No one paid Monica any attention. In a moment of awareness she saw that they were all gathered around Winifred.

She heard Stevens say, "Stand back, please. No, don't do that, Mrs. Veach. I've already attended to her tongue."

Monica raised her head. The blond woman had stepped back from Stevens. She was shaking her head and smiling, as if in apology for offering to do something that had been unnecessary. She had on a lavender organdy dress and a big yellow straw sun hat. Very dressed up for the mountains, this fisherman's lady, and there was something else about her, something that made Monica's nose twitch. A smell. An odor of perfume. It stained the air around her.

I've got to think, Monica said to herself. There's something I've got to remember. Ungrammatical. I must remember: That would please Miss Tooley, who taught us English. Miss Tooley, she had freckles on her arms, and I hurt. I hurt like hell, and to hell with remembering anything. I'm going to grit my teeth—

A long, roaring, breathless time went by.

Out of the vacuum Stevens said, "She's coming around all right. I'm going to take her inside. Open the door of that last cabin for me, will you, Mr. Brill?"

Mr. Brill. A man Monica hadn't seen before, one of the hunters perhaps, went ahead. Stevens followed. Winifred's legs dangled from the crook of his elbow.

The blond woman was bending over Monica. "Can I help you, honey? Would you like to stand up?"

Monica raised her head enough to shake it. "No, thanks. I'm all right."

Still the woman lingered. "Was it cramps?"

Monica looked at her fuzzily. Some fugitive thing nibbled at her brain, something she was supposed to know, to recognize. "Was what—"

"The little girl. Did she have a spell of cramps in the water?"

Monica said, "No, I think she must have stepped into a hole."

The blond woman used heavy make-up. In the heat, sweat stood out on it in beads. "That's bad," she said, keeping her bold blue eyes on Monica.

Monica turned her head and forced her eyes to focus on the flat, bright water. "Your husband was fishing in a boat. I don't see him now."

"He came ashore when the excitement started."

"I don't see how he helped hearing the rumpus we made."

The woman blinked, rather slowly; there was almost, to Monica's imagination, the effect of a cornerwise closing, like a snake. "He's pretty deaf."

Monica put her head down. The sun was beginning to warm her through, to make her feel drowsy. The blond woman went away.

She became gradually aware, at length, that her skin was too hot. She staggered to her feet, went on through the pines to the cabin. Winifred was in the bed, propped up with pillows. Stevens sat in a chair, talking to her. When Monica came in, both of them looked up. Winifred smiled, but there was unmistakable anger in Stevens's eyes.

Monica went to her own cot, sat down gingerly, felt of the ribs, and winced. "Thanks for helping," she said to him.

He rose from the chair and took a few steps to stand over her. "Why did you let her go out that far?"

She was surprised at the amount of anger in his tone. "I didn't. She was hot and bored, and I told her to go in but to stay close. I don't see how she got out where she did."

"You ought to have your head examined." His chest rose in a panting breath under the wet, clinging shirt.

Monica tried to control her rising temper. "Keep a civil tongue in your head, lout."

"I have a civil tongue for anyone but a fool."

Monica started to count to ten, and then gave it up. "If my ribs weren't giving me hell, I'd slap your damned face," she told him.

"Try it." He rolled on the balls of his feet, his hands moving at his sides; she sensed how fury drove him, possessed him. An irrational rage. He was going to be out of hand in a moment.

There wasn't anything close but a box of dusting powder on a shelf over the cot, where she'd put it to use now and then to relieve the itching of the tape. She reached for it suddenly with a swinging motion that continued into a toss that carried it directly into Stevens's face. He must have seen it coming and been too surprised or too mad to duck. The box hit him above the eyes and popped open with a snapping noise; the next moment a shower exploded over him, a covering of perfumed talc.

Winifred crawled snickering from her covers. Then, in a voice suddenly as angry as Stevens's own, she said, "Serves you right! You leave my aunt Monica alone!"

The box fell, and he just stood there. The powder caked in his damp hair, clung to his eyebrows, and settled thickly on his shoulders. Monica turned her head; she was still shaking with rage, and she wanted to laugh. He began beating the powder off his clothes, savagely, making a cloud that drove Monica and Winifred to the ends of the cots. He ran his hands through his hair; his cold eyes flickered from one to another. To Winifred he said, "You—why did you go out into deep water?"

Winifred squatted on her haunches on the cot and appeared to reflect. "There was a little bitty bird," she said at last. "It got in the water and couldn't get out."

"Where?"

"Close at first. Only when I tried to catch it, to save it, the bird sort of wobbled away on a wave. It was going to drown."

"Did it make a sound?" Stevens demanded.

Winifred rubbed her wet mane. Her eyes were puzzled. "No. I guess it didn't."

"Which way did it go? Did it go toward the boat?"

"What boat?" Winifred asked innocently.

In Monica's mind a picture re-created itself: Veach, bent over, reclaiming a draggled something from his line. She stared at Stevens, at his close-mouthed, unreadable face; she felt a pulse start up, hard, above her collarbone. "What are you hinting?" she demanded.

He gave her the wise, knowing look again, the one that infuriated her. He didn't answer. He walked over to the window and looked out and whistled a ragged tune through his teeth. Monica got the idea that he was thinking.

He spoke over his shoulder. "Your car's okay except for the glass. You'll have to replace that in town. A bent fender—it's not bad. The lights work."

"Thanks," she said mechanically.

The lights ... She had an image of the car, the good sound little Buick, tooling its way securely along the dark highway. She said, "If you'll get out now, I'd like to get Winifred and myself put of these wet suits."

He went on whistling for another minute, then started for the door. He turned there. "I owe you an apology, Miss Marshall. I shouldn't have shot my mouth off about the kid going in the lake. You weren't to blame; you were laid up, all but crippled. You did a wonderful job saving her."

Monica gulped in astonishment. Winifred's face crinkled in a smile; her hero was redeeming himself.

"I'll be back after a while," he finished, "to see about getting you both some lunch."

He shut the door. A moment later Monica was up, peeling off her suit. "Get your clothes on, Winifred. Your good clothes. We're clearing out of this place—fast."

"You ought to go back to bed," Winifred worried.

"Nuts to that. I can't even feel those ribs now, I've got such a tizzy in my head. I don't care who Veach is, who the blonde is—"

"She's Wanda."

"Wanda go to the bathroom, or whatever," Monica went on grimly, "or what went wrong with the car, or what kind of a bird you saw on the water, or what Mr. Stevens's mysterious little game is—we're leaving. We'll go back to Los Angeles, sell the car, and hop a train to New York. City kids may not breathe much fresh air but they're notoriously—even unnecessarily—healthy. You'll be a city kid and to hell with Raboldi's."

She grabbed the suitcases, propped them open, and began stuffing them with clothes. Infected by the hurry, Winifred skittered about. "Here's Boozer's traveling box. But where's Boozer?"

Monica stopped, her hands full of clothes. A tickling sense of cold drifted up her spine into her scalp. "Didn't he go to the lake with you?"

"Yes, he did."

"He wouldn't go in the water." A stupid remark. Boozer's antipathy for water fitted his alcoholic name.

Winifred tiptoed toward her, eyes big, face paling. "*They've* got him!"

"Who?" Another stupid remark; she knew who.

"*Them!*" Winifred jerked her head significantly toward the row of cabins to their right.

This was the snapping point; ridiculously, it was the idea that her cat might be in danger that gave Monica a lion-like purpose and courage.

She walked from the cabin, her clothes all but thrown on, limping with the pain in her side, her wet hair tangled and messy. She went up the path to the Veach cabin, up the steps to the screen door. And was stopped there by the innocent scene inside.

The blond woman and Veach sat at a table in the center of the floor; there was food on the table before them, a lunch of canned stuff and crackers, but they weren't giving it their attention. They were watching Boozer.

Boozer was lapping from a white dish near the door.

The blonde tittered; then she must have noticed Monica's figure against the light. She looked up, squinting. "Oh, hello."

Monica had no words to say; she stood rooted to the porch. The noise

Boozer made, the slupping and splashing of his gluttonous tongue in the beer, was the only sound in the silence. The glare off the water reflected through the trees and into the Veach cabin; the interior had a sort of glow in which Veach sat illuminated, his face turned toward her, his eyes fixed on her face.

They were peculiar eyes. Yellowish, and with a motionless quality that made them seem strangely aware and alert and not quite human. She had, Monica remembered, glimpsed something much like them in a den at the zoo. "I came for my cat."

Veach rose. "Oh. Is the animal yours?"

"He's so *funny!*" chortled the blonde. "We were here eating, and having a cold glass with our lunch, and all at once he was at the door, begging. He's just bulging! This is his third dish!"

"I know," said Monica.

The blonde got out of her chair, picked up Boozer and stroked him, and came to unhook the screen. "I'll bet he has a hangover."

"He never seems to." Monica backed down the steps with Boozer in her arms. A wave of violet sachet flowed from the blond woman through the screen into the outer air. A fog of fragrance. Too much.

Monica wanted to run.

Now I know, she thought; and her mind began backtracking, picking up details as it went. The steps in the hall at the hotel. Mrs. Lannon: *She knows things....* The blonde, clicking her teeth. Mr. Veach, who was smaller and younger—with those eyes he could do anything; he probably refreshed and renewed himself from time to time in the way of vampires. The face at the window of the lodge. The brakes that mysteriously went to pot. The little bird on the water, drawing Winifred out to drown.

"You look a little pale," the blonde said through the screen. "I'd take it easy for a few days. Quite an experience you had in the lake this morning. Things like that leave you weak, you know."

"So they do," Monica said. She turned and walked away.

At the cabin she found another surprise waiting. Stevens was there, in dry clothes, sitting down in the middle of the obvious preparations for flight. He had a bottle of whisky on the table, some ice in a bowl, and a siphon of soda.

6

"What's wrong?" Stevens asked, giving her a stare.

"Nothing." Monica put Boozer on the floor, rubbed her temples, then sank down on the cot and took a good look at the cabin. She felt that she had never seen it clearly before. The shabbiness now seemed sinister, the aloneness of the place frightening. Why had she been so stupid as to come here? And—incredible blunder—how had she managed to find the very people who must be bent on doing Winifred harm?

Then she remembered the clerk at the hotel, so anxious, so solicitous and eager to make all arrangements for her. And so eager to turn over to another, for a fee, the information of where she meant to go.

"It strikes me that you could stand a drink," said Stevens.

She nodded mechanically; then her eyes swung to fasten on him. She felt a rush of the initial antagonism and suspicion. But no. If he were in on the thing, whatever it was, why should he have pulled Winifred from the water? And why should he have been so genuinely angry and insulting over what he considered Monica's carelessness?

She took the drink he offered, sampled it. The whisky was good scotch, smoky, warming.

"I take it you have something on your mind," Stevens commented. "Mind telling me what it is?"

He'd seen the suitcases, anyway. "I'm leaving for L.A."

He took his drink down by a couple of inches, then sat thoughtful. "Yes, I thought you might be. You haven't had too good a time of it."

She shuddered—a motion he must have noticed. She was remembering the downward lurch of the Buick high at the top of the grade, the nightmare panorama of flying shrubbery, curved road, trees.

"I want to look your car over first," he said.

She was stung anew by suspicion. This morning at the lake, had he seen that she was rescuing Winifred anyway, and decided to put on a show to win their confidence? Or had the hunters been on the verge of coming in sight of the lake, so that Stevens had known she would soon have help and that his had better be first?

"I'm going to Bishop late today. I'll drive you that far," he added.

"Oh, good!" cried Winifred happily.

Monica frowned. "You won't have any way of getting back."

"Yes, I will. There's a party coming through on their way here."

It didn't sound convincing; it was a lie. She made up her mind to be rid of him. "I'm afraid the car will be pretty full with all of our stuff."

"Full—with just suitcases?"

"Too full to give you a lift," she said firmly, looking him in the eye.

He assumed an indifferent manner. "Okay, then. Drink up."

The whisky masked the pain of her wrenched side and the fright that had filled her mind. She began to think optimistically of the trip to L.A. She'd make it in one jump, driving straight through. She should be out of the hot part before the night was over, if she started soon. She'd drive carefully, but fast where there was little traffic and the highway was straight.

Then her thoughts returned to Stevens, to his inexplicable actions and his possible motives. "How long did you say you'd worked here?" she wondered cunningly.

"I didn't." Stevens bent and picked up one of Winifred's pinecone men off the floor and dangled it in front of the cat. Boozer gave it a jaundiced eye and burped.

"You're not what you pretend to be," she said, probing.

"Neither are you." He kept his gaze on the dangling toy.

"Neither is Mr. Veach." There was a sense of foolish daring in thus hinting at her suspicions. The whisky was loosening her tongue; she had sense enough to realize it and stop drinking.

But Stevens poured her a new drink and she didn't protest. It was good to feel calm and relaxed. I'll quit after this one, she thought.

"That's right," said Stevens, agreeing with her last remark. He looked at Winifred. "How do you like Mr. Veach, kiddo?"

"He has wolf's eyes," said Winifred, as if that disposed of liking Mr. Veach.

Stevens smiled on one side of his mouth. "A pretty good description." When he thought Monica wasn't noticing, he poured some fresh whisky into her glass.

He's trying to get me drunk, she thought with inward amusement. She gave him a tipsily drowsy smile, and laughed inwardly at the way he brightened up. He's got something up his sleeve— a plan—some sort of monkey business. If Stevens hadn't centered his real interest so obviously on the child, she might have considered that he had designs upon herself. But that wasn't it. She decided to try him out a bit. She let him make more drinks, and put on a show of becoming sleepy. What he didn't know wouldn't hurt him, and what he didn't know was that Monica carried her liquor like a gentleman.

She stretched out languidly on the cot after a bit, propping her head up with the pillow. Stevens said guardedly, "I thought you said you were leaving?"

"Am leaving," she insisted with the careful distinctness of the drunk. "Am leaving; taking the kid. Going to L.A."

"Hadn't we better be getting started?" he wondered.

"That's right." She let her eyes close for a moment, then jerked them wide. Stevens was bending toward her. His tanned face was expressionless. He might have been watching the struggles of a fish he expected to have for dinner.

"You coming along?" she mouthed, as if puzzled.

"If you want me." His tone was clipped and businesslike; she could read whatever she wanted into the bald words. Monica decided that she was expected to read a lot.

She reached out, caught his fingers in hers. "Like you a lot. You're aw-ful big—awful quiet. But cute."

Winifred giggled and hopped about, her eyes wide and excited.

Stevens winked at Winifred as though they shared a joke. "Sure I'm cute. You just didn't notice it before. Have a new drink." He mixed one that would have taken the fur off an Eskimo's parka and held it out to her. She took it, looked into it as if with indecision. "Drink it," he urged. "It's good for you."

She looked around woozily. "Where's yours?"

"Right here." It was, she thought, the one he had started with, rein-forced with fresh soda.

"Right *where?*" She wriggled on the cot, twisted, and sat up, reached over and poured the drink from her glass all over his pants.

They were brown cotton work trousers. The smell of whisky rose from them in a stench that made him turn his face. He stood up quickly, and she saw suspicion flicker in his eyes. Monica said, "Hadn't you better go change your clothes? We'll wait." She gave him a hiccupy smile. "Mix me a new one to work on while you're gone."

Her desire for further liquor reassured him. He used most of what was left in the bottle to make a new drink with the wallop of the one she had spilled. "There you are. As good as new. I won't be long."

"Remember—I like you," she said sentimentally.

Boozer, aroused by the smell of the spilled liquor, had come out of his beer coma and was trying to climb Stevens's leg. Stevens put the glut-tonous animal back upon the floor, went out, and shut the door behind him. A moment later Monica went to work in a frenzy. She stuffed the last of the clothes helter-skelter into the suitcases, put Boozer into his box, checked Winifred's appearance, and then reconnoitered the front door.

"Are we running away from something?" Winifred asked.

"We are leaving Mr. Stevens in what is known as the lurch."

"Mr. Stevens? Isn't he a nice man?"

"He's a boor and a cheat, plus other probable things which I won't put into your innocent young ears." With a staggering rush, burdened by the bags and other paraphernalia, Monica led the way to the car. The door hung open, as Stevens must have left it when he raced for the lake. Mon-ica stowed Boozer and the bags in the rear seat, put Winifred in front with her, slid in behind the wheel, and closed the door with sly careful-ness. The car didn't look too bad, except for a dented left fender and the windshield gone. The car being as old as it was, the fender bump had-n't ruined the headlight. Monica turned the switch and spun the mo-tor like mad.

Nothing happened.

All of the frantic rush, the deception, had been for nothing. By and by Stevens came out of his cabin wearing a suit, carrying a bag, and stopping casually to light a cigarette. The motor ground and ground, and then Monica leaned on the wheel and cursed to keep from crying.

"Move over," said Stevens.

"It won't start," Monica flung at him, raging.

"Oh yes. That thing. You damaged the automatic choke. Wait a minute." He lifted the hood and did something to some gadget in the motor. Then he came back, crowded Monica over, stepped on the starter, and the motor roared. Monica looked around for something to hit him with, but this time there was nothing. Besides, Winifred was admiring him.

"You're smart," Winifred said. "You fixed it."

"Oh, I'll get by," Stevens said, with a sidelong look at Monica.

She was in such straits to show him what she thought of him that she found herself sticking out her tongue.

Stevens gunned the motor several times, with what seemed an almost deliberate effort to draw attention to their leaving. Then they rolled out of the camp, climbed the road that led to the end of the valley which opened to the pass and the highway to the town of Bishop. Monica was surprised at the conditions in the car with the windshield out. The rush of air was terrific. She had Winifred get into the rear seat; she tied up her head and the child's with scarves. Still there was a lot of discomfort. Stevens's hair blew about his face. He kept his eyes narrowed.

They had passed the summit and started down when Stevens suddenly gave a jerk to the steering wheel that sent them into a dim side road.

A frightened lump rose in Monica's throat, choking her. She put a hand on the door, crouching far from Stevens. He gave her an impatient glance. "Keep your shirt on." The car crawled into a clump of low, stubby pine trees and rolled to a stop. Stevens got out from behind the wheel, opened the rear door of the car, and unsnapped his suitcase. He put something in his belt, under his coat, patted the coat into place, and said, "Come on. No, not you, kiddo. You stay here." He took Monica's hand and guided her with him into a thick clump of brush.

Some paralyzing things rushed through her mind.

"You can just forget what you're thinking," Stevens said. "I wouldn't try it with a kid along."

"You're a beast," Monica said heatedly.

"Look," said Stevens.

From the clump of brush they could see the road. She heard a rushing sound, and a moment later a Cadillac swept by below with Veach and the blond woman in the front seat.

They waited. There were no sounds except faint ones made by the birds in the brush, chirrupings and the rustle of feathers. After a while Stevens touched Monica's arm. "Let's go."

She had forgotten him; her mind had been taken up by a panorama of evil, a tenor that she hadn't believed which had come true. She collected her wits. "Won't they realize that we've stopped somewhere?"

"Not for a while, anyway. And we're not going to follow them. We're going back, over the ridge to the lodge, and down the other side into San Joaquin Valley. It'll be a hell of a drag, but worth it."

She looked at him angrily. "All that business about your needing to go to Bishop, about getting a ride back with people who were headed for Raboldi's—"

"Just as phoney as your drunk," he offered grimly. "Come on."

"You can drive us back to Raboldi's. Then you can stay there. We'll go on over the ridge."

"No, I'm going with you."

She stuck her chin out. "I don't intend to remain in L.A. I'm going to sell the car and take a train East, back to New York, where Winifred will be safe."

"The kid won't be safe anywhere." He was taking the thing from his belt. It was a gun, a surprisingly big gun.

"You're not scaring me with that," Monica snapped. "And you seem to know an awful lot of things, all at once."

"I've always known them." He stuck the gun back into his belt and took her by the shoulders and shook her, impatiently and hard. "Get it through your thick skull that I'm trying to help you."

"Th—thanks for being so nice about it," she stuttered, jolted.

"Just don't be so God-damned independent."

"Why not? You're not doing this because you give a damn for me."

"No. Just say I'm nuts." He pushed her ahead of him to the car.

"Are you a detective?" she hissed at him.

"Shut up. You'll scare the kid."

They got in. Winifred was sitting up straight, her gaze curious. With a half-grin Stevens said, "I thought I saw a lost dog over there."

But Winifred was sharp. "There was a car went by on the road," she told him. "They followed us, I bet."

This was the pattern, Monica thought: Winifred with her eternal bogies. Only they were real, they were fearfully real, and Winifred right along had been speaking the simple truth.

"Who are those people?" Monica demanded. Stevens gave her a sharp look and shook his head; he wasn't going to talk in front of Winifred. She flung around to face the child. Here was a source of information all too ready to divulge what it knew. "What did you mean when you said Veach was smaller? How could he be?"

"He wasn't *much* smaller," Winifred qualified. "He was flatter on his feet—sort of."

Stevens was looking straight ahead, through the frame of the windshield, his eyes narrowed against the rush of air.

"I don't get it," Monica said in exasperation. "I don't understand why they should want to—"

"Save it," Stevens cut in.

Her mind went on: Why should anyone want to hurt Winifred? Who was she, that she should be shaken up in an accident, half-drowned in the lake? A half-orphan, soon to be a whole one, with a father sitting in the condemned row of the state penitentiary, a mother murdered, a dim-witted aunt—

Well, for one thing, Monica's own thoughts answered, she's the only one on earth who believes that Jerry Huffman didn't kill her mother.

But how could that be it? A kid's simple belief, reasonless, built up on nothing but faith.

She was distracted by seeing Stevens take the gun out of his belt and lay it on the seat between them. She drew away. He seemed a violent and unreadable man. "Do you expect trouble?"

"I don't know." They had come out of the defile; the camp lay below in its cuplike valley. There seemed to be no one stirring. The car in which the hunters had returned the day before stood beside the space the Cadillac had occupied.

"But Veach and the woman are gone."

He went on squinting into the wind. "They could have friends."

But they passed the camp without incident, without even seeing anyone. The lake looked lonely and peaceful. The boat from which Veach had fished was tied to the end of the pier, rocking a little. The terns and mud hens were busy at the edges of the reeds. "Aren't you going to give me any information?"

"Yes, I think so." He drove in silence for a while. They began to climb the steep grade to the ridge. The rushing wind smelled clean and woodsy. "We'll stop at the first good-sized town and get this glass fixed. We can't drive all the way to L.A. without a windshield. When we get to the city I'm going to take you to a place where you and the kid will be safe. At least I think you'll be safe." He frowned, and a spot twitched in his cheek. "Then I want you to meet a man I know. His name is Demarist. He is a very rich man."

"Are you working for him in this thing?"

Stevens didn't answer except to shake his head.

She went on, her voice picking up heat: "Don't you think you're taking us over in a high-handed manner? I haven't asked for your help or your protection. I'm grateful, of course, for the help you gave this morning in the water, but I was making it okay when you showed up—"

"You were getting ready to drown the kid and yourself," Stevens said. "I thought for a minute there that I'd have to go back for you."

"So thoughtful of you to notice!"

He gave her a glance out of the unreadable gray eyes. "Let me set you straight about something. You brought this all on. *You!* If the kid had stayed at Mrs. Lannon's place, she'd have been safe; nothing would have happened to her."

"Now I know who you're working for!" Monica cried.

"The Lannon woman?" He laughed, gripping the wheel, his face thrust forward and his eyes screwed up. A thoroughly detestable man, Monica thought. "No, I'm afraid I'm not in her set."

"And your name probably isn't even Stevens!"

He shrugged. She could think what she wanted. What she thought wasn't important, anyway. Monica raged, "Why don't you tell me the truth? Are you simply a congenital liar?"

"Wait until you talk to Demarist," he said. "Then you'll know as much as I do."

7

The house was in the San Fernando Valley, south of Ventura Boulevard, in the fringe of the Hollywood hills. It stood at the end of a winding road, no other houses were close, and the place must have contained a quarter acre of ground fenced throughout in steel link with a padlocked gate. Inside the gate a couple of police dogs lay on the green lawn. When the car drew up and stopped, the dogs lifted their heads and their ears rose.

Through a few scattered eucalyptus trees Monica could see the house. It was low, sprawling, Spanish, white stucco and red tile, with a broad, deep porch facing the drive. Stevens got out of the car and went to the stone gatepost and pushed a button. Presently a woman in a white dress came out upon the porch of the house and opened a box on the wall. Stevens opened a cubicle in the stone post, took out a small telephone receiver, and spoke into it. By and by a man came around the house from the rear, walked unhurriedly down the drive, and unlocked the gate. He was a big man in gardener's overalls. He watched without curiosity as the car went through, then relocked the gate.

The woman in the porch shadow was about fifty, well-built, well-preserved, with a pleasant face and neat gray hair. The white dress was a nurse's uniform and there was a nurse's cap on the gray hair. She smiled when she saw Stevens, then glanced with a touch of interest at Monica and Winifred.

Stevens went up the red-tiled steps. "I called from Bakersfield. You weren't in, but they took a message."

"Yes, I was expecting you." She came down toward the car. In the sunlight she looked older, more lined, though the impression of good health and steady intelligence remained.

Stevens opened the car door for Monica. "This is a nut house," he said matter-of-factly. "A private booby hatch. Nobody gets in or out without some difficulty. You'll see what I mean. Mrs. Adams, this is Miss Marshall. And the kid is Winifred."

The woman gave Monica her hand. "You must be very tired."

Monica nodded. Her head buzzed with the steady sound of the motor; her eyes burned from the long hours of watching the highway. The tape had become an intolerable agony, gripping her flesh. "There's a cat in the back seat. He's pretty hungry by now." She rubbed a hand over her face; she felt gritty, unwashed. I stink, she thought. And no doubt I look a fit patient for a private—or even a public—insane asylum.

"We'll take care of everything. Don't you worry for a moment," Mrs. Adams said. She had a soothing, professionally mothering voice. "Come inside and I'll show you your rooms."

They went into a pleasant small parlor. At the opposite door was a desk, at which was seated another woman in white—this one square-jawed and big, with beefy shoulders. The bouncer, Monica thought. The woman was sizing up Stevens, Winifred, and herself in a thorough and unabashed manner. "This is Miss Wice," said Mrs. Adams. "Miss Wice, this is Miss Marshall and her niece, Winifred."

Monica, in spite of the tired fuzziness, tried to look sharply at Stevens. No wonder he'd kept calling her miss; he'd known all along that she had lied about Winifred being her own. She tried to rouse anger in herself over it, but Stevens's appearance distracted her. She hadn't noticed before how he looked; there was a stubble of beard over his face and his eyes seemed hollow and burned out. The hand that had touched her elbow a moment before was trembling.

I'm too tired to hate him right now, she told herself. I'll save it for when I'm rested. But he needn't think I'm going to take his bossing lying down.

She wanted to fall into bed without preamble, but the nurse Mrs. Adams summoned to help wouldn't let her. No, first the old tape had to come off. After it was off a conference was held over the condition of the skin under it. Then she must bathe. She fell asleep in the tub and the nurse roused her before she drowned. Then she had to submit to being daubed with sticky ointment where the tape had rubbed her raw. The ribs, freed of the binding, at first felt good and then felt horrible. She was coming apart bone by bone. She gritted her teeth. The nurse saw it.

Another conference. The sticky stuff was removed and more tape was applied. Not so much and not gripping in quite the same tender spots; but tight, making her feel like a mummy again.

After all this rigmarole, when she was in a nightgown and in bed, a young and timider nurse came in and tried to stick a thermometer in her mouth. This was the last straw.

"I'm not *sick!*" Monica raged. "I'm beat. I'm dying for some rest! Now get out!"

She turned over, and sleep rolled through her like a tide.

It was morning. Early. A lot of sparrows were making a fuss in one of the eucalyptus trees outside the window. The light was thin and milky, and objects in the room stood out with a stark perspective like a Dali painting.

Monica got out of bed and went to sit on the window seat. There were iron bars fitted into the concrete sill. She rattled them absently, a gesture of defiance. I'm in a nut house, she reminded herself. Just suppose there was a deep, dark plot hatching to declare me incompetent and to take Winifred away. What could be neater as a start? Here I am, already shut up.

This line of thought made her nervous. She went over to the wall near the bed and punched a button. By and by the timid nurse of the thermometer episode stuck her head in. Monica went out of her way to sound civil. "Is it too early to have something to eat?"

"Breakfast isn't quite ready yet," the nurse said. "But I can fix you a cup of instant coffee."

"Fine."

"Cream and sugar?"

"Black this time, please."

The nurse went out. When she came back with the coffee, Boozer walked in at her heels. He seemed possessed of a cynical lassitude. He looked up into Monica's face and licked his jowls. It was his beer signal.

"He won't drink milk," the nurse said. "He ate some liver, though."

"You wouldn't have what he likes to drink. Not here," Monica told her. "He's alcoholic. He started very young, when he was just a kitten."

The nurse stooped to rub Boozer's ears. "Poor kitty. You wouldn't like our wood alcohol we sterilize things with."

"Don't let him even get a sniff. He'll drink your sterilizers dry and beg for more. Nothing fazes him. Is Winifred up?"

"She's still asleep," the nurse said. She gave Monica an under-the-eyelash look. "Mr. Stevens was asking for you. He wanted to know how you felt."

"Tell him I died during the night," Monica replied. Boozer jumped up on the bed and thrust his yellow face close to hers, purred loudly, and half-shut his eyes. Monica petted him and he pretended to bite her. He was trying all of his tricks. He must have spent a very thirsty night. "I'm going to get dressed," Monica told the nurse.

"Would you like a shower?"

"I'm wearing a lovely new batch of tape. I'll do without the shower."

"If it was put on here, Miss Marshall, I'm sure that it's waterproof tape."

Monica shook her head. "Don't let them fool you. There's no such thing. Try wearing some and see."

The nurse went out, and she dressed. The clothes had been hung neatly in the closet and most of the wrinkles had fallen out. Monica put on a gray silk knit dress with a dark blue belt. She brushed out her black hair and powdered her nose. With lipstick, she thought, she didn't look too bad, considering the way she had felt yesterday. The nurse came back with breakfast, made the bed while Monica ate at the window seat, and admitted Stevens when he knocked.

He still looked tired and a little pale, though he was freshly shaved and had on clean clothes. He took a chair close to where Monica sat eating. He lit a cigarette, waiting for the nurse to go. He looked, not at Monica, but through the window above her head, as if he were thinking.

When the nurse had gone he said dryly, "I'm glad to see you pulled through."

"Curiosity kept me alive. I'm waiting to hear who you are and what your business is."

He went to the bedside stand for an ash tray. "You know who I am. My name's Stevens."

"What did you do with Mr. Raboldi? Put him in the lake with some old tire irons? Can't you at least explain the stuff at the resort?"

He came back carrying the glass dish. "Yes, tell you that. You were being followed. The clerk at your hotel on Wilshire was paid to keep track of you. I was paying him, but so was someone else. He didn't mind selling information more than once."

"And the real Mr. Raboldi?"

"He didn't mind taking a few days off when I convinced him there might be trouble coming."

"Plus a hammer lock or two," Monica surmised.

"Oh no, he was very friendly. He wanted to visit his sister, anyway." She thought it over. "You got to Raboldi's ahead of Veach?"

"That's right. I flew to Bishop and hired a car there. Raboldi took the hired car to make the return trip, leaving me the truck."

"So there you were, all set. Doesn't Veach know you?"

"Not yet. When he does, I won't be sitting so pretty."

She frowned. "What does Veach want? What's his motive?"

"I don't know," Stevens said surprisingly. "The kid obviously represents some danger to him. But I don't know what it is." Stevens crushed out his cigarette, got up to walk impatiently across the room and back. "Why didn't you believe the kid when she told you she knew Veach?"

"She said he was smaller and younger," Monica answered. "Besides, she'd already told some whoppers—that Mrs. Lannon had followed us to the hotel, that my sister left her outside a bar while—"

"What bar?"

"It wasn't true!" Monica flamed. "Biddy didn't drink!"

He studied her levelly. "Why the fuss? You do."

"Yes, but she was younger, and—and always a lot more conventional and scrupulous. She wouldn't have left Winifred outside a bar while she went in to lift a few!"

He shrugged as though it didn't matter, and went on walking the floor.

Monica's mind returned to something he'd said. "Why were you paying the hotel clerk to tell you where we went?"

"Let's say I just wanted to know," he answered aggravatingly. "I thought Veach was going to be interested, and I had a hunch I'd better be ahead of him. It meant coming out where he could see me, but that couldn't be helped."

He wasn't going to tell her what she wanted to know, the basic reason for his interest and intervention. She changed her tack. "Why did you bring Winifred and me to this place? How did you know of it and how were you able to get in?"

"When I first contacted Demarist—the man I mentioned, the one in Beverly Hills—he was here."

"Then he—he's been—"

"No, he's quite all right mentally. He went through a bad time. You'll understand when you meet him today."

She looked at him impatiently. "It's all so foolishly mysterious, so asinine. I don't see why Winifred and I should have to hide or be afraid. I can go to the police and tell them everything."

"Tell them what?"

She stopped. What did she have for the police? Footsteps in a hall ... A bird upon the water ... "My—my brakes. They'd been tampered with, to go out like that. There must have been some evidence."

"The brakes were damaged," Stevens said, as if explaining to a child. "They could have been damaged in other ways than by deliberate tampering. If they were worked on with the idea of killing you and the kid on the grade—who did it? Where was it done? Did you catch anyone at it? Do you have proof? In other words, what can you pin on Veach?"

She tensed all over with anger. She didn't want to acknowledge it, but what he had said was true. "Nothing. Dammit."

He stood over her, implacable, commanding. "Unless you want to keep the kid locked up behind bars like these for years"—he motioned toward the window—"you're going to have to string along with me."

She let him see the scorn in her eyes. "And you're doing—what?"

His face twitched; then he turned and went to the door and put his hand on it. He stood there for a moment. She thought he meant to walk out of the room. But he came back. "What gives with you?" He leaned over her, and slammed a fist down hard. The tray containing the breakfast sat on a small table across her knees; it rocked, threatening to spill. "What's the eternal chip on your shoulder all about? Did some man stand you up somewhere—sometime? You look the kind who wouldn't forget. But give the kid a break, even if you are a man-hater."

A pulse began to beat through her temples. She felt almost ill at his insolence. "No man ever stood me up," she managed to say evenly. "I can take men or leave them alone. You with the rest."

"It sticks out all over you," Stevens insisted, his face close to hers. "The first moment you met me, you had your claws out. You didn't even know me. I hadn't done a thing."

Her face felt hot, burning. "You remember you criticized me for bringing a cat to a place where hunters already—"

"That's it! You won't take a breath of criticism! You're not a man-hater. You're an everybody-hater. Everybody who doesn't agree instantly with you."

She felt tears—tears of rage—ache in her eyes. "You'd have let me drown when Winifred and I—" She cut it off, biting her lips. She wouldn't let him see how she felt. Or, rather, how much she felt it.

He withdrew a little, the mask look on his face. When he spoke it was calmly. "Let's agree to an armed truce, Miss Marshall. For the little girl's sake. She's a—a kind of a nice little kid." He made an abrupt, oddly broken-off gesture.

"Why are you interested in Winifred?"

His eyes stayed on hers blankly. "Don't you think she needs friends—any friends?"

"You're asking me to take you on trust—on nothing," she insisted. "I have a right to know your motives in this business."

He turned back to the door. "I'll be ready to leave for Beverly Hills around nine. I'll meet you in the waiting room then."

She bit back a retort. There wasn't anything you could impress on a man such as Stevens, a close-mouthed, stony-eyed man who didn't give a damn about anything you said.

She poured and drank the last of the coffee in the silver pot. Then she retouched her make-up, and from the closet took a light coat and a scarf for her hair. Boozer watched from the bed; when he realized that she was getting ready to leave and that no beer would be forthcoming, he set up a howl. An instant later the door popped open and there was Winifred. She was in pajamas, slippers, and robe. The child and the cat greeted each other like exiled compatriots. You'd think, Monica told herself wryly, that they were comforting each other for my common meanness to them. "I'll bring you a bottle of beer," she promised the old cat.

Winifred crooned over him for a moment. "We're in jail. I saw the bars over the windows, just like in the movies."

"It's a nut house," Monica corrected. "Didn't you hear Mr. Stevens explaining yesterday?"

"Are we crazy?" Winifred wondered.

"I wouldn't be surprised. Not for myself, at any rate. I guess you and Boozer are just a little bit queer." She went to the bed and stroked the tumbled yellow hair. "When I get back I'm going to have a talk with you."

A wary light settled in Winifred's eyes. "What about?"

"Lots of things."

"Mrs. Lannon, I bet," said Winifred.

"You're psychic, kid," said Monica, rubbing her cheek against the small hard head.

Winifred took one arm off the cat to circle Monica's waist. "Will we stay with Mr. Stevens?"

Monica stiffened. "Why do you like that fellow?"

"I don't know," said Winifred, on the defense. "I guess maybe it's because he listens, though. When we went out in the boat to fish I told him lots, and he listened to every word. He even believed it, I bet."

For some reason Monica was aware of acute mental discomfort. She gave Winifred a final pat, then went to the mirror and put on the coat and adjusted the scarf.

"You look nice," Winifred assured her. "I bet Mr. Stevens likes you."

"Just like arsenic," Monica agreed absently.

"Will you be gone long?"

"Not any longer than I can help."

"Don't you like Mr. Stevens?"

Monica was aware that her hands had clenched into fists on the dresser top, that the knuckles had turned white. How silly, she thought in anger, to let the fellow get you down. "He's quite a guy," she said to Winifred, keeping her voice casual. She walked to the door. "You and Boozer stay indoors and be good. You won't find Mrs. Lannon peeping in any windows here."

8

They climbed the canyon road. "It's a little off the beaten path and out of our way," Stevens said. "But if anyone's following, I'll spot them."

But no one followed. The crest of the grade was hot and sunny and deserted. The flanks of the hill gave off the smell of wild sage, spicy with heat. The downward road was winding, closed in, shaded with eucalyptus, and bordered with masses of Ragged Robin.

Monica took a slip of paper and a pencil from her purse, and began to make notes. Stevens looked at her sidewise. "A shopping list?"

She shook her head. "I'm making a check on everything I didn't believe before. I'm going to talk to Winifred when I get back."

"I'd like to be there too."

She shrugged. "I don't mind."

They weren't in Monica's car, but one that Stevens had had sent out from a rental agency. It was a black sedan, not too new, and inconspicuous. After a while Monica noticed that Stevens had slowed down a bit and that he was watching parked cars, and the rear-view mirror, with narrowed attention. He swung off the main drive into a side road. Here were cement and stucco walls shutting in big estates. Monica was not aware that she betrayed any particular feeling, but Stevens—who must have eyes in the side of his head—said, "Prejudiced?"

"Yes, I guess so," she admitted.

"Demarist is going to surprise you."

"There's nothing I loathe more," she told him, "than a rich hypocrite pretending to be democratic."

"My, my," he said. "We're very opinionated today."

"My father was an industrial chemist," she said without expression. "He spent his life making another man rich. My father left twenty thousand in insurance when he died. The other man left more than twenty millions."

"I see," said Stevens, watching the road. "What line was your old man in?"

"Paints—varnishes. He invented some stuff a three-year-old kid could throw at a wall and make it look like a decorator's job. The paint company owned the formula, of course, when he had perfected it. It made millions. My father was paid a little more than three hundred dollars a month."

"You have a point," Stevens said, "but I wouldn't brood over it."

"My father died of a poisoning contracted in his work."

Stevens drove for a minute or two in silence. Then he said, "I'm beginning to get it."

"What?"

"That chip on your shoulder."

"You can stop trying to figure me out," she said coldly, "and do some explaining about this man Demarist."

Stevens didn't answer. He turned the car into still another side street and then into a private drive. The house was big—a colonial mansion sitting on a little knoll. Wide lawns glittered from a fresh sprinkling. The roof of a greenhouse showed through some trees. A fountain near the drive had a bunch of nude marble girls pouring water from stone pitchers. Birds splashed and fluttered in the marble basin. "Yeah, it's pretty awful," Stevens said, following her glance. "But Demarist is getting ready to turn this place over to a religious order for an orphanage. They'll take down those naked women."

"I'm not prudish. The naked women don't offend me in the least."

"Something's making you grit your teeth."

"My ribs hurt." Her glance informed him how dense and insensitive he was.

With an air of apology that was obviously spurious, Stevens helped her from the car. They crossed a broad terrace, then entered the porch between two columns. Stevens pushed a button in an ornate decoration on the door. Presently the door was opened by a pleasant-looking man in a white uniform. Monica glanced at Stevens cynically; so he isn't nuts, the glance said.

Apparently the man in the uniform knew Stevens from some previous visit. "Hello," he said. "Come this way, please. Mr. Demarist is waiting for you in the den."

The long hall had a floor of dark waxed parquet, with a few chairs and decorative tables here and there against the paneled wall. The chairs weren't the kind anyone would care to sit in, except perhaps a monk doing penance, Monica thought, remembering the remark about the religious order. The man in white led the way to a door halfway down the hall, threw it open, and stood aside.

It was quite a den. Stuffed animal heads and mounted fish adorned the walls. Hunting prints flanked a huge fireplace. A small coal fire burned in the grate. The room was hot. Monica began to remove her coat.

Across the room near some windows were two men, one in a wheel chair. One rose as she and Stevens entered. The man in the wheel chair sat where he was. He was a big, bony old man in a faded blue cotton-flannel bathrobe, his legs wrapped in a white blanket. The other man, the one who stood up, was in his thirties. He had on a silk sport shirt and cocoa-colored slacks. He was dark, slender, and extraordinarily good-looking. Stevens didn't know this second man; Monica saw his quick, appraising stare.

The man in the wheel chair held out a hand. "Hello, Stevens. This is Miss Marshall, I take it?"

"Miss Marshall, I'd like to present Mr. Demarist," said Stevens.

The flesh hung on the old man's face as if it were tired and was getting ready to drop off. His eyes were tired, too, tired and pale; but in their depths glittered a feverish impatience, as though he knew he was short of time and had to be about things while he could. He turned to his companion. "This is my nephew and attorney—Mr. Richard Aldeen. Miss Marshall, Mr. Stevens." He took a minute to watch the reaction among them. Stevens held out his hand; he and Aldeen looked at each other steadily for a moment, a measuring stare. When Aldeen took Monica's hand, he did it with a certain flourish, an effect of heel-clicking and bowing, though he did no more than incline his head. There was a certain flamboyance about the man that Monica found amusing. Mr. Demarist went on, "Since I'm feeling none too chipper these days, and since the affair concerning my ward must go on even if I am dead, I wanted Mr. Aldeen in on the investigation."

Stevens obviously didn't like it. His flat stare fastened on Demarist. "I thought for safety's sake we had agreed to limit our information to as few people as possible."

Demarist touched the sagging flesh of his face with fingers that shook a trifle. "I'm not really a *person* any more. I'm a hulk, a ghost— a spook without sense enough to lie down where I belong."

"I'll withdraw, if you find my presence objectionable," Aldeen said stiffly, his dark face flushing. "I'm as eager to find Margaret as anyone is. I wouldn't want to hamstring the investigation."

"No, no," said Demarist brusquely. "The estate—Margaret's estate— must be represented after I am gone. I no longer have any hopes of living until she chooses to come back to us." He swung the wheel chair to face the room more squarely. "Sit down, please, all of you. Would anyone care for coffee?"

"I would," Monica said. Aldeen echoed, "I too." His tone was bristling, offended. Well, Stevens simply had a gift for making people dislike him at first sight.

"See if you can locate Henry," Demarist said to Aldeen.

"You ought to have bells put in," Aldeen grumbled.

"There were bells," Demarist said absently. "I didn't like them. It made me feel as if I were summoning a robot."

Aldeen went out, returning in a moment or two with the man in white. "Yes, Mr. Demarist?"

"Do you suppose Irene is still in the kitchen?" Demarist asked.

"I don't know, sir. I could find out. If she isn't there, I could fix whatever it is you wish. Is it coffee, sir?"

"Yes, we thought we might have a pot of it in here while we talk." Demarist's tone was tentative, almost apologetic, as though he feared to
overwork the people he had hired.

Oh, he's putting it on, Monica thought. He probably has a bull whip
stuck up behind that elk's head, and uses it regularly when he's irri-
tated.

Demarist was looking at her with a surmising glance. If he could read
minds— But no, he was smiling. "I'd like to hear about the little girl,"
he said.

A touch of fear fled through Monica's thoughts. So many people
seemed to be interested in Winifred, so much curiosity was shown
about her, so many minds in such odd places seemed waiting to soak up
knowledge concerning her. Even here, in this immense house which
must belong to a man at least a millionaire, there was someone wanting to know ... "What is it you'd like to hear?"

"What has she told you about the man named Veach?"

Monica found herself glancing at Stevens. He wasn't looking at her,
however; he was watching Aldeen, who had seated himself after the departure of the man in the white uniform. Monica said, "She dislikes
Veach. She says he has wolf's eyes."

"Mr. Veach is, indeed, a very terrible kind of wolf," said Demarist. "I
believe Mr. Stevens, on the phone, made mention of some incident at the
lake in the mountains. What was Veach's part in it?"

"Veach was in a boat, fishing or pretending to fish," Monica told him.
"Winifred went into the water, went far out, stepped into a hole, and almost drowned. She said that a little bird had fallen into the lake and
couldn't seem to get out, that it wobbled ahead of her on the waves, just
out of reach. I saw Veach take something from his line, a draggled thing
I thought to be a piece of weed." She stopped, aware of her own heart's
thudding; she was remembering that moment when Winifred in her
struggles had broken the surface of the lake—she saw again the streaming hair, the thin arms beating the churning water, heard the strangled
cry.

"You are afraid, just thinking of that," said Demarist, studying her.

"Yes, I'm very frightened."

"But there was no proof that Veach had done anything?"

"No."

"Did the child seem to connect Veach with her misfortune?" He
watched Monica shake her head. "But she recognized him?"

"In a way." Monica frowned, feeling baffled. "She said that he was
smaller and younger. She insisted on it."

"That's very odd," said Demarist reflectively.

"Couldn't there have been some mistake?" Aldeen wondered.

"There was no mistake," Stevens put in. "It was Veach all right."

Demarist looked at Stevens, as if expecting him to go on, to make an explanation of Veach's appearance, but Stevens said nothing further. He seemed in an unpleasant mood over Aldeen's presence. Demarist said, "I should be very cautious, Miss Marshall, in giving Veach the opportunity to get at the little girl. He is an unscrupulous and evil man. I would like to tell you—"

Stevens interrupted. "Miss Marshall knows none of the details concerning your ward, Mr. Demarist. You'll have to start at the beginning."

Demarist lifted his eyebrows. "Does she know Veach's profession?"

"No."

Demarist rubbed his knuckles together, looking at Monica. "Veach is one of the human vermin who have taken advantage of the interest in, and the recognized need for, psychological guidance. He is not a physician. At one time he studied for the ministry in a small eastern interdenominational college. He didn't finish the course, but from it he seemed to acquire a manner of authority and righteousness. He took up Yoga and other autosuggestive cults briefly, finally abandoning all of them to set himself up boldly as a psychiatrist. Under the present lax laws governing the practice of this branch of medicine he is able to operate, taking in many dupes and extracting their money and sending them away again no better, if not actually worse." Demarist's sagging face grew grim. "You see, I know much about him, since I was one of his victims."

Stevens, Monica recalled, had said: *He went through a bad time ...*

"It took me some time in a sanitarium to get over the effects of Mr. Veach's ministrations. My troubles hadn't been serious—until I went to him. In my absence here he gained the confidence of my ward, a girl I had adopted and raised " Demarist broke off to turn to Aldeen. "Get Margaret's photograph from the study, will you, Dick?"

Richard Aldeen went out of the room. While he was gone Demarist was silent, sitting hunched in the wheel chair with a brooding, regretful air. Aldeen came back with a large picture in a plain gold frame. Monica took it from him. The girl in the picture was slight and young, with a simple and obvious type of prettiness. She was blond; the tinted photograph showed deep blue eyes on a childish and rather expressionless face.

"That picture was taken when Margaret was seventeen," Aldeen offered. "She's twenty-two now, and looks older."

"She seems very innocent," Monica commented, giving the picture to Stevens.

"Innocent she is," said Demarist. He rubbed a flap of skin beside his mouth. He was obviously deeply distressed. "A trusting child, always. There was no way I could wisen her to the ways of the world. She is— handicapped."

Monica's eyes dwelt on him blankly.

Aldeen said, "Margaret is a little slow. Not much. Not enough that you'd notice it immediately on meeting her. But, as Uncle Dem says, trusting. She believes anything she's told, the way a child does."

Monica's throat grew dry. She was remembering Veach as he had looked in the strange illumination of the cabin. "And Veach—*has* her?"

Aldeen shrugged. "She went to him willingly. Uncle Dem was ill. I couldn't hold her here."

"We heard from her just once," Demarist said. "She asked us not to try to find her. There was a desperately pleading tone to the note. I sensed that some dreadful trouble was hanging over her. It was almost im- mediately after the Huffman murder. I wouldn't have connected the two events, except that Veach was called as a witness in the Huffman case. You knew that, didn't you?"

"No. I didn't follow the trial. She was my sister and I—I didn't want to know."

"You believed in Huffman's guilt, then?" Demarist asked.

"It seemed certain."

"There is something very strange under the surface of the case," the old man said slowly. "I am sure that if I could locate my ward, she could cast some new light on it. She is afraid to come to us, afraid for us to find her. I am sure she has some guilty knowledge."

"I'm not sure that I agree with Uncle Dem," said Aldeen. His dark eyes were narrowed and introspective in his handsome face. "There are a lot of coincidences possible in a thing like that. Veach wasn't an important witness at the Huffman trial. I've studied the case records." Aldeen paused to shift on his chair and to clear his throat. "My own opinion is that Margaret may have been subjected to experiences which shamed her and made her reluctant to come home."

There was a short silence. It's queer, Monica thought—we all know what he means, though he didn't put it into words. She thought of the trusting, not-quite-normal young girl with Veach, and goose flesh came out along her arms. "Haven't you gone to the police?"

"We have no grounds for police action," Aldeen answered. "Margaret is of legal age. Uncle Dem would never attempt to have her declared in- competent, even if her condition made it possible. She had a consider- able amount of money of her own—we suspect that Veach has it now. Any other funds left to her by Uncle Dem will be put in trust."

"I have a plan—" Demarist began, but he was interrupted. The door opened at that moment and the man in white came in bearing a large silver tray. There were fine china cups and saucers, deeply embossed silver spoons, sugar and cream in ornate containers. "I'm going back for the coffee, sir," Henry said to Demarist. "I couldn't quite bring it all at once."

"Blasted heavy stuff," Demarist complained. "Why didn't you pile it together on the small aluminum tray?"

"You want to show off your nice stuff now and then, Mr. Demarist," Henry said. He went out, came back a minute or so later with a large silver coffeepot. The odor of coffee stole out upon the warm air and began to pervade the room. Henry poured, passed the sugar and cream.

Demarist probably keeps him chained in the cellar when he's not working, Monica told herself; but there was no vindictiveness behind the thought. She was beginning to like Mr. Demarist. Something about his tired, friendly manner reminded her of her father.

When Henry withdrew, Demarist put down his coffee cup and resumed what he had been about to say. "I have a plan which will, I think, force Veach to show his hand. I'm going to write to Margaret in care of him, and tell her that because of my state of health I am ready to turn over to her a substantial part of what will be her inheritance—*provided* she can account for the whereabouts of the money she had when she left. I'm not going to mention Veach, or cast any aspersions; I'm simply going to state that I know she has closed out her bank account and that I'm wondering if she used the money wisely." Demarist's pale eyes seemed to burn in his sagging face. His voice was husky and urgent. "Veach is going to be on the spot. He's going to have to restore the amount of that bank account in order—as he will think—to get his hands on a much greater sum. He's going to have to let Margaret present the proof of that restoration."

Demarist straightened and grew tall in the wheel chair, as if already savoring his triumph over Veach. But it seemed to Monica, listening, that there was danger in the plan—nothing definite that she could put her finger on—but danger nevertheless.

9

"I have seen Veach only a couple of times," said Aldeen, "but he impresses me as being shrewd enough to smell a rat in that scheme."

Demarist shook his head. "You have no idea of the man's avarice. I want you to write the letter and get it into the mail at once."

"As you wish, of course, Uncle Dem."

Demarist reached for his coffee and sipped it. The thought of what he was going to do to Veach had brought a faint color into his face; he sipped the coffee with relish. "There is a woman named Lannon—" He paused as if to choose his words.

"I've met Mrs. Lannon," Monica told him. "She was keeping Winifred when I came for her. She claimed to have been a close friend of Biddy."

A glance passed between Stevens and Demarist. Demarist's look was questioning, Stevens's blank and negative. It was as if the old man had asked Stevens if Monica should be told something, and Stevens had said no.

Monica went on, "Winifred's repeated statement about Mrs. Lannon was that the woman *knew things*."

Demarist was looking into his cup. "There is a close relationship between the Lannon woman and Veach. I do not know whether it is simply a business tie or some other. When he was treating me at his home, I saw her more than once. She had an air of ease and familiarity in the place. Have you seen Veach's house?"

"No," said Monica.

"Let her see it," Demarist said to Stevens. "Let her see the house that madness built. Let her see the gardens manured with broken brains."

"Please, Uncle Dem, you're being rather grim for our guests."

"Yes. And what Veach does is grim."

"Do you think he has your ward there?" Stevens asked.

"No." Demarist made an abrupt motion of dissent. "He wouldn't have Margaret at his house. He keeps patients about, if they're wealthy enough and not too far gone to make trouble. He wouldn't take the chance of keeping a girl around whom he'd robbed—perhaps wronged in other ways." Demarist brushed at his white hair. "I'm beginning to feel a bit tired. I'll be brief with my ideas. Miss Marshall, since you know the Lannon woman and took the little girl from her house, couldn't you return there on some pretext or other?"

Monica remembered the dusty, silent street, the cavernous porch, the house that had seemed like a prison. "For what reason?"

"As a spy," Demarist said frankly. "I think, since the child is gone, that Veach may be keeping Margaret there. I can't endure to think of her—of him—" His voice broke; he put a hand over his mouth to hide its shaking.

Aldeen looked at Stevens, a look that suggested he and Monica leave.

Monica said, "I could go there, I suppose, but I wouldn't get any farther than her front room. Why don't you put private detectives on these people?"

The old man shook his head mutely. Aldeen said, "Uncle Dem is afraid that such tactics would bring reprisals upon Margaret."

"Reprisals?" Monica echoed hotly. "You handle that murderous snake as if he were made of glass."

"If Veach had Winifred, you'd handle him very gently," Stevens said in a monotone. "Try the shoe on. You'll find it fits." He rose from his chair. "Mr. Demarist, Miss Marshall and I will discuss how and when she is to go to the Lannon woman's house. We'll contact you as soon as the plans are made."

"Talk about gall—"

Stevens took her arm and guided her to the door. "Don't look back," he said. She heard a thudding noise, as if the old man were beating the arms of the wheel chair, and a high, animal-like whimpering wail.

Some instinct must have summoned the man in white; Henry passed them at the door in a hurry. "We'll let ourselves out," Stevens said to him. Henry jerked his head in assent without looking at them. He had eyes only for the room beyond, where Demarist shuddered in his agony.

"Demarist has angina. The attacks are pretty bad," Stevens said in the hall. "He hasn't long to live. His mind is tied up in knots with his desire to find his ward and make sure that Veach hasn't—hurt her. It isn't the money, in spite of the emphasis he put on it in the plan to trap Veach. Demarist doesn't give a damn for money."

There was a breeze, once they had passed through the door to the broad porch under its pillars. "He didn't say who Margaret really is, or how he happened to adopt her."

Stevens nodded. "He hasn't told me, either. There's a story back of it somewhere."

She stopped to face him in the sunny drive. "Look. Why are you so damned willing to offer me as a sacrifice to Veach on Demarist's business? Do you think I'm going to that house, stick my neck out, invite violence?"

He took out a handkerchief and mopped his temples; in that moment, she thought, he looked almost as weary as old Mr. Demarist himself. "Huffman didn't kill your sister. He was framed, but good. Aren't you willing to go a little way to keep the kid's father alive for her? Doesn't the kid mean a Goddamned thing to you?" He didn't touch her, but Monica saw the rage in his eyes.

"How do *you* know Jerry didn't kill Biddy?" She was yelling; the sound seemed magnified in the overrefined quiet of the neighborhood.

"Skip it," he ground out. "Get into the car. I'm going to do what Demarist suggested—take you to look at Veach's hacienda. It's quite a joint. You didn't think much of him as a fisherman. Wait till you see how he's doing as a psychologist."

For no reason that she could think of—except being scared stiff and so mad she could spit scorpions—Monica found that she was crying. Stevens offered a handkerchief; she threw it in his face. He shrugged. He drove the car down the drive and out into the tree-shaded street.

"Don't you ever for one moment think of anyone except yourself?" he wondered. "Weren't you touched by the misery of that old man, helpless in a wheel chair, almost crazy with worry about his ward?"

"He's got *millions!*" Monica hollered, as if Stevens were in the next county, or stone deaf. "He can hire squads of goons ... gangsters ... hoodlums—men who would make Veach look like a baby."

"And Veach could revenge himself by working on Margaret Demarist."

"You've got the imagination of a sex fiend!" Monica gritted.

"I don't imagine Veach lacks in that respect, either," Stevens said, keeping his voice obnoxiously calm and quiet. "How would you like to be kind of fuzzy in the head and at the mercy of Veach? Don't you think he has a few tricks that would make your hair curl?"

The tears flowed without stop. "Let me go to a phone and call that sanitarium. I've got to be sure Winifred's all right."

"She's all right." Stevens's tone was unexpectedly gentle. He pulled the car to the curb and stopped it. There were no houses here, only the long, high walls that bound the big estates. He turned to face Monica. "Let's have that truce. You can slap me if you want, if it'll make you feel better. One good swat. Then we'll start over."

She hit him. It was better than good; it was terrific. A wave of pain fled through his eyes; the side of his face welted and grew red.

He didn't say anything for a couple of minutes. Nor did he raise his hand to touch the reddened place. Monica had the uncomfortable sensation that he was appraising her in some subtle way. Then he said, "Did it make you feel better?"

"It's something I've wanted to do for ages."

"Yes, I thought that." He stayed turned toward her, his eyes steady in his lean, uncommunicative face. "No truce, though?"

"I'm drawing it up mentally right now. One of the terms is that I'm going to know about you. Who you are, and why you're interested in the Huffman case—that's back of your interest in Winifred, I've discov—"

He reached for her quickly. His hands gripped her throat, her shoulders, jerking her roughly in his direction. She went off balance on the seat. Her hair swept forward, obscuring her face. Then she found herself pushed and rolled to the floor, and Stevens crouching over her.

She opened her mouth to scream. At that instant a car roared past in the street outside, the wind of its passing peppering the steel door behind which she lay with bits of gravel. There was a squeal of brakes at the corner, the roar of low gear, then gradual silence.

"I'm sorry," said Stevens. He pulled her up and tried to brush the dust off her coat.

She was suddenly dry-eyed. Her head ached with a pounding pulse. She fumbled with her disordered clothes. "Who was it?"

"I don't know. I didn't have time to see. I caught the car in the rear-view mirror—it seemed to be coming at us, and damned fast."

"You thought it was—someone after us?"

"Yes. False alarm." His blank eyes hid his thoughts. Had he been really afraid of danger, or hadn't he wanted to answer her questions about himself?

She reached for the silk scarf, crumpled on the floor. "One thing I'll never understand—when Winifred and I first appeared at Raboldi's, why didn't you warn us against Veach and the blonde?"

"I wasn't sure what Veach's game was. It could have been simple surveillance. Then, too, I thought the kid would tell you she knew them, and that you'd tumble something was up. I couldn't understand why you stayed. I kept testing you. For a while I even entertained the idea that you were acting with Veach, an impostor perhaps, and going to help him get rid of the kid."

"That's why you made those enigmatical remarks—gave me those blank stares as if I were an idiot." She rubbed her temples; she felt sick, and then faint, as if a wave of feathers were floating through her head. I'm damned, she thought, if I'll fall into Stevens's arms. She rammed herself back into the cushions so that if she passed out she'd slide down on her spine, not topple forward.

He started the motor, glanced at her—a glance that turned into a steady look. "Feeling rocky?"

"I'm quite all right, thank you."

Something twitched at his lips. He wanted to grin at her. Well, no doubt he would think any sign of weakness very funny.

It seemed no more than a moment later that she roused to find herself flat on the seat cushion, her head downward a little in the direction of the curb, Stevens outside looking thoughtful.

She pushed herself up and wedged back into the corner.

"I'd better take you back to Mrs. Adams," Stevens said reflectively.

"No, I want to see Veach's domain," she answered. Her voice was okay, the feathers were out of her head, and the sickness was gone. "It must have been a delayed reaction to that long drag we made getting out of the mountains."

"Or perhaps you're just human, after all," Stevens said, getting in and starting the motor.

He drove down the canyon boulevard to Sunset, turned right toward the coast. The wind that blew in at the windows began to take on the salt-and-kelp smell of the sea. The road dipped, rose, wound among hills. Stevens turned off into a wide street that seemed to lead nowhere. There were no houses here, though paving and curbs were in and trees set out in the parkways. Then Monica saw stakes driven here and there in the brown earth. It was a new subdivision in Los Angeles' everlastingly growing city landscape, just getting ready to build. "This isn't the direct way to Veach's castle, but we'll have a good view," Stevens said. He guided the car through a little grove of eucalyptus trees and they emerged on a sort of headland. Below was a canyon tangled with wild growth and leading down to the Pacific. The water was very blue, the light dazzling. Cars that seemed the size of toys whizzed by on the highway that bordered the beach. Then Stevens touched her arm and pointed.

To the right, across the narrow canyon, was another headland, closer to the sea and slightly lower than the one on which the car stood. At its tip, at the end of a winding drive, was a big two-story tan stucco building. Monica observed the wide, red-tiled roof, the Portuguese balconies, the ornate trimming of scrolls and moldings, a wide sun porch facing the sea. "It isn't what I had expected," she said. "I thought it would be something like Mrs. Adams' place—low and modern, and shut in with a steel fence to keep his nuts from running wild."

"He doesn't have to worry about the patients—it's pretty certain he keeps them all mildly doped. The house belonged to a big movie star, a hero of the silent pictures in the twenties. It was quite the castle of its day, and the reputation clings a little, I suppose. Now it's dated, but Veach probably feels quite lordly out there above the sea."

The grounds about the tan stucco house had been extensively landscaped. Monica could see an overalled gardener guiding a lawn mower and hear the staccato puffing of the motor that turned the blades. "Do you agree with Mr. Demarist," she asked, "that Veach wouldn't have his ward here? The place looks big enough to conceal a battalion."

"Demarist knows Veach better than I do. I've merely spied on the guy. Demarist was his patient."

"You think that—that Veach killed my sister?"

Stevens's fingers tightened on the wheel. "Yes, I think so."

"Why? What earthly connection could a decent girl like Biddy have with a man like him?"

"She knew him pretty well."

Monica tried to pierce the expression on Stevens's face. There was a mixture of anger and stubbornness, she thought, plus a kind of reserve, as if he disliked what he was thinking. "I don't believe that."

"I'm not saying she *liked* Veach," Stevens argued. "She might have become entangled with him without realizing just what she was getting into."

"You mean—he had some sort of control over her?"

He gave her a look—one of the how-dense-can-you-be? looks. "If your sister got involved with Veach, she did so for money. Don't tell me she didn't care for the green stuff." He waited; Monica's face must have betrayed the sudden memory of the letters Biddy had written, the letters whose only complaint had been the lack of ready cash. "Veach needs steerers for his racket. He can't stroll down the street and buttonhole somebody and say, 'Look, old man, it seems to me you're on the skids a bit and need psychiatric treatment.'"

"Biddy—Biddy wouldn't—"

Stevens continued as if he hadn't heard her. "Veach's principal digging is done among the alcoholic brethren. No reputable doctor sends him anyone to work on, of course; he recruits his suckers at the source. At good, high-class gin mills. All he needs is a name, an address—a quick check can tell him if the too-steadily inebriated one has family or money enough to make stripping him profitable."

Monica shook her head determinedly. "I know that the state of California controls sanitariums for the cure of alcoholics. Such places have to be licensed and inspected. He can't set himself up as a doctor without—"

"No, no, no," said Stevens impatiently. "He's a psychological adviser. He supposedly gives no physical therapy, merely consoling talks and a comforting analysis of one's difficulties. You can't forbid a man to talk and get paid for it. In addition, Veach has other protection. He has a pseudo-religious organization to back him up. The officers of the outfit are all people he has cured. Oh yes, it surprises you to learn that he *does* sometimes cure." Stevens's laughter was chopped off, bitter.

She thought about it. "No, it doesn't surprise me. Even witch doctors have their cures. But where is your proof that Biddy was mixed up in this horror?"

"We'll have to go back to the case against Jerry Huffman," said Stevens. "We'd have to eventually, anyway; you know far too little about it." He took out cigarettes, offered Monica one, lit both hers and his. "Huffman and your sister and the kid had an apartment in Hollywood. It's significant, I think, that they'd moved out of Mrs. Lannon's house about six months before and into a much more expensive establishment, though Jerry hadn't had any increase in wages. He was working in a garage at sixty dollars a week. The rent on the apartment was two hundred a month. Your sister had some pretty sizzling clothes."

Monica felt the color drain out of her face. "You knew her before she— she was killed. Who are you?"

"I'm not really anyone you'd care to know," Stevens answered in the aggravating way he had of saying things that meant nothing. "Jerry Huffman believed that the money was coming from some trust fund your parents had left his wife."

"That was gone years ago," Monica put in. She wondered, suddenly, if

Biddy could have spent that final settlement on herself instead of in a garage venture as she had hinted. Her sister's image was beginning to shift, to seem strange to her. The memory was not of the little girl with the soft, blowing feathery hair, but of a woman she had never known.

"Jerry and the little girl lived in the apartment, of course, but they seemed to get no other benefits from the sudden riches," Stevens said. "Jerry wore coveralls at his job. His taste in clothes was simple. The kid's things always looked a bit short and a bit tight, as if she were starting to outgrow them."

Monica rubbed her eyes to relieve them of the dazzle from the sea. "If you knew them as you seemed to have, why didn't Winifred recognize you as she did Veach and the blonde?"

"She did remember me—after we talked that morning in the boat. I hadn't seen her for quite a while, remember—her dad had been arrested, tried, and sentenced during that time, and she'd been with the Lannon woman. Anyway, I came to the apartment only when your sister wasn't at home. Barbara didn't like me." His level glance met Monica's startled one.

"If Biddy didn't like you," Monica said slowly, "there must have been a reason."

He didn't offer any defense, any argument. He just went on smoking, as if Biddy's opinion of him hadn't mattered. Monica felt a slow red creeping up her face, and with it a kind of panic, a desire to get out of the car and run—before she heard anything more about her sister.

10

"The principal witnesses against Jerry at his trial were the manageress of the apartment court where he lived and the janitor there." Stevens crushed out his cigarette into the dashboard container. He turned toward Monica. He looked cool and disinterested, as if he were talking over the score of a baseball game. "You see, Barbara was killed at around four o'clock in the afternoon. Ordinarily, Jerry would have been at work at that time. But a telephone call came for him, asking him to come home in a hurry. It was a woman's voice. The girl who answered the phone in the garage office said that she knew Barbara's voice, and this was it. Anyway, Jerry seems to have cleaned up a little and gone home."

Monica's mind painted a picture: the tall blond boy who'd married Biddy, grimy in overalls and fresh from the greasy underside of a car, entering a court where the apartments rented for two hundred dollars a month. She tried to imagine the place. It was as if Stevens read her mind.

He said, "It's a new building, very nice, two stories high, built in the shape of three sides of a square with a wall to shut out the sight of the street and a big parklike patio in the middle. The apartments on the second floor are entered from a balcony which is open to the court. There are palm trees in the patio, and patches of ivy geranium, and a pool, and a paved space with beach umbrellas and little tables beside the water. All very Californian, and exclusive. Naturally Jerry didn't use the patio entrance in his work clothes. His place was upstairs, and it would have involved mounting the steps in full view of the loungers at the pool and parading along the balcony in front of these people of leisure."

"But *you're* not prejudiced," Monica said dryly.

"I'm a realist," Stevens said. "I can understand why Jerry didn't use the balcony entrance to his apartment when he came from work without getting hot under the collar over it."

She ignored it. "There was another entry?"

"Yes. Down each side of the building is a service walk leading to the alley, and each four apartments has a door and an inside landing for milk and paper deliveries and so on—this also applies to the apartments on the alley. Inside stairs lead to the upper apartments, each pair having an upper landing. Jerry, when he arrived home, went down the left-hand walk to the second door and opened it. He claimed that that is when he found Barbara, dead, lying face down on the staircase."

"No one believed him."

"No. No one believed that he'd found her like that because of the testimony of the janitor and the manageress. Just before four the janitor was sweeping the service walk below the back windows of the Huffman bedroom. He heard Barbara's voice raised in argument and weeping. He heard her speak Jerry's name. A crashing sound followed. The janitor, whose name was Wilfred Spriggs, went for the landlady. The things he had overheard didn't sound 'very proper'—this was the phrase he used in court. He thought the manageress might need to take a hand to keep the situation under control."

In spite of the conviction Monica held that Jerry Huffman must be guilty, she found her interest quickening. "Then what?"

"The manageress went into the inner court and used the balcony to reach the Huffman apartment, front-door talk being more authoritative, apparently. She rang the bell repeatedly. Presently Barbara opened the door a crack and peeped out at her. The manageress stated that the policy of the house was quiet at all times. Barbara said that she'd try to remember it, that her husband was abusing her but that she thought she had him calmed down. This testimony was bitterly attacked by Jerry's attorney in court as being hearsay, and was, I think, thrown out, but not before it had made its impression on the jury. The manageress, acute for the stupid woman she looked to be, asked Barbara if she thought she was in any danger. Barbara hesitated."

Monica shifted uneasily in the seat. "That's the sort of thing people always remember—afterward."

"So it is. Barbara hesitated, and then said that if things got any worse she'd take steps. The landlady was not specific. I suppose she meant 'call the police.' The door closed, and that was the last time anyone but Barbara's murderer saw her alive."

Monica thought about it. "There should have been some sort of proof in the time angle—what time Jerry Huffman checked out of the garage, how long he might have taken walking home, and so on."

"He was out of luck there. Since he was leaving early, at the special permission of the garage foreman, he didn't check out with the time clock. The idea was that a friend would do it for him at five-thirty—a favor that would keep him from getting docked. So there was no exact check possible. He acknowledged that he didn't rush, as the call from Barbara had requested. They'd had words at the breakfast table and he was, in his own expression, 'fed up.' He anticipated more quarreling."

"That admission couldn't have helped his cause in court."

"No, it was damaging."

Monica frowned. Her eyes were on the stretch of sand at the far end of the deep, tangled canyon, on the sea glitter and the rushing swarms of toy-sized cars; her mind was in a courtroom where a slender and bitter blonde young man sat on trial for his life. "There must have been some other evidence that Jerry had been home before finding Barbara's body."

"Evidence of the most crucial sort," Stevens agreed. "Under the body of his wife were two fresh spots of auto lubricant. You may be sure that that grease got the works, and it came up, sure enough, as the type used in the garage where he worked. His overalls were pretty well saturated with it. You see, he claimed not to have touched the body. If he'd had sense enough to say that he'd turned her over, the grease wouldn't have meant much."

"It seems such a little thing."

"Things much smaller have trapped murderers before."

"Were there—other things?"

"A couple. A smudge of grease across the back of her neck and a touch of it in her hair. You understand it was hard finding traces like that, since the weapon had been a hammer and the method thorough."

"I know," Monica said hastily. Into her memory swam the image of a paper she'd picked up at a newsstand, the way she'd stood reading it in the windy street, her heart at once dead and yet bursting: HUFFMAN

HAMMER VERDICT, and under the heavy print a picture of Jerry with a single word, *Guilty*. "Were there fingerprints?"

"No. Hidden in the lining of a suitcase was an insurance policy on Barbara's life, with Jerry as the beneficiary, to the amount of ten thousand dollars in the event of accidental death—one of these mail-order policies you can write in for without a physical examination. You know, seven to seventy, come all. The night before Jerry had complained to the manageress that there was a slick place on the back stairs where Barbara had almost fallen. He admitted it; he said Barbara had asked him to speak about it."

She shook her head. "He couldn't have thought such injuries would be taken for the result of a fall."

"They made it look as if he had."

"What about the weapon?"

"It was a ball-point hammer, very greasy, which showed evidence of having been used in a garage. It was at the bottom of the clothes hamper in the bathroom, along with a couple of towels which seemed to have been thrown over Barbara's head while the beating went on. No blood splashed, you see. The stairs, except for the area immediately under the head, were clean of bloodstains. So was Huffman—until they turned his pants inside out. They found a faint smear on the inner surface, near the knee. The prosecution's theory was that he rolled up his pants to keep them from any chance of being soiled."

"There's a conflict in the testimony. The business about the slick place on the stairs and rolling up his trousers point toward premeditation. But Biddy's phone call wasn't anything he could have arranged."

Stevens shrugged. "I thought of that. It didn't appear to worry anyone else. They went all out on the premeditation angle, with the insurance as a motive. Jerry said he hadn't even known about the insurance, that Barbara must have taken it out herself. A weak defense—it didn't make any difference."

"Where was Winifred during all this time?"

"Can't you guess? At Mrs. Lannon's house."

"That seems a bit queer."

"They made it fit into the case against Jerry. He'd taken the kid over in the morning, early. Barbara had worked intermittently—they didn't say at what—and the Lannon woman had cared for the kid during those times."

"And what was Veach's evidence?"

"As a friend of Barbara, he testified that she had told him frequently of her fear of Jerry. He wasn't the only witness along this line—several unsavory characters, who have, significantly, disappeared since, gave the same evidence." Stevens straightened suddenly in the seat, his eyes narrowing. "Wait a minute. I think we've been spotted. Look at that top-floor window at the left. Do you see a spot of light now and then like a reflection on the lenses of field glasses?"

Monica watched, and a dim glimmer came, a twin glow like the peering eyes of a ghost. She felt a sense of shock, as if something from the house had touched her, had fingered her flesh. A shiver started between her shoulder blades. "Yes, I caught it."

Stevens started the car, backed it, circling the way they had come. The dim greenery of the little grove swallowed them. He looked ahead, at the road that led down the hump of the small headland and on into Sunset Boulevard. The road was empty, empty and sunny and full of peace, and the neat pegs staked out by the builders and roped with twine were like whimsical mazes made by children. Still the cold feeling remained with Monica, chilling her bones.

On the boulevard the traffic was fast. Stevens maneuvered the car into the outer lane in the direction of downtown L.A. before he spoke again. "I want to locate that bar where Winifred waited for her mother. I have a funny hunch about that. Some days Mrs. Lannon may have had other business and Barbara might have been stuck with the kid. Then she'd have to take Winifred along, I think, and probably she parked her in the car while she went in. Did you know about the car?"

"No," said Monica.

"A Cad convertible. Very snappy. Jerry sold it to help finance his defense."

Monica's lips tightened. "It was Biddy's car, though," she said.

"Oh yes. Earned by steering suckers to Veach."

Monica shook her head. "Whatever the truth was—that wasn't part of it. Biddy had an old-fashioned sense of what was right."

"She'd been corrupted, then. How long since you'd seen her?"

"A long time." Monica counted mentally. "She and Jerry married at my apartment in New York during the war. They left immediately after."

"Anything could have happened in those years."

"Not—not what you think happened." But there was panic under her words, and she wondered how much of it showed in her voice. Hanging on to her will to disbelieve took a special effort. The memory of the years when she had been building a career—when she should have been checking up on Biddy—was a bitter taste in her mouth. In that moment she hated Stevens more than she ever had.

He drove for a while without talking. "I'm going to take the kid for a drive after we get back to Mrs. Adams' place. She just might recognize that bar where she waited outside. I'm not asking you to go along because I know you think I'm lying."

Monica wouldn't answer. She kept her eyes on the unwinding boulevard. They came to the university, big and sprawling on its hills, its grounds lush under the heat of summer. The paving was flecked with eucalyptus shadows. She thought suddenly of Boozer, of his impatient thirstiness. "Stop at a liquor store. I want to get my cat some beer."

Stevens began to watch the buildings as they passed them. "When do you want to go to Mrs. Lannon's place?"

"I don't."

He raised his eyebrows a bit, as if mildly surprised at her objection. "I'm sorry I can't go with you. That would be a giveaway, of course. They know you're on guard because of the way you lit out and gave them the slip at Raboldi's, but I'm hoping my identity is still a mystery to them."

"I don't need you to come with me," she said, clipped and businesslike. "I've remembered something I really want from Mrs. Lannon. Biddy must have left some personal things and Mrs. Lannon should know where they are. I want them."

He offered her a cigarette. She shook her head without looking at him. He began to light one leisurely for himself. "You won't give away the fact that you're onto Veach and his racket?"

"Why should I? I'm going for Biddy's things, not to inquire about Veach. I don't think Veach wants to harm Winifred because of the murder of her mother. I think it may be because of something the child overheard while she was at Mrs. Lannon's."

"You think that Jerry Huffman killed your sister?"

"I'd have to have definite proof that he didn't."

He shook his head, as if at her stupidity. "Watch yourself while you're at Mrs. Lannon's. She's a hard, shrewd character."

"You wanted Winifred left with her," Monica reminded, remembering what he had said in anger at the lake.

He didn't defend himself, didn't even bother to answer; his attitude seemed to imply that if Monica wished to she could figure out the answer for herself. He pulled to the curb in front of a liquor store. "Do you want me to get it?"

"I'll get it." She opened the car door hastily, before he could offer to be polite and help her, and crossed the pavement to the open door. Inside it was bright and cool, with fans humming and a radio playing, and a short man in his shirt sleeves putting canned beer into a big glass-front refrigerator. He looked back at her. "Yes, miss?"

"I want some beer."

"I got all kinds. What do you like?"

She found herself looking at a telephone on the wall. A quick glance toward the street showed her that Stevens could not see her from the car. "Wrap up four cans of Acme. Take your time. I'm going to phone." It had struck her, in that moment of entering the store, that in all of this fantastic business there was one person who saw things approximately as she did. Aldeen—Mr. Demarist's lawyer-nephew. She knew, instinctively, that Stevens hadn't liked him. It should be a recommendation.

She looked in the thick book for the phone number, took a nickel from her purse, dialed Demarist's house. Henry came on the wire; she recognized his professionally pleasant and soothing tone. "This is Miss Marshall. I would like to speak to Mr. Aldeen."

"Yes, miss. Just a moment," Henry said.

Aldeen's voice was brisk, friendly, warming. "Hello. Miss Marshall? What can I do for you?"

Now she felt suddenly at a loss. "How—how is Mr. Demarist?"

"He's resting now. You understand—these attacks are nothing new to him. He became overexcited, talking about Margaret—"

"It was in that regard that I called," said Monica, suddenly seeing her way clear to common ground. "He asked me to go to Mrs. Lannon's house. I've decided to go this afternoon."

"Uncle Dem had no right to make such a request, Miss Marshall."

"I'm going anyway, on an errand of my own. If possible, I'll try to find out whether your uncle's ward is there."

"I don't feel at ease over your going there alone," Aldeen said slowly. "If these people are all that Uncle Dem says they are— Wait a minute. I have an idea. What would you say to my coming along?"

"It's very kind of you to offer."

"It occurred to me—if there are two of us, one may get a chance to look around, more likely to at least than if one goes alone."

"That's right," Monica agreed. Aldeen's friendly thoughtfulness was a refreshing change from Stevens's reserve.

"I'll pick you up at Mrs. Adams' place," Aldeen offered.

"Fine. Say—in a couple of hours?" She wanted to give Stevens time to get away with Winifred. She had a hunch he wouldn't care for her bringing Aldeen in on her errand.

"This woman won't know me, of course," Aldeen warned. "You can introduce me as a friend. Veach would recognize me, but I think it's worth taking the chance that he won't be there."

"This is all very decent of you."

"No, no. It's little enough, considering all that Uncle Dem has done for me. Frankly, I don't think we'll find Margaret, but if you go I want to go with you."

"I'll be waiting for you."

"Good-by, then."

"Good-by."

She turned from the telephone. The proprietor of the store had put the beer in a brown sack, folded the top down neatly to fit the contents, and was ringing up the charge on a small machine. She opened the change purse in her hand and was removing a dollar bill when her eye fell upon newspapers in a rack beside the counter. Someone had taken out the first paper, glanced at it probably, and put it back in upside down, so that the lower half of the front sheet showed instead of the headlines. A minor thing; she noted it without interest as she put her hand on the counter. Then she saw the item in the left-hand corner, the tiny black heading that leapt out at her, stabbing her mind.

Huffman Appeal Denied, it said.

She reached for the paper mechanically. *San Quentin, July 21: The appeal of Jerry Huffman was denied by the governor today. Huffman is under sentence of death for the murder of his wife, Barbara, in Los Angeles, and is due to die in the gas chamber four days from now ...*

Four days.

"Are you feeling all right, miss?"

"Quite all right," said Monica stiffly. She picked up the coins the little man had laid down as change, put them into the small purse, put the small purse into her bag, and lifted the beer in its brown paper sack.

Stevens was standing by the open door of the car. He gave her a hard look. "Who'd you meet in there—Dracula?"

She got into the car. He closed the door and came around to slide under the wheel. "Four days isn't enough," she said through wooden lips.

"It's not much." He stared meditatively at the street, the traffic; his face was blank, uncommunicative. "We'll do the best we can and, when time runs out, we'll forget it."

She closed her eyes and rubbed them hard with her knuckles. The sun was too bright, the street garish in the strong light, the rush of traffic seemed unendurable. Through her head ran a little refrain: Four days. Tomorrow, three. Next day after, two. Then one. Then none. "Let's go," she said to Stevens.

The refrain began again, senselessly: *Four days. Tomorrow, three ... Next day after, two ...*

11

Winifred met them at the gate, looking warm and worried. "Boozer caught a grasshopper and ate it. Mrs. Adams says they'll give him fits. Now he's asleep, but he twitches."

"He's dreaming," Monica told her, handing her the sack. "Go ask the cook to open one of these. Put some in a dish and stick it under his nose. He'll quit twitching."

Winifred eagerly grabbed the sack and ran away.

Stevens was closing the door of the car. "You wouldn't care to go with us?"

Monica shook her head. "I'm not even sure I should let you take Winifred." Her tone reminded him that he hadn't been honest about himself; she'd meant it as a simple dig, and was surprised when anger flared in his eyes.

"You don't have to worry about the kid when she's with me." There was subtle irony under the words. Monica was forced to recall the accident on the grade and the terrifying fiasco in the lake; she flushed hotly.

"*Touché*," she said softly, and went in. The Amazon at the inner door nodded a greeting. In her room she threw the scarf and coat over a chair and flopped on the bed. The new tape was beginning to pull and rub as badly as the old. She shut her eyes, and a desire for sleep stung behind her eyelids. She took a deep, relaxing breath; the bed was soft, the room quiet and cool. Then the door flew open, and Winifred bounced in with the cat and a soup bowl of beer. The cat had one eye open, and his expression was leering. The beer dripped. Monica took one look and lay back.

Four days. Tomorrow, three ...

"The rest is on ice," Winifred informed her. "The cook thought I was going to drink it myself. She said she was afraid I was a—a al-colic."

"Nothing should worry her, working where she does," Monica said.

Next day after, two. Then one. Then none.

"Now you set here, baby," said Winifred in the oddly protective tone she used with the old cat. "Don't spill it." She put Boozer on the wide window seat and pushed the beer into place before him. Boozer opened both eyes and took a longing but cautious sniff. Apparently he had resigned himself to a life of thirst. He gave several investigative slurps before settling down to his usual gluttonous lapping.

Winifred watched with a doting motherly air. "When did he start liking beer, Aunt Monica?"

"I think his mother must have weaned him on it."

"Does he drink whisky?"

"Or gin or wine or rum or even vodka. I don't suppose he's a good pet for a nice little girl like you."

"I love him," said Winifred frankly, rubbing the yellow-and-orange fur. "At first I didn't like him. 'Specially when he wouldn't eat my chicken salad." Her eyes dwelt on the wall, full of thought.

Now was the time, Monica thought—her mind's on Jerry Huffman this moment. "Tell me about your father," she forced herself to say.

The old response came, unhesitating, quick as a whip stroke. "He didn't do it."

"How do you know he didn't?" The question she should have asked days ago, Monica told herself. She raised on an elbow to watch the child.

Winifred shook her head. "He didn't."

"But that day—you were at Mrs. Lannon's house."

Winifred's gaze crept off the wall and fixed on Monica's face. An expression of distrust tightened the child's mouth, settled in her eyes. My reward, Monica thought, for never believing. "Come on. Tell me."

Winifred licked her lips. "He wasn't there. He wasn't in our rooms."

There was always this sensation of fighting fog or feathers; you thought you were coming to grips with something solid in Winifred's narrative and then it dwindled in your grasp. "Look. You weren't at home. You went to Mrs. Lannon's house early in the morning. You were there all day; in fact, you probably just never did go home, since your mother was dead and your father had been taken away. How could you know your father wasn't there when your mother died?"

"You called her Biddy before." There was a hint of injustice, of lost faith, of defection on Monica's part.

"—when Biddy died, then," Monica corrected.

"She talked to me on the telephone."

It was a moment before Monica realized what Winifred had said. "What?"

"Mama called me on the phone. She said, 'How are you? What are you doing?' I told her, and she said, 'Be a good girl.'"

Monica was sitting up in bed. "When was this—what time of day? Was it late?"

Monica's ferocious interest seemed to repel the child. She drew back into the window seat. "It was four o'clock," she said firmly.

"How do you know what time it was?"

"I was taking a nap, and Mrs. Lannon came in and said, 'Your mama's on the telephone. She wants to say something to you.' We went into the front room. It's not very light in there. There are a lot of curtains and things. Mrs. Lannon got up close to her old clock and then she yelled, 'My God, it's four o'clock!' Then she acted like she was going to grab the phone, but I was already talking to Mama."

"And—and then what?"

Winifred touched the tip of Boozer's tail. "You won't believe it."

"Tell me! Try me!"

"I heard Mr. Veach. He was there with Mama. He said, 'Hang up that damned phone and leave that brat alone.' I'm not a brat, am I?"

Something had tightened in Monica's throat, almost choking off her breath. "Did your mother hang up?"

"She said, 'Be good. Be a good girl.' Then she made a noise like crying. Then she hung up."

Monica leaped off the bed and raced for the door. In the hall she almost ran over the timid nurse, who was carrying her usual rack of thermometers. "Which is Mr. Stevens's room?"

The nurse made shocked eyes at her, as though Monica had unspeakable designs on the man. "Really—miss. Patients are supposed to rest just before lunch."

"I'm not a patient and neither is he."

The nurse's glance flickered guiltily toward a door at the rear of the broad hall. "Shall I check for you, and find out if he's awake?"

"He's awake." Monica ran to the door and flung it open. Stevens was by a window, looking out, smoking a cigarette. He turned as she shut the door hastily behind her. "I—I've learned something important."

"From Winifred? What is it?"

"About Veach. He was with Biddy at four o'clock the day she died."

"And?"

"He ordered Biddy to get off the phone and quit talking to Winifred."

Stevens's face grew very quiet, all expression washed out of it. His hand, taking the cigarette from between his lips, was very steady. The breath on which he exhaled smoke seemed no more than a sigh. "I thought it might be something like that."

"We must take her to the police at once."

He took time to think about it. "We can do that, as a last resort. We'll be accused of coaching the kid, of course. There's not much meat in what she says—perhaps not enough to save Jerry. But we'll use it when we have to. Let me talk to her a little more." He followed Monica back into the hall. "Just me," he said at her door, his glance dismissing her.

"Why?"

"I think I might get more out of her alone."

"But there—there isn't time to beat around the bush. There's only four days!"

"I've always been aware of just how much time I had," he said levelly. He went in, and the door closed behind him.

She felt shut out, unwanted, unworthy of trust, outraged. She looked behind her. The timid nurse was standing there with a rubber-wheeled cart holding a rack of dinner trays. "Would you like to eat in the sun porch, miss?" The veiled eyes had a smirk in them; the nurse had heard Stevens's curt dismissal.

"Anywhere," said Monica, hating her. "Just anywhere at all, so long as I'm not near Mr. Stevens."

The nurse smiled, very smug. "As you say. This way, then, miss." A side corridor led to a brick terrace which had been roofed in and partially enclosed in glass. A lot of potted fuchsias and ferns lined the balustrade. A painted metal table held magazines and playing cards and a portable radio. Two other people were already there, in lounge chairs, wrapped in robes: two elderly women who conversed in low tones and gave Monica and the nurse not so much as a glance.

Monica sat down in a wicker chair near the exit to the grounds. The nurse put the tray on a redwood stool beside her and went back into the hospital building. Monica began to investigate the contents of the covered dishes. There were creamed sweetbreads on toast, mashed potatoes, buttered spinach, two hot buns ...

Next day after, two. Then one ...

She jerked her mind away from the senseless chant and looked at the two old ladies. One was talking earnestly, punctuating her speech with a pointing finger. In the middle of a sentence the other gripped the jabbing hand and examined the outstretched finger minutely, the way a monkey examines another monkey for fleas. "I'll be right there with you before long," Monica told them under her breath. She put the lids back on the dishes and carried the tray outside. Under a tree was a shed, propped against the shed was a none-too-steady bench. She sat there to eat the lunch.

The grounds were pretty and peaceful under the bright sunlight of noon. A faint breeze blew from the direction of the coast. The birds in the trees had lost their morning frenzy and sat, looking somewhat stuffed, in the shady spots among the branches. Monica surveyed the wide driveway, the locked gate, the road outside. Pretty soon Mr. Aldeen would be driving up that road to take her to Mrs. Lannon's house. There wasn't any reason she shouldn't walk down to meet him.

She went back into the enclosed terrace. The nurse was there now, giving lunch to the two indifferent little old ladies. Monica spoke, her tone excessively pleasant and civil. "I want some fresh air. Would you mind bringing my coat and scarf from my room? I'm a bit cool out here."

"Surely. Just a moment." The nurse spread napkins on the little old ladies, pointed out the excellence of the sweetbreads and the goodness of the spinach. To Monica in passing she muttered: "They never eat anything but the mashed potatoes."

When she returned, Monica put on this coat and tied her hair into the scarf. Then she strolled idly back to the shed, beyond which were other outbuildings: the garages, a lath house, and miscellaneous storerooms. She went on to the edge of the grounds, to the fence. There was a back gate here, a small one giving on a footpath. A very businesslike-looking padlock hung through the chain. She looked about. Just coming from the lath house was the gardener who had admitted them yesterday. "Hello," she stammered, wondering if he would give an alarm at seeing her try to escape.

He fished for a key on the end of a leather leash. "You want out for a bit, miss?"

"Yes, thank you." Was it the coat? Did they keep the real nuts in their nightshirts so that he knew at once she was not one of them?

"Mrs. Adams told us you was to come and go as you pleased," the old man explained, loosening the lock and chain. "You and Mr. Stevens, she said. The patients here—well, you understand we couldn't let them traipse out when they felt like it. They're sick folks. Some of them would never find their way back. Some would get into trouble. They're like little children."

"They get well, though," she said, thinking of Mr. Demarist.

"Oh, sure. Some do," he qualified. "Will you be coming in again soon?"

"I'm going for a stroll. I'll be gone for a while—don't wait here to let me in again."

He nodded. "Give a whistle when you come back."

"I'll do that." She walked away. The feeling of freedom was unexpectedly vivid; she had the sensation of having been shut up for a long time. It was the steel fence, she decided. She scuffed the dirt with her shoes, feeling reckless. To herself she admitted a childish desire to worry and annoy Stevens by her absence. If he kept shutting her out of things, she'd repay him in kind. She looked back at the long, low building with its air of safety and refuge. For a moment she was tempted to return.

Creep back to him, she told herself scornfully; lick his boots. She went on. The footpath crested a little rise that gave a view of the San Fernando Valley. The hills were covered with dead grasses which were tall, headed with seeds, burned pale by the sun. Here and there were clumps of dwarf oak, desert laurel, and manzanita. Below lay a few large homes, then the business district bordering Ventura Boulevard, then the thickly-settled level portion extending for miles. The broad valley lay under a haze of heat smoke, the little houses and streets foggy and far away.

She walked on. She was out of sight of the sanitarium now. The street curved in close under the rise. She gained the pavement and stood to cool off in the shelter of a eucalyptus tree. Presently she heard the motor of an approaching car in the direction she had come. She stepped out of sight behind a bushy oleander—it was Stevens and Winifred in the rented car. Winifred was on her knees in the front seat, peering ahead as if expecting some gigantic surprise. Monica couldn't see Stevens's face; he was opposite the side where she stood watching.

For a moment she wanted to hail them, to demand to be taken along. When the car had vanished she felt very much alone, a little frightened. Well, when you were nutty enough, even rudeness like Stevens's seemed preferable to emptiness and silence.

She walked steadily downhill. Though there were no houses here, the paving had been laid long ago. In places it was broken. She scuffed through dead eucalyptus leaves and drifted soil. Any of Mrs. Adams' patients who managed to get over that steel fence were in for a hike.

She thought about Mr. Demarist, about his sick old sagging face and the fear he had for his ward, who wasn't quite bright and who was at this moment at the mercy of Mr. Veach. She thought about Mr. Aldeen. He was nice, she decided; he had good sense. He knew what had probably happened to Margaret but he wasn't rushing off madly in all directions to her rescue. He knew that getting her away from Veach must be done delicately and would take time. Time.

Four days. Tomorrow, three. Next day after, two ...

She pulled her thoughts out of the rut. Suppose we find Margaret, she speculated, and get some sort of testimony out of her concerning Biddy's murder. Would the evidence given by a subnormal person be admitted in court? Would Margaret stand up under cross-examination? Wouldn't the prosecution try to bring out what she'd suffered at Veach's hands and use it to cast doubt on her motive in testifying? What chance have we, anyway, to help Jerry Huffman (provided he's worth helping), when the only two witnesses in his behalf are a little kid and a semi-moron?

She remembered Margaret's photograph: the shy, believing face, the blankly trusting eyes, the soft chin, the attitude of innocence. She thought then of Veach, of the way she had seen him clearly at last in the cabin, illumined by the glare off the lake; she recalled the congealed evil in his gaze. And again she experienced the prickling sense of horror.

She shut her eyes and leaned against one of the tall eucalyptus trees that bordered the parkway. The dry air stung her throat. The tape that bound her and kept her bones from falling apart was a white-hot vise. She was trembling. "I'd hire a goon squad," she found herself saying out loud. "I'd get me a bunch like—like Al Capone. I'd blast that damned yellow monstrosity of a house right into the sea."

A car drove past slowly, paused, began to back up toward her. She waited, watching with a feeling of dullness. It was a new Dodge with the top down, a blue and shining car. Aldeen leaned from behind the wheel to smile at her. His teeth looked very white in his dark, handsome face.

She managed to smile back. Aldeen parked, got out, and approached her. "Hello. I hope you haven't walked far in this heat."

It was hot, she realized suddenly. She began to pull off the coat and scarf. Aldeen took the coat, folded it neatly, and laid it in the back seat of the car. "I'm all right," she said.

"You're a brave and generous person to do this for Uncle Dem."

"I have an errand of my own at Mrs. Lannon's."

"Decent of you to put it that way." His hand under her elbow, assisting her into the car, was firm and somehow intimate. He smelled of shav-

ing lotion, a crisp, heathery odor. His black hair was full of little curl-
ing lights under the sunny glare. "Would you rather have the top up?
Only takes a minute."

She rubbed her temples. "Yes, I believe I would."

He got behind the wheel, touched a button, and allowed the canvas top
to rise. He backed the car, turning it; they began to roll in the new direction, downhill. His glance was subtly observing. "You seem a bit
wilted. What do you say to a tall, cold drink before we go too far?"

She looked at him gratefully. "It sounds wonderful."

He stopped at a place on Ventura Boulevard; it was air-conditioned,
coolly lit with dim blue lights. "How about a Collins?" he offered.

"It's fine," she agreed.

He beckoned a waiter, gave the order, turned back to her. "That place
you're staying—Mrs. Adams' place." He chuckled. "Don't the inmates
sort of get you?"

"They're a little odd," she said, thinking of the two little old ladies and
the monkey-like scrutiny of the finger.

"I used to visit Uncle Dem when he was there," Aldeen added. "It was
quite a show." He made amusing small talk about the things he had
seen.

She felt herself relaxing under the influence of Aldeen's normal, casual attitude. The memory of Veach's motionless eyes, the hideous urgency of Jerry Huffman's vanishing days, the horror and mystery of
Biddy's murder began to submerge themselves in her mind so that she
could look at them measuringly, calmly. The nervous trembling went
away. The Collins was set before her; it was cold and sharp.

In the bar with Aldeen she felt better than she had for days.

12

The street was still the same: there was still the sense of deadness,
too much quiet, too much dust on the windless air. Mrs. Lannon's porch
echoed their steps from the walk, a faint beat like a far-away drum. The
rampant lantana brushed their clothes as they passed and left dirt on
them. Aldeen looked around, surveying the neighborhood; he wrinkled
his nose at Monica and she saw that he shared her opinion.

Monica looked at the house more closely than she had before. There
was an attic room, she saw, with a single window in the peaked gable
above the porch. A net curtain hung behind the glass. There was a base-
ment too. Tiny cobwebby panes were set into the foundation on either
side of the steps. The place was bigger than it looked, bigger than she
had thought it to be.

She touched the black button on the wall and stood back.

Mrs. Lannon opened the inner door and looked out through the screen. The jet eyes gleamed; she took in all details of Monica and Aldeen's appearance before she spoke. "Oh. Miss Marshall. How d'you do?"

"This is a friend, Mr. Aldeen," Monica said.

Mrs. Lannon seemed to peer into the crannies of the porch. "You didn't bring Winifred?"

"No. I came about something else. May we step inside?"

"Oh. Sure." Mrs. Lannon unlatched the screen and stepped back. "Come in. It's warm today, isn't it?" Her glance on Aldeen was approving, even friendly; his glossy, immaculate appearance had taken her fancy. "Have a chair, won't you?"

They sat down. Monica was aware all over again of the closeness of the room, its unaired smell. There were too many draperies, too much heavy claw-footed furniture. The potted fern had been sprayed for its sickness. The runty fronds gleamed under a coating of oily liquid and there was an antiseptic stench. Mrs. Lannon smoothed the black silk of her bosom. "Is there anything I can do?"

Monica said, "It's about Biddy's—my sister's—things. Her personal belongings. There must have been some. I thought you might know where they were stored. Or—if I'm lucky—that you might even have them here."

There was no surprise in Mrs. Lannon's manner; she was nodding, almost smiling. "Yes, there are a couple of boxes and a suitcase. The maid at the apartment court packed Barbara's things after her death and I just put them away without disturbing them. I've had them all this while, and wondered now and then how to get in touch with you. Funny I didn't remember, that day you came for Winifred—" She turned to Aldeen in a manner that implied an apology. "Putting you out—an extra trip like this!"

He grinned at her. Plainly he knew how to handle the Mrs. Lannons of this world; their steel turned to butter under his touch. "No trouble." He looked lazily at the scene through the open door. "I haven't been in this part of town for ages. I was beginning to wonder what it looked like down here."

"This part of L.A. never changes." Mrs. Lannon looked over her furnishings and her room with an air of complacent satisfaction.

"It has atmosphere," Aldeen told her. "It has the flavor of the old city, the way I recall it as a kid. We lived close in on West Adams when West Adams was in its prime. I don't remember much of it except the feeling of old-fashioned comfort; and this reminds me of it."

She almost purred, Monica thought. Aldeen was an artist in handling

people. He had soothed Demarist, cautioned him on his plan to draw
Veach into the open, tried to act as a buffer between the old man and
Stevens's determination to have action—something Stevens hadn't
loved him for. Now he had Mrs. Lannon lapping out of his hand like a
house cat.

She rose after another moment and glanced at Monica. "The things
that belonged to your sister are upstairs. Would you like to look them
over, or shall I just bring them down?"

"I'll look at them," Monica said, seeing the chance to leave Aldeen alone
on the lower floor. He should have time to take a quick look through the
rooms here, perhaps even a peep at the cellar. She winked at him mean-
ingfully behind Mrs. Lannon's vanishing back.

He jerked up a hand, thumb and finger circled in a gesture of knowing conspiracy.

The hall was dim. They passed several doors, one of them to the room
in which Monica had first seen the child, and at the end reached a small
open space some five feet square. This was the bottom landing for a tiny
staircase that mounted into gloom. Mrs. Lannon had paused to wait for
Monica. "He's nice, isn't he?" she said, nodding in the direction of the
front room.

"Very nice," Monica agreed, hoping that they moved on before Aldeen
should come tiptoeing in to the hall.

"He reminds me of my late husband—sort of," Mrs. Lannon decided.

"A brunet," Monica said idly.

"No. The politeness." Mrs. Lannon started up, her skirts rustling. She
was heavy inside the rigid corset; by the time they reached the attic
landing she was puffing a bit. Two doors faced them across a space in
almost complete darkness. Above, a grimy skylight let in a dim gray
glow. One door, Monica realized, led to the front room whose curtained
window she had glimpsed from the street. But it was not this door, but
its opposite, which Mrs. Lannon opened.

The room inside was small and crowded. Its unshaded windows faced
the rear yard and the fenced alley. Monica found herself looking at a
dressmaking form, an ancient treadle sewing machine, a long table piled
with boxes and cartons and a miscellaneous litter of paper, and a large
mirror which reflected the room. "I used to sew in here," Mrs. Lannon
explained. "Then I just sort of gave it up and started buying ready-made
things. Is Winifred in town with you?"

The question, slipped in at the tag end of the casual remarks, put Monica on guard. "She's with friends."

"Bring her around sometime," Mrs. Lannon said. "I miss her a lot." Her
tone and manner were almost indifferent; it was only in the depths of
the black eyes that some emotion glittered—anger, avarice, perhaps a

combination of the two, Monica thought.

"She's not the easiest kid on earth to manage," Monica observed.

Mrs. Lannon paused with her hands on one of the cartons. "Does she ever mention me?"

"Oh yes," said Monica thoughtlessly.

"What does she say?"

In spite of herself, Monica hesitated: a blunder, a betrayal. She found Mrs. Lannon's gaze searching her face. "Just—just little things you used to do for her. She hasn't forgotten, you know." Did it sound as false to Mrs. Lannon as it did to her? A weak, stammering lie.

Mrs. Lannon pulled two cartons forward to the edge of the table. "Here you are. Tied tight with twine. One had a damp spot on the side, and I was tempted to open it in case of damage, but then I sniffed, and it was just cologne leaking, so I left it be. The suitcase is in a closet. I'll get it. It's locked. I never had the key." She went to a door under the eaves and snapped a catch, and brought out a blue cowhide dressing case. She rubbed dust away with her hand. "Nice. This cost money."

It had cost money. Its weight was solid in Monica's grip as she took it from Mrs. Lannon. Monica examined the twin catches at either end of the lid. They were locked. She lifted the case and shook it. Apparently there was something heavy and solid inside wrapped in clothing; a muffled thud reverberated the heavy cowhide.

Monica put the case on the end of the table. "I'm curious about this. I think I shall see what is inside. Do you have any stray keys hanging about? Something I could try on it?"

This was giving Aldeen a lovely lot of time. The cartons were still to be investigated.

"I used to." Mrs. Lannon's black eyes seemed to turn inward in introspection. "Old keys, tied up on a shoestring. In a drawer somewhere." She frowned, tapping her toe. "Wait a minute. I used to keep them in a drawer of the machine."

Monica felt a surge of triumph at the way things were working out for her. She waited while Mrs. Lannon went to the sewing machine and opened several drawers and finally lifted from one a dirty string on which an array of keys hung, all shapes and sizes. Mrs. Lannon started to hand her the keys, then paused. "I ought to tell you what I think. When Barbara first began to worry about her husband and the way he was acting, I loaned her a gun. It was never returned. I forgot about it. But when you shook the case, and that sound came, I thought of it. I remembered."

Monica smiled pleasantly. "If we get the case open, and if it is a gun, you shall have it back," she promised.

She took her time with the keys—none were an exact fit but two of them gave promise. One of the two, with twisting and pressure, finally snapped the catch. Inside was a ruffled mass of silk underwear and nylon hose. Monica lifted a nightgown of black chiffon, one of blue crepe, white brassieres, pale tan hose—these she pushed out of the way. Rolled into a cylindrical bundle was a flame-colored dressing gown of heavy silk; it had a solid core whose weight sagged in Monica's hands. She unrolled it—caught the gun that slid out.

"Is this the one?" She held it toward Mrs. Lannon.

The woman didn't offer to take it; her face puckered as if in dismay. "I've wondered—I hope it wasn't the cause of that final trouble between them. She might have showed it to him, you know, trying to protect herself."

The grip fitted solidly into Monica's palm. She turned the gun this way and that, touching the cold steel; there was a deadly look about the thing, though it hadn't, after all, done Biddy any good. "I wish—" She thought of Biddy, her back to the wall in terror and madness, pumping bullets into Jerry Huffman. "No, I guess I don't. I just wish there hadn't been any difficulty between them at all."

Mrs. Lannon walked to the unshaded window and looked out at the yard as if deeply troubled. "So do I."

"Where shall I put it?"

"Just lay it on the machine."

Monica put the gun down on the dusty lid of the sewing machine and turned her attention to the cowhide case. There was nothing else in it except the tumbled lingerie. Monica fiddled with this, stretching out the time she could give Aldeen. Then she touched one of the bound cartons. The twine was thick and taut, resisting her efforts to loosen it. "Do you have scissors?"

"If I were you, I'd take the boxes along as they are," Mrs. Lannon offered. "You'll need time to sort all that stuff."

But Aldeen might be in the middle of something interesting, Monica thought. "I won't unpack here. I'll just glance in."

Mrs. Lannon stretched her lower lip between thumb and forefinger. "My scissors are downstairs. I'll bring them up."

Monica was afraid that Aldeen might be caught in the rear of the house, until she heard the noise that Mrs. Lannon made on the stairs. The heavy, jarring tread should give him plenty of warning.

She stepped to the open door and waited, her ear tuned to catch any least sound from Mrs. Lannon—knowing that this would be her chance, her only chance, to explore the other room!

Mrs. Lannon had reached the bottom of the stairs, had paused there to draw her breath and exhale a gusty sigh. Monica darted out upon the upper landing. The other door seemed to gleam at her through the dim gray light. Mrs. Lannon, out of sight beyond the turn in the stairway, grumbled something half under her breath, the muttered words echoing in the stairway's dark tunnel. Then she walked on down the hall, her feet thudding. A bedroom door opened and shut.

Monica put a hand on the knob of the door to the other room. It turned under her grip, turned easily and silently. The door drifted inward without a sound, and she looked at the room beyond.

The gable window let in the afternoon sun in a great bright patch upon the rag rug and the shining floor. The net curtains blew a little on the draft; there was a faint odor of lilac sachet. A bed under a fresh white cotton counterpane occupied one front corner, a painted dresser the other. On the dresser was a clean white scarf and silver toilet articles, bottles of perfume, a jewel box, and a pair of dark sunglasses. Monica took a single step inside. To her right she saw an open closet in which hung an array of dresses, a sport coat, a dressing gown of pale green chenille.

A sense of hot excitement seized her. Though there was no one in the room at the moment, it was undoubtedly lived in. In addition, it had a sparkling brushed-and-dusted cleanliness which the rest of Mrs. Lannon's house lacked. Monica pushed the hair from her pounding temples; she was convinced that this was Margaret's room. As old Mr. Demarist had shrewdly surmised, Margaret had been brought here when Winifred was out of the way. Here she remained cooped up, her money gone, feeling puzzled and bored no doubt, perhaps frightened and shamed also, keeping the little room gleaming and immaculate as a method of whiling away the dreary hours, or as a protest against other things which she was helpless to deal with—the things Mr. Demarist had feared for her. A kind of dirt which wouldn't scrub off.

Monica went to the closet, took out one of the dresses on its hanger. It was of lightweight pale rose crepe with a wide black patent-leather belt. The moment Monica touched it, she knew that it had cost a good deal of money. There was high style in the subtle cut, a hint of lovely daring at the neckline, a silken cobwebby feel to the material. She examined the tab in the back of the neck. *House of Monaco, Beverly Hills.* A famous shop, noted for its original creations. She frowned, knowing that she should have remembered to ask old Mr. Demarist how much of her clothing Margaret had taken, the sort of things she preferred, and where she had bought them.

Would Veach have bought the girl new things? Monica thought not. These gowns were important. She must fix them in her mind.

She returned the first dress, took out another. This was a dull blue taffeta; there was a bodice with flaring sleeves, a row of tiny red buttons down the bosom, a full, bias-cut skirt. *House of Monaco* again. In the back of the closet, in a clear plastic envelope, hung two fur coats. Monica pulled them forward into the light, unzipped the side, put in a hand. She'd never felt such soft, silky luxury.

Hats sat in a row on pedestals on the shelf above. Monica looked at them, trying to visualize the innocent face of the not-quite-normal girl under each of them. They were, she decided, rather sophisticated. Of course Mr. Demarist's ward was older than she had been in the photograph.

A row of shoes sat on the floor under the gowns. Monica picked up several pairs; though none were new all were of expensive make and showed thorough care. They were of a size smaller than her own, some of them of rather extreme cut, with elaborate lacings and exaggerated heels. Of course you couldn't judge the taste of someone like Margaret Demarist from her appearance in a photograph, Monica thought. If old Mr. Demarist hadn't supervised her shopping, the clerks might have been able to sell her what they chose.

Monica backed from the closet. A sudden feeling of uneasiness sent her out upon the landing. She tried to walk silently, to still even the rustle of her clothing. The house below seemed to be empty of life. She could not recall having heard the bedroom door open and shut again, but of course she had been engrossed with the things inside the room.

She was so tense that the sound of Aldeen's and Mrs. Lannon's voices came, with shocking loudness. Apparently they were in a room just below, the kitchen perhaps. Monica caught the noise of chipping ice, of the ice being dropped into a container. "... and in this heat, it'll be real nice," she heard Mrs. Lannon say.

"Awfully kind of you to think of us," said Aldeen.

Mrs. Lannon: "I'll run up and ask Miss Marshall to have a glass."

Monica bit her lip, strained to hear. "Oh, let me go and tell her," Aldeen said, rising to the emergency.

Monica turned, raced across the empty room to the dresser. She had a moment or two left. Aldeen, when he arrived, would understand and would keep his mouth shut about where she was. She opened dresser drawers hurriedly, finding neat stacks of underthings, a box of hose, one of handkerchiefs. The lilac sachet had been sprinkled in the drawers, so that everything was dimly fragrant.

She even took time to lift the lining papers, but there was nothing of unusual significance anywhere. The last thing that might give proof of Margaret's presence would be the jewel box. Monica lifted its lid.

There had been jewels here. The velvet tray was marked with the impressions of rings, the padded inner lid showed the stab marks left by heavy pins. Now there was nothing but the dark red lining and a few flecks of dust. Veach, Monica thought. Of course he'd cash in any jewelry. She took the tray by its small center bar and lifted it out.

A single ring lay in the lower compartment—white gold with a tiny span of diamonds. Monica took it upon her palm, frowned over it. In her mind something was struggling to make itself known.

She heard Aldeen tiptoe into the room, heard his whisper of question. She shook her head, remained staring at the ring. It was important that she should know, should remember. Frightfully important. She knew that.

"Is this Margaret's room, do you think?" Aldeen's voice was no more than a breath beside her ear.

She nodded without looking up.

"Good. Let's get out of here and go tell Uncle Dem. Mrs. Lannon isn't going to wait all day down there beside the pitcher of lemonade. The old bat's going to get suspicious."

She closed the ring inside her hand, shut the jewel box, walked to the door and shut it silently. She knew now. There was no use trying to remember any longer—the picture had come back. The image of Biddy in her wedding dress, her hand outstretched, the ring on her finger.

This ring. She caught at the stair wall, felt Aldeen's touch instantly under her elbow. Veach *had* killed Biddy. He had killed her and taken her ring and after robbing Margaret he'd given the pitiful token to her to keep her still.

13

Old Mr. Demarist's face looked more sagging, older, frightened, dull-witted, and gray with a slick sweat. When Aldeen bent above the bed and said, "We think we found something important, Uncle Dem," the old man merely turned his head to stare with half-shut eyes. Aldeen looked at Monica. "Henry gave him something to ease the attack. He's still a bit fuzzy."

"I understand," said Monica.

The old man brought a hand from under the bedclothes, a clean, knotted, shaking hand, and touched the cuff of Monica's sleeve. She was in a chair beside the bed in the big plain room. The Venetian blinds let in very little light. Henry sat reading on the other side of the room, too far and too indifferent to overhear what they said. The room smelled faintly of medicine and floor polish. Old Mr. Demarist gave off odors of rubbing alcohol and soap. Everything was clean, bare, shipshape.

Mr. Demarist said, "Not much time. Can't fuddle this. Got to do it right. Right the first time. You didn't see her?"

"We didn't see Margaret, but I'm sure we found her room in Mrs. Lannon's house. I want to tell you about the clothes I saw there."

"Clothes?" The old man's voice was a husky, disappointed whisper. He spread his fingers on the rim of the sheet, shut his eyes, sighed.

Monica gathered her thoughts. The ring in her clutched hand was a distraction—the white gold made a circle of ice against her flesh, a brand. She'd held it all the way from Mrs. Lannon's—held it even in the house, while she stared into Mrs. Lannon's jet-black eyes and drank her lemonade. Her heart had pounded; there hadn't been much feeling in her head, just a sick, dull awareness of what was going on, of the chatter between Aldeen and Mrs. Lannon, of their getting ready to leave, and of Aldeen carrying down the cartons and Biddy's blue cowhide bag. Then the cool wind on her face as the car raced for Beverly Hills. And now old Mr. Demarist's regretful whisper—he didn't care about the clothes, he wanted the girl who wore them.

He spoke before she could begin. "We didn't know what was wrong until Margaret was almost eight years old. She had been a lovable baby. Obedient, friendly, trusting. Small, with yellow curls and a mouth like a rose. Kitty and I made no demands—Margaret talked or she didn't, she walked when she got ready to. It was late. Then, when she was seven and a half, we took her to a specialist. We'd had trouble with the private school, with the reading teacher who said Margaret wouldn't learn. The specialist told Kitty and me in his office—a very decent man—and it wasn't the teacher, it was Margaret. Our little Margaret wasn't—wasn't—"

How had the specialist phrased the bitter verdict, Monica wondered? Kindly, she judged. Kitty—that would be Mrs. Demarist—would have cried, perhaps, and Mr. Demarist would have comforted her. But there would have been a wound, the kind that never closed. How do you feel about a child who will never be able fully to protect itself? She thought of Winifred, the alert, self-sufficient, opinionated brat. Suppose—

She knew then.

Old Mr. Demarist opened his eyes. "Tell me about the clothes."

She forced her thoughts back to the closet in Mrs. Lannon's house. "If I describe them, you might recognize something of Margaret's. That would make it certain that she's there."

"Yes?"

"There was a dress of pale rose silk with a, wide black leather belt. The neckline was low, the skirt full and pleated. Another dress was a smoky blue, taffeta, and had red buttons down the front of the waist."

"She wore it for my birthday," old Mr. Demarist whispered.

"There were two fur coats—a gray squirrel and a black Persian lamb."

"She had four," said Demarist. "Those two, and a mink, and a blue-fox cape."

"I didn't see the mink or the cape." Monica looked down at the hand which was clenched about her sister's ring. "There were hats and shoes. These were sophisticated, elaborate, and very high-style. Most of the shoes had unusually high heels."

Old Mr. Demarist frowned, as though some detail had struck an objection in his mind. He puckered his lips in thought. "Any jewelry there?"

Her clenched hand tightened. The ring might be evidence, but she intended to keep it. It had been Biddy's—now it was hers. The last link between the two of them; the first goad in her private vendetta with Veach. "There was a leather jewel box on the dresser. Nothing in it, though there were marks left by jewelry which had been kept there."

Old Mr. Demarist's sick eyes searched out Aldeen's face. "This is much worse than we thought, Dick. Worse than just the money. Besides the things I'd given Margaret, there was all of Kitty's collection too. The diamonds, that ruby gadget with the hanging pearl, the emerald clips, those earrings we bought in London—" The flesh under the sick eyes twitched and grew taut. "Did you mail that letter to Margaret in care of Veach?"

"Yes, I mailed it," Aldeen said soothingly.

A grim, fanatic humor crossed Demarist's wet face. "We'll have an answer soon, then. He'll be on tenterhooks for a while, not quite decided what to do—to risk returning the stripped bank account so that Margaret can come into a bigger sum, or to let the gamble slide. I'm betting that he'll gamble. He'll gamble, and I'll get him."

"Perhaps so, Uncle Dem. Or he might smell the trap. We'll know in a little while."

Mr. Demarist coughed and twisted on the pillow. In a moment Henry was there, his face full of watchful concern. "Before you go—" Demarist tried to rise on his elbow; his shoulders shook with the effort. "Miss Marshall, I don't quite know how to say the things I feel—an immense gratitude, a humbleness for the risk you took. I feel sure that once we find Margaret, and get her free of Veach's influence, we will know the truth about your sister's death."

"In a little while," Aldeen repeated. "Just a short time."

Four days ...

Monica said, "I understand."

"I must plan the next step very carefully. If you're willing to help contact Margaret—"

"I'll be glad to."

Demarist's eyelids fluttered; his throat swelled. Henry interposed himself between the bed and Aldeen and Monica. "You'd better let him rest now. It's a strain on his heart, even thinking about the girl and Veach.

He oughtn't to talk about it, ever."

"We're going, Henry," said Aldeen. He gave Henry a smile that implied that Henry was the wisest and most faithful guardian his uncle could have had, and Henry smiled back, briefly, in pleasure.

They went out of the house to the broad porch. Aldeen paused to light a cigarette for each of them. "It's going to kill him," he said softly.

"At least he knows that the girl is alive," Monica pointed out. "She fared better at Veach's hands than my sister did."

Aldeen stared at the sunny drive, at the fountain whose waters splashed gold under the late sun. "I don't think Margaret will come back. She's easily controlled, easily kept in check, lethargic. Uncle Dem should be glad to know that she's alive and well, and at least not living under the same roof with Veach."

"It struck me," Monica said, "that your uncle, unknowingly and in kindness, had made a sitting duck of his ward."

Aldeen's black brows rose in question.

"He shouldn't have given her so much personal property," Monica pointed out, "since she was incapable of protecting it or herself from predatory people."

"That's right." Aldeen nodded. "That's exactly what I've told him, over and over. I wish you had said it to him in there. The more he gives Margaret, the more she hands over to the people preying on her. This new scheme, this bait to force Veach to restore Margaret's money—it won't work the way Uncle Dem thinks it will. Margaret is stupid, but the people behind her are clever. She'll have the bank account put back, Uncle Dem will kick through with the amount he's promised, and she'll end up with nothing while Veach and his gang pocket the dough." Aldeen's mouth was bitter, his dark eyes flintlike.

"What do you think he should do?" Monica's mind was not wholly taken up with the question; her thoughts were centered on the small gold band in her clenched fist, on Biddy, on the horror and degradation of Biddy's dying. Veach had been in the apartment; he'd forbidden Biddy to call her little girl; he'd performed a hideous murder ... Biddy must have had a foreboding. It was the reason she'd called Winifred at four o'clock. Everything about that last conversation spoke of farewell. It should, she thought, be legal to shoot a man like Veach. She remembered the gun that had been in Biddy's cowhide bag, and a hot sense of fury swept her. She should have managed to keep it, taken it and gone to see Veach, forced her way in, killed him as he had killed her sister.

Only—killing Veach wouldn't remove Jerry Huffman from the condemned row at San Quentin.

Aldeen was speaking. "Uncle Dem would never do what I think he should, so I've just kept my mouth shut about it. But if I were he I'd cut

Margaret off without a dime, I'd sue for the return of Aunt Kitty's jewels, and I'd put a private eye on the job of digging up enough on Veach to run him out of the state. If things got uncomfortable enough, he'd drop Margaret like a rag."

"That would take time. And it would simply drive Veach underground. You still wouldn't have any evidence against him."

Aldeen nodded. "You're thinking of your sister's murder."

"Yes."

"Uncle Dem raised your hopes that Margaret must know the truth about it. I wish he hadn't done that. It was unkind on such slender proof—"

"No—it's certain!"

The handsome face smoothed out to blankness. "You have evidence of your own?"

"Yes. It's true. I *know*. Veach did the killing. He planted evidence which implicated Jerry Huffman. I don't quite see how he managed part of it." Monica was remembering the testimony of the janitor and the manageress. The janitor had heard sounds of a fight, with Biddy crying Jerry's name. The manageress had heard a direct accusation. Could these people have been paid by Veach to give such evidence? Or could Biddy, in the grip of some terrible fear, have covered Veach's presence to the bitter end?

She rubbed her temples, trying to ease the pounding inside her head. It was warm; the fountain made hazy rainbows in the heat, and the few blackbirds scouting the lawn for bugs had an indolent air. "I'd better get back to Mrs. Adams' place. I'll look through Biddy's belongings, and if I find anything further that concerns Margaret, I'll call you."

"Do that." He ushered her to the car with an air of concern. "It's been a sticky afternoon. I hope you're not overtired."

"I'll be quite all right," she said, grateful for his courteous interest.

"Call me anyway this evening—just to talk," he said as if on sudden impulse.

There was something new in his voice—warm, personal, cajoling. A little bit of wolf cropping out, Monica thought. It amused her. In the midst of her fright and terror for Winifred, the ugly mystery of her sister's death, and Stevens's bullheadedness, she had almost forgotten that she was a woman.

The gardener carried the two cartons and the blue case into her room. Monica put them in the closet. She wasn't up to looking at them just now. The tape was becoming an agony; her bones ached, funny cold fingers played at the back of her neck, and her head buzzed. She stretched out on the bed in her clothes and shut her eyes. Then the young nurse came in with the rack of thermometers. Monica opened her mouth; she was too tired to argue.

The nurse went away. She came back in a little while, removed the thermometer from under Monica's tongue and looked at it. She didn't say a word, but a sudden attentive stiffness in her posture didn't escape Monica's drowsy eye. The nurse went out quickly, and Monica sat up. A dizzy nausea clutched her.

Mrs. Adams returned with the young nurse. She was smiling with a brisk, confident, casual air which wouldn't have fooled anyone. She sat down beside the bed, twinkled professionally, and said, "Let's count a little pulse here."

"I'm quite all right," Monica said. This is my tag line, she thought. I'm always telling people that I'm all right. They don't believe me, but I go on telling them anyway. The room swam.

"How have you felt today?"

"Fine. Splendid." Oh, just ducky—I passed out in Stevens's car, of course, and I thought I was going to drop on Mr. Demarist's veranda. Being picked up and carried around by handsome Mr. Aldeen shouldn't be an unpleasant experience. She looked dreamily at the ceiling. It wriggled.

"The—the accident in which you hurt your ribs—any severe bumps you might have overlooked?"

"No. Not a one. I sort of half caved in one side of me against the steering wheel. And I think my skull did things to the windshield. But this feels more like the flu. A very mild flu which will go away if you give me five or six aspirin."

"Your ribs hurt, of course."

"Well, I keep remembering them."

"Let's have the tape off."

They turned down the bed and undressed her while she grumbled at them. The tape seemed to want to take the skin with it—the two were everlastingly welded in fire, fused in agony, interlocked cell by cell. Monica bit her lips for a little while and then she let it out—a scream that lifted the roof.

Someone looked in the door in a hurry. Mrs. Adams threw a sheet over Monica, and Stevens's voice said, "Sorry."

The tape was off. Monica lay on her face and squeezed her eyes shut and said, *"Dammit! Dammit! Dammit!"* into the pillow. Cool fingers poked and probed.

"Let's have Dr. Shattuck take a look, shall we?" Mrs. Adams crooned at Monica.

"I'm all right," Monica ground out.

"He'll know what to do."

"I want my clothes on before that damned Stevens comes back in here!"

"I'm awfully sorry. Miss Raymond was standing between you and the door, though, so you needn't worry."

"It's the principle of the thing!" Monica yelled.

"Of course," said Mrs. Adams. "Please don't cry like that. You're only causing yourself unnecessary pain."

"Who's crying? I'm gritting my teeth!"

"Good girl! Just lie quietly until we get Dr. Shattuck."

Mrs. Adams went out swishing her white skirts. The other nurse remained, looking solemn and big-eyed, as though Monica were developing symptoms of beriberi or elephantiasis. Winifred popped in for a moment, yapping about the trip she'd made with Stevens; she managed about a dozen words before the nurse had her shoved back out into the hall. During the eviction, Boozer squeezed in between the nurse's ankles. He came to the bed, jumped up, marched to the middle of Monica's stomach, and looked curiously into her face. He had a leering, debauched look, she thought. He smelled strongly of beer and fish.

"Go away!" Monica gritted at him.

He sat down on her stomach and burped.

Some time later, after the doctor had taken his little satchel and his hypodermic needles and gone, and Monica was sitting propped up eating dinner off a tray, Stevens put his head in at the door. "Hello." He looked wary and embarrassed. Damned snoop, Monica thought. She ignored him.

He came in anyway. "Where did you go this afternoon?"

"To Mrs. Lannon's house," she said, inspecting the broiled sole.

"Alone?"

For some reason the look she gave him made him flush. Or perhaps his thoughts were making him flush. "Mr. Aldeen kindly went along."

Stevens sat down, though she had in no way indicated the chair. "Why did you scream like that?"

It was her turn to blush. "My skin was coming off with the tape."

"All right now?"

"It seems I have a touch of pleurisy. That's why I keep wanting to pass out with fever, and why my breathing hurts me, and perhaps even why I—I hate you so damned much."

The mask look came over him. She hadn't realized until then that it had been gone, that an opener and friendlier expression had taken its place. She puzzled over it, wondering, until she remembered the incident of the suddenly opened door. Her mind seemed to throw up a wall; she stiffened on the bed. Stevens asked hastily, "Did you find anything important?"

"Margaret Demarist is living there in an attic bedroom. I didn't see her, but I found clothing which Mr. Demarist identified. I found this too." From under the pillow she took Biddy's small gold band.

He took it; it looked small and shining on his brown palm. "Whose is it?"

"It was Biddy's wedding ring."

He looked at her—a funny, half-shut look that seemed trying to read her face without knowing. "What do you think it means?"

"Veach killed Biddy. He robbed Margaret Demarist even of her foster mother's jewels. In return, as a sop, he gave Margaret this ring."

Stevens's voice seemed hoarse. "It could mean other things."

She thought it over. "You mean that Veach could have gone through some hocus-pocus pretended marriage ceremony with Margaret?"

"Perhaps."

"He wouldn't need to. She wouldn't be strong enough mentally to hold out against him, marriage or no marriage." In sudden impatience Monica changed the subject. "What results did you have this afternoon?"

"We found a bar." Stevens was sitting hunched, as if he were tired; his eyes were still on the ring. "My idea was to take you back there this evening. You were to be my alcoholic wife, over whom I was worried. I thought we might run into someone who was scouting for Veach, and who had known your sister."

Monica shook her head impatiently. "There must be more direct methods than that."

Stevens didn't argue. "I'll figure out something," he said.

14

Three days ...

Monica inched cautiously over in bed so that she could see the window and the gray early light. The birds were at it again in the trees outside. A convention of sparrows. The air smelled damp and fresh, and the iron bars looked very black.

Tomorrow, two ...

She had on a great deal more tape now. The doctor had explained the mechanics of pleurisy: one layer of your lungs rubbed against another when you breathed, and since in pleurisy both were sore and infected, it was like the rubbing together of two boils. So you wore a casing of tape as stiff as cement to keep you from expanding when you breathed. Where did the air go? Into your stomach, probably. It was nice to have something to speculate over. She'd spent the long night thinking about

Biddy.

She remembered that Biddy had been a moody and difficult child. Their parents had indulged and petted her because she'd been terribly ill when she was small. Monica remembered the pale face on the big white pillow, the bottles of medicine, the quiet dim room, the weeks of waiting. What had Biddy been ill of? Polio? T.B.? She couldn't recall; it had been very serious, and when Biddy had recovered her presence among them had always seemed a miracle of giving back from Death.

Monica was eighteen when their parents had died in the car wreck. She had worked her way through art school. The money her parents had left, the modest savings and the money from the sale of the house and the twenty thousand in insurance, had been put aside to keep Biddy in a sheltered place. Biddy at fifteen had had a fragile pixie loveliness— not a girl who would challenge the world. Monica saw that Biddy stayed on in the good expensive school, and that worry, excitement, and grief didn't touch her. A good sister. I was, Monica thought savagely, a damned fool. Why didn't I bring her to New York and introduce her to the wolves of the world and teach her to protect herself from them? I let her marry a dumb kid, whom she seems to have ended up treating like dirt; I let her get herself innocently involved with a creature like Veach.

In her anger Monica rolled a little without thinking; it seemed in that moment she was aware of every bone in her sick body. When Jerry Huffman rolls on his prison cot, she wondered, does he feel all his bones? Is he struck with the idea of how fine and sturdy Nature made them, so that they long outlast the flesh? Does he touch his skull in the night and think of its grim look, its fine, grim lines in the dark of the grave under the prison churchyard?

Such thinking was unendurable. It was better to wrestle with something else—with the problem of sitting up, for instance. When the nurse came in some minutes later she found Monica ramrod straight in the bed, panting with exertion.

This was an elderly nurse with jowls and a freckle beside her nose which was growing hairs. "You're not supposed to be sitting up, Miss Marshall." She made it plain that she intended to do something about it, so Monica lay down again. "Penicillin," said the nurse. "Turn over."

"I haven't even had breakfast."

"Lots of things before that." *Stab.* "Washing up, brushing teeth, using the pan."

Privately, Monica was damned if she would. When the nurse went away she propped herself up, got her legs over, staggered to the bathroom. There she did all of the things the nurse had itemized minus benefit of help. Then she went to sit firmly in the window seat.

The nurse came back, took one look, and went out again.

Presently in walked Mrs. Adams, very crisp and irritable. She stood over Monica. "We admitted you as a favor, Miss Marshall. Even though you are now ill, you are not ill in the way with which we expect to cope, and you *are* occupying space which may become necessary to people who badly need it."

It wasn't too awful, sitting up, Monica thought, so long as she didn't move her upper torso quickly. It could be endured.

Mrs. Adams tapped her toe. "We ask co-operation—no more—so that you may get well and prepare to leave."

"I am prepared," Monica said stubbornly. "Just pack me up and ship me along to a hotel somewhere. I'll be fine."

Mrs. Adams flushed. "Your attitude is unworthy of you. It's childish and silly." She half-turned; she wanted to stamp out of the room and make a lot of noise slamming the door; the desire flamed in her face. But training won. She said civilly, "Just go back to bed and stay there for a day. Then Dr. Shattuck will look at you and decide how you're getting on."

Monica experimented, letting her body sag inside the cement casing of layers of adhesive tape. By relaxing, letting the muscles go flabby, all of the pain seemed to float away; it was as good as being in bed.

Mrs. Adams said, "We admitted you because Mr. Stevens said you were in some sort of danger—"

"Stevens is apt to say almost anything," Monica put in. She wasn't trying deliberately to rile Mrs. Adams. She wanted out of this place because if she stayed here she was going to be sick and there wasn't time for it.

"And the little girl?"

The words were a flare in Monica's mind; she tried to figure out what she could do about Winifred. Stevens was no fit guardian for a child, though he showed unmistakable signs of being willing to take over. Funny. She had never managed to get out of him his exact place in the scheme of things, though it seemed obvious that he was interested from Jerry Huffman's point of view. He was Jerry's friend, or a relative—there was nothing impersonal in his feeling about the case.

Monica studied Mrs. Adams and decided to pull in her horns. She could not afford to have the woman evict them; she would have to slip away by herself, leaving Winifred in the shelter of the strong house built to hold madmen. She rubbed her hands over her heavy black hair. "I'm sorry. I'll be good and go back to bed."

"That's better," said Mrs. Adams. The victory made her feel good; she touched Monica's shoulder consolingly. "It won't be long; you've suffered out the most of it. As soon as the penicillin takes down the infection you'll be better than new."

"May I see Winifred?"

"Of course."

Mrs. Adams went out but the older nurse remained; she straightened the bed and changed the water in the bedside pitcher and inspected Monica out of the sides of her eyes as if wondering how good a job she'd made of the scrubbing. "You can hop in now, Miss Marshall."

Monica went to the bed and fell upon it lengthwise like a log; it kept her from hurting and it also ruined the neat, tidy effect. The nurse stifled an exclamation and went out. When she returned she had Winifred and a tray. "I'll bring yours. You sit here."

Winifred sat down; she looked fresh and scrubbed and healthy. An obnoxious friskiness kept her bobbing on her chair. "I'm going to eat with you."

"Sit still. What did you do yesterday on the trip with Stevens?"

"We rode around. We found a place where Mama used to go. He went in. I ate me a popsicle and a little box of raisins."

"Not ate *me*," Monica corrected. "Just ate. You ate a popsicle."

"It dribbled on me," Winifred added. "I sucked the juice at the wrong places."

The nurse returned with Winifred's tray, put it on a stand, took the napkin and tucked it neatly into the neck of Winifred's dress. "Poached eggs. Aren't they nice? And melba toast with jam. Let's see, milk, orange slices—"

"When I get out of here I'm going to have waffles again," said Winifred in a tone that implied she was serving a stretch in jail.

The nurse swished out and shut the door. Monica said, "Go on about yesterday. Did anyone go in or out of the bar that you knew?"

"No, but Wanda waited on the corner for the bus."

"Wanda!" Forgetting herself, Monica tried to jerk erect. "Did she see you?"

"No. I scrooched down in the seat. She was fanning herself with a paper. When no one was looking, she scratched—right down *here!*" Winifred demonstrated, leaving no doubt as to what Wanda had done.

Monica thought about it. Was Wanda a spy, a messenger of Veach? "Do you suppose she lives nearby?"

"I don't know."

"Mrs. Lannon used to meet her at that same bus stop?"

"Sometimes. Sometimes other places. Do you like poached eggs? They're like eyes, aren't they?"

"What did Wanda and Mrs. Lannon talk about?"

Winifred paused to consider. She bit into the dry toast with a crunching noise. "It was jokes sometimes, because they laughed. Once in a while Mrs. Lannon would get a little cross at Wanda, and twice she said,

'Keep your lip buttoned.' When they talked about my daddy they called him George. They thought I didn't know. Once Wanda said, 'How long has George got?' And Mrs. Lannon said, 'Not time enough to figure it out.'"

Not time enough … No, not enough. Three days.

"Did you ever meet Wanda there with your mother?"

"No. I never saw Wanda till after Mama was gone."

Monica ate, not tasting the food. If Wanda had appeared on the scene after Biddy's death, it might mean that she was some sort of replacement, taking Biddy's place. Biddy had become involved with Veach because of an innocent desire to have more money, to live richly. That had to be it—Veach had gradually involved her in his schemes; she'd spent the money on the better apartment, on clothes. This would have been like Biddy. She'd always been spoiled and petted and indulged. When the last of the money from the estate was gone, she'd looked around for a way to get her hands on more. Like a child. Veach had taken advantage of her, and in the end she must have revolted; then he'd killed her.

I have two little shreds of proof, Monica thought: the thing Winifred tells about Veach being in the apartment at four, and the ring I found in Mrs. Lannon's house. I've got to go to the police with them, or to a lawyer. She put the tray aside. "When Veach came to Mrs. Lannon's house, what did they say to each other?"

"Mrs. Lannon told him everything I'd done."

"Such as?"

"Was I talking to strangers. Things like that."

Into Monica's mind came the clear picture of Mrs. Lannon's unwillingness at Winifred's departure. Was Veach unsure of what Winifred knew? Why had he let her go unharmed from Mrs. Lannon's house? A possible reason crossed her thoughts—Veach wouldn't have wanted anything to happen which would draw the attention of the police to Mrs. Lannon or her house. She was far too important a link in his organization. A dead or missing child was too risky. He had decided to wait, to strike after Winifred was with her aunt and it could be made to look like an accident. The importance he had placed on the job might be judged by the fact that he had undertaken it himself.

This had to be the right line of reasoning. His murder of Biddy had been long planned and deliberate. Winifred's story of the telephone call had one point which revealed as in a clap of light the study and stage-managing of the crime—Mrs. Lannon's exclamation on seeing the time: "It's four o'clock!" What else could this have meant but that Biddy was due at that moment to die and the evidence be planted swiftly to involve her husband? The oil spots under the body, the trace of blood inside his trouser leg, the hidden ball-point hammer which had been used around a garage—all of these things were no more than a cheap trickery once you realized how the thing had been built up to incriminate another man.

There was a polite rapping at the door, then Stevens looked in.

Winifred jumped on the chair and grinned at him and sputtered melba toast crumbs in his direction. Monica felt a surge of irritation. She wanted time to think—she needed most of all to plan a method of getting away and of contacting someone official. It had to be done carefully; she must be believed. There wouldn't be time for delay or doubt. And Stevens might hinder her. She had no faith in his roundabout schemes.

He came to the bed, pulled up a chair, and sat down. He looked tired, and the blonde hair, damp from combing, seemed to have lost its gleam. "I hear we had a revolt."

"The grapevine must be spinning this morning," Monica said.

He ignored it. "I'm glad you're that full of pep. I want you to help me."

"Doing what?"

"I think I've got a lead into Veach's web."

"What good will it do you? Once he catches sight of you, he'll remember you from Raboldi's."

"The people I want to contact are his subordinates. I'm going to stay out of Veach's way as long as I can and talk to his lower-grade help."

She frowned at him. "For what purpose?"

"I want a line on that woman in Mrs. Lannon's house. I went out there last night around ten o'clock. There's someone in that upper room all right. A girl. I caught a shadow on the blind. I checked to make sure it wasn't Mrs. Lannon herself—she was in the parlor playing solitaire. I looked in through a nick in the curtains."

"It's Margaret Demarist," Monica agreed. "But I don't think we could get enough out of her to swing things for Jerry Huffman."

"We have to try," he argued. "The one thing that stumps me, that makes me suspicious, is that you got into that room so easily."

"I just outsmarted Mrs. Lannon."

"No one outsmarts her. She let you go into that room for a reason."

Monica pointed to the dresser, where Biddy's ring lay on the scarf. "I don't think I was meant to find that. It's too damaging."

"I don't think you were meant to find it, either—it was a slip perhaps. If so, it was the only one. You were meant to see the other things."

She puzzled over it. He was looking at her with the surreptitious, studying look she had noticed before—trying to read her expression without her knowing. "They must have wanted old Mr. Demarist to know that Margaret was all right, that she wasn't living openly with Veach. This might soften the old man up and make him release more money to her."

"Possibly." His eyes flickered over her.

She pleated the bedclothes nervously, hating herself because he could break the icy front she wanted to present. "What else did you do last night?"

"After I left Mrs. Lannon's place I went back to the bar on Santa Monica Boulevard. It's a very nice place, for a bar, and lots of nice people in it. I was worried—I was looking for my wife who was a dipso and who hung out there when she could get away from me."

"Someone talked to you about your wife?"

"Yes. A steerer for somebody. I'm hoping it's for Veach. He's a little guy, professional-man type, well-dressed, wears glasses, speaks with authority. I wasn't the only one he had his ear out for—a woman was trying to control her husband, and this little guy helped her with him. They had a short talk on the curb before she got into her car. I rather imagine that he told her he knew someone who might straighten out the husband. Psychiatric treatment is accepted everywhere now as the antidote for alcoholism."

She wanted to pick at him. "You don't think that it is?"

"Not universally." Winifred had crawled into his lap and he was stroking the yellow curls; for the first time, at that moment, Monica saw it—the resemblance.

Their faces were close, the features lit by the same light.

The knowledge brought Monica nothing but fear. She had begun to think of Winifred as belonging to herself; a possessive affection had taken root. Here was someone—an interloper—whose very face branded him as having a claim upon the child. She shrank back into the pillows.

He never missed anything, of course. "What's wrong?"

"Nothing. A twinge," she said hastily. "What is your lead to Veach?"

"The little well-dressed guy gave me an address. I'm supposed to take my wife there tonight. It may be a sort of screening process. Or it might be—something else."

"What?"

"A trap. I'm asking you to take that chance."

She reached out a hand to take one of Winifred's. "Come sit over here." She pulled the little girl to the edge of the bed and put an arm around her. Stevens's eyes had followed every move; they seemed to hold a knowing light. "I'm not sure what I should say," she told him. "I'll have to think."

He took out a pack of cigarettes and turned it in his hands, idly. "You want to rush to the police and start sirens and things. You mustn't do it. The results would make you very unhappy."

"What results?"

"We wouldn't find the woman in Mrs. Lannon's attic room. She has a way out of the house—proved by the fact you didn't catch her there yesterday. Without her we get nowhere."

Monica stirred; pain stabbed her under the heart. "You keep calling her 'the woman.' Why don't you say Margaret Demarist?"

"We haven't seen her face," he said quietly.

Monica started to argue and then did not. What he said was true. In the attic room she had found clothing, had seen the results of labor, had felt the impact of a personality. It was as if she had caught a half-glimpse of someone in the distance on a foggy evening—someone who had quickly vanished and left only the impression of a faint familiarity, a teasing memory.

"Tell me what you want me to do," she said.

15

At a quarter past seven it had begun to grow dark. The birds had quit squawking and fluttering in the trees, the lights in the grounds were turned on, and the pale twilight in the sky had died to a bright patch in the far west. Monica borrowed a pair of scissors from a nurse on the excuse of clipping something from a magazine. When the nurse left she took the scissors into the bathroom, removed her gown, and started to work on the tape. Parts of it could be clipped away, she had decided, without damaging the important section that kept her lungs immobilized.

She sat on the lid of the toilet seat and writhed this way and that, using the scissors. She'd had five injections of penicillin, plus sulfa and other items. There was no longer the dizzy inclination to drop unconscious, but sitting on a hard surface was a discomfort. The sadism of modern medicine, she thought. When are they going to perfect that gadget which shoots hypo injections in on a squirt of air? You'd think they'd work on it night and day.

She rose and tested the tape. It wasn't bad now. She was a little weak from lying in bed, but that feeling would go away with a bit of exercise. A loose coat would cover the bulk around her torso.

She crept into bed again, and presently the nurse came back to give night care. Monica had her back rubbed with alcohol and dusted with powder; the light was adjusted for reading. "There. All tucked in," said the nurse.

That's what you think, Monica told her silently. When the door shut, she was out of bed and jerking into her clothes. She slapped a powder puff at her nose, used a lipstick, tied her hair into a scarf. How does a dipso look? How would Stevens's wife look if he had a wife and she were a dipso? Silly questions. She gave herself a searching look in the dresser mirror. "You're not trying to fool anyone, are you, my wench?" She studied her reflection while doubt chewed at the edges of her mind. Any wife of Stevens would be, she decided: (1) a moron; (2) a doormat; (3) a dipso in self-defense. I'm not any of those—I hope.

There was a faint tap at the door—Winifred. Monica let her in. They spoke in whispers. "The nurses are having their dinner," Winifred told her. "Mr. Stevens has it fixed with the gardener. The car is already out in the road."

"You'll stay here? Promise you won't stir outside?"

"I'll stay," said Winifred. "I'll look after Boozer."

Monica hugged her in farewell. Then she went out into the hall and walked quickly and silently to the terrace. In the gray light she saw Stevens. He was leaning against one of the posts at the entry. She saw his eyes move, taking her in. She walked close to him, and suddenly he roused—his arms shot out, his hands gripped her shoulders. He pulled her toward himself. She felt a start of surprise; this wasn't anger. There was a kind of despair in his eyes. "I can't take you there."

"I'm going anyway. You can't leave me out. Biddy was my sister."

In the half-dark his face seemed tight, bitter, brooding. "There's something you'd better know."

"About you?"

"I'm not on your side or your sister's side. Barbara never liked me. I didn't like her. I always thought she was a cheat."

Monica's mind closed against him. There had been a moment, there at the beginning of their meeting, when a wild new thought had beat inside her brain. Now it was gone. Stevens was the enemy. "I'm still going."

He thought she hadn't understood. "Don't you see—the thing can turn out nastily from your point of view. We might find out that your sister wasn't what you thought she was."

"I know that." This was bitter knowledge, gained through a long day of lying abed, thinking. "I'm not going to let it stop us."

"If I find out—what you wouldn't want known—I can't keep it a secret. Not if it's important to Jerry's defense."

"Promise me you won't take Winifred away from me. That's all."

He took his hands off her shoulders. "Why should you say that?"

"I know you have some claim. Perhaps one as good as mine. When you held her today, when her face was close to yours—"

He cut her off abruptly. "Someone's coming inside. It's you they'll be looking for. Let's go."

They hurried to the back gate where the gardener waited. He looked with deliberate innocence in the opposite direction as Monica passed through. The car was parked below the rise, at the spot where Monica had met Aldeen yesterday. Stevens put Monica in the car, then went around and slid in behind the wheel. The last of the faint gray twilight shone in his eyes. "I won't ever take Winifred away. She's yours—if Jerry can't have her."

"Thank you."

He started the car, drove down to Ventura Boulevard, and joined the traffic going east. They swept through Cahuenga Pass into the fringes of Hollywood, then west again on Sunset. Stevens slowed down now and then, and studied the rear-view mirror. "We're going to be early. They wanted us at nine-thirty. We'll beat that time by a good half-hour and see what's doing. It's a place in a canyon, a side road. I went up part way this afternoon. I don't like the isolation. It looks phony."

"Veach would have to be careful about who he took in for treatment," she pointed out. "He couldn't admit just anyone. He'd end up with charity cases and stool pigeons and an order from the police to cease and desist."

Stevens grunted, weaving through traffic in a burst of speed. "It was too easy. It should have been harder."

"You were in luck."

He shook his head. "I don't believe in luck." They were on the Strip now; neon signs glowed, shattering the dark, and feverish, overdressed people hovered at the doors of the expensive night spots. Beyond Beverly Hills Stevens turned the car right and found a road that wound among trees. It looked much like the district where Mr. Demarist had his house. There were walls, iron gates, an air of exclusive quiet. Then, suddenly, the surroundings changed. Monica caught sight of a couple of shacks beside the road, then others as the car's lights hit them—this was outside the city limits, outside the control of the building restrictions set up to keep the neighborhood slick and glossy. This was county, and it was shabby and helter-skelter. Still the road climbed, leaving the cluster of shacks behind. It wound between sharp little hills, skirted a reservoir whose waters glittered faintly under the stars. The wind searched its way into the car, a desert wind with sage smells and a touch of dust. Stevens doused the lights. The car lurched and crawled, feeling its way up the steep grade.

Monica moved away from the door and toward Stevens. She was beginning to share his feeling about the trip—it was indeed queer that Veach would ask a prospective patient, someone whose nerves were supposedly raddled with liquor, to make this long drive to such a lonely spot.

With a wrench of the wheel Stevens pulled off the road into a pocket of utter blackness. Shrubbery pushed and scratched at the windows. Monica smelled the sharpness of crushed sage above the oily odors of the motor. She felt Stevens's hand touch her arm. He said, "Follow me out this way." She slid over, under the wheel, and out. He steadied her; his touch seemed firm and alive though in the dark he had the invisibility of a ghost.

"I don't see any sign of life," she complained in a whisper.

"We're early, of course." His touch guided her to a level spot in the road. "We're going to crawl through a hole in a fence. You might snag your clothes. Don't complain above a whisper if you do."

She snatched the coat tighter. Stevens said, "Duck down a bit. We don't want to be conspicuous." They went forward between clumps of sage. Monica felt twigs grind underfoot; the strong tang of the crushed herb filled the air. The ground rose and broke into tiny gullies. Stevens reached out, taking her hand and putting it against wire netting. "There's a hole here. You'll have to wriggle through after me." Then he was gone, the silent dark swallowing him, and Monica had an instant of panic. She stumbled in a hurry and felt her way to the ragged break in the wire. Stevens's hands found her again, settled on her shoulders, pushed her down, and then pulled her forward. She dropped to her knees, crawled, felt her nylon hose disintegrate to rags.

Stevens put his mouth against her ear. "The house is above us, a little to your right. See it?"

She squinted, straining her sight against the dark. The star-shine mingled with the faint reflected glow from the city; against these she saw the bulk of a dwelling. Not large. Something in its line reminded her of the clustered shacks in the canyon. "What sort of place is it?"

"It's a dump," said Stevens.

"Then we've come into a trap," she told him. "Veach wouldn't bring a prosperous patient here."

"He may let the subordinates do the screening on the pickups in the bars. We'll take a chance. Or I will."

"What are you going to say?"

"Not much. Most of it will be up to you. Think of the worst hangover you ever had, and act it. A semi-stupor. I'll ask you questions as if I want you to make a good impression. You ignore me, or grunt."

It sounded vulgar and stupid; Monica felt herself stiffening.

"I know—you're too good for the part," Stevens said dourly. "Play it the way you want."

"I'll do anything you tell me to."

"You're out of character."

"I loathe you."

"I loathe independent women."

"You hate anything that isn't a doormat."

"Shut up. Somebody's coming."

They crouched by the fence and waited while footsteps passed some distance away. Several minutes later, far down the hill, a car's motor started, and then there was the soft crunch of tires. Stevens peered down that way. "No lights. I didn't see the car on the way up, but then I wasn't using my lights, either. I don't like this. Someone's cleared out."

"Leaving the trap?"

"Let's have a look at what they left."

She tried to get to her feet silently, slipped on gravel, and almost fell, making a lot of noise. "Dammit!"

"Don't worry. We'll go quick, not quiet." He pulled her with him into a level pathway. They found wooden steps set into the side of the hill and went up, making no effort to hide their walking. The house had a smell that met them—an old smell, a tired and undusted and overused smell. People had been here weekends, Monica decided, and had done a lot of drinking and smoking and hadn't aired or cleaned up afterward. The porch had a faint unsteadiness underfoot, as though the foundations were beginning to weaken. She knew without being able to see that the paint was peeling, that the windows were dusty, that the place exuded a secretive dirtiness. Stevens opened the door without knocking. There was no light inside, only more of the same smell.

"I'll find the light switch," Stevens muttered. She heard his hand rubbing the wall. "No button by the door. Might be a drop cord in the middle of the room." He went away, leaving her alone with the night at her back.

She found herself shivering in spite of the stricture of the tape, the woolly warmth of the coat. The feeling of being on the verge of a trap was making her heart hammer, was putting a sick taste in her mouth. "Where are you?" she demanded.

"Right over here. I've found something." The next instant the light sprang on—it was a floor lamp beside a divan. On the divan was a woman who looked at Monica and smirked.

It was Wanda, the blonde.

She was all wrapped up in a gray fur coat. Her legs were half off the couch, as though she might be getting ready to sit up. Her yellow hair was fuzzy acid unkempt and the make-up needed fixing. There were dark patches under her eyes where the mascara had run. Wanda had been crying.

"What's the matter with her?" Monica whispered.

"She's dead," Stevens answered. He stood looking at the body with a cynical expression, as though Wanda had played him exactly the kind of trick he had expected.

"How?"

He reached with a forefinger and flipped the edge of the gray coat, so that the things Wanda had on underneath were visible. She was wearing a green satin dress; the blood on its bosom was like the blooming of a gigantic flower. "Shot through the heart. The coat doesn't show much—she was brought here afterward, the coat put on her, propped up to wait."

"For us to find her?"

"Something like that." He began to walk around the room. It was a narrow room, perhaps ten by twenty, stretched across the front of the house. There were two doors. Stevens went through one, snapped on a light, came back out. "Kitchen. Lots of dirty dishes. No weapons, unless she was killed with a wooden fork." He went through the other door and spent some time there. Monica crept across the room, avoiding the divan, to peer in at him. There was a bed—Stevens had the mattress upended and was looking through the springs at the floor. He glanced at her. "Come here."

She went to stand beside him, to look where he pointed. On the floor in the midst of dust rolls was a gun.

"I don't get it," Stevens muttered. "The whole thing smells of a trap, of a plant, except for the gun being where it is. We couldn't be expected to pick it up, to handle it." He glanced at the watch on his wrist. "Nine-twenty. We're supposed to be coming through Beverly Hills about now." He let the mattress drop and stood staring at the wall in bitter reflection.

"We have to get away from here," she urged.

"Not yet."

"It's dangerous. We might be found here."

"We'd be found here at nine-thirty, much to our embarrassment," he agreed. "I wish now I'd risked taking a look at the gent who walked down the hill in the dark."

"Was it Veach?"

Stevens went on frowning. "Somehow—I didn't think so. A heavier guy than Veach." Stevens worried his lip, then took out the inevitable cigarette and began the process of lighting it.

"Give me one."

"Sorry. Mind's on other things. You haven't seen Wanda in your travels since coming back to town?"

"No, but Winifred caught a glimpse of her while you were in the bar."

"She mentioned it."

The silence closed in after his words. Monica's cigarette seemed dry and tasteless. Her mind kept re-creating for her the scene on the divan—Wanda, with her hair all screwed about on her head as if from a struggle, with the stains of mascara spotted on her cheeks. She'd spent some little while in fear, in terrified weeping. She'd known what was coming. Why had Veach sacrificed her to the scheme of trying to trap his enemies? Were they so close to the truth—was Winifred's little story so damaging—that he had to get them out of the way at all costs?

Wanda ... Monica recalled the rocklike stare, the impervious self-satisfaction. A woman who thought well of herself. Mrs. Lannon had warned her to keep her mouth shut. Wanda had proved expendable.

But Veach's reasoning was faulty. There was no link between Stevens and herself and the blonde woman, except the fact that they had been at Raboldi's together. It wasn't enough. He couldn't expect the police to know it, to take a charge against them seriously.

She moved restlessly away from Stevens, walked back into the other room. Stevens was cutting the time too close. They had to be down off this hill before the trap sprung shut on them. She went to the doorway, pushed the screen ajar, looked out at the night. It was velvety and deep, that darkness. It could hide many things. A murderer, for instance.

She heard Stevens's step behind her in the room—and then, far away, another sound. A siren. It sounded thin and lonely, floating up to the twisted reaches of the canyon.

Stevens's hand on her arm jerked as he caught the sound. "It could be for us. We'll go now." He went back—she didn't look at him, nor at the divan—and clicked off the light. A moment later he was beside her again. They went out upon the faintly shuddering porch. There was no siren, no bird twit, no breeze. They began to walk downward on the path that led to the steps and the level reaches and the hole in the fence. It's too quiet, Monica thought. There's too much silence—and the cruel business inside that cabin hasn't any sense to it. Wanda was killed for something which isn't going to come off. Some inner part of her mind whispered: *It'll come off and you won't like it.*

She threw down the cigarette; it spattered sparks on the dark ground. I'm turning Veach into a superman. He can make mistakes—he's already made one. Biddy's ring. He shouldn't have let me find it in Margaret's room, he shouldn't have let me get hold of that pitiful proof of his hold over my dead sister. Because no matter what happens to Jerry Huffman, I'm going to see that Mr. Veach gets his just deserts. It may take years, it may ruin me, but I'm going to attend to him personally. She felt her breast swell with the great resolve.

The siren came again, briefly, just enough to clear a knot of traffic at an intersection. Not enough to startle two guilty people on a hillside above the city. Stevens was at the hole in the fence. He crouched, pulling her with him through the broken wire. They felt their way through the thicket of sage, across the road, into the car. The smell of it was familiar and safe. Monica slid in, Stevens following. He started the motor.

The car started to roll, and Monica cried out, a wordless yelp full of sudden fright. Stevens jammed on the brakes. "What is it?"

"The gun!"

He peered toward her in the dark. "What of it?"

"At Mrs. Lannon's house—it was in Biddy's suitcase. Mrs. Lannon said she'd given it to Biddy because Biddy was afraid." She shook Stevens's arm, trying to make him understand. Fear was like a hand jamming back her breath.

"You touched it?"

"And she didn't—she had me lay it on the sewing machine."

"Oh, God. Your prints are all over it. That's why it was under the bed. We weren't supposed to see it; the police were." He opened the door on his side of the car.

"What are you going to do?"

"Go back and wipe it off."

"There isn't time!"

He hesitated for a moment. "You'll have to get out of here and take the car. I'm going to try something. Go straight to Mrs. Adams' place. Wait a minute." He stood with the door open; she could barely make out his figure under the starshine. "There has to be another trail. The finger-print angle needs backing up." He beat his fist on the rim of the window. "Those things you brought from Mrs. Lannon's place—you'd better go through them at once. It's the only thing I can think of right now. Hurry up and get on it."

He shut the door and vanished into the dark.

16

She parked the car at the curb under the hill and began the climb to the back gate of Mrs. Adams' place. Fear was a thudding weight behind her eyes; she trembled with it, shook with the effort to control it. Every instinct commanded her to crouch, to hide, to be small and silent. The clean and lonely night, filled only with starshine, was a cunning mechanism for re-echoing her footsteps. Rocks slid away under her heels, made scrabbling noises as they dropped, struck other rocks to mock her efforts at caution. The night was full of noises, and at the same time filled with nothing. A waiting nothing. She paused at the crest of the rise to suck breath into her lungs and to look back. The car and the hollow in which it stood were smothered in darkness, but San Fernando Valley, beyond, was a sea of little lights. Out there people were safe, were at home; panic wasn't dogging them, nor monstrous phantoms at their heels.

She staggered on, to touch the fence, to follow it to the gate at the rear. She shook the iron frame softly. Inside, out of reach, the padlock grated on the mesh, the chain rattled. "Let me in!" She hissed the words at the dark. There wasn't any answer.

She looked up. The fence was about eight feet in height. They were clever, these nuts—Mrs. Adams was giving them something to work on. Monica took off her shoes, tossed them over, and tried digging her toes into the spaces between the steel mesh. The pain was excruciating.

She took off her coat and flung it upward by the collar. The collar caught at the top of the mesh and hung there. She tested it with her weight, and it held. Mrs. Adams, you're not so good as you thought you were. I've found a way into your fortress.

And others might, said a part of her mind.

She writhed and scrambled her way upward, clutching the coat, digging her toes into the spaces of the steel mesh. Her hose snagged and tore, the hem of her dress ripped with a snapping of stitches, the catch of her brassiere popped under pressure of her heavy breathing. Then she was teetering at the top of the fence. She was up; now she had to get down. She probed the dark space under the fence. Beyond the outbuildings were the lighted grounds, but this was all in gloom. I could break my neck, she thought, if there's something there and I hit it. She wriggled over the stiff fringe of the mesh. Her ribs stabbed her, and she let go and dropped.

There was a sharp pain in her left calf, a flame like the running of a little knife. She lay on the grass, conquering the urge to yell, then felt behind her to find what it was. A rose stake. A neat little stick to keep a thorny plant upright. I would get that into my hide, she muttered to herself. Monica the magnificent. Never misses a thing. She touched her left leg. The hose was in shreds, and it was sticky with a warm wetness. The welt on her flesh was beginning to throb. Then the ribs began again—a steady burning. She forced herself up, found her shoes, began to hobble toward the terrace. Then she remembered the coat and went back for it.

She took the rose stake and hooked the collar with it. The fabric was firmly wedged into the spiked edges of the steel mesh. She tugged and swore. When it came, it fell over her head and she fought it as if it were alive. "You're cracking up, old girl," she chattered. Then she laughed. It would be easy to go on laughing; a lot of hysterical giggling seemed crowded just inside her throat. Then the sobering thought came that Mrs. Adams had strait-jackets in her little closets and wouldn't have any hesitation about using them if it seemed necessary.

Monica wrapped herself in the coat and headed for the terrace.

There was a man on the terrace, a fellow in a white jacket, evidently one of the help whom Monica hadn't seen. He was a short, chunky blonde and he was stretched out in a lounge chair, snoring.

She tiptoed past and went into the hall. The quiet, she thought, had a slyness about it, as though Mrs. Adams and the nurses might be hiding and spying on her. She stuck out a defiant tongue, then went to her room. The light was on, the bed made, everything in lovely hospital order. Also, her bags were packed and sitting in the middle of the floor.

Mrs. Adams had had enough.

There wasn't time to lie down but she had to, anyway. Besides, there was an evil satisfaction in falling on the new crisp counterpane, feeling the covers give and disarrange themselves all the way through to the mattress. She rolled, smiling to herself, her eyes shut. The rubber sheet was a slickness she could feel under the spread, the blanket, the two sheets, and the mattress pad. Why did they always expect you to wet the bed? Silly people....

She opened her eyes. It had been only a moment. Or had it? She looked at her wrist. Her watch had stopped.

She got up and went over to the heap of bags and boxes. Biddy's blue suitcase was on top, as befitted the most expensive piece of luggage. The cartons were underneath. Monica pulled them out, rummaging in one of her own bags for fingernail scissors, then cut the heavy twine.

A smell of moth repellent rose from the packed things. Filmy curtains, a chiffon spread embroidered in pink roses, a sterling-silver dresser set—this was bedroom stuff. It had cost money, lots of money. Monica dug deeper. There were knickknacks rolled in fluffy throw rugs, nothing else. The apartment obviously had been furnished—Biddy had decorated it with these little things to give a personal touch. At the bottom of the box was a piece of writing paper. In black ink in an angular hand the articles in the box were listed in a row.

At the bottom of the sheet were two signatures:

Rowena Charles, Manageress
Mary Cassidy, Maid

Protecting each other. Mary had done the work of packing while Rowena watched. No question of pilfering from the dead, from the poor young woman who had been afraid of her husband and had been beaten to death by him on the stairs.

Monica felt the pressure of hurry. She cut the twine on the other box and dumped the contents out on the floor, helter-skelter. She saw more little rugs, a few delicate china dishes, tablecloths, a couple of bright-jacketed novels, shoes ... Just one pair of shoes, red patent-leather pumps, the heels studded with rhinestones. They were just a touch shabby. Biddy had worn them a lot; she'd worn them to bars, Monica thought with a stab, doing Veach's dirty business.

Monica took the shoes to the bed and sat down there to look at them. One of the heels was loose. It twisted as if on a pivot, then dropped off into Monica's hand. The heel was hollow; there was a space the size of a large pencil in its center. As Monica lifted it, a few grains of a white powder drifted out, lost themselves on the white counterpane. Monica sniffed at the little opening. There was no odor but that of leather. She shook the heel. More of the powder fell into her palm.

With sudden unaccountable revulsion Monica wiped her hand on the edge of the bed.

She set the shoes together—their red glitter was bright as blood against the aseptic white spread. There was something naughty and daring about them. They had life, high style, a foolish recklessness. She knew how Biddy had felt buying them. Get it now—you may not be here tomorrow. Claw into life with both hands. These were night-life shoes, dancing shoes, barroom shoes.

Oh, Biddy, I kept you in school uniforms too long!

She went back to the box, draggingly, her mind heavy with guilt. She turned over some of the household stuff—little pictures which had hung on Biddy's walls, gay towels, bath mats. Then she saw it, tucked into the folds of a peach-colored sheet—a purse, and not one that Biddy would have owned. A straw bag, worn and misshapen, with garish embroidery in wool, the eternal lazy Mexican sleeping under a cactus. Tijuana was stamped all over it; it was the kind of thing indiscriminating tourists were forever bringing back from over the border. Monica grabbed it, jerked at the soiled bamboo catch. The contents spilled out upon the carpet.

There was a shabby gilt compact, two lipsticks, some wadded facial tissues, a scattering of coins and bills, and a lot of little paper packets folded to a uniform size and thickness. But these were not what held Monica stiffened above the bag, her face tight, lips thinned with fear.

The thing which stunned her was the smell. A violet odor, strong as sheep dip, rose like a miasma from these things. Wanda's smell. Monica closed her eyes; inwardly she saw Wanda at the door of the cottage at the lake and was choked again by the overpowering perfume.

She jerked her thoughts back to the present, turned the white packets over, selected one, prodded it with her nail.

A small amount of white crystalline powder seeped out through the hole.

She saw it all now, saw how neat and complete it was. Wanda was dead, and here was Wanda's handbag in her room. No one had to spell out the meaning of the white powder. Wanda had been killed with a gun containing Monica's fingerprints, and now Monica had possession of Wanda's little hoard of heroin. Or whatever the stuff was....

It was fine. It was tighter than a miser's clutch on a ten-dollar bill. It was almost beautiful. She saw how it would knit itself up in the eyes of the police. Her sister had owned a pair of slippers with a false heel in which were traces of a drug. That made her sister a drug peddler. Monica had come to L.A. to take over what had been her sister's—the business end too. Two of a kind. Wanda had tried to muscle in as a replacement (you can bet there'll be no lead to Veach, Monica thought grimly) and hadn't wanted to give up the trade. An argument had ensued—Wanda had lost it. The source of supply? Oh, you can get the stuff anywhere.

A hot pulse began to throb behind Monica's eyes. She grabbed up all of the little packets and limped into the bathroom. When she had disposed of the stuff, she came back and studied the straw bag and Wanda's other belongings. They weren't as easy to get rid of. She'd have to figure something.

There was a brisk tap at the window. Monica saw the pale blob of a face against the glass. She went to the pane and pulled it inward on steel hinges. Winifred was on the other side of the bars.

"What the devil are you doing out there?" Monica demanded.

"Boozer and I are keeping watch," said Winifred. "I hear sirens coming."

Monica gripped the bars and leaned against them to listen. The sound of the sirens was thin and remote; it died when the vehicle reached what would approximate the entrance to the road from Ventura Boulevard.

Monica ran for her discarded coat, her bag, then Wanda's purse. She hurried down the hall, meeting a single nurse who was standing still, frowning over a patient's chart. The terrace was deserted. Winifred and the cat stood together just beyond the perimeter of one of the lights. The child was fully dressed and wore the navy-blue jacket which Monica had bought her. The cat was switching his tail.

"This way," said Monica.

"Are we running from the cops?" Winifred asked interestedly.

Monica didn't answer. She ran for the back fence, threw her coat to the top of the steel netting. "Up with you," she said to Winifred. Winifred mounted with the agility of a monkey. Monica picked up Boozer, set his claws into the coat, gave him a boost. He went over, dropping lightly.

They hurried. Instead of taking the path which led straight down the hill, Monica headed for a little grove of eucalyptus trees on a rise to the left. They skirted the deep shadow, walking in twigs and fallen leaves which crackled underfoot. Winifred slipped a hand into one of Monica's.

"I was lonesome for you."

Monica bent to rub the small fingers against her chin. "I missed you too."

"Are we going to meet Mr. Stevens?"

A shiver went over Monica. "If we're lucky."

"He's a nice man," said Winifred.

"Why didn't you tell me you knew him?"

"You didn't like him."

They had paused at the edge of the hill. Here they were sheltered by the overhanging branches, the deep night under the trees. Ahead was the broad glow of the Valley; behind, the little island of light under the black bulk of the hills. A car rocketed out of the defile and stopped swiftly and silently at Mrs. Adams' gate. A man opened the door of the car and went to the gatepost and rang the bell there. He wore no uniform, but Monica knew what he was.

They waited. The car inched forward as the gardener came to open the lock. Monica asked, "Why were you outside?"

"Boozer wanted out."

"What gave you the idea there might be trouble?"

Winifred pressed closer. "I don't know. I sort of got a cold feeling in the middle of my back. I looked in at your window and you were sleeping. Then I felt queer."

Monica remembered with a stab that seeming moment when she had lain on the bed. "Did I sleep long?"

"It looked long," said Winifred.

Monica ground her teeth together. She'd lain sleeping while the police spread their net for her—while Stevens stayed to rub her prints from the gun and to get out the best way he might. Fine, fine. I'm sharp, she thought. I sleep, and an infant with more sense than I watches over me.

The cat made a lonesome, querulous sound in his throat, a protest against the dark and the hurry and the stuff that kept him from walking in silence the way cats like to.

"I saw you looking at Mama's shoes," said Winifred.

"The red patent-leather slippers," said Monica. She tried to read Winifred's expression through the dim light. "One of the heels came off."

"It didn't come off when Mama had it," said the child, "because I used to wear them when I played sometimes, and nothing happened."

The car had vanished into Mrs. Adams' driveway. "Come on. Quick and quiet. Watch for stones and don't fall down." Monica pulled the child after her. The path was difficult and winding, the reflected light from the valley thin and deceptive. Winifred was inclined to slip on gravelly spots. But at last the three of them were on the lower sidewalk and ahead were the scattered lights of the big homes. Monica approached the car with caution. She stood beside it for some moments, listening. She opened the rear door and examined the space there before she and Winifred got into the front.

Winifred knelt on the seat to look at the road behind. "Mama had a lot more shoes."

The cat was inclined to balk; he didn't like the strange car. Monica tossed him in, scarcely listening to what the child had said. "Were there?"

"Mama liked bright-colored shoes. She liked buckles and little bows and fancy laces."

The curb slid away; the car crept downward between the homes toward the bright, busy intersection. Monica glanced at the instruments; the gas gauge was registering low. She drove for some distance on Ventura Boulevard before pulling into a service station.

It was the first moment of letdown, of time for reason, since the moment she had awakened on the bed in her room. She crossed her arms at the top of the steering wheel and laid her head on them. The attendant came and said inquiringly, "Yes, ma'am?" and she answered, "Five gallons" without even looking up.

What utter insanity had she been guilty of, taking the child and the cat with her while she tried to dodge the police? Winifred had been safe with Mrs. Adams; Monica had removed her from that safety. The sudden cold light of logic, illuminating her actions, shook her with dismay. She'd been a fool.

Tossed into the rear seat was Wanda's bag. Bringing it away with her was the one sensible thing she'd done, but it was time now to get rid of it. She got out from behind the wheel, took the bag from the back, and went to the ladies' toilet. There she checked the bag's shabby interior, wiped any possible prints off the compact and the lipsticks, felt the lining for any hidden things which might lead back to Wanda. In a tiny pocket of the lining she found two items: Wanda's California driver's license and a snapshot of a fox terrier dog. The picture of the little dog brought a stab—Wanda had loved something, had kept its memory with her. She'd been a gross and conniving crook, and Veach's hireling, but a part of her had been human and loving.

With lips pressed together grimly, Monica tore the license and the snapshot into tiny bits and flushed them away. Then she stepped outside the lighted room and looked around. Across an alleyway was the service entry of a café, with trash containers ranged beside the door. Monica walked over quickly and put the purse among the other debris, then returned to the car.

She paid for the gas, pulled out again into traffic. To Winifred she said, "Tell me about the other shoes."

Winifred had had her attention distracted; it took a moment to orient herself to the question. "Mama's shoes? They were pretty."

"I know. Do you remember any particular pair?"

"No."

How could she remember, Monica reminded herself, after all these months? I'm asking too much of her.

They passed near a hamburger joint, its façade bright with neon, and Winifred said, "I'm hungry. All I had for dinner was some creamed stuff on a bun. I think it was part of the insides of a chicken." The doubt in her voice implied that she had not cared to eat it. "Besides, I think Boozer wants a drink."

Monica parked the car and they entered the small café. Winifred wanted a double hamburger with pickle. Boozer drank beer from a paper cup. The place had a boiling aroma of fried meat, onions, and strong coffee. The juke box ground out one tune after another.

While the kid ate and the old cat licked his lips, Monica thought out what she must do. When the plan was complete, she outlined it to Winifred.

Thirty minutes later she left the car under a street light a half-block from Mrs. Lannon's house.

17

The upstairs window had a light behind it, a light which threw upon the shade the frilly tracery of the curtains. Downstairs, Mrs. Lannon's parlor held a soft glow deadened by heavy draperies; in Monica's mind rose the picture of the overcrowded room, airless and prisonlike, and she wondered at Mrs. Lannon's satisfaction with it. Surely if Veach were prospering and Mrs. Lannon was as high in his organization as old Mr. Demarist seemed to think she was, she could afford better than this.

Some quirk, some pretense of clinging to an old-fashioned respectability kept her here, Monica decided.

She crossed the lawn and approached Mrs. Lannon's windows. Under the skimpy shade she managed a look at the room. The glow came from a big glass-canopied lamp on the center table. Mrs. Lannon was sitting under the light in a chair with a wooden frame propped into her lap. In the frame was a square of heavy cloth, drawn taut, and to the material she was sewing loops of beads. Her unhandsome face held a placid happiness, as though the beading pleased and relaxed her. Only the jet-black eyes looked sharp and alert.

Monica went around to the rear of the house, feeling her way cautiously in the dark. Stevens had said that there must be a secret way in; she meant to find it. She discovered a back stoop and some steps, but the door at the top was securely locked. Monica prowled like a hunting cat, but there were no other doors and no cellar entrance.

She investigated the garage, even daring to switch on the lights. Mrs. Lannon sported a blue Cadillac; it was new, spotless, shining. There were no secret rooms to the garage. It opened to the back yard, and to the alley, and none of the doors were locked, though the car was.

Monica turned off the garage lights and crept through the dark yard to the house. At the moment when she reached the foot of the steps Mrs. Lannon came out into the rear porch and switched on a light there. The porch was enclosed in glass down to about waist level; there was a good view of Mrs. Lannon. For a roaring instant Monica stood rooted, the glow reflected into her face, and Mrs. Lannon's advancing figure took on the proportions of a dragon's.

Monica ran blindly, tripped, rolled into shrubbery in an effort to get out of sight. She found herself under one of the lantana bushes, breathing the musky fragrance and the stirred-up dust, her shoulders tight against the foundations of the house.

Mrs. Lannon walked with a slow, deliberate step that reverberated in the wood above Monica's head. She loosened the catch on the door, rattling the knob, came down a step or two—the steps creaked—and deposited an object, then another, which clanked together.

Monica rubbed her face, feeling the dirt there. She was aware in that moment of several things she had almost forgotten—the weakness left by the fever, the deep scratch made by the rose stake, and the binding torture of the tape on her ribs. She lay still, getting her breath, while Mrs. Lannon returned inside and relocked the door. Mrs. Lannon had put out her milk bottles, something so commonplace and so domestic that it seemed a little ridiculous.

The house above grew quiet again, as though Mrs. Lannon had gone back to her beading. Monica reached out to push herself up, and then an idea occurred to her. If there was a hidden way in it might be under this rampant shrubbery. Lantana was tough, it could stand passing through with a minimum of damage. She began to crawl along the line of the foundation, touching the cement and the overhanging wooden siding as she went. It was dirty, unnerving, itch-provoking work. Dust sifted down invisibly in the dark, from the lantana into her clothes, under her collar, to the depths of her underwear. The lantana blossoms gave off their musky perfume. Monica wanted to sneeze, to scratch, to dive head-first into a cleansing bath. She wondered if she were making a noise that Mrs. Lannon might hear inside the house. At about midway up the side of the house, and about the time when she was ready to say to hell with it, she found the little door. It was small, set into the cement. She ran her hand over the dry, worn-feeling wood and found a knob and pulled, and the wooden square swung out silently.

She found herself looking in at Mrs. Lannon's cellar. It was brick-walled, floored neatly with broken tile and concrete, and from a rafter hung a light bulb in a dark blue shade. The brightest spot was on the floor; there would be nothing to show outside, Monica thought, through those narrow panes at the front of the house. She squeezed through, found toe holds in the brick, and crept down.

The place had a barren look because of the expanse of floor, though there were a few things stored here. Several pieces of old-fashioned furniture stood in a corner, and there were stacks of newspapers and three orange crates which Mrs. Lannon had thought prudent to save. Across the open space were the steps to the upper floor. Monica went up, put an ear against the door, and listened. There was no sound. She tried the lock; the door moved inward across the narrow landing. She was now in Mrs. Lannon's kitchen.

She crossed the kitchen to the hall she remembered.

At its other end, toward her left, was the glow from the lamp in the living room; there was even a shadow on the wall, the shadow of Mrs. Lannon's bent head and the edge of the beading frame. Ahead, a few steps away, was the little flight of stairs that went up to the attic.

The least sound would betray her, would lift that bent head and send the beady eyes searching for her.

She had a curious sense of floating as she crossed the strip of hall. At the same time she entertained a feeling of inevitable failure—there *would* be a board creak, or she *must* sneeze, or something would fall with a crash.... Even at the top of the stairs, facing the door to the room that had been empty of all but Margaret Demarist's clothes, she had a queer feeling of disbelief. As of itself, her hand reached for the knob and turned it and pushed the door inward.

The room was not empty now.

A woman sat on the edge of the far side of the bed, her back to Monica. She wore only a pink satin slip over some under-things; her bent shoulders were bare, her face hidden by the wings of yellow hair which had drifted forward. Like Mrs. Lannon, she was working with something in her lap.

She was counting money.

A space no more than the width of the bed separated them now. Monica caught a hint of perfume, the murmur of the woman's voice.

The money had the crisp new look of a green vegetable. No wonder they call it lettuce! As it slipped from the woman's hands into the little pile on her lap, it had a hissing sound like the rustle of silk to Monica.

Monica's knees were against the bedframe. She spoke then. "Look at me," she said.

The other woman gave a convulsive jerk, and one hand swept up to brush at the fallen wing of hair and then stopped, remaining there, the head not turned, the body small, crouched, animal-like in its sudden tenseness.

"Turn around," said Monica.

The hand crept downward, away from the concealing hair. "What do you want?"

"I want to see your face."

The hand spread itself on the heap of bills. "Go away."

"Turn around," Monica insisted, "and let me have a look at you."

The woman crouched lower, her body tensing and gathering itself as if for some sudden action. Her head moved from side to side within the wings of hair. But she remained seated on the counterpane.

Monica worked her way along the end of the bed by holding the metal footpiece, the clean, cold steel painted white. She pulled herself as a swimmer might against a tide. When she stood beside the other woman, the blonde looked up at her quickly. Hot blue eyes glittered in a face without color.

For a long moment Monica stood as if frozen, then she said, "How could you?" and one hand slashed out to strike the woman on the bed.

The stony face didn't flinch under the blow, nor the eyes falter. "It's none of your damned business."

"You're letting him die for something he didn't do." In Monica's voice was incredulity as well as fury.

The slender hands covered the money, as if to shield it from some danger. "I hate him. I've hated him for years. He was just always a jerk."

"And Winifred? Do you hate her too?"

"She'll get along all right." The tendons under the flesh pulled the pale features this way and that; the effect was of a mask worked from within by strings. "She's got you!"

Monica's eyes squeezed shut, then flew open.

"I'm still here," said the other woman.

"You're a monster!"

"Names don't hurt, Monica."

"Why did you do it? For the money, wasn't that it? Veach promised you much, much more than you'd ever seen before. You didn't care that he intended to let Jerry be executed for a crime he hadn't committed, nor that he meant to murder your child."

"Winifred would have been all right," said the other venomously, "if you hadn't come snooping and insisted on taking her away. She was here where I could even get a peek at her once in a while. And Veach would-n't really have hurt her. He just wanted her taken East for safety's sake."

Monica, standing rigid, her brain pounding, realized how she had almost fitted into this plan. But she shook her head at Biddy. "No. Winifred came as close to drowning in that lake as anyone could, and live."

"I don't believe it."

"Veach hasn't any plans for you, Biddy, outside the same sort he has for Winifred. Can't you see that? Can't you realize what a danger you are to him? At any time you reveal yourself, there'll be an inquiry into the death of Margaret Demarist. And no one's going to think Jerry killed *her*."

The other woman drew her lips back with a kind of hiss.

Monica, advanced one step, then another. "You're coming with me now."

"No, I'm not." The hands clutched the money, lifted it, pressed it to the bosom of the soft satin slip.

"You're coming with me to the police while there's time. You're going to prove to them that Jerry Huffman isn't a murderer. You're going to make them let him out of the death house."

The pale lips curled. The absence of make-up on the other woman's face gave her a look almost of illness. To match the golden shoulder-length bobbed hair there should have been rouge, powder, heavy mascara, bright crimson lipstick. "I'm staying here, Monica. If you're smart you'll get out before that old dragon downstairs catches on you're here. She's really tough when she wants to be. Tough and mean."

"You're coming, Biddy." Monica, moved closer, but the other woman inched away suddenly in the direction of the pillows. A bill slipped loose from the mass of money in her hands. She snatched at it, catching it before it had reached the counterpane.

"You touch me," she said evilly, "and I'll scream. I'll turn you over to them and they'll make you wish you were dead." The pale eyelids drooped slyly. "I hate you just about as much as I hate Jerry, anyway. You were both such stinking jailers."

Monica reached out to touch Biddy's shoulder; not harshly, but as if to emphasize what she meant to say. "I did what Dad and Mother wanted done for you. And then, too, I always loved you dearly. I made sacrifices—"

The other woman made a face like a cat's, showing her teeth. "Yeah."

"What poison could have crept into your mind—"

"You were just too dumb to see, Monica. I hated those dull, proper schools and the frigid old maids who ran them. I envied you like hell, being in New York, meeting men—" She broke off to laugh. A few drops of spittle ran out upon her chin; she brushed at them with the back of a hand that never let go of the money, bending her head, her eyes bitter and mocking. "When I got out of the damned school at last, I tried to let you know how I felt about you. I left hints all over the place. You never did tumble. Don't you remember that wedding bouquet you bought me?"

Monica's forehead furrowed. She recalled the dead stinking flowers she had found in the depths of the closet.

"You thought I'd take it with me, or put it in water as if it were precious. Jerry was broke. You made a big show of buying those damned white orchids. But I got back at you."

"Yes, you did," said Monica.

"I've only started on you," said Biddy. "I was going to let you know I was alive, once Jerry was out of the way and you'd settled down to raise the kid. You'd do a lot to keep the world from knowing the sort of mother she had—to keep her from knowing her mother was alive. You like Winifred, don't you?"

"Yes, I love Winifred very much," Monica admitted. "She reminds me of you when you were very small."

Now the first chink appeared in that ferocious armor. The pale face stiffened, the eyes dulled. The mouth moved, forming words, but no sound came. A couple of bills tumbled off the heap to lie on the bed. "You shut up," Biddy said.

Monica pulled at the stubborn fingers. "Let it go, Biddy. It isn't worth what you're doing to get it. There isn't that much money in the world."

The next words came through clenched teeth. "I'm going to yell for Mrs. Lannon!"

"No, you won't." Monica went on prying at the fingers. One hand came away, the money it had held tumbling to the bed and the floor. "Let go. It belongs to Veach and there is blood on it. Why did they murder Margaret Demarist?"

Biddy's fingers writhed inside Monica's. The hot eyes were frightened and unsure. "You let me alone. You get out of here."

"Why, Biddy? Surely she couldn't have been a danger to them. She was like a child in her mind, docile and willing. Why did Veach have her killed?"

Biddy swallowed; her mouth trembled. With her free hand in which the remaining bills were wadded she tried to gather up the fallen money. The whole thing opened and popped apart and the money made a green cascade over the pink slip, her legs, the fur-trimmed mules to the floor.

Biddy sat looking at the money; then her eyes moved, and she turned her head to look back at the door. "Get down. Get on the floor."

Monica dropped and inched in under the bed. She heard the soft sound of the door catch, the faint squeak of a hinge. Under the scalloped border of the counterpane she had a narrow view of the floor and the far wall. The door had opened a little way and one of Mrs. Lannon's feet had inched in over the sill.

Biddy was motionless on the bed above; she made no sound of greeting. She was obviously pretending that she didn't know Mrs. Lannon was there.

There were several moments of silent observation from the door. Then Mrs. Lannon said, "Are you alone up here?"

Biddy jumped as if startled, and the bed squeaked as she turned quickly. "Huh? What're you doing? Snooping again? Can't you leave me in peace?"

"I thought I heard voices." Biddy's querulous anger had no effect on Mrs. Lannon; her tone was flatly assured and cynical. "You aren't pulling a fast one, are you?"

"I'm counting my money," Biddy told her.

"Yeah—as usual." Mrs. Lannon moved into the room. "The green stuff certainly fascinates you."

"You get out of here before some of it turns up missing," Biddy snapped.

Mrs. Lannon put a hand on the bed; a ring on her finger made a metallic clatter. "This is my house."

"And a lousy, rotten place to be shut up."

Mrs. Lannon came a couple of steps farther. "What was that?"

"You lay a hand on me," said Biddy, "and I'll claw your eyes out."

Mrs. Lannon sniggered. "It's high time you learned who's boss here."

Monica began wriggling soundlessly toward the opposite side of the bed. She heard Mrs. Lannon pounce on Biddy, heard the girl's enraged yelp, and the struggle that followed. She crawled out on the side next the door. There was a stool, a three-legged maple stool—she'd noticed it on the way into the room.

She got a good grip on one leg of the stool and then lifted herself suddenly. Biddy was on the edge of the bed, arched backward; Mrs. Lannon had Biddy's throat squeezed in her heavy hands. Biddy was clawing the air in the direction of the jet-black eyes but her movements were frantic and uncoordinated, and Mrs. Lannon avoided her hands with almost a look of amusement. Biddy's face was beginning to turn blue.

As Monica moved at the edge of her vision, Mrs. Lannon jerked up her head and looked back. The mixed anger, and pleasure washed out of her face; the jet eyes took on an expression of disbelief. Plainly she hadn't really thought that Biddy had a visitor; some sound had brought her up, but her purpose in staying was to torment the girl.

Mrs. Lannon's lips tightened across her teeth. She let go of Biddy when she saw the stool in Monica's hand. As soon as Biddy drew a breath, her hands were back in Mrs. Lannon's face; but this time they did the work she meant them to do. Mrs. Lannon sucked in a whistling moan and lifted her arm. The realization of danger caused her skin to pale. She must have seen that now she was outnumbered and that Biddy's fury was like a flame. She half-turned, flung out a hand, looked toward the window.

Monica hit her with the stool at the base of the skull.

She let out a choked sound and dropped like an ox. The floor shook when she hit it. Biddy bent over her. "I hope you killed the bitch."

"I didn't hit her hard enough," said Monica. "I just want her out of the way for a while." She thought swiftly. "Let's tie her up and put her into the cupboard in the other room—the place she kept your blue suitcase."

Biddy shook her head. "I've got a place for the old bat. In the cellar. It's all lined with brick. Soundproof. My hunch tells me it's where they kept the Demarist kid those last few days."

18

Those last few days ... The final days that Margaret Demarist had been permitted to live. Monica looked at the woman on the floor, at the hard face gone slack and senseless, at the cruel hands outspread. Then she lifted her eyes to Biddy's, this was her sister, this was the small loved child grown up—Winifred's mother.

"What's the matter with you?" Biddy queried. She ran to the dresser and took scissors from a drawer, then stripped back the bedding and attacked a sheet with the sharp blades. "What're you waiting for? Come on—help me. We'll tie her just enough to keep her from making any trouble on the trip downstairs. Then we'll stick her in that little room. I'd give a million to see her face when she wakes up in that black hole."

The overhead light shone in Biddy's pale hair, glittered in her yellow lashes. She ripped at the sheets, tearing off long strips of cloth, then worked swiftly at Mrs. Lannon's wrists and ankles. The hurrying efforts brought out a frost of perspiration on her face.

"Come on!" she cried. "Don't just stand there!"

Monica moved forward. She stood above Mrs. Lannon and felt a shiver run through her.

"I know," said Biddy, "she's a snake. We'll just drag her."

They pulled the heavy form to the stairs.

"Down you go!" said Biddy cheerfully. She gave the limp body a shove and giggled as it bobbed and wove its way to the bottom of the staircase. One of Mrs. Lannon's slippers came off; Monica picked it up and tossed it down. The thing was warm from Mrs. Lannon's foot. Monica found herself scrubbing her hand against her skirt.

In the cellar Biddy pulled away the stacked orange crates to display a small, low, but solid-looking door of heavy planks set into the brick-work. She tugged at the catch and the door swung out. The light that hung from the beam in the middle of the cellar cast only a thin reflection this far, but Monica made out a rough brick-lined nook not more than four feet square. Someone had hollowed out the earth here to make this crude little prison. The floor was stained with filth and what looked like the remains of food. Biddy bent above Mrs. Lannon, tugged at her shoulders with cheerful energy. The woman's head rolled like a melon.

"Happy dreams," said Biddy, giving a final shove with a foot.

"She'll smother in there!"

"No, she won't. There're a couple of air holes. She'll be as snug as a bug. Say, that binding on her wrists looks kind of tight. Maybe—" Biddy looked at Monica, frowned a little, nibbled her lip.

"I'll see." Monica went forward unsuspecting; she caught the scratch of Biddy's shoe on the tile floor behind her, and a sharp sense of danger made her turn—not soon enough. The next instant Biddy's ferocious heave had thrown her in, she'd stumbled on Mrs. Lannon's prone body, and fallen against the brick wall. She threw out her hands, clutching for a hold, found none, fell to her knees. She fell upon Mrs. Lannon; the woman's breath went out with a coarse grunt. In that moment it grew dark. Then it was pitch black.

"Biddy!" Monica felt round the narrow space until she found the door. "Biddy, let me out!"

There was a crack beside the lintel; she felt a narrow breath of cool air from the outer cellar, though no light penetrated. "Biddy, don't leave me here!"

"Sorry, darling." Biddy's voice was smug and far away. "I couldn't let you turn me over to the cops, now could I?"

"There isn't air enough for both of us in here!"

"I think there is," said Biddy, as though it didn't matter much anyhow. "If you're smart you'll tighten up the old hag's bindings right now. When she comes around and gets loose it might not be too nice in there. Get busy!"

Monica didn't say anything; she leaned against the door in the dark and rubbed her temples. She was sweating. Her eyes were wide, though there was nothing to see. She was aware of the hammering of her heart against her ribs, and of the painful stricture of the tape.

Biddy scratched a little, like a mouse, at the edge of the door. "Hey! Monica!"

Monica didn't reply. There was nothing to say. There were thoughts to think and memories to dredge up—some of these rose of themselves like ghosts and paraded through the dark. She remembered Winifred, breaking the surface of the lake, and Veach's little boat motionless in the midst of the glaring light. It was hard to understand how there could have been so much sun. It was so dark here, it was like a tomb.

"Listen, Monica, I'm not going to leave you there forever," Biddy said, her tone conciliatory. "I'm going upstairs now and pack a few things. I have to get dressed and put on some make-up, then I'm gathering up the money and clearing out. I'll telephone for someone to help you—any-one you say—after I know I'm safe."

A faint smile touched Monica's lips.

"Do you hear me?" Biddy demanded.

Against the dark Monica saw an image of herself as she had been on that long-ago day, poking aside the clothes in the back of a closet and picking up the withered bouquet. How hideous the dead orchids had looked! There had been something spiderish about their twisted brown petals. The white ribbon streamers were stained and crushed. The whole thing reeked of decay.

"Just one thing," Biddy commanded, "you're not to start yapping that you saw me here. They won't believe you, but it might delay what's go-ing to happen to that jerk, and I just don't want it. Promise?"

Monica was seeing a vision of Stevens, his face set and bleak, saying, "I'm beginning to get it. That chip on your shoulder—"

Stevens! Wouldn't he come here soon? Once he learned that she had fled Mrs. Adams' place, wouldn't common sense tell him—

Biddy rapped impatiently. "Good-by for now, darling! Thanks for whacking her with the stool."

"Wait!"

Biddy stopped speaking, waited a moment, then asked cautiously, "What is it?"

Monica pressed her face toward the cool breath of air, tried frantically to marshal her thoughts. "It's about Winifred. I have to pick her up be-fore it gets much later. Let me out, Biddy. I've learned my lesson. I won't try to keep you from leaving, and I'll keep my mouth shut."

Biddy apparently took time to think it over. "Where *is* the kid?"

"Not where you could get her—and she mustn't catch sight of you, Biddy!"

In the dark, on the floor, Mrs. Lannon groaned in half-wakening, a sound like a rousing animal. Words came out, grumblingly. Her feet scraped about, hitting the brick walls.

"Please, Biddy!" Monica pounded the door softly with a closed fist. But she forced her tone to remain subdued and wheedling.

"You better not try anything!"

"No, I won't. I'll do just as you say."

"Is the old battle-ax coming out of it?"

"She's beginning to."

"Okay. Out with you, and we'll shut her up quick." The door was jerked open; the thin light striking Monica's eyes seemed like a midday glare. She stumbled through the low doorway. Biddy slammed the door shut, fastened the catch, and pulled the boxes into place.

She looked over her shoulder at Monica. "You can go."

Monica drew a deep breath of the fresh air. "I dropped my bag upstairs when I crawled under your bed."

Biddy eyed her narrowly. "I'll bring it and toss it down to you. Stay here." She turned and hurried toward the cellar stairs. In the silk slip her figure looked childlike, slim and unformed. She whirled when she heard Monica following. "Don't come close. I'm warning you." Her face was suddenly savage, the cheekbones high and white, the lips puckered in hatred.

Monica slowed, pausing at the foot of the steps. "Are you really going to let him die, Biddy?"

"Am I? Wait and see!"

"No matter what your married life was like—"

The mask of loathing broke open to show Biddy's perfect little white teeth. Like a meat-eating animal's, even and sharp and clean as bone. "He's a sap. He's just too dumb to live! When I remember the years on end that I had to endure living with him—"

"Biddy—think what he's going through tonight, this instant!"

Biddy wagged her head. "I'm thinking of myself, of the years when I was young and wanted to have fun, and of how he'd preach, preach, preach. He didn't want me to drink. He didn't like for me to go out alone nights. I couldn't have a friend that he approved of! He's a stinker, a dirty, rotten stinker, and I only wish I could be there to see him die!"

The mask that looked down at Monica from the top of the stairs was nothing she had ever seen before. Somewhere under it was what was left of the small child who had been her sister. The bitterness of the voice, the triumphant hatred that flamed in the eyes, were scalding poison. Monica turned her head, fighting for control. "You wish—don't you, Biddy—that I was there with him and going to be executed as he is?"

Biddy's mouth jerked. She moved her gaze off Monica to the depths of the cellar.

"Why didn't you tell me that you hated the schools? Why didn't you demand that I bring you to New York and turn you loose to fight your way in the jungle you hoped to find waiting for you? I'd have listened. I'm human. I'd have let you come. Nothing is worth killing over, Biddy. Don't let Jerry die for something I should have done."

Biddy said, "Shut up!" She moved uncertainly in the shadows at the head of the stairs. "I want a drink. I want whisky."

"Biddy!" Monica took a step toward her. "Let me come up and go out one of the doors. I don't want to crawl out the way I came in."

The change of subject attracted Biddy's attention. She slid backward through the door at the head of the stairs. "Come on up, then. Don't try anything funny. I don't trust you—not a damned bit."

In the kitchen they faced each other. Biddy had known where to look in the few moments she had preceded Monica—she now held a short knife in her clenched right fist. "Pour us a drink," she said. "She keeps the whisky and the mix, too, in the refrigerator."

The refrigerator was big and white; a breath of solid cold drifted out against Monica's face as she readied in for the bottles.

"Get ice cubes too," Biddy commanded.

Monica put the makings on the sink, took glasses from a cupboard, dropped in ice cubes, poured whisky and ginger ale.

Biddy picked up her drink, then moved away cautiously. "I heard Veach talking," she said to Monica. "You've got a guy with you."

Monica looked across the rim of her glass. "Stevens. You know him."

Biddy lifted her drink, pretending to measure it with her eye, then glanced sidewise, as if trying to study Monica. "How did you meet him?"

"Through Winifred. He was interested in seeing that nothing happened to her. He has a claim on her as good as mine, of course." Monica, kept her tone matter-of-fact; she waited for Biddy's reaction.

The ice rattled in the glass when Biddy's hand shook. "No. I don't even want the kid to know him. He's a rat, just like—" She stopped, shrugged, her expression wary.

"Who is he?"

It grew very quiet while Biddy looked at her with a touch of amusement. "You don't know?"

"I know that if it weren't for Stevens, Winifred and I would both be dead—we'd be at the bottom of that lake where Veach intended us to drown."

"You're so damned afraid of Veach!" There was chilly scorn in Biddy's voice, an accusation of cowardice. "Veach isn't anybody! He's a dope. I'm tired of hearing you yap about him and how dangerous he is." Biddy turned up her glass, swallowing the last of her drink. "I'm going up to the bedroom now. I'll throw your purse down to you."

"Biddy—"

"Quit harping about Jerry. If I wanted to do anything, I'd have done it long ago. I'm paid off, see? My job's done."

She ran for the stairs to the upper room. At the upper landing she looked down, checking on Monica's whereabouts. Then she disappeared.

Monica stood in the little hall at the base of the stairway. She held out the glass in which some liquid and the ice still remained—she held it at arm's length and let it drop. It shattered on the bottom step.

An instant later came Biddy's yelp. Biddy pounded out upon the upstairs landing. "Monica!" But now there was nothing to see except the rolling shards of the broken glass and the spreading liquid. "Monica! Hey! What happened down there?"

The silence closed in eerily. Monica was flattened against the wall beside the entrance to the stairway. Biddy would not be able to see her until she was all the way down and into the lower hall. It was dimly lit; such light as there was came from the kitchen, from the landing at the top of the stairs, and down the length of the hall from the living room.

"What are you doing, Monica? Why did you drop that drink?"

No answer. Biddy came down a step. She must have known that there was apt to be a trap, and yet curiosity and uncertainty were bringing her down. If something had happened to Monica, it might happen to her—she had to know.

She came down a few more steps; her voice took on an edge of angry fright. "Who's down there?"

Monica tried not to breathe. There mustn't be any warning; she had to take Biddy by surprise.

Biddy emerged from the stairway and peered toward the kitchen. Monica stepped behind her, threw her arms around her sister in such a way that Biddy's arms were pinned to her sides. For a moment the thin figure stiffened in surprise. Then Biddy looked over her shoulder and snarled in fury.

It had been the denouement she had half-expected, and this added to her rage—knowing that she had acted in spite of her own caution and common sense. She kicked backward, arched her back, tried to break Monica's grip by leverage under the elbows. "Let me go!" It was a gasp, a hiss. "Damn you!"

They struggled, and the thin silk slip burst apart and left Biddy half-naked, in rags. She dragged Monica into the kitchen. Monica clung doggedly, head down, against Biddy's back, her teeth clenched. "You're going to tell them!"

"Like—*hell!*" Biddy forced a hand free, then an arm. She gripped the edge of the tiled sink, pulling herself and Monica toward the cupboards. A drawer opened with a rattle of cutlery and Biddy's fingers searched among the tools inside. Monica caught a glimpse of spatulas, cooking spoons, and knives. The next instant Biddy had turned like an eel, twisting Monica off balance.

Monica's hold broke; she went down on one knee. In her hands were only the ragged pieces of Biddy's slip. She looked up. Biddy stood against the light, her body poised and whiplike, and in her upraised hand something gleamed with a steely brightness.

Monica lifted a hand. "No, Biddy! You couldn't!" She tried to rise, then to turn and dodge as the blade swept downward toward her. The leg she had stabbed on the rose prop buckled under her. She felt herself begin to fall. The next instant something struck her under the heart.

She found herself sitting on the floor. Biddy was still bent over her, but now there was utter quiet, a breathless and waiting silence.

Monica shut her eyes; she had a sudden sensation of utter weariness. I ought to sleep, she thought, only now there isn't time—there won't be time until it is all over for Jerry Huffman, either one way or the other. She fumbled with the bosom of her dress, where something seemed wrong.

Biddy screamed then, and Monica opened her eyes and looked up. Biddy's face was a caricature; there was such terror and revulsion in it that it seemed a mockery of these emotions. It was a paper mask that someone had made and then crumpled and torn up. Biddy was pointing. She was pointing at Monica.

Monica glanced down. She saw, with a feeling of surprise, that there was a steak knife sticking from her ribs below the left breast. She touched it. It was in solidly; it didn't move.

I must be dying ...

Biddy got down on her hands and knees and crept toward Monica, the way an animal sneaks up on something that is strange, and in a chattering voice she said, "Monica—honest, I didn't mean to!" She squeezed her eyes half-shut and reached out with a hand that wobbled like a withered leaf in a high wind, and touched the tip of the knife handle with one finger. Then she withdrew the finger swiftly, as if it had been burned. "I didn't really want to kill you, Monica! It was just—I got excited. I know all that you did for me when we were young. It was something you thought you ought to do—the schools and all—and I couldn't want to hurt you for it." She covered her face with her hands and began to rock back and forth on her heels. "Oh, God. Oh, God!"

Monica put a hand on the knife handle and pulled at it—pulled hard. It didn't budge. The blade was stuck into something inside and wouldn't come out. There was no blood as yet; but the queerest part was that Monica felt no pain. There was a kind of numbness from the blow, nothing more. It wasn't going to be too bad then, after all—this business of dying.

Biddy remained crouched there in her pants and brassiere, looking more like a skinny child than ever—looking, as a matter of fact, remarkably like Winifred with the sharp bones thrust up against the fresh white skin. She panted, "I'll do what you want, Monica—anything. I'll tell the cops what I did—what Veach made me do—"

"Then go to the telephone," Monica said tiredly. "Go now. Call the police and tell them who you are."

Biddy rose, pushing herself up from the floor as she backed away. "If you'll forgive me—"

"I forgive you. Go on."

Biddy turned to go. At that moment Mr. Veach walked into the kitchen from the back porch. His wolf's eyes held an expression of indulgent humor. "Sorry, Barbara. I can't have you using the telephone. It would be most inconvenient for me. Besides, don't you realize that the first thing the police would do would be to arrest you for murdering your sister?"

19

Veach walked farther into the room and leaned against the door of the big white refrigerator. "You were always on the impulsive side, Barbara, but tonight you really overstepped. I had other plans for Miss Marshall—nothing so crude as this impromptu knife work of yours." He hefted the small, deadly, blued-steel gun in his hand with an air of testing its usefulness. "Don't make a dash for the telephone. Don't even try to leave this room. I shall dispose of you quite shortly if you become troublesome."

Biddy didn't seem overimpressed. She pulled the remaining shreds of her silk slip this way and that, as if wishing to deprive Veach of the sight of her nakedness.

Veach frowned. "I judge that you have incapacitated Mrs. Lannon."

"She was picking on me." Biddy stuck out her lower lip. "I didn't feel like taking it."

Veach's cold yellow eyes became introspective. "Women are not constituted to carry out intrigue. Their emotions get mixed into the business at hand. Wisdom is overruled. My cousin is like all the rest—she dislikes you, and so she takes advantage of the chance to harass you. I should have foreseen it."

Monica was studying the man. Height-building shoes made him considerably taller, lengthening his step and changing the way he held himself. The tint or dye had washed out of his hair, and the loss of color made the hair seem thinner, a silver-gray through which his scalp showed. His whole appearance had shifted—there was a patriarchal calm; his movements were deliberate. He gave an impression of gentleness and courtesy even, ironically, when he was threatening Biddy with the gun. He was, Monica sensed, back into the character he had created for himself—the psycho-religious adviser, the haven for broken minds.

He moved the gun slightly. "Where is Mrs. Lannon?"

"In the upstairs closet," Biddy lied. Her attitude toward Veach had more spite than fear. "She's okay. She yelled for a while. Now she's sulking." Biddy's glance shifted to Monica. "I want to get a doctor for my sister."

"You have no more chance of getting a doctor than you have of getting the police," Veach told her. "Besides, Miss Marshall is dying. It is quite possible that she will live for a little while, wounded as she is, but you may be sure that the internal bleeding will shortly be fatal."

"But a doctor—if she were operated on—"

"No one, even a surgeon, could do more than ease her misery. And she doesn't show any indications of undue pain." His cold eyes studied Monica's face. "Are you suffering, Miss Marshall?"

"I feel—chilly," Monica said.

"That's to be expected. Where is the little girl?"

Monica laughed under her breath.

"You don't intend to tell me."

She shook her head. "And there's very little you can do to make me." She put a hand to shade her eyes from the bright overhead glow and to conceal the knowledge that must be blazing in them. For, of course, she was in no danger of dying; in the excitement of the struggle with Biddy she had forgotten the heavy casing of tape that bound her ribs, and the tape was what held the knife. If the knife had penetrated beyond it, the wound was no more than a scratch.

"It doesn't matter," Veach decided. "The child has no way of acting alone."

"She isn't alone," Monica said.

A touch of interest sparked the cold eyes. "Stevens has her?"

"No." She said it too quickly; she saw conviction spring up behind Veach's mask off casual irony.

"Just what does the child say about her father?"

"That he didn't kill her mother."

Veach rubbed a hand across his smooth gray hair. Something like a smile twitched at the corners of his mouth. "Nothing more definite? No proof? Nothing she—overheard, shall we say?"

Whatever she told him now might mean life or death for Winifred. She chose her words slowly, kept her voice faint. "Mrs. Lannon seems to have carried on some revealing conversations with a woman named Wanda. They thought that Winifred wouldn't know what they meant. They underestimated the child."

His face grew still and attentive. "Then the child has no evidence, but only hearsay."

"You're quite safe," Monica told him, "since Mrs. Lannon is your tool and the woman called Wanda is dead."

The yellow eyes grew glacial in Veach's stiffened face. The man was a superb actor; if Monica had not been aware of the inner workings of the plot, she would have sworn that the knowledge of Wanda's death was a surprise to him. Even his breathing changed. He seemed to shudder, a motion that suggested that something cold had touched him at the spine. "Do you say so? What makes you think this?"

"That Wanda's dead? I found her. But you know that, Mr. Veach."

He moved away from the refrigerator. He came close and looked down at her. "Where did this occur?"

"Aren't you being a little ridiculous?"

She coughed, then—it was a genuine cough, and it racked her sore lungs—and she took the opportunity to half-fall against the low door of the sink cupboard. She didn't like Veach's close surveillance.

If he stayed close to her it would not be long before he would begin to suspect the truth. Monica put begging appeal into her voice. "Biddy— water! I feel I'm strangling!"

Biddy, suddenly galvanized again by guilt, ran for the faucet. Veach's gun jerked round to cover her. "Be careful, Barbara."

Biddy ran water into a glass. "Give it to me," Veach commanded. A moment later he bent above Monica, held out the glass to her, and his voice seemed almost out of control—high and womanish. "Miss Marshall, where did Wanda die?"

She looked up at him in spite of her need for caution—looking directly into the pale eyes like a wolf's, over which the thick white lids drooped and trembled. What was wrong with the man? You'd almost think that he was fond of that dead woman. Monica said, "You know where she was killed. In that little house at the top of the canyon road, out beyond Beverly Hills. You know all about it, Mr. Veach!"

Her scorn made no visible impression. He separated his lips, licked them, sucked them. "When?"

"Don't you remember walking down that hill in the dark tonight?"

He shook his head slowly. His free hand reached out to strike her face. The glass, an inch or so from her lips, flew across the floor and struck the bottom of the refrigerator. "When?"

Biddy dived for him, a small and feral shape, and he swung on his bent knees, the gun came up—the next instant there was an explosion. Biddy kept coming.

He jerked himself straight and tried to back away. Monica kicked out. Her shoes struck his ankles. Still Biddy came, but slowed now to a crawl. She arrived at a spot directly in front of Veach and then she fell. On the floor with her thin limbs outstretched, with the gilt hair spilled, she looked no bigger than a child.

For a long instant Monica stared into the muzzle of the gun. She wasn't aware of fear, though she expected Veach to kill her. His arm shook; he tottered this way and that. Suddenly he seemed to pull himself together. A look of savage humor crossed his face. "I leave you to your dying, Miss Marshall. Take your time at it."

He swung around and walked out of the room.

Monica crept to her knees and reached for Biddy to turn her over. The thin, colorless features were slack now. There was a glaze on the clear blue eyes. Biddy's lips moved a little, and Monica bent over and put her ear close. The knife got in her way, twisting this way and that. She pulled it out with a vicious jerk and looked for an instant at its tip: there was nothing except the rubbery stickiness from the tape. She caught Biddy up and bent above her face again. A gushing warmth ran suddenly between her fingers, crossed under Biddy's back.

Biddy's whisper was loud and hoarse. Monica waited, her breath stopped in her throat. There would be something about Winifred, there would be a last message for Biddy's little girl. But Biddy said, "Go get that money, kid. I earned it." Then she went flaccid all over, as if somewhere inside a string had pulled loose and disconnected all her joints at once—like the coming apart of a puppet.

Monica let her down slowly, let her down softly, so that there should be no noise to disturb the immense silence that now filled the kitchen. It seemed as if something frightful, evil, and violent had blown through the room, had taken Biddy's life with it, and now was gone. A wind from hell, leaving a vacuum. Monica sat quite still; it seemed impossible to move.

Inwardly she flinched, for Biddy's words re-echoed in her mind, *I earned it.* Yes, Biddy had earned all that Veach had given.

She'd earned her reward by giving up her husband and her child, by betrayal, by avarice, by playing a part in a cold, cunning design.

A panorama unfolded in Monica's stunned mind, the story of the crime from its beginning. Months ago a girl named Margaret Demarist had fallen into the hands of a man who wanted her money. Though she allowed herself to be stripped of all she owned and though she was docile, timid, and almost helpless, it was decided finally to do away with her. The crime had to be well-managed, for the girl's guardian was wealthy, and once there was a suspicion of foul play Veach could expect no mercy from a man financially much more powerful than he.

Veach must have plotted with extreme care, building slowly, testing, considering alternatives, selecting his tools. Choosing Biddy must have come early in the game—physically she closely resembled the dead girl, she was money-hungry to a high degree, and she had a husband whom she wouldn't mind involving in a murder.

For of course there had to be a murder—an open, admitted murder. It was the simplest and most logical way of managing the thing. The body could be disposed of as a body; no dangerous hocus-pocus was necessary to cause it to disappear.

As if upon a stage, Monica's numbed mind painted the actors and their actions. Biddy obviously had prepared part of the trap for Jerry the night before—the blood spots inside the trouser legs had to be planted while he was out of his clothes. In the morning an argument was stirred up at the breakfast table, an unsettled argument that left Jerry seething—this in order for him to be in a bad mood when Biddy phoned later, to cause him to delay on the way home and help put the noose around his neck.

The thing progressed with the inevitable timing of a well-written play. The janitor, working in the areaway where his position could be checked, was allowed to hear something which alarmed him, which suggested danger. Monica's imagination re-created what must have been the man's dismay as he heard cries and weeping in Biddy's voice, then the crashing noise. The interview immediately following between Biddy and the manageress had been plotted on exactly the right note, with Biddy apologetic for her brutal husband, forgiving yet afraid. She'd turned down an offer of help without allaying any of the manageress's disquiet.

Once the stage was set and the phone call made to Jerry, how swiftly the work must have gone! There was much to do. Margaret, smuggled in during the morning and kept quiet, most probably, under drugs, was quickly dressed in Biddy's garments and killed. Not on the stairs, of course—too much chance of interruption there, but in some place which could be easily cleaned. The bathtub perhaps, the evidence sluiced away with gallons of water. The grease spots were dropped on the steps, other grease smears put upon the body, the murdered woman was carried to the stairway and left for Jerry to find.

No doubt when Jerry discovered the dead thing on the stairs the terrible condition of the head and face sickened at the source any possible questions he might have asked and any doubts as to identity.

One little slip—Biddy had kept her wedding ring. Who looks for a wedding ring on a body in the condition Margaret's had been?

Who raises his voice to question identity when the police are yelling that they've just found an insurance policy for ten thousand dollars?

Who could do anything but sit dumbfounded while a hammer and towels are displayed, fresh from their hiding place, and while bloodstains are found where no bloodstains could be?

Monica lifted a hand at last, rubbing her temples. With a dazed, slow awkwardness she got up off the floor and went to the sink to run water over her hands, to rub them dry against her thighs. From one of Mrs.

Lannon's drawers she took two clean towels.

Biddy was dead. The thought was a blazing pain behind Monica's eyes. She returned to where Biddy lay, taking the towels, and knelt down. She brushed Biddy's hair with a soft touch, feeling its feathery texture. Her face twisted; she shuddered with the repression of grief. Sweat came out on her temples and across her upper lip. When she drew a breath it was light and sighing. She leaned over and put her lips against Biddy's forehead for a moment in a gesture of good-by. Then she shook out the towels and spread them, covering Biddy's face and the small, thin torso.

Whatever Biddy's part had been in the murder of Margaret Demarist, the score was paid.

Monica went to the drawers and inspected the array of knives. Each in its slot, they were bright and gleaming. Monica picked one up, then turned toward the door.

There was a stream of fresh air flowing in the hall. The front door must be open, Monica thought. She could not recall any sound from the front part of the house. She had taken it for granted that Veach had stayed to release Mrs. Lannon. She moved cautiously in the shadows. Then she heard Veach's voice, the light, trembling, womanish tone that, she realized now, betrayed a thinly balanced and deadly anger. She gripped the knife and stole forward, scarcely aware of Veach's words.

"... *but not Wanda!* You had no right to sacrifice her!" He said it loudly and furiously, and there was a sound afterward as if he'd stamped his foot or slapped a hand down hard on the table.

Another voice answered in a cautious monotone.

Veach almost shrieked his next reply, and Monica suddenly recalled Biddy's attitude toward him and her summation of him. *He's a dope.*

Biddy had not underestimated Veach. In some subtle way she had known the weak, uncertain side of him, concealed though it was by the suavity of his pose as a mental healer. The thing she had misjudged was his deadly quickness when he was rattled. Biddy had jumped him from the back; in an almost instantaneous reaction he'd shot her.

Monica's thoughts broke off at the impact of the thing Veach was screaming.

"*I planned it for you ... staged it ... put it off on Jerry Huffman. I turned butcher for you. Worse, I would have killed the kid. Do you think I liked these jobs? Don't you think even my stomach turned a bit? And whom did I turn to for comfort? Who helped me forget? Wanda did. And you killed her!*" His voice broke into heavy sobbing. "*You did! You did!*"

Veach, with his heavy-lidded wolf's eyes, with his cold, murderous efficiency, had loved someone after all. He'd loved Wanda, and he really hadn't known that she was dead.

Monica took two steps and looked into the living room through the open door.

The first person she saw was Richard Aldeen, across the room by the entry as if he had just walked in. There was a flush of anger and excitement on his dark face. The muscles of his jaw knotted as though he were clenching his teeth. His hair was tousled, his manner harried. He had a gun in his hand. It was a much bigger and more dangerous-looking gun than Veach's, and when he saw Monica in the doorway he twitched the weapon as if to center it on her. At that moment she became aware of Veach. He was off to her right, his back to her. At the moment Aldeen's gun moved, Veach fired his. Then he leapt toward the big center table, crouched behind it, waited for Aldeen to fall.

Aldeen shut his eyes for a moment. He seemed to be thinking, or dreaming; something like a smile hovered around his handsome mouth just before he opened his eyes again, took careful aim, and shot Veach dead center between his hairline and his nose.

Veach straightened with a jerk and rose high on his toes. He nodded twice, as if in terrific agreement with some unheard remark. Then he collapsed on his face on Mrs. Lannon's beadwork which was spread out on the table. He stayed there for perhaps a minute while his body gathered downward momentum. Then he slid off upon the floor.

Monica, didn't move, nor did Aldeen. One of Aldeen's black eyebrows rose a little; he seemed to be asking a silent question of Monica or of the room. A vial of beads had been overturned on the table; they began dripping off a few at a time and bouncing on Veach's upturned face.

Aldeen nodded in the direction of that face. "I had to come, Miss Marshall. I couldn't let you walk alone into such danger."

"I didn't tell you where I was coming," she said.

"No, but—" He shrugged. All the while his eyes had searched her; they had a waiting, expectant expression. "Winifred is perfectly safe. She's with Uncle Dem. He wanted me to come."

Aldeen stopped talking. The room became very quiet except for the slight noise made by the little dropping beads. Aldeen's black eyebrow rose again, and the faint smile hovered at his mouth.

"It isn't going to work, is it?" he asked.

"No. I know what you are. I heard Veach accusing you of Wanda's murder. Even before that—when Mrs. Lannon was ready for us, when you brought me here—I should have guessed." Monica lifted a hand to rub her head; she saw the knife gripped in it, stared as if surprised.

"A knife?" Aldeen wondered. "Really, it won't do you any good."

"You'll have to kill me," she told him dully.

"And I had hoped not to," he assured her. "I *do* like you. Stevens saw that, you know. It made him jealous."

She let the knife slide out of her fingers. It didn't matter. She felt gray and numbed inside; there were only a few things important enough to rouse herself over—old Mr. Demarist was one. "Why did you let your uncle go on thinking that Margaret was alive?"

He shrugged again. "Margaret was not to be presumed dead until I had solidified myself with him. Uncle Dem wasn't always so friendly or dependent, nor willing to be close to me—until Margaret left and he was unsure about her."

"How filthy! Why did she have to die?"

His black eyes met hers flatly, unanswering. Monica herself supplied the answer. "She saw you with Veach, she knew you were part of the organization."

His vanity couldn't resist correcting her. "She knew that I was the head of the outfit. She got quite excited. In her limited way she could be stubborn and determined. We tried corrective measures, but that mental limitation of hers—it made her a little immune to pain, I guess."

"You didn't have to sacrifice Jerry Huffman! You could have made it a suicide!" Monica heard her own voice, marveled at her own stupidity—arguing with a murderer who sees nothing but cold logic in his crime.

"There were—uh—traces of our corrective measures, and it was necessary, of course, for the face to be mutilated so that identity might be confused. Suicides are hard to arrange from that point of view." His faint smile took on almost the hint of apology. "If you hadn't found out, if Veach hadn't quite lost his head and killed your sister—I was going to ease out and leave him holding the bag. And I had hopes that you and I might mean something to each other."

His bright, dark eyes went on studying her, and all at once she got it—this was a proposal!

She heard her own voice, husky and intimate, saying the incredible. "You mean—even yet—you'd take a chance on me?"

"You're very pretty. Do you know that?" His hands quivered. He put the gun into the pocket of his coat. He held out his arms.

She went to him. She thought afterward that it may have been curiosity. He was a splendid big animal; his dark looks had that faint touch of brutishness that somehow made him more a man. It was going to be interesting just to see what sort of love he might make to her before she disillusioned him about keeping her mouth shut, and he had to kill her.

He put an arm around her waist, against the stiffness of the encasing tape. She saw a flicker of surprise go through his face. He touched the underside of her chin with the fingers of his free hand, turning her mouth up to his.

"Didn't Veach hit you at all?"

It annoyed him. It wasn't the thing to say for this moment, for this time when they were to investigate their passion. "No." He said it shortly. His lips bent toward her.

"You'll see that Jerry goes free, won't you?"

He wanted a stagy perfection to surround this first kiss; she sensed irritation leaping in him at her questions. "We'll talk about Jerry afterward. Right now—"

Right now he was going to kiss her, and apparently what he had said about Stevens being jealous was true, for Stevens came in from the dark at that moment and, with the maddest-gesture Monica had ever seen anywhere, felled Aldeen with one blow.

20

Stevens looked at her scorchingly and laughed. "Don't you know that in another instant he'd have been strangling you?"

"It that why you hit him with your gun?"

He ignored the question. "Have you forgotten the frame up he fixed for you in that cabin tonight?" He seemed to want to communicate to her some of his own loathing for Aldeen. He made chopping motions with the gun. His eyes were hot, his mouth cynical and sneering. All the same, she sensed his utter tiredness; there were drawn spots under his eyes and the blonde hair seemed faded and dusty.

He's interested in me, after all, Monica thought, and I don't even know his first name. "What do people call you, besides just Stevens?" she wondered. "Gareth. Lousy name." He went over to inspect Veach, grunted at the hole in Veach's head, then went over to Aldeen. He kicked Aldeen to see if he might be shamming, then went on into the hall.

Monica saw a chair against the wall. It was a straight-backed chair with a red plush cushion. She sat down in it and looked at Aldeen and Veach. Then she shut her eyes. There were prickles of cold, or tiredness, or perhaps the returning fever, all over her skin. Stevens must have come in silently; when she opened her eyes he was there again. He put a hand down to take up one of hers. "I saw Barbara in the kitchen. I'm sorry I popped off."

"It's all right."

"Who killed her? Veach?"

"He slapped me to make me talk and Biddy jumped him."

"Because of you?"

"I don't know." She felt the ache in her throat. "Yes, I do. It was because of me." No one would ever get out of her what Biddy had said, there at the end.

"You've had it rough. I ought to be kicked." He squatted beside her. Now that she was close to him, she saw that he was very dirty. He had rolled, or crawled, through dusty brush. There were traces of leaves and twigs in his hair. His clothes gave off a smell of earth.

"Is there time to help Jerry?"

"Yes, plenty of time."

She inspected the hand that held her own. The knuckles were cracked and skinned, the nails broken. "What happened at the cabin?"

"I wiped off the gun and put it into Wanda's hand. Then the cops came. They chased me through half of Los Angeles County before I got away. My imitation of Superman was the only thing that saved me. I jumped from one eucalyptus to another, about fifty feet up."

"You mean Tarzan."

"I guess I do."

He was so close that she could see the thick dust in his eye brows. "Mrs. Lannon is in the cellar, in a little brick room with a secret door."

His mouth twitched. "That's good. What do you say we give her about twenty-four hours down there before we remember to tell the cops?"

"I think it's a swell idea."

He didn't say anything for a minute. He had, Monica noticed, begun to breathe as if he were excited about something. Then he said, "Were you really going to let Aldeen kiss you?"

"Well ..."

"He was forcing you," Stevens decided.

"That's right. I was paralyzed with fear, and he took advantage."

Stevens was getting very close. His rough hand stroked her fingers. "I shouldn't try to make love to you, either. Not right now. But tonight, after you'd left me there—and I couldn't be sure but what you were running right into some trap of Veach's—well, I sort of figured out a few things. About myself, for one. I don't dislike independent women as much as I thought I did."

"No, you were right. I was wearing that chip on my shoulder from the first minute I saw you." She studied him by the light of Mrs. Lannon's fringed lamp. "I guess I was afraid I might fall for you and you wouldn't fall back."

"Still afraid?"

They looked at each other, a steady and intriguing look, and things would have become very interesting, except at that moment Aldeen began to show signs of coming around. It was a nuisance, but he had to be tied up for the police.

At about the time the sun was coming up Monica was ready for bed.

There had been long and confusing interviews with the police, with detectives, with reporters. Winifred had to be taken from Mr. Demarist's house, with Boozer. They didn't see the old man at this time; he was extremely tired, Henry said, and needed the sleep, the little brief sleep he would get before he awoke and learned that Margaret was dead. Winifred and the old cat acted stupefied, and curled together in the back seat on the ride to Mrs. Adams' place.

At Mrs. Adams' they were told politely, but firmly, to go elsewhere. Their bags and baggage were brought out, in the middle of the night, by the old gardener. In a voice which implied that she could say much more than she chose to, Mrs. Adams informed them that their stay had been disruptive to her hospital routine.

They drove off to search for a hotel. "We couldn't get back in there even if we *were* nuts," Stevens decided. "Why do you suppose she got so down on us?"

"All I did was fall on the bed," Monica defended. She yawned. A part of her mind was wide awake and twitching with impatience. "How long ago did you suspect Biddy wasn't the dead girl?"

He shrugged, his eyes on the sides of the street; it was late and such motel signs as glowed invariably contained the phrase, No Vacancy. "It just never did seem real to me for Barbara to be the one to get it. That's why I cultivated old Mr. Demarist and tried to get every last detail about his niece. I knew it must be Margaret."

"It was the shoes made me suspect," she told him.

"The shoes?"

"The ones in the closet. Biddy could keep Margaret's dresses, alter them a bit, leave them there for me to find when Aldeen staged his little play-acting—but the shoes were another matter. They had to fit, and she had the choice of buying what she wanted. So she got high heels and fancy laces. Old Mr. Demarist frowned when I described them to him."

They drove for a while. Stevens put an arm around her and pulled her against his shoulder. "Should be a hotel before too long."

She yawned again. "Thank God I can sleep without dreaming about Jerry. When will they let him out, do you think?"

"Pretty quick."

"You're some relative of his, aren't you?"

"Half-brother. I'm older. He was always a helpless kind of kid."

"You two were like Biddy and me."

"I guess so." He turned into a side street, drove for several blocks, then swung to the curb. Monica looked out. The building was low, dingy, and secretive behind a row of starveling potted evergreens.

"It looks like a cat house," she protested.

He rubbed his bristly chin and sighed. "You're taking a cat into it, aren't you? What're you crabbing about?"

"Besides," said Monica, "we sort of need a chaperon, don't we? A nice, middle-aged lady, or somebody."

There was a moment of silence. Then: "Mrs. Lannon, I bet," said Winifred from the back seat.

Stevens and Monica looked at each other blankly. "We *did* forget her!" said Stevens incredulously. "She's still down in her cellar!"

For just a minute the memory of Mrs. Lannon's house and all that it had held made a shadow behind Monica's eyes. Then Stevens snapped his fingers in front of her face. "Remember me?"

The little girl and the old cat were sitting up and stretching themselves in the back seat. The dawn smelled crisp and clean. Long ago there had been another little girl with soft feathery curls; and it was this child whom Monica intended to think of when she thought of Biddy.

"I remember," she said to Stevens.

THE END

Terror Lurks in Darkness
by Dolores Hitchens

CHAPTER ONE

The street had narrowed into a kind of lane. When she had turned into it from the boulevard, it had been broad, well paved, and well lighted. Now there was neither pavement nor lights, only a curving track between low shrubby trees which bent toward the car, and were wet with rain, whipped by the wind, tossing in the beam of her headlights. She had climbed the winding drive expecting to find a way over the hill and down into the traffic of West Los Angeles.

Now she was lost.

There was nothing to be afraid of. She was annoyed more than anything, and teased by the memory of Sunny's voice assuring her of the ease of finding the shortcut. *You turn on Du Moyne and zip on over the hill and there you are....* Either this was not still Du Moyne, or Sunny was a liar, or there had been a sudden deterioration in the road.

The rain slipped aside under the lash of the windshield wipers, giving a clear view; if there had been any sort of signpost, she would have seen it, even a notice that this wasn't a through street—someone should have had the decency to put *that* up. The trees pressed in, rattling on the fenders. The dark had swallowed up the outline of the hill, and the rain concealed the reflection of light from the city. It was like being a million miles from nowhere, instead of a hop, skip, and jump from Sunset Boulevard. There was just this mean narrow track, the two ruts into which her tires fitted, the drumming noise on the roof of the car.

Lost. This was being lost, this funny lonesomeness, this odd chill under your skin, this wish to see a fence, a light, a house.

Only you're in town, you nut, she reminded herself. You're on a halfway spot between the Valley and West L.A. You're a little north and a little to seaward from Hollywood. You're on Sunny's marvelous new shortcut. She made an impolite noise for Sunny's benefit, even though Sunny wasn't there to hear.

The dog seemed to materialize instantly out of the night, a yellow phantom filling the middle of the road. She slammed on her brakes as her lights hit him; the car rocked forward, slowing, the wheels spinning a little on the mud. He was a very big dog and he stood in a way that suggested this part of the road belonged to him.

She got the car stopped and began to roll down the left window to coax him out of the way; she had her lips puckered to whistle when she saw him move. He was a streak. He slashed past the window she was lowering and she caught his hoarse growl and the snap of his teeth not five inches from her face.

She rolled the glass up in a hurry.

Curious, she waited for his next move, wondering if she'd somehow got into private territory. He was savage and assured as if trained to keep out trespassers. By and by she caught movement again at the side of the car. Then he stalked out to face the headlights. She gunned the motor, letting her foot off the brake so that the car crept forward a few inches. He bared his teeth.

"I don't *want* to run over you, dammit," she told the dog under her breath. "Get out of the way!" The car crept on a little further, a foot or so. Then he leaped again, this time for the hood of the car. The next instant he was looking in at her. And now she was afraid.

There was no sense to this fear, as a heavy shield of safety-glass protected her. The dog had no way of getting in. He could stare, he could show his fangs, he could claw at the glass; but he couldn't bite. And there were several things she could do to get rid of him. She tried the first that came to mind: she blew the horn.

It didn't faze him. In the light reflected from the dash she could see his eyes, shining and watchful, and the white glitter of his teeth.

"Nice gums you've got there, old boy," she said, trying to joke away the fright she felt over him. "I've seen them, though, so you can get off the car and let me pass." She waved at him, and he snapped at her hand, as close as the glass let him. Then she rocked the car, bracing herself in the seat and throwing her weight from side to side. He balanced himself skillfully; the slight motion she was able to set up didn't dislodge him. He put a paw on the glass and she saw the big toenails and the mud on his pads, and through the sound of the rain she heard his growl again.

She put the car into gear hurriedly. She would throw him off with some erratic driving. The chassis shuddered as the engine took hold; she swung the wheel quickly, jerking the wheels upon the shoulder of the road. He fell against the glass. His wet fur plastered itself there. He was trying to get his feet under him again. He was falling, sliding off to the left. She reversed the wheel to keep from running over him in case he fell close to the car. The car jumped under her, bouncing in the ruts. Then there was a tearing crash and the lights went out.

She stepped on the brake. It took a moment to realize what had happened. The memory of the sights she had just seen lingered in her eyes; it was as if by blinking she would see them again. The dark produced a sudden fright as shocking as the attack by the dog. She waited, clinging to the wheel, listening to the purr of the motor and the drumming of the rain. She didn't know if the dog was still on the hood or was gone. He could be lying there staring in at her; she had no way of knowing.

She put the car into reverse and cautiously backed away from whatever it was which had caused the impact. A boulder beside the road, probably; she'd passed more than one, seen them shining gray and wet among the shrubby trees. The car moved sluggishly and there was a steely clanking from the vicinity of the right wheel. The sound sent panic thudding through her. She'd wrecked her car because of the brute on the hood; and the noise made by the wheel warned her that she couldn't get far. She was pinned here in the rainy dark, with a ferocious animal waiting for her to emerge from the shelter of the car. Nice, she told herself bitterly; I've fixed myself up thoroughly.

Now what do I do?

In despair she experimented with the light switch, pushing it in, then jerking it out sharply. A miracle happened. The lights came on.

The view was just what it had been before, the wet trees and the shabby road, but now the left headlamp was tilted crazily, shining up the hill, and in its round beam she caught the corner of a house. It was a white house built low against the rise of the hill. There were vines, not yet leafed out, which made a knuckly pattern on the stucco wall.

There was something else new, too. There was another dog.

The two big yellow brutes stood together in the road, looking at the car. One must be the dog she'd knocked from the hood. Or had there been two of them from the beginning, the one which had leaped and snapped, a second one which had jumped up to face the windshield and look through at her? She studied them, trying to search out any difference, and so became aware of what was happening to the lights. They were going out again, not quickly this time, but with a slow ebb like the stealing away of a tide.

She tried snapping the switch again; it didn't do any good. The glow faded moment by moment. She had the strange impression that the car was bleeding to death.

While there was still a trace of the glow to see by, she rattled the door handle. The reaction was instantaneous. One of the dogs took off in a snarling leap. The other stayed put. He sat there, having dropped his haunches suddenly, looking mildly puzzled while the other beast chewed and growled at the rim of the door.

"Go away!" she yelled through the narrow cleft and in reply she heard the chop of his teeth. He's mad, she thought; this was the first time this idea had come to her. She was penned in by a mad dog. She'd be here, a prisoner, until someone whose car was in running order happened to come and find her.

She jerked the door to snap the inner latch. The lights died completely. The dark closed in like the shutting of a tomb.

She beat the horn with her fist, causing three sharp blasts. Then she began to cry. She didn't want to weep with fright; it was a silly and useless course of behavior, a nitwit's answer to danger. What she really wished to do was to find a wrench in the car and get out and beat the brute senseless. She wanted to take out on the dog the fear and the dismay he had caused. She could with the greatest of pleasure have split his skull. This was the moment when sheer rage overcame her, so that she did something quite foolish. She grabbed her handbag off the seat and turned to the door, ready to give one chopping blow.

The door opened too suddenly. Perhaps the dog had thrust his head in—she couldn't see. For a moment the handle slipped from her grip. She sensed the thing that was coming in at her, the teeth that meant to find her throat. She dropped the purse, grabbing for the door and kicking out with her feet.

A roaring panic confused those next few moments. She was aware of a grip on her toes, as if a shark had taken hold of her foot. The rest was a melee of fright, struggle, strain. The door slammed shut at last; she crouched there, numb, rubbing her left foot. The shoe was gone.

The smell of the night had entered the car in the brief while that the door had been ajar; this odor was the first thing she noticed as her senses began to reorganize themselves. The air was fresh and sweet, washed clean by the rain. But it smelled lonely, too, and a long way from the traffic fumes of the city.

Were there people in that house? She tried peering toward it through the rain; she thought that she could make out the dim impression of a white wall, a paleness like a ghost's. But no light showed. She risked lowering the pane a little, cautiously so as not to rouse the brute that leaped. The night-smell came in stronger than ever, and moisture touched her face. It was very dark out there. She felt cut off from everybody, and bewildered.

The motor hadn't faltered. Perhaps it would be better to risk further damage to the ruined wheel, even another crash in the dark, just to get away from here. But behind lay a long stretch of vacant hillside. She'd have to back the car, feeling her way in the ruts. Ahead somewhere was Sunset Boulevard ... maybe. But how far?

Her thoughts stumbled here and there, trying to fight a way through the difficulty. She rubbed her temples. Her fingertips were cold.

All at once a light bloomed in the dark, quite close, and shone in on her through the rain-spattered pane. A man's voice spoke. "Well, what have we here? A stranger at the gate?"

She wasn't sure that she liked this new development very much. He had come up without warning, without any sound of walking. She moved away a little and let there be a space between her and the door.

"Hey in there! Open the window, will you?"

She thought of locking the doors quickly, rolling the glass to the top, defying him.... But that would be silly, an extension of the foolish panic that had led her to try to wallop the dog. The man did sound friendly, somehow, and as if he wanted to help. She rolled the glass down a bit further, tried to make her tone commonplace as she spoke. "I seem to have discovered a dog, a very bad-tempered dog. He blocked the road, and then jumped on the hood of the car, and in trying to shake him off I ruined a wheel."

The light disappeared from the window. The man went to the front wheels and examined them. She could see something of him in the reflected glow. He had on a raincoat and a soggy felt hat. She thought he was rather good-looking, with a square face in which thick brown eyebrows almost met over deep-set eyes.

He came back to the window. "I think you hit a stone."

"Yes, I thought so."

He flicked the light in at her for a moment as if checking up. "You said something about a dog. What sort?"

"A big yellow dog. There are two of them hereabouts."

"What do you mean?" The flashlight darted aside, and in its beam she saw one of the brutes; he looked mild now, pacified; but she thought she knew those teeth.

"That's one of them."

He laughed. "Not Saki. You wouldn't be talking about him, not this mutt. He's like a lamb."

"He has a brother, then, that's not a lamb."

"Saladin?" The light twitched over to the second dog. He too was grinning in a mockery of friendliness. "Here, boy!" The dog came over, not with a leap, not lunging with his teeth bared, but walking meekly. The man's hand came down into the cone of light, patted the dog's head. The dog didn't try to take the hand off in one gulp as she had half-expected.

"You'd better check up on them and find out how they behave when you're not around," she said with a touch of heat.

"They hunt coyotes and rabbits in these hills. Perhaps you just happened to interrupt something," he offered. "Look, you seem to be in trouble. The radiator's smashed, and I think your right axle is bent. The car shouldn't be driven until it's been worked on. It ought to be towed out."

"I'd drive it anyway, if the lights worked," she flung at him.

He waited a few moments as if considering what should be done. "It's too late to rouse anybody from a garage. Even if there is an all-night place reasonably close, I doubt if they'd come up in rain like this. What I wanted to offer was to drive you home in my car. You can come up in the morning and attend to things by daylight."

"My car might be stripped, leaving it here alone."

"No one will even see it. This isn't a through street."

Now I find out.... She was flooded with hot anger at Sunny, at the stupidity of city departments in charge of labeling streets, and at the yellow brutes who had bullied her into wrecking her car. "I won't come out with the dogs there."

She saw his smile in the half-light. "They won't hurt you."

"One of them has my shoe."

He cocked his head as if amused. "How did that happen?"

"I stuck a toe out and he fastened on. The shoe stayed with his teeth. Fortunately I got my toes back inside."

He didn't believe her; she sensed that. Probably he thought she'd tried to strike one of his pets, that the shoe had flown from her hand, and that this was just what she deserved. But while she watched, he went to search. Presently he came back. "No shoe. Sorry."

She risked opening the door and stuck out her foot in its bare silk stocking. "Do you have anything I could borrow?"

He spotlighted her foot and it looked silly and a little indecent, she thought. She pulled it back inside. He said, "I don't want to wake them up inside the house. If you'll let me, I'll carry you to the garage. You'll be dry from there on home. Unless home is somewhere you can't walk in half-barefooted."

"Home is a very broad-minded place," she assured him.

He pulled the door wide. He had an air of confidence, she thought; he'd figured this out and now everything was settled. She slid forward on the edge of the cushion and he lifted her. The raincoat had been deceiving. He was thinner, wirier than she had thought. He kicked her car door shut and began to walk up the hill. Gravel made crunching noises under his shoe. The dogs padded behind; she could hear their pads slapping, and the breathy whines they gave now and then. Saki and Saladin.... At first they'd tried to eat her up. Now they were shy as mice. She couldn't figure them out.

He said, "I ought to introduce myself under the circumstances, shouldn't I? I'm Edmund Linder."

She couldn't see his face; he'd turned off the flashlight and put it away, probably into a pocket of the raincoat. She couldn't decide whether the situation warranted coolness, straight manners, or humor. She said, "My name is Katherine Quist."

"They call you Kitty," he said instantly.

"Yes, how do you know?"

"We have mutual friends."

"I've never heard of you."

"The DeGraffens call me Lin." He stopped. The gravel had ended; they had reached the slope of a cement ramp. She made out a dim white square not too far away—the garage, shining under the rain. "It's a small world. Just how small is it? Don't tell me you just came from there?"

"Yes, that's right. I was trying to find a shortcut that Sunny Walling claimed to know all about. Du Moyne, she said."

He put her on her feet; she teetered, not liking to put down the shoeless foot on the wet cement. "Do you know Sunny?" she asked.

"No." He threw the word over his shoulder. He had walked to the side of the building. She heard the metallic rattle of a hasp. Then the garage door began to yawn upward, showing a black void to match the rest of the night.

"She's a very good friend of the DeGraffens. She practically lives at their house in the summertime, when they're using the pool."

"Is that so?"

He had disappeared into the blackness of the interior. She was out here with the dogs. She couldn't see them but she could sense their presence. Or perhaps it was the faint odor of wet dog-hair that warned her of their nearness. They were looking at her; she was sure of it. She hugged the coat tight and took a firmer grip on the heavy handbag.

The lights came on in a car inside the garage. There were spaces for three cars, and each was occupied. The one he was backing out was a station wagon, a small car; it looked new.

She looked around at the scene which was lit up by the backing-lights on the car. The dogs weren't anywhere near; she couldn't see them. She saw the edge of a lawn bordered with geraniums—no blooms now; this was February. Dimly in the distance she could make out some of the house. There were people up there, since he had said he didn't want to wake them getting her a shoe.

The car stopped opposite her and he jumped out and came around. She thought he meant to pick her up again, so she said hastily, "I'm fine now. What's a wet sock between friends?" She saw that he was looking at her, that he was sizing her up now that she stood in a brighter and completer light than that given by the flash. She felt herself flushing.

"Kitty Quist," he said, and it seemed as if he were connecting her with something that was already in his mind, something the DeGraffens might have told him. There was so little to know—the job at the University, the tiny flat, the very limited social life, the dead love affair with the DeGraffen cousin, Arnold. One of these must interest him.

He opened the car door and she slid in. He shut down the garage, fixed the hasp, got in beside her, behind the wheel. The car swung downhill, backed on the gravel. For a moment she saw her car, crippled there among the shrubby trees.

One of the dogs was sitting on the hood.

CHAPTER TWO

Ardis peered into the hall from the door of her bedroom, her black hair tousled, fair skin pink with sleep, her small body lost in the crazy nightgown she affected. "Is it you, Kitty? Or is it a burglar? If you're a burglar there isn't any money but there's a bottle of whisky in the kitchen cupboard with the cereals. Take that, you bad man, and go."

Kitty stuck her head out of the bathroom. "Oh, you nut—corrupting burglars now, no less. I didn't make enough noise to wake you."

"I had a nightmare." Ardis cut off a yawn to squint at her. "What happened to you? You looked drowned." Her eyes widened. "You can't be washing your hair at this hour. So somebody must have pushed you into the swimming pool." She nibbled a lip. "Only they don't keep water in it in the winter."

"Go back to bed."

"No, I'm wide awake now. Tell me."

"It's raining outside." Kitty had gone back to setting the witch-locks that clung to her throat. She pulled open a bobby pin, transfixed a curl with savage hurry. She was tired, she wanted to be in bed. But tomorrow she'd look a freak if she didn't attend to this. "I took a shortcut over a hill. I ended up putting the car out of commission. A kind Samaritan brought me home. His dog stole my shoe, only he said not."

"The dog?"

"The man. Mr. Edmund Linder."

"I might know him. What's he like?" Ardis was getting interested. She came to the bathroom and leaned in the open door, and stared.

She would make a thing out of it if she could. Ever since the breakup with Arnold, she'd been sniffing out romances for Kitty. So Kitty was carefully nonchalant when she said, "Oh, eyebrows ... very. Brown hair—I think. Knows the DeGraffens. Feels muscly under a raincoat. Loves dogs, big mean ones. Drives a station wagon."

"You didn't like him?"

"He's all right."

"What about the car? How bad is it?" Without waiting for an answer to this Ardis rattled on, "Oh, and for grief's sake how'd you happen to take a shortcut you didn't know anything about?"

Kitty said, "Sunny told me about it," before she thought. She caught the flicker of hatred in Ardis's face before the mask-like look came to conceal it. "She did it on purpose," Ardis said after a moment.

"No, I don't think so. She wouldn't do that. It was a mistake. She said to turn on Du Moyne, I thought. I either misunderstood or she forgot the name of the right street. It ended in a kind of trail, just one house there. I'm going up in the morning, early, before it's time to get on the job, and see about the car."

"You always stick up for her," Ardis said, turning away. The door of her bedroom shut with a click.

Kitty looked at her own reflection in the mirror. "You're so stupid," she told herself; it should be easy to remember not to mention Sunny in Ardis's presence. There was so much rankling bitterness even yet. It might even be better to drop the friends she had who were also friends to Sunny. Because Ardis was more than worth all of them. Ardis had proved her loyalty in a thousand ways. She was the kind of friend you might never find again. And Sunny Walling ... well, after a while, under all the fun and laughing and the sense of mischief that had given her her name, you sensed the utter lack of honor, the emptiness of soul, the heart like a small cold stone.

Kitty slipped into bed with a grateful sense of ease. She thought briefly of her car as she had seen it last, spotlighted against the rainy dark, the big dog sitting on its hood; and she remembered Edmund Linder and the feeling of safety and strength she had drawn from him. Then, it seemed, she must have slept at once, deeply and tiredly. Some long time later she was awakened by the ringing of the telephone.

The ringing from the niche in the hall penetrated her tired slumber, and under its blanket of sleep her mind began to count the rings: *one ... two ... three... four....*

Ardis must have answered then. Kitty waited, still less than half awake, wondering if the call was for her. And then, sometime during the waiting, sleep rolled in again like an all-obliterating fog.

The rain had turned to mist during the night. The morning was lowering, dark, and cold. Kitty ate a hasty breakfast in the kitchen, nibbling toast and an egg, gulping a cup of instant coffee. Ardis was still asleep.

By telephone she found a garage open, then called a cab to take her there. At the garage she explained to a man in coveralls where the car was and what she thought had happened to it. "A wheel, huh?" he said, turning to the big tow truck in the shadows of the garage. "Well, we shouldn't have any trouble. I know the road. You don't have to go up there with me unless you want to."

She debated; up to now she had taken it for granted that it would be necessary to show the garage-man the way through the winding hillside streets to the queer rutted lane where Edmund Linder had found her.

Curiosity was her worst fault; Kitty admitted to herself how much it dictated her actions, and how many scrapes it got her into. She wanted to see by daylight the road shut in by shrubby trees, the house whose corner she had glimpsed, and she wanted to figure out just where she had taken a wrong turn, and what had happened to Du Moyne Avenue.

Most of all she wanted to see those dogs.

There was no accounting for the behavior of those brutes, their outright viciousness followed by grinning quiet.

Of course, she assured herself while the garage-man waited for her answer, she had no interest in Edmund Linder whatever.

"I think I'll go with you," she decided.

"Hop in, then," he said.

They rumbled westward on Sunset Boulevard, then turned abruptly into a street that climbed the hill. She read its name and gasped. Du Moyne, the pixyish avenue which had vanished and left her on a dead end ... here it was, sedate, lined with eucalyptus, some nice houses looking out superciliously over the vast expanse of West Los Angeles and Beverly Hills.

The truck worked its way farther into the hills, through branching canyons and over small divides, and came at last to a ridge where houses were far apart, where the stony crust had been scoured bare by the wind. "I'll bet you turned wrong here," the tow truck operator remarked. "There was a sign here up until last week. Slide took it out, along with part of the paving."

She looked where he pointed, downward and to the left, and saw how Du Moyne made a loop here, avoiding an outcropping of rock, and how at the sharpest part of the turn the paving was washed over with dirt, so that the side street seemed naturally a continuation of the avenue. The dirt track led down between small trees. It was sheltered by the bare ridge to the south. There were grassy spaces beyond the trees, green now in California's brief spring.

Ahead, near the edge of the yard of the white house, there seemed to be several cars beside her gray coupe, and quite a group of men.

She leaned forward, puzzled, trying to make out the reason for the group and their possible business with her car. At the same moment she was aware that the garage-man was staring at her. He said through his teeth, "Cops. What kind of accident was this, anyway? Hit and run? You sideswipe somebody?"

"Of course not," she answered impatiently. But what he had said about the police being there was true. The black-and-white sedan blocking the road at an angle was unmistakably the law. The tow truck crept forward with caution, came to a stop. The garage-man made a face of distaste; Kitty thought that he had not believed her claim of innocence. With a grunted word, advising her to stay put, the trucker got out and walked toward the group of men.

Kitty felt a growing alarm; she scrambled out of the truck and waited to take in the scene ahead, still baffled by it, still trying to understand. There couldn't be anything for which she was to blame, she assured herself. But the ominous quiet of the men, the lowering sky, and the dead dark light sent her hurrying to see. There were two other cars; one had crushed a path through the shrubby trees to outflank her car and get beyond it.

She studied the house for a moment. There seemed no sign of life in it. In order to get around the black-and-white sedan, she stepped into the trees. Their leaves still held traces of rain, and brushed her wetly. She went on, passing her own car. The group of men still hadn't moved. The trucker had joined them, stood speaking with one of them—a tall man with red hair—though the attention of both seemed directed toward something Kitty couldn't see, upon the ground.

There was the whine of a siren in the distance.

Kitty came out from between her car and the one flanking it ahead, and saw the huddled shape covered by a blanket. Someone lay there in the middle of the graveled lane, and the covering blanket told its own story. This was death. At this moment the trucker and the red-haired man turned to look at her. There was something in the eyes of both she couldn't fathom. A feeling of helpless fright jerked at her nerves. "Who is it?" she whispered.

The trucker raised his cap, something he hadn't done before; it was as if, Kitty thought, he suddenly took notice of her, seeing her in a new light. He said, "There's been some kind of trouble, Miss."

The other man also touched his hat. "I'm Lieutenant Doyle of the Sheriff's Office. Are you Katherine Quist?"

"Yes."

"This is your car?"

"That's right. I had an accident here last night. A man from that house"—she pointed to the low white house against the hill—"took me home in his car."

"What time was this, please?" He had direct brown eyes under red brows; his face had freckles on it. There was something young about him—the fresh cynicism, perhaps—but the watchful attitude betrayed the years he had put in at this kind of work.

"I had left some friends' house at about eleven-thirty," Kitty told him. "I must have been ten minutes or so getting here. I wasn't familiar with the road. I stopped often to read street markers."

"Will you see if you know this woman?" He walked briskly to the huddled figure and flipped back the edge of the blanket. Kitty saw the great spread of tawny hair, the ruffled blue chiffon, the small wrist with its glitter of diamonds, and she cried: "*Sunny!*"

She stumbled closer. In that instant it seemed impossible that Sunny could be dead. Sunny wasn't made for lying cold and still; she was a sky-rocket giving off sparks in a world made only for hilarious fun. This was unreal. It was nightmare. Even as the sense of dreaming washed across Kitty's mind, masking the sudden shock, she caught a glimpse of Sunny's throat.

She turned to stumble away. Black waves roared in behind her eyes. She was buffeted, falling. She heard the trucker's sudden yell of warning. Somebody grabbed her. "Dammit," said the voice of Lieutenant Doyle. "I didn't mean for her to get that close."

When things came back to normal somewhat, she was sitting in the front seat of the Sheriff's car; the door was open and Doyle was there to keep her from falling out. "Why is she—like that?" Kitty managed.

"We haven't a full report from the medical examiner as yet." He was putting her off; there was knowledge behind his eyes. "Will you give me her name and address and tell me when you saw her last, please?"

"Her name is Sunny Walling. She lives in Studio City, on Sierra Drive—I don't know the number. She's a radio and television actress. I saw her last night at the home of some friends, a party —" Kitty stopped; she had to have time for getting control, for fighting down the panic and sickness.

"She had on those clothes?"

"Yes."

"There isn't any coat or outside wrap here. Do you know if she had one?"

"She had a mink stole. She was very proud of it. Please, I—I'd like to sit quiet for a few minutes."

He walked away, readjusted the blanket, spoke to one of the other men. Kitty realized that there was a search going on. These other men were looking for something.

By and by Doyle returned. "Did Miss Walling own a car?"

"Yes, a dark blue Packard sport coupe. It was new."

"Do you know if she was driving it last night?"

"I think she was." Kitty made an effort to remember. She'd been on the terrace, talking to Maud DeGraffen, when Sunny had appeared. There had been a number of new arrivals at that time, a lot of greetings and chatter, the mounting excitement when people first see familiar faces. Sunny always sparked a party, gave it sudden gaiety. Too much, sometimes—the kind of fun that wears thin after midnight, though Sunny never seemed to tire or be bored with it. "You might talk to the De-Graffens, our hosts. They'd know."

A man emerged from the trees at the right and beckoned to the Lieutenant. They went away together, out of sight. Kitty studied the group near the body; she saw that the men kept changing. A squat, square-faced plainclothes man in a brown suit was the only constant factor. The others came, spoke to him, left again.

The siren whined, close this time. She heard the crunch of tires on gravel and looked back. This was an ambulance.

They took Sunny away.

When Doyle came back, he seemed to have lost his curiosity about Sunny. He said, "Will you tell me about your accident here, Miss Quist? Start with your leaving the party."

She marshaled her thoughts, tried to give him a clear and concise account of her efforts to find the shortcut, the mistake in getting off Du Moyne Avenue, her scare over the dogs, Edmund Linder's fortunate appearance. He stood and listened, literally—Kitty was reminded of the old expression—not batting an eye.

When she had finished, Doyle asked, "Was Miss Walling acquainted with these people, the Linders?"

"Mr. Linder said not. I asked him. It seems he knows the DeGraffens, so I thought he might know Sunny, too."

"Just how explicit was she about this shortcut?"

"Sunny wasn't ever explicit about anything. She made it seem like nothing at all, a mere hop, skip, and jump over the hill to Sunset Boulevard."

"Do you think she herself had driven it?"

"She didn't say so."

"Now ... the dogs. Do you know one breed from another?"

"I don't know what kind these were. They reminded me of Great Danes, only they hadn't the gentle look a Great Dane has. They were fierce." She looked toward the house. "They must be up there. They belong to the Linders."

"Temporarily missing," he said in a sharp, clipped tone; and his gaze on the Linder house was cold as stone. He turned back to Kitty. "I'm going to let you get your car out of the way now. You can go back with the tow truck. I'll want your telephone number at home, and at the job, if you work."

"Of course I work," said Kitty. For an instant she puzzled over the detective's tone; there had been some implication there, some hint of cynicism. Then she thought of Sunny, and all at once the truth hit her. They had already known who Sunny was. They'd recognized her. Well, the newspapers had given last November's night-club fracas a pretty thorough coverage, plus some hints about Sunny's mode of living, rather lush for a radio actress who worked as little as Sunny. Doyle thought Kitty was a part of that group. She felt herself flush. "I have a job at the University. I'm a secretary there."

"I see," he said without any change of expression. "Telephone numbers, please?" He had a piece of a pencil in his fingers, a card in his palm.

She gave him the numbers and he wrote them down.

"I'll see you later," he said. He walked over to talk with the tow truck operator, and Kitty saw that they were figuring out how her car could be moved. She saw Doyle looking curiously at the hood of the car, as if for some evidence of the dog's being there, and she sensed his doubt.

She tried to shrug off the feeling. Let Doyle think what he pleased.

She got out of the car and stood in the cool, damp-smelling air. The tow truck man lifted a hand in her direction, a brief gesture that said, *Buck up, we'll soon be out of here*. Something had taken the suspicion from his eyes—her stunned reaction when she had seen Sunny, perhaps.

She looked up at the Linder house, wondering who might be there, and whether the police had ordered them to stay indoors while official business went on.

Doyle had said that the dogs were missing. For the first time Kitty thought definitely of the savage dog in regard to what had happened to Sunny. She saw again in her mind's eye the hideously torn throat. The cool air still flowed about her but now her skin prickled with heat, stung with sudden sweat. She rubbed her palms against her skirt. Her dry mouth seemed to congeal, cutting off breath.

She turned away and stumbling, half-running, she hurried down the lane. The shrubby trees, the dark sky, the narrow track, seemed to frame some horror she couldn't face. She would wait on Du Moyne for the truck and her crippled car. Later, when she was calm, she would think of something to do—telling the detective most logically. Just now the impulse to get away was overpowering.

Someone came out of the trees just ahead, a man in a raincoat. She all but ran into him before she realized that it was Edmund Linder.

CHAPTER THREE

His hands caught her, steadying her shoulders in a grip that was almost cruel. "I must see you later. How about ten o'clock—your place?"

It seemed important for him to understand what had happened here; she took for granted that he had been gone, that he didn't know. "A girl is dead, killed in a dreadful way—the girl who told me to take this cutoff last night. I can't help wondering if the dogs—"

He broke in harshly. "The dogs didn't have anything to do with it!"

She stammered lamely, "But they're gone!" as if this proved their guilt.

"I know. I've been out in the hills looking for them. Poor devils, if I can't find them first it will go badly with them."

She studied him, meeting the gray eyes under the thick brown brows. His face had tired lines in it, though there was angry determination in the set of the mouth. It seemed that he was being *too* oblivious of the dogs' possible guilt. He was deliberately ignoring that chance; there was a touch of obstinacy in his attitude. Kitty felt a stirring of irritation rising to meet

"They have to consider everything."

"I guess so. Will you be home at ten?"

"I don't know that I can. I have a job at the University."

"Make an excuse." He was, urging; no, more than this, she thought—he was commanding. "Be there. I'm bringing someone to see you."

She opened her mouth to ask who, but he had turned without even saying goodbye and vanished into the trees. She listened for his steps; she ought to run after him, to tell him that she had to be at her job. But the sodden earth, the thick grasses, deadened any sound. Behind her the truck roared. She looked back. The black-and-white police car had been drawn aside and the trucker was maneuvering to get in line with her car. She walked on slowly, trying to organize her thoughts.

She resented what seemed like trickery on Doyle's part—letting her tell him the long story of last night's trouble, keeping his face blank, leading her to believe that she was giving him new information. And all the while he already knew that there were dogs here, he suspected that they were vicious, and probably it hadn't been long since Edmund Linder had told him her experiences second-hand and had incidentally belittled the idea that the dogs could have actually frightened or endangered anybody. She decided that she didn't care much for Mr. Doyle, and that Edmund Linder was out to make her seem a fool.

Her thoughts swung over to the thing she'd been subconsciously avoiding—Sunny's death, the strange circumstance that had brought the girl here to die so soon after she had advised Kitty to take this route home. What possible reason could lie behind the coincidence? It could be presumed that Sunny had recommended the cut-off because she was familiar with it, had used it. But how had she discovered it? And why was she on the side road leading to the Linders' house? She had not been acquainted with them, according to Edmund. Of course, there were other houses, not close but within walking distance.

Only, Sunny wouldn't have gone walking in that storm.

Where was her car? Where was the mink wrap of which she had been so proud—a gift, Maud DeGraffen had said with sly indulgence, of an advertising executive who must remain anonymous because he had a wife? Would Sunny have gone even a short distance out of doors without either of these, the car or the wrap? Knowing Sunny, her love of ease, Kitty found it inconceivable that she should.

At the garage, while the trucker made an estimate on the damage, Kitty looked for scratches on the hood of the car, some sign left by the dog. There were some, quite visible to her, but the car was not new and Doyle might not think the marks significant. There were other, older scars on the paint. Kitty knew that these scratches were fresh, but would Doyle believe it?

When the trucker had finished his estimate, Kitty approved the order, gave him the name of her insurance company, and took a cab for home.

She walked in and looked first at the clock in the living room. It seemed impossible that it was not yet nine, and that still by breakneck efforts she could make it to the University and Professor Galem's office. For a moment this prospect seized her mind, but only its surface; all the while that she made plans—rush here, fly there—her feet were taking her toward the telephone in its niche in the hall.

Professor Galem's voice was pleasantly dry and husky, and called up his kindly image, a small, stout man with gray hair as curly as a poodle's. Kitty explained what had happened, and that she might be expected at a kind of inquiry. It was only partly a lie; Doyle would probably be here.

Professor Galem expressed his regret and said that she shouldn't worry, he'd make out with a temporary girl, one of the students perhaps.

She was putting the telephone in its cradle when a movement in the door of the bathroom, a shadow that shifted and grew dark, sent quick chills racing along her nerves. She dropped the phone, more quickly than she had meant to do, and the loud rattle of its falling jarred the silence in the dimly lit hall.

"Who is it?" she asked from a dry mouth, and then felt foolish—it was Ardis, still in the great flannel gown with the pattern of cabbage roses, the pink ribbons at her wrists, ruffles high about her throat. She came into the hall and the poor light didn't conceal the fact that she looked white and sick.

"I couldn't make it to work," she said. "Headache. Ghastly. I've taken a half dozen aspirin and a sleeping pill. Look in on me in an hour or so, will you? If I'm dead from all this dope, take care of everything." She went to the door of her room and turned there. She seemed to be getting up her courage to say something, and trying to seem elaborately casual doing it. "What were you telling the professor on the phone? Someone's dead?"

Kitty was struck by, the falseness of Ardis's attitude. Ardis was usually just frankly nosy. "Sunny Walling has been killed."

Ardis moistened her lips. "And high time, too," she said at last, "don't you think?"

It was no time for fun, even though she knew the justification Ardis had. "It was horrible."

"Yes, I judge so. You've turned quite green, Kitty. Want a drink? Or one of my aspirin? Who did her in?"

"They don't know." Kitty felt cold and weak. "I think I'll have some coffee, thanks."

"I still don't know the details." A certain edge in Ardis's tone struck Kitty's ear. It was as if Ardis had underlined the remark, had asked Kitty subtly to remember it. "Where was this? How'd it happen?"

"They found Sunny in a road in the hills above Sunset, on the cut-off she advised me to take last night. I don't know the details either. Her car wasn't there. She wasn't wearing a wrap, though she was out of doors."

"Sounds very mysterious," Ardis commented with a flippancy as false, as strained, as had been her casual air. "Somehow, though, darling, I can't get excited over anything happening to that bitch."

The sharp buzz of the doorbell cut across her words. She flinched at the sound and Kitty thought that a shiver rippled the Victorian nightgown. Ardis whispered, "If it's for me, say that I'm not here. I can't see anybody." With a sudden air of fright she stepped into her bedroom.

"I'll see who it is," Kitty said. She sensed that Ardis waited behind the partly shut door, listening while she went to the entry to check on their visitor.

Maud DeGraffen stood on the outer landing. She was a tall, spare woman, always crisp and chic, dressed now in a severe black wool suit, a tiny red hat, and red shoes, with a big, black carryall handbag. Her gray hair lay in a smooth knot at the back of her neck. She came in; her long-legged step reminding Kitty of some elegant water bird, some flamingo or heron, stalking at the edge of a pool. She turned to face Kitty. "I'm glad I caught you at home. I came about this thing which has happened to Sunny. Do you know?" Her stare was cool and searching.

"I damaged my car on the shortcut she told me of, went back for it this morning, and ran head-on into the police."

"They called me by telephone, very early. A certain Mr. Doyle is coming to see me shortly. First I thought I'd do a bit of checking up." She dropped the big bag on the couch, sat down, began to take out cigarettes. "First, this: did you meet Sunny there last night?"

Kitty felt a sense of shock. "On that hill? No. Why should I have?" She sat down facing Maud.

"Right after you left Sunny got herself into a terrific tizzy. There was something about that shortcut she should have told you, and hadn't."

Kitty's mind supplied that answer. Sunny had remembered the washout, the missing signpost, the pavement covered with dirt just before the opening to the side road. Sunny, then, had known every detail of that street....

Maud continued after puffing at her cigarette. "Sunny took off in her usual mad fashion to go after you. She seemed sure she'd find you lost, stranded."

Kitty asked curiously, "Was she driving her own car?"

Maud shrugged. "Darned if I know. I didn't go outside with her when she left. I'm not sure that anyone else did, though she and Arnold had been holding hands just before. I thought the whole thing was a little silly. I couldn't see what the excitement was all about. After all, you're not a fool."

Maud didn't have any way of knowing, of course, just what that lane had held. Thus Kitty made excuses for her friend. "Perhaps it was just an excuse Sunny used to get away," she offered. It suddenly seemed quite false to her that Sunny should be concerned over whether she had lost her way or not.

"It could have been," Maud said thoughtfully. "And since you didn't meet her—" Her glance was sharp, quick.

"I wasn't there long," Kitty said. "A kind Samaritan brought me home."

"Someone who lives nearby?"

"You know him," Kitty remembered. "Edmund Linder."

A perfectly blank expression seemed to congeal upon Maud's face. She tapped her cigarette into Kitty's ash tray. "Is Lin in this?"

"Not directly. But there is one way he might be involved." Kitty told Maud about the dogs, the fright she had had over them, the damage to the car. "Of course Mr. Linder made fun of me. He said the dogs were perfectly gentle and well behaved—and they were, while he was with me. Only ... the—the way Sunny looked—the way the body had been damaged—"

"Spare me the gruesome tidbits," said Maud sharply. "I gather it looked as if the dogs might have been at her. That could have happened *after* death. And it might have been some wild thing, a coyote for instance. There are lots of them in these hills and they aren't afraid to come close to houses, either. We've even seen them from our back porch in broad daylight."

Again Kitty felt as if someone had pointed out to her, patiently and reasonably, how foolish she was to try to convict Edmund Linder's dogs of wanting to hurt anyone.

"Of course I shan't say anything to the police about Sunny's erratic behavior," Maud was saying. "It's just the sort of thing they'd pounce on, make your life miserable over. You didn't meet Sunny; probably she didn't even follow you, immediately at any rate. So I won't mention it."

"Perhaps you'd better," Kitty said slowly. "It would look suspicious if they found out later; it would seem as if you and I had conspired to hide something. And Doyle is shrewd. He'll know much more than you think he does, and in his mind he'll be checking what you say against what other people have told him."

Maud was staring. "Really? You make him sound devilish, Kitty. By the way, I thought I heard some sound from the hall. Is Ardis still here?"

Kitty had heard nothing. But Maud was sharp; there could have been some faint noise that only she had caught. "Yes. She isn't feeling well."

"She knows about Sunny?"

"Yes. I told her." Kitty was uncomfortable under Maud's steady regard. Then Maud said, in almost a whisper: "Was she here all of last night?"

Kitty felt the heat that rushed to her skin. "Of course she was!"

Maud laughed. Then she rose and stalked over to the hall door and closed it, and went over to the windows and stood there looking down at the yard and the frostbitten garden. She looked lean and elegant against the light, a slim silhouette, the heron at rest—regarding his inferiors with amusement. "Don't be a baby, Kitty. There is going to be a good deal of unpleasant publicity about Sunny. Her death will smear us all. Do you think you can conceal Ardis from the police or the newspapers?"

"You said we didn't have to tell the police what they didn't know."

"Not telling something you might logically have forgotten in the excitement of a party isn't the same as pretending you don't know who her enemy was."

"She had more than one."

"She had one real enemy. Ardis. Ardis never forgot the Burns kid, nor what Sunny did to him."

Kitty wrung her hands. "I wish I had quit going anywhere that Sunny might have been! I wish I'd given up knowing her."

"You mean you wish you'd given up knowing us," Maud said wisely. "And to tell the truth, I used to wonder, too. We both like you immensely, Kitty. We wanted you to come to our shindigs whenever you could. But looking back, I can see how you must have felt about Sunny. Of course I gave you credit to figure out the answer with Arnold. With him, it wasn't Sunny; it was boredom. It was seeing the gambling and the all-night drinking and the drive-in waitresses and the bar blondes go down the drain together. It was seeing decency close in—your kind of decency. So Sunny was an excuse, a ticket out of jail."

"I knew all that before you did," Kitty said through stiff lips.

"Of course you did. The fiasco over Arnold wouldn't have made you hate Sunny. But you and Ardis are good friends. You must have thought of Ardis every time you looked at Sunny."

"I wish I could say that I did," Kitty answered, "only I wasn't that loyal a friend. I needed a little of Arnold's kind of fun, just to get over him, the way you take a drink to help a hangover—and yours was the best brand I knew. And I like you and Hal, really like you as human beings, the way you say you like me."

Maud came over and patted her hand. "Nice little Kit." She sat down then on the couch, in the spot she had vacated, and went on, "We must plan our stories so that they hang together. That isn't conspiring, it's plain common sense. I shall remember hearing Sunny tell you about the shortcut, since you've already told the police she recommended it to you. But I won't recall her saying that she was tearing off after you unless someone else does. After all, I'd had a few drinks and they could have affected my memory. Shall I remember that it was Du Moyne Avenue?" Maud meditated. "Or shall I be vague about the direction? Who else was around at that time? Not Arnold. He was at the bar, I'm sure. Hal was with that little brunette, that Sylvia somebody, the one who keeps her mouth puckered as though she's getting ready to suck an orange."

"I don't think anyone heard Sunny tell me about the shortcut except you," Kitty decided.

"Well, you can be sure that more than I heard her say she was running along to set you right," Maud said with a touch of snap. "But I can't recall who. Old Dena Frayne was skulking about, on the trail of a producer, if I remember correctly. Hal had already told her he couldn't use her, so it might have been Chesterly."

At one time Kitty had been entranced by this professional chitchat about the radio and television merry-go-round, the Hollywood jealousies, the dirt-digging, self-promotion, and back-stabbing activities which made up the usual background of a rather mad-house industry. Now she just felt sorry for Dena, a middle-aged woman who was trying to cling to her bit of fame as an actress; and she could see in her mind's eye Dena of last night, the tired, overpainted face, the anxious stare, the coppery bob so beautifully waved and dyed—and so unbecoming.

"I'll call Dena and tell her to keep her mouth shut," Maud decided. "I may as well use your telephone and save time."

She got up from the couch, went to the hall door, and disappeared behind it, staying for several minutes. When she came out, she was frowning. "I thought you said Ardis was home."

"Yes, she is."

"Her bedroom is open and empty. I checked on the bath, and your room, too; she's gone. She must have slipped out by the back way while we were talking." Maud waited as if expecting an explanation from Kitty.

Kitty hurried, aware of a strange uneasiness, to check on the rest of the apartment, the kitchen, the rear hall. It was true, Ardis was gone. Perhaps she'd begun suddenly to feel better—though Kitty's common sense told her that this was unlikely, even as she thought it.

There was something queer about this quick recovery ... and something even more queer about the illness which had preceded it. For Kitty realized, looking back, that Ardis's principal symptom had been an enveloping terror. The white face had been the mask of fear. The trembling hands shook with fright, not with fever; and the shivering body under the loose gown had been like that of a hunted animal who hears the footfall of doom.

CHAPTER FOUR

They were in the kitchen now, she and Maud. The place seemed too quiet, almost eerily silent. As if deliberately wishing to break the stillness, Maud went to a cupboard, took down a glass, ran water into it at the sink with a rushing noise. "Well, I don't see why she should run off just because I came."

"It couldn't have been that," Kitty said. "Ardis likes you. She must have decided not to miss a day's work, after all. You know, it's credit accounts at Weidmann's, the florist, and there's always a lot of bills to post after the week-end. She'd feel that they needed her."

"Speaking of Weidmann's," Maud began, "did you know that when the Burns kid fell overboard for Sunny, she insisted he buy flowers for her at Weidmann's so that Ardis would see the bills?" Maud began to light a new cigarette. "It was so characteristic of the little fool."

"No, I didn't know," Kitty said, her voice sounding to her as if she were trying to lie, weak and hollow. Perhaps Ardis had told her about it, during those frantic days when just living was an agony, when the Burns kid was due to go overseas, when Sunny had moved in on the small, mild romance and made it a joke—Ardis had been all but out of her head with shame and fury, and sometimes Kitty had wearied of hearing about the affair; it could have been one of those times that Ardis had mentioned the cruel refinement of having Weidmann's post the bills for Sunny's flowers. Kitty couldn't remember.

Maud continued, "At the time Ardis was still wearing his ring, still clinging to a last-ditch hope that he'd wake up, see Sunny for what she was—rotten, of course—and come back to her. It would have worked if the Burns boy hadn't been sent overseas so soon, might even have worked after that if he hadn't been killed."

Perspiration came out on Kitty's temples. "If the police knew all this, they'd arrest Ardis, of course."

"Oh, I don't know," Maud said, almost idly. "How could Ardis have met Sunny on that empty road in the hills? How could she have known Sunny was going there, that she'd have a chance at her where no one would see?"

"The real murderer might have telephoned, might have lured Ardis out, in order to cast suspicion on her ... might even have enticed her up to Du Moyne Avenue on some excuse —" The words had bubbled out; Kitty checked herself when she saw the sudden light in Maud's face.

"If there was a telephone call, you should have heard it."

Kitty shook her head stubbornly. "Anyway, there wasn't a real murderer. It was the dogs."

"Sticking to that, hmm? I might as well warn you—Edmund Linder won't like that theory, nor will his brother nor his aunt."

"I can't help it. I believe that the dogs must have done it."

A look resembling ironic pity flickered in Maud's eyes. She touched Kitty softly on the shoulder, a reproving tap. "If I thought for an instant the police would go for it, I'd back you up." She stood thoughtful, reflective. "Only it seems much too pat. So many people felt unloving toward our little Sunny. So many people had legitimate beefs over the way she'd treated them. And having a couple of mutts do her in would be much too convenient to be real. No, Kit, the cops won't take it. Not after they start digging. Not after even a whiff of Sunny's remarkable reputation. Don't back those dogs. They aren't going to be in the running long. And you'll be left out on a limb. Settle now for a good anonymous suspect. Like a tramp you might have seen lurking in those little trees."

"I didn't see a tramp," Kitty pointed out.

"Think back, dear," Maud said sweetly. She crushed the cigarette in the sink, led the way out of the room and back to the front entry. Her manner was gentle and advising. If she sensed Kitty's boiling confusion, she gave no sign.

"You want me to deliver Ardis up to the police," Kitty flung out as Maud opened the door to go.

Maud looked back, her green eyes regretful. "I'm not saying so, Kit ... only, one of them is it—one who knew Sunny. One we know. Goodbye." She went down the stairs to the street, her heels tapping a hollow echo up the stairwell.

Kitty stood on the small back porch. She saw without noticing the rather unattractive yard below, the circular clotheslines hung with wash, the plots of geraniums and the bordering ivy looking rather sick because of a recent spell of cold weather. The morning was beginning to clear; beyond the narrow rows of houses were the Hollywood hills,

green now, and up there in a general northwesterly direction was Du
Moyne Avenue, where she had sat last night, imprisoned by the dogs,
and where Sunny Walling had died, sometime between when she had
left and morning.

She tried to remember with meticulous detail anything that might
have indicated uneasiness on Sunny's part, but there had been nothing.
Sunny had paused in the middle of a dance with Hal DeGraffen, had
pushed him off, as a matter of fact, had tossed her shoes into a chair,
and had begun to chat with Kitty and a man named Chesterly, a television producer. She'd broken in upon their small-talk without any excuse, just naturally, the way a child breaks in with a self-centered
thought, and then Chesterly had drifted off as Maud had joined them.
And the talk had turned to going home, since Kitty had to work next
day and was on the point of making her excuses.

Kitty remembered Sunny's face; its overanimation, its quickness to
squint, to grin, to raise eyebrows, that had always made her think somehow of a monkey. A beautiful monkey, of course; Sunny had had an as-
tonishing perfection, physically; voluptuously built in the right places;
ripe, soft, creamy. She recalled Sunny's voice, the flippant assurance
about the shortcut which stilled any questions, any doubt. And as
Sunny's memory swam in her mind, she forced herself to face the question: was she really as understanding about Sunny's conquest of Arnold
DeGraffen as Maud said she was? Did she see quite clearly that Arnold
had simply been afraid of matrimony, and had used Sunny's wiles as a
lever to pry himself loose from danger?

When Arnold had broken their engagement six months ago, hadn't she
thought a little about some of the unpleasant things which might happen to Sunny?

Of course I did, she thought. And I didn't murder her. So Ardis didn't,
either. Ardis is like me; she was sick with hurt, ashamed that a man had
dropped her abruptly for a woman like Sunny. But murder didn't figure in it. Ardis had had even longer to get over her anger than Kitty had;
the incident with the Burns boy had happened almost a year ago. He'd
been dead five months. If you're going to kill a person like Sunny, you
do it when anger is at its fiercest heat.

Not afterward. Not now.

The breeze was colder than she had thought. She felt gooseflesh
come out along her arms. The wind that sang about her seemed to hold
an echo of Maud's words. *One of them is it. One who knew Sunny. One
we know.*

She jerked about as she heard the bell ring, inside the house. Someone was at the front door. She thought at once of Maud. Maud had come
back to say that she was wrong, that a little thought had shown her her

mistake, had brought belief in Kitty's theory. Kitty ran through the apartment and threw open the door, and found herself face to face with a woman she had never seen before.

This woman was not at all like Maud DeGraffen, whom Kitty had expected to see. She was not slim and crisp; she was a small, soft dumpling of a woman, and her clothes were far from the tailored strictness of Maud's; they were rather frumpy, as a matter of fact, with too many little frills, too many dangling bits of trimming, too much lace and braid. The woman smiled, then looked back over her shoulder. On the step behind her stood Edmund Linder.

Kitty backed from the door, saying, "Won't you come in?"

He said, "Aunt Dru, I'd like to present Miss Quist."

"How do you do?" Aunt Dru put out her hand, which was warm and moist and even a trifle sticky, as though recently she'd been eating something sweet. Her round blue eyes crinkled at the corners. "I'm pleased to meet you, Miss Quist."

Kitty stammered a reply, trying to orient herself to this surprise. She led them into the front room, gave them chairs, supplied ash trays— Aunt Dru looked at hers as if wondering what it might be. She asked, "Do you know of my adventure last night?"

"With the dogs?" asked Aunt Dru. "Yes, Edmund told me a little about it. He's quite firm that it had no connection with Miss Walling's death. I'm not so sure. I want to hear you tell it."

"The dogs belong to my nephews," Aunt Dru was saying in her small sweet voice. "They were darling as puppies. We spoiled them dreadfully. Saki was Edmund's dog, and Charles always claimed Saladin. Now they've grown up to be practically identical, and I can't tell one from another, though Edmund claims that he can." Her round eyes took on a serious, worried look. "But recently I've begun to suspect that one of the dogs is developing very bad manners. A man who was sent out by the county to work on our road said that one of them tore his pants leg." She stole a glance at Edmund, as if apologizing. "The truth should come out before someone is hurt, badly. If one of the dogs is vicious, he should be chained up." She turned again to Kitty. "Now—let me hear your story."

Kitty told it swiftly, phrasing it as she had for Doyle, starting with the party and Sunny's glib description of the shortcut, ending with Edmund's taking her home. She expected some comment from him, at least some brief word of agreement; but he said nothing. His face stayed blank, with displeasure obviously hidden under its reserve.

Aunt Dru, on the other hand, showed a lively interest. She looked scared when Kitty told of that first dive the dog had made for her, and she sucked in her breath sharply when Kitty described the loss of her shoe. She was such an oddly Victorian little old lady that Kitty half-expected her to bring out a bottle of smelling salts to revive herself from the fright.

She did take a lace-bordered handkerchief from her purse and dab at her temples. Violet cologne stole upon the air. "Edmund ... you didn't tell it at all like that!"

"Because it couldn't have happened like that!" he burst out. "You weren't there, Aunt Dru! You didn't see any such attack—"

"I did," Kitty broke in stiffly. "I'm not an imaginative person, Mr. Linder. My job at the University allows no flights of fancy, and the attitude I've had to cultivate there in the physics laboratory has carried over into my private life. I'm quite hard-headed, quite without delusions. Your dogs did just what I say they did." Her eyes dared him to call her a liar.

Instead he smiled all at once, and all the grimness went out of his face and she was reminded of those moments last night when he had carried her through the rain. "I must have sounded a boor. Of course the dogs did what you saw them do; the thing I'm trying to bring out is that their intentions were not what you thought. Probably you broke up a rabbit chase, or a fight with a coyote."

"Yes, you said that last night," Kitty put in, determined that no softness should betray her.

"Snapping teeth seem unfriendly, too," Kitty added with irony. "But I do venture to suggest that when you find your dogs again, you keep them chained at your house, especially at night. Even if it turns out that they had nothing to do with the death of Sunny Walling, chaining them up would be the safest course. They're going to get you a suit for damages sooner or later."

Edmund took out a checkbook. "Of course I'll pay for the repairs to your car," he said stiffly.

But Aunt Dru interrupted, breaking in at a moment when Kitty thought that open enmity would flare between her and Edmund. "That name—Walling. It sounds so familiar in a teasing way. There's something I should remember, and can't. I didn't want to mention it in front of the police, Edmund, but didn't you or Charles know a girl by that name?" She fanned herself with the cologne-scented kerchief. "It's the strangest sensation, like a kind of echo I'd heard a long time ago. Walling ... Walling ..." Her dumpling figure was straight, poised at the edge of her chair. Her face was puckered, oddly baby-like in its perplexity.

"I didn't know Miss Walling," Edmund said, in a tone that sounded ominous.

"Couldn't she have come to the house during the time Charles was acquainted with all those radio people?"

"I don't think so."

Aunt Dru explained to Kitty: "My other nephew, Charles, wrote a book, a very cute book everyone said, and there was a lot of talk for a while that one of the big broadcasting chains would base a series of programs on it. We had so many radio people in and out of the house then—"

"Aunt Dru," Edmund said sharply, "I think before you tell this to anyone else, you should check with Charles, and find out definitely whether Sunny Walling was among his radio friends. You can't scatter stuff like this. It's poison."

"Did … did I say something I shouldn't?" The smooth hands fluttered at her beribboned throat; and Aunt Dru's eyes swam with dismay and hurt.

"Of course you didn't," Kitty said, feeling sorry for her. "Walling isn't an uncommon name. It's quite likely you met someone with the name and now can't recall who, and so confuse them with Sunny." At the same time, in Kitty's thoughts were other things: the quickness with which Edmund Linder had denied, last night, that he knew the dead girl. He hadn't stopped to think about it, to check through the many people he must have met through the DeGraffens. He'd cut her off with a quick denial. Too quick, now that she thought about it. Too sure. And now he was telling Aunt Dru to keep her mouth shut.

Aunt Dru was saying helplessly, "I wish that I didn't sleep so soundly. There couldn't have been such a horrible crime, right below our house, without some disturbance, some outcry. If I could have awakened—I might even have saved that girl's life. If not that, I might have seen something useful to the police. At least I could have placed the time for them." She was rolling a bit of ribbon between her fingers.

"We don't know where she was killed," Edmund pointed out.

"I don't think it was anywhere very far away," Kitty told him. "You see, after Sunny had told me about the Du Moyne shortcut and I'd left the party, she remembered some detail, probably the missing signpost, and hurried off to follow me. She must have come right to Du Moyne, right to that spot where the paving is covered, at the entrance to your lane."

He didn't like this; Kitty thought that he covered an angry reaction with difficulty. He wanted to lash out at her; and yet something, perhaps the presence of his aunt, held him back.

Aunt Dru said softly, "It's very strange, isn't it, that Miss Walling sent you there?"

Kitty explained, "She thought I'd reach home so much quicker."

Aunt Dru's round eyes were worried. "A very weird theory has occurred to me. Suppose Miss Walling knew that she had an enemy, a dangerous enemy, and so had deliberately made a date to meet him in an isolated spot—our road, for example. She made the date, and then sent a decoy. Suppose she meant your going there as a test—"

On the arm of his chair, Edmund's hand made a spasmodic movement, a thrashing jerk, and the lamp on the table beside him jumped into the air under the blow, then crashed to the floor. What Aunt Dru said in finishing her remarks was lost in the breaking of the china standard. He rose to his feet, staring as if dazed at what he had caused to happen.

Kitty rose, too, but Aunt Dru cowered back into her chair as if the violence of the noise had shocked her.

"I'm ... awfully sorry." His voice was flat, the words dragged out. He went on staring at the crushed stuff on the floor. Bits of the bulb and pieces of the fat white china base had scattered over a wide area. The silk shade was torn.

Kitty was at a loss. Angry words boiled in her mind; she wanted to dress him down, but good, for his clumsiness. The lamp belonged to Ardis; it was one of the expensive knickknacks she had collected when it seemed that she would shortly marry the young soldier, Burns. Its breaking would be a final wrench, a last reminder that her hopes had been vain, her dreaming useless. But you can't fly at a man who won't even hear what you say to him.

Edmund was still staring at the lamp, but his mind was somewhere else. He wasn't thinking of what had happened here. He wouldn't care what Kitty said to him.

Aunt Dru got to her feet uncertainly. "Aren't you well?" she demanded of her nephew. "Can't you apologize to Miss Quist about her lamp?"

"I said I was sorry." He looked from her to Kitty. "Come on, Aunt Dru. Let's go home." He opened the checkbook, which was still in his hand, signed a blank check, threw it down on the table where the lamp had stood. "That's for you, Miss Quist." He stalked out of the room.

"He's just upset over something," Aunt Dru murmured distractedly, patting Kitty's hand as though she were a sulking child. "Don't feel bothered. He always was hot-tempered, even when he was little. The bad one who had to be spanked a lot." Her eyes pleaded for him.

Kitty took grim pleasure in ripping up the check and putting it into Aunt Dru's moist palm. "Give him this. Then he should feel better."

Aunt Dru's chin quivered. "Don't misjudge him."

"I'm sure that I haven't."

With a squeak of dismay, Aunt Dru hurried after Edmund. Downstairs the door had slammed, a car's motor was roaring.

CHAPTER FIVE

Kitty brought a broom and a dustpan from the closet in the kitchen and swept up the remains of the lamp, the crumbs of china, pieces of the electric bulb, twisted wire.

There was a feeling of guilt, of embarrassment, in doing it. She was helping to erase a little part of Ardis's hopeful longing, burying a bit of that picture Ardis had painted for herself and the man she loved: a small home, lovingly furnished, the small things gathered one by one, each with its story, its separate bit of planning. Now the lamp was gone.

Poor Aunt Dru. The little dowdy woman had been brought along, obviously with the idea that she would back up whatever Edmund chose to say. But her innocence had been his undoing. She hadn't seen where he had meant carefully to lead her. She'd blurted out her impression that the other nephew, Charles, might have known Sunny Walling. And she'd been struck by that strange idea which seemed to have upset Edmund—that Sunny could have had an engagement to meet someone she distrusted, and that Kitty had been sent as a decoy, a test for danger.

Kitty remembered what Maud had told her about Sunny's rushing away as soon as she was gone. This would fit in with Aunt Dru's strange surmise. Was there any way of checking it? Kitty wished that she had someone she could question, someone whose observation was sharp and whose memory could be trusted. Maud had seemed vague on some points, almost oddly so.

Then Kitty recalled Dena Frayne.

In her wish to be ingratiating, in her hope of making a good impression, Dena had been everywhere; she'd passed drinks for Maud, coaxed out the wallflowers and the sulkers, played nursemaid to a little blonde who'd had too much to drink too quickly, checked the record-player for the dancers in the rumpus room, done everything but mop up the floors—she'd have done that, too, Kitty thought, if it could have helped a producer notice her. Dena must have seen a great deal, contacted a lot of people. And she was observant, quick to catch on, hanging as she was by her toenails to an industry that no longer wanted her.

I should go to see Dena, Kitty thought. Now. Before Doyle gets here to pin me down, to make me say things I shouldn't say, to ferret out the story of Ardis and Sunny and the young soldier. She ran into her bedroom for her hat and coat.

Dena Frayne lived in an older section of Hollywood, a narrow street crowded up against the hills, only a minute or so by car from Hollywood Boulevard and Vine, the nerve-center of the networks. The crooked street was bordered with closely fitted stucco houses, two and three stories in height, built in the fashion of the early twenties. Once it might have been a rather fashionable neighborhood of movie people. Now it was a backwater, the houses split into flats and inhabited by those who had not yet arrived or who were on their way out. If you were anybody, you wouldn't live in Amaryllis Lane. If you were Dena Frayne and wanted to be close to that world whose door was slowly shutting in your face, it was ideal.

Kitty took the red streetcar to Hollywood and Vine and walked.

Kitty rang Dena's doorbell and heard the ringing echo in the apartment. It took a while for Dena to come to the door. She was wearing an atrocious red kimono. She hadn't put on any makeup and her pale, sagging face looked almost sick. The coppery hair was tied carefully into a net.

"Hello, Kitty." Without any sign of surprise, Dena unlatched the screen and stood back. "I haven't got dressed as yet. Don't look at the apartment, it's a mess. Sit over there. Want a cup of coffee?" she sidled over to a door that must lead to the kitchen. "Excuse me. I have to watch these eggs. I'll only be a minute."

"Don't let me interrupt breakfast."

"It's all right." Dena disappeared into the other room.

The place smelled stale and overlived-in. There were newspapers scattered over a cocktail table, a beaten-looking davenport, an old-fashioned radio console, the kind with carved mahogany doors and high legs, and on the walls some framed photographs of Hollywood celebrities. In the corner on an iron stand was a fern, almost dead from lack of sun and water, the earth in the pot scattered with cigarette butts.

Dena didn't live here in the accepted sense of the term, Kitty surmised, but merely waited as she would in a depot for some vehicle which would take her on to something better.

Dena came back, wiping her mouth with the back of her hand. There was a faint odor of whisky. She sat down at the other end of the couch and smiled in a way that meant to be conciliatory. "Gosh, I'm sorry you saw me looking like this."

"You look all right," Kitty said, wanting to explain if it were possible to do it kindly that no one any longer expected Dena to be young. "We all are just witches in the morning."

"Yes, that's right." Dena patted her jaw-line absently, something she must spend a lot of spare time at. "I'll bet you came about that awful thing that happened to Sunny."

"I'm confused," Kitty admitted. "No one seems to have seen the things I saw, or even believe that I saw them. I'm beginning to doubt my own senses. And Maud tells me a queer story about Sunny rushing off to overtake me, after I'd left the party last night. I want *you* to tell me about it," Kitty insisted. "I want to know how Sunny acted, how she looked, exactly what she said. I know you're observant, Dena, and you know all those people. Who heard Sunny declare that she was going to catch up with me and set me right about that cut-off? Who left when she did, or immediately after?"

Dena rattled the newspapers, found a pack of cigarettes under them, offered Kitty a cigarette, showed no reaction to her refusal, lit one with elaborate care for herself. "I'm trying to think," she said finally.

"I'd been in the bar for a while," Dena began quietly, "taking care of a teen-age kid who thought she had a hollow leg and found out otherwise. I left her for a minute because I had a kind of hopeful hunch that Hal DeGraffen might get me into the new show his agency is casting—an 'old troupers never die' kind of deal on the order of the old 'Blackouts.' Well, DeGraffen gave me the brush-off in a nice way, and I went for more ice for the kid's head, and finally managed to get her away from the wolf she was with and into a bedroom. Poor little devil. Then I thought I'd butter up old Chesterly. You know him. The fat little wart."

"I know him by sight."

"Lucky you. That's well enough." Dena made a face. "I was in the hall, looking for him, when I heard all this squealing from the powder room. You know, the nook at the end of the hall—just a dressing table in there. Well, the door was open and I saw Sunny Walling and Maud DeGraffen. Sunny was yipping about having to run after somebody—you, obviously—and Maud was telling her there wasn't any hurry, to stay put."

"Were other people within earshot?"

"Must have been," Dena replied. "The door of the rumpus room isn't more than a few feet away. Then there's the dining room across from it, and people were in there at the buffet. Sunny's voice was plenty loud enough to carry. She came out of the powder room and sailed for the front door. She had on her wrap, that mink thing."

"Did she, Dena? Are you positive?"

"God, I think she must have slept in it!" Dena flung out; then her eyes grew still. "Why? Why'd you ask that?"

"The mink stole is missing. It wasn't with Sunny's body up there on that lonesome road."

"Mmmm ..." Dena smoked for a little while in silence, her thoughts obviously busy. "Any official theories floating around?"

"The police didn't let me in on what they believe. The detective who interviewed me, a man named Doyle, pretended to be much more ignorant about things than he really was. Only I did gather the stole was gone because he wanted to know if Sunny had been wearing a wrap."

"What about her car?" Dena asked. "Wasn't it in that?"

"I don't think they have the car, either, though I can't be sure."

Dena thought some more. "Would Sunny have picked up a hitch-hiker, taken a shine to some presentable sort of snake who'd throw her out of her car, even kill her, if she resisted him? But no, no.... Sunny had too many people gunning for her to need any such coincidence."

Studying Dena's withdrawn, slightly ironic expression, Kitty was reminded of what Maud had said, and in much this manner; both women had looked on, with dry amusement, at the havoc Sunny had made of other people's lives. "You said Sunny sailed out the door," Kitty reminded, getting back to the original subject. "Did anyone follow right away?"

"Oh, yes, several. Maud even went out, I think. About that time I got a glimpse of Chesterly—I think he'd been avoiding me, the little toad— and I went after him."

"Was there any clue as to whether Sunny was driving her own car?"

"Oh, she must have been." Dena paused all at once. "Yes, I'm sure of it, since she was holding a set of keys, dangling them beside her skirt."

"That was the last you saw of her?"

"It's probably the last almost anyone saw of her," Dena pointed out, "except, of course, the person who killed her. Tell me, Kitty, just what is your interest in Sunny's death? I'm sure it's not just your accidental connection with the scene of the crime. You've got a bigger stake in it, somewhere." Dena's eyes looked calm, incurious; but this was the mask she was able to wear to conceal her curiosity.

Kitty searched for words, aware now that she should have had some logical story prepared.

"Not love for Sunny, surely," Dena went on as if sensing Kitty's intention to lie. "You've known a lot of her friends, though—or should I say victims? Like Ardis Lake, for instance, the nice little girl who was engaged to the kid in the Army. What was his name?"

"Burns."

"Don't flinch so. There's no one here but us. I don't know your friend Ardis; I don't think I saw her more than twice. But she impressed me as a sort of intense little thing."

"She had time to get over her hurt. She wouldn't have killed Sunny."

"Hurts don't always improve with time," Dena said wisely.

"Ardis was at home last night with me."

Dena drew a deep breath. "Nice—you both have an alibi."

"I wouldn't have given Sunny so much as a frown over the business with Arnold DeGraffen. He wanted to break off our engagement, and he was a coward, so he took a coward's way to do it."

"Well, somebody's got good sense," said Dena approvingly, "though often a bitch like Sunny could get under the skin of the most level-headed. She certainly had the ability to put on the screws."

Kitty thought of Ardis, posting the bills for the flowers young Burns had sent Sunny. Yes, Sunny had had a gift— She almost missed what Dena was saying.

"—like wearing that stole. I used to wonder how she had the nerve. Of course, not many knew where it came from. But she was turning the knife, but good."

"Who gave her the stole?" Kitty asked quickly. But Dena had jumped up with a sudden gasp of dismay. She murmured something about the breakfast which was supposed to be cooking in the kitchen, and rushed for the other room.

She came back, coughing into a handkerchief. Again there was a faint flavor of liquor. She said evasively, "I'll tell you about that mink one of these days. I've always thought women placed a silly value on furs and jewels. No fur can do more than keep you warm—like any other coat— and no jewel can do anything but sparkle. And women make fools of themselves over these things, and risk the enmity of other women." She coughed again; her eyes were bright. "You have more sense than most, Kitty. Hang onto it. Now ... how about some breakfast?"

Kitty shook her head. She wondered what would happen if she simply sat here, refusing to leave until Dena had told her the truth.

Dena sat down on the couch, tucking the untidy kimono in about her knees. She had trouble getting a new cigarette lighted. Then all at once she fell back against the cushions and said, "I'm not cooking anything. I'm sneaking drinks. Do you want a drink?"

Kitty said grimly, "Yes, I don't mind if I do."

Dena didn't quite cover her surprise. This new line, the embarrassing confessional tactics, had been intended to send Kitty running. "Gin," Kitty instructed. "With limes. I don't like whisky in the morning."

After a moment of collecting herself, Dena went off to mix the drink. She came back holding a tall, slightly dirty glass in which swam a greenish liquid.

"I'm out of ice," she apologized. She set the glass down on the table by Kitty's chair and waited.

Kitty reached for the glass, looked over it at the sagging face framed by coppery waves. "Who gave Sunny Walling the mink stole? Was it Arnold DeGraffen?"

Dena made a long face of wry amusement. "Well, we're a little green around the edges, after all."

"I'm not jealous. Don't be a fool. This is evidence, a part of the picture. Sunny went out of her way to show off her power over men—if you want to dignify her shenanigans with such a phrase—and she enraged a lot of women in the process. Maud DeGraffen let it out that the stole was a gift from a married man—"

Under the mask of ironic half-indifference, something flickered—a flash of surprise, or interest, or even possibly anger—which Dena could not quite cover. It was as if, Kitty thought, you looked into a pool and sensed movement under the water, currents that never rippled the surface. The empty eyes that stared into her own had not moved; but there had been some change. Kitty thought for an instant that Dena was afraid.

"I can't tell you his name now," she said slowly. "It might not bear on this affair, and would only cause trouble if it were let out."

This attitude was false, out of character. She was protecting somebody. But why? Dena was tough. In her world it was every man for himself.

Into Kitty's mind swam the memory of last night, and Dena's desperate efforts to make herself agreeable. If Dena knew the name of the man who had given Sunny the missing stole, and if the fact of its being missing could be made significant enough, Kitty had a sudden conviction as to what use Dena would make of her knowledge.

"I want to do a bit of snooping on my own," Dena went on. "I'll have to make sure that this man and his wife are in the clear."

There was a lie behind the words. Dena had no interest in justice, in bringing into the clutches of the law the person who had murdered Sunny Walling. Her attitude was from first to last one of self-preservation.

"Let me know what you find out," Kitty said, rising to go.

"I'll do that."

Kitty had called Dena's attention to the stole, telling her that the police were looking for it; and Dena saw, or thought she saw, some opportunity here. Kitty was aware of a sense of guilt. The woman was too wrapped up in her own aims to be as wary as she should. No warning would penetrate. She probably didn't even think of her intended actions as blackmail.

CHAPTER SIX

Kitty stood on the corner of Hollywood and Vine, looked at the street whirling with traffic without seeing any of it, her mind full of questions and conjecture.

Ardis was behaving much too peculiarly. A sense of worry shook Kitty's composure. She went into the big café, to the telephone booth, and called the apartment. There was no answer. Then she telephoned Weidmann's and asked if Ardis was there. They said no, she wasn't; she was at home, ill.

Kitty went back to the street; she thought of Hal DeGraffen. His agency office was only a few blocks south, on Sunset. She could at least partially check Dena's story in that quarter. Of course he would wonder, as Dena had, why Kitty was running around asking questions. What should she say? That she herself was under suspicion? Could she give an impression of a zany girl who thought she might solve a crime before the police came for her? Would he believe it?

He was shrewd and alert, honed keen in the cut-throat advertising game. But he was also inclined to underrate women, a trait Kitty had at times noted with irritation. She might make him think that the police had scared her, that she was pulling a Philo Vance to escape them.

She walked down to Sunset, crossed in front of the vast green bulk of NBC, got tangled briefly in a crowd ready to storm the doors for a quiz show, finally made it to the nearby low Spanish stucco building where several minor agencies had offices.

She went into the main hall, turned right, opened a door to *Waddell Brothers*—there were, she knew, no longer any Waddells left in the place. They'd been bought out by a man named Baron, and the agency had changed sharply under his management. It had once been dignified, pompous, and stuffy, with a few large long-term accounts; now the place gave off a sheen like polished chrome and its offices operated like well-oiled machinery and there was no account too small for Mr. Baron to pounce on like a cat. The main entry was stark in the modern manner, tricked out with Swedish furniture and a silver-blonde who looked quite intelligent behind her glasses. "I'd like to see Mr. DeGraffen if he's in," Kitty told her, and gave her name.

The girl punched a lever in the interoffice phone-box on the desk. Meanwhile she stole a second look at Kitty. Kitty knew that look; you met it everywhere in Hollywood, and it asked if you were anybody. In Kitty's case, it always decided not. She had wondered what would happen should she manage to get herself up as a perfect duplicate of Hedy Lamarr.

The blonde spoke into the wired box, then spoke to Kitty. "He's not engaged. Upstairs and to the left." Kitty tried to analyze the tone as she walked upstairs; was it a shade too emphatic? Wasn't it putting over a little hint that Mr. DeGraffen wasn't too much in demand? Kitty remembered in that instant that of late on occasions she'd seen a worried flicker in Maud's eyes.

She rapped at Hal's door; his voice told her to enter. She opened the door. He was across the room at the window, facing into the room; she got a quick impression that he was not pleased to see her. He was a tall, lean man in his fifties. He had a wide, quick smile and a good handclasp, fine assets in his trade, where so much depended on personal contacts, good first impressions. But it seemed to Kitty now that the smile cov-

ered other things than pleasure. "Good to see you, Kit. What are you doing downtown?" He came to the desk, pushed a chair forward for her,
sat down opposite.

Kitty told him a rigmarole about being on the spot and afraid that if
she didn't try to find out who killed Sunny, the police would take her.
He listened gravely.

"Maud telephoned a little while ago. She told me about seeing you."
He paused to tap his nails on the edge of the desk, to think, perhaps to
pick out words. "There was something about the dogs, Linder's dogs. I'm
very curious about that incident, Kit."

She told him in phrases that were becoming settled, almost stale, almost worn out and with no flash of the real terror she'd experienced. And
she concluded with a complaint: "No one seems to believe that this really happened. Linder least of all—of course they're his dogs."

"And they've disappeared?"

"They were missing this morning. This Detective Doyle didn't like it.
But—thinking back—I'm inclined to think that even he put small
stock in my yarn. He thinks I made it up to cover something else."

Hal was frowning, rubbing the spot between his brows where the thick
gray hair knitted together. "Let's go back over it. You saw the dog before
you stopped the car. That's right?"

"He was in the middle of the road. I had to stop, or else run over him.
Then, as I said, I thought I'd whistle him to the side of the car so that
I could drive on. Because of the dark and the rain I couldn't see that the
road was a dead end. And so, when I whistled ..." She stopped abruptly
to correct herself. "No, I hadn't even done that. I'd merely rolled the glass
down a little when he came for me." She felt her hands twisting together
in her lap, a thickening in her throat. Silly, of course. You're here, with
Hal, she told herself; it's daylight, an ordinary office in downtown
Hollywood, and around you, a baffle to danger, are thousands of human
ants scheming and planning to get into television and radio, or at least
to get tickets to Groucho Marx.... She jerked her attention back to what
Hal was saying.

"—almost seems as if he were set to wait for somebody in a car. Any
car. Though, of course, it would be highly unlikely that anyone would
take that road except someone going directly to the Linders'."

"Y-yes, that seems so." She added a question. "I'm trying to get impressions from others who were at your place last night and who might have
seen Sunny before she started after me."

"I saw her." Hal glanced at the clock on his desk. "Let's run over to the
Derby. It's not too early for lunch. Frankly, I'm fagged from last night.
Something hot will pep me up. How about it?"

Ten minutes later they were in the Brown Derby. The place was beginning to fill up. Some of the faces in the booths were famous, and Kitty stared at them like a native—in a way she'd have been too embarrassed to do when she'd first come here. Hal ordered a martini apiece; when the drinks came, he sipped his in a way that somehow gave an impression of trying to hide a raging thirst. Kitty was faintly uneasy; there was a feeling here that things were going wrong for the DeGraffens. She waited for him to tell her about seeing Sunny last night, but instead he broke into a new line entirely.

"Do you know anything about the Linders, the two young fellows, their aunt?"

"I met Edmund Linder last night, as I told you. This morning he brought his aunt to see me. I think she was supposed to convince me the dogs couldn't have done it."

"Of course they'd take that attitude. A dog can be a danger to the neighborhood; the owner will be the last to admit it. Will fight others for saying so, in fact. No, what I mean, Kit, was whether you knew of them otherwise. Gossip, I guess I mean."

"Very little. Charles Linder wrote a book, didn't he?"

Hal groaned in a basso voice. "Oh, Lord, don't mention that. I got mixed up in the mess when they were trying to make a radio program out of it. If you want to see temperament, get writers together—I mean especially somebody who writes a book and somebody else who can make a radio play out of it, but wants to change a few items. I'll tell you, I sat in on conferences whose very memory makes me want to tear my hair. Baron cooked it up because a possible sponsor had read the damned book and liked it, and we worked the networks—well, we had some promising leads there for a while. You know how Hollywood is. All at once the bottom dropped out of the thing, and Linder practically took me and Baron apart. He was due for three hundred a week, you see, when it went on—just for using the characters." Hal looked around sourly at the busy restaurant. "A rat-race if I ever saw one. But getting back to the subject. I guess you know that Edmund Linder served time in prison."

Kitty felt stunned, at a loss for words.

"Yeah," Hal went on, motioning the waiter for another drink. "It goes back to the war. Some nasty business on Saipan, or somewhere, a rotten officer that got some of his men killed through stupid mistakes. Edmund laid for him when he got out of service and beat the bejasus out of him. If he'd done it *in* the Army, of course, it would have been life in a military prison, or worse. As it was, he served a year or so for assault. He's quite a character."

Kitty said, out of a numbed mind, "He holds a grudge."

"Like a bulldog." Hal started on the second martini. Again there was a strain, a holding-back, as if some terrible inner tension must be denied. "Now he and his brother own a photographic-supply business and a store. You must have passed it—Sunset, along about the eighty-five hundred block. Charles handles the store, oversees the help and so on, and Edmund does the leg work, the sales on the supply end. I can't imagine shutting that wild man up in a store; I guess he knew better than to try it."

Kitty tried to organize her thoughts, to fight out of the inexplicable dismay that seemed to have seized her. "About Sunny, last night—"

"Yeah, we're coming to her. And in that connection—Sunny, I mean—do you know, I have a queer impression that she figured in that fracas about Charles Linder's book, the radio deal. I think he met her while that was on the fire." Hal was sitting quite still, his frown erased, as if chasing inwardly some illusive impression. The rattle of silver and crockery, the murmur of voices all around, seemed to shut them into a small island of silence. "Funny. I can't think where I got that idea. It just came to me then, though; I believe he mentioned her name."

"It's odd that you bring it up," Kitty told him, "since the aunt, Miss Dru Linder, said the same thing, that she thought Charles may have known Sunny."

Hal's glance centered on Kitty's face sharply. "What did Lin say?"

Kitty remembered that this was the name the DeGraffens used for Edmund. "He warned his aunt not to spread such gossip."

"Ummm ... Do you think it upset him?"

"No, not especially. He just commanded her to shut up, hurt her feelings—I thought the poor little old lady was going to cry."

"I pity her, living with those two," Hal said briefly. "Where were we? Oh, yes. Sunny's leaving. Let me think. Somewhere about then I got mixed up with poor old Dena, wanting a part in the show we're casting; and I more or less gave her the brush-off—tried to do it decently. The show isn't for has-beens. Then I remember going to the dining room and looking over the buffet. I decided to check on what the maid was doing in the pantry, since we seemed low on some items, the curried eggs I remember particularly. I looked into the pantry and found Chesterly. You know, the little fat guy, produces those horrible Go-for-Gold Shows. He's got something new coming up, just as bad I'll bet, and he knew Dena was after him for a possible part in it. He was hiding from her in the pantry. He'd found the Scotch and was peacefully getting liquored up. I told him to go on out and face her, treat her human, but be firm." Hal's face took on a sudden bitterness. "I hate that kind of thing, chicken-livered producers with the power almost of life and death over some poor wreck like Dena. She might almost have a chance if she got a break again."

"Can't something be done to help her?" Kitty cried, remembering the sad shabby apartment, the smell of whisky, and Dena's ideas of blackmail.

"I don't know. I'll see what I can do, the next few days." He looked anxiously into Kitty's cocktail glass. "Ready for another? No? Mind if I do— I'm coming unkinked, gradually."

The drink came. Hal said, "What did you want to know, exactly, about Sunny's clearing out?"

"How she looked—what she said—who went with her ..."

"Oh. As far as looks went—" He grinned wryly. "I wonder how many men ever got their eyes above Sunny's bust-line? Damned few, I'll bet. I recall, now you ask, that she seemed excited. I'd come back from exploring the pantry. I stepped into the hall, and to my left, near the front door, were Maud and Sunny and two or three others. Maud and Sunny seemed by themselves, and they were arguing."

"Was Sunny holding a set of keys?"

He waited for some little time before answering. "I'll have to admit, I don't know."

"Is there any way of making sure that she drove off in her own car?"

"Oh, Maud ought to know that."

"She says not."

"I ... I had a funny idea that Maud went out with her." He was frowning again, twirling the stemmed glass in unsteady fingers.

So had Dena thought that Maud went out.... "Why did you think that?"

"I'm trying to remember." He moved uneasily on the curved bench of the booth. "But come to think of it, I didn't hang around; that little brunette, Sylvia Marsh, beckoned to me from the rumpus room bar."

It seemed to Kitty that she was trying to put together a jigsaw puzzle, and that over and over again she came across the same pieces, and that each time they had different shapes. Now Hal was mentioning Sylvia—Maud's *Sylvia somebody* "who keeps her mouth puckered as though she's getting ready to suck an orange." Only, Kitty was sure that Maud had said that Hal had been with her earlier, when Sunny was giving directions about the shortcut. Or had there been two interludes with brunette Sylvia? A coincidence, if Hal had been with her during each departure.

"What are you thinking about?" Hal said sharply.

"Oh, I don't know. My head's buzzing," Kitty cried.

"Are you afraid? Did the cops bully you?"

Kitty remembered the line she was supposed to follow. "I—I guess they have me at the top of their list of suspects."

He examined her with a touch of suspicion. "It's nuts. Why won't they go for the story about Linder's dogs?"

"I don't know. As a matter of fact, Doyle didn't exactly disbelieve. He was just secretive and … and ominous."

"Stock in trade. Automatic by now," Hal assured her. "Don't let them get you on the run." His gaze took on sudden curiosity. "How many people have you gone to see, so far?"

She saw no need to hide the truth from Hal, and yet— "Can you suggest someone I ought to talk to?" she evaded.

He took it to mean that she'd gone to no one. "I wouldn't do it, Kit. I'd leave it alone. Stick by your story of what happened up there. They can't pin anything on you."

"Do you think Linder may have hidden his dogs to keep the police from taking them?"

"I wouldn't be surprised if he had. My guess is, the cops will be more and more interested in those hounds as time goes by."

When the food was served, Hal toyed with his portions; and Kitty thought that there was an air of impatience about him, and that his mind was on other matters, probably something relating to business. She had met the DeGraffens when she had first come to Hollywood, had liked them both, had continued being friends even after her engagement with Arnold DeGraffen had ended in a fiasco. They were fun, and they seemed so genuinely devoted to each other in a rakish, mocking way. Now some change had taken place. Perhaps the pressures of Hal's employment were gradually taking a toll. He and Maud, Kitty realized, were both tense and on edge, trying to conceal a deep uneasiness.

She had not sensed that something of the DeGraffens' old cocksureness, humor, and mockery was gone until this frightful incident of Sunny's murder. It was as if, she thought, you suddenly looked at a picture you'd had hanging on the wall for months, and found it different, found that details were blurred and changed, the colors transformed into something unpleasant.

When the food was taken away, Hal excused himself on the grounds of business appointments. They parted on Vine Street, and Kitty started for home.

CHAPTER SEVEN

Kitty had stepped into the lower entry and begun to mount the steps before she realized that someone was waiting for her. She looked up, drawing back a little, and then saw the red hair gleaming like a light and saw Doyle's expressionless face. She thought, on a surge of irritation: he's probably been trying the door.

"Mind if I come in for a minute? There are a few things I need to know."

He sounded innocent; he sounded like a third-grade kid who wants to know how to do the multiplication tables. But this time Kitty wasn't fooled. She'd been taken in once by that careful ignorance. Now she walked ahead into the small flat, her whole body wary, her feet as cautious as a cat's. She took off her hat and coat and dropped them over the arm of the couch. "How can I help you?" She turned, looked at him eagerly as if wanting to offer him the whole contents of her head, every thought, every impression, every secret.

His mouth twitched. Perhaps he was wise enough to guess her imposture. He sat down, swinging his hat in his fingers. "I want to meet a friend of yours. She lives here. Ardis Lake."

"Ardis isn't here now."

"She isn't at work either," he said, as if perplexed.

Kitty didn't make any comment. She sat down opposite, trying to seem helpful but confused.

"When did she leave?" Doyle wondered. "Did you see her this morning?"

Kitty wanted to lie to him just for the hell of it, but the truth seemed about as confusing as anything she could make up. "Ardis was here when I returned from that trip with the tow truck. She wasn't feeling well. I don't know just when she went out. Often a headache will go away when you walk in the fresh air," she explained.

He nodded. "Yes, so I imagine. Do you think she knew Miss Walling?"

"Oh, Sunny Walling inherited one of Ardis's old beaux. Of course you'd run into that story."

"A soldier," he said slowly. "Went overseas. Got himself killed. He wrote Miss Walling some pretty frantic letters there near the end. We found them among her belongings."

This was something none of them had known. Kitty's heart thudded with fright. What accusations had young Burns made? Had he seen at last what Sunny had done to him and Ardis? Had he outlined any of the story of those bitter last few weeks, when Ardis had watched with sick eyes the slow ruin of her love? "What ... what did he say?"

"I can't tell you that, naturally. I would like to get Miss Lake's side of the story, to fill in what I know." He was warning them, Kitty saw; he was saying, indirectly, that he wouldn't take any lies. He already knew too much for them to attempt to fool him.

She let her shoulders droop. There had to be a way to throw him off, even for a little. "It was terrible for Ardis. But I suspected, even before Burns began acting erratically, that he was not dependable, that she was making a mistake in falling for him."

"How erratic was he?"

Kitty shrugged. "So many of the young soldiers have a kind of—of reckless hurry in their attitude. And this quality seems to keep them from seeing anything but the surface, especially as far as women are concerned. This Burns boy was like that to a striking degree. And I might add that Sunny Walling's romantic technique had all the finesse of a gorilla's with a baseball bat. She had him doing nip-ups in no time."

She couldn't tell how much impression she'd made. Doyle's brown eyes remained innocent and wondering. He rose as if to go, then turned back as if with a sudden thought. "I wonder if you'd do us a favor."

"Sure, if I can."

"It's about what happened last night." He looked as if he hated to say that he doubted her word; an act, Kitty assured herself. "I should have done this when you were up there this morning. A complete re-enactment. A picture of just what did go on."

She said slowly, "You want me to show you just how and where I met those dogs, what I did, what they did?"

"Yes. Whatever you can remember. I saw some scratches," he said carefully. Kitty saw that he reserved a doubt about them. "Please don't think I'm trying to prove you in the wrong. You might give us a clue, if you'd go up there, act out what happened —"

She interrupted. "Have you found the dogs?"

"No, they're still missing. There's a lot of lonely territory in those hills. Lots of hiding places."

"Who'll act out the part of the dog, then?"

He bit his lip, perhaps to tell her he'd had enough of her sass. He walked over to the door, pulled it open. It occurred to Kitty then that he had made no search of the apartment; Ardis could be hidden here and he wouldn't know. He'd taken her word that the girl was gone. He looked back at her. Kitty was standing, reaching for her coat and hat again. She followed him downstairs without another word.

In the car on the way west on Sunset, Kitty asked, "Do you know now what actually caused Sunny's death?"

He kept his eyes on the traffic. "Autopsies take a little time."

The car swung into Du Moyne and began to climb the hill. The rainy night, the dark morning, had left a chill in the air; but now the sun had come out and lay on the hills in patches, interrupted by the pattern of clouds moving before the wind. Raindrops sparkled in the grass. Kitty decided that Doyle must have some well-founded suspicion of the dogs, or he wouldn't be taking her back to check her story.

The sunlight brightened the Linder house. Its white walls were clean as bone, the low tile roof a brilliant red. The lawns stretched down the hill to the border of geraniums; it all glittered with the drops left by last night's storm. She saw that the garage was open; two cars were gone. But contrary to what she had expected, Doyle went past the entrance to the Linders' lane. He sent the car to the top of the barren ridge to the north, turned there, looked over at Kitty. "It was raining last night. How much could you see from here?"

She tried to squeeze past that interlude of terror in the lane, to recall what had immediately preceded it. "I realized that I'd crossed some sort of ridge. I remember working the brakes—there was mud on the street. But I can't remember any lights ahead, any indication of people—if that's what you mean."

"Was there a light at any time in the Linder house?"

"I didn't see one. There could have been a light in the back of the house, though."

"Rain is funny stuff, reflects light when there is any—I think you'd have known if there was a light inside anywhere."

He let the car creep on the grade and Kitty felt the pull of the incline. There was a slight crook in the road; Kitty clenched her hands convulsively. Doyle, with eyes like a fox's, said, "Remember something?"

"Yes. There was a car on the ridge behind me."

"Just recalled it?"

"It was what you said about the light, about rain reflecting it—in the rear-view mirror there was a sort of glow, as if a car were cresting the ridge from the north, from the way I'd come."

"And then?"

"There wasn't anything else. It must have turned aside somewhere."

"There is no cross road near the top of the ridge," Doyle pointed out patiently. "Are you sure it wasn't the general blur from the city?"

"Not last night. The dark was intense. I remember how shut-off I felt, when I'd stopped."

He let the car swing into the entry of the lane leading to the Linder house. "Do you think you would have noticed a car going past on Du Moyne?"

"Oh, yes. I was quite lost by the time I turned in here. I needed help. I'd have flagged down anyone."

Doyle stepped on the brake. "Well, it gives us a fragment, I guess. You think someone approached the ridge from the other side, then turned around up there and went back the way they came."

She frowned into his eyes. "No, it couldn't have happened like that. A car turning would have sprayed this whole little valley with light, even in spite of the rain. I couldn't have missed that."

He drew the corner of his lips into a quirk. "I'll have a look for possible tire-marks—later. Right now I'd like to go through this thing that happened with the dogs. Two of them, you said."

Kitty didn't answer. She was looking at the road ahead. A big yellow dog had walked out of the low shrubby trees and squatted in the road, baring his big white teeth in a happy grin.

"Well, well," Doyle muttered. He opened the door and got out from under the wheel. The dog didn't move. Doyle clucked and snapped his finger. The dog rose slowly, almost reluctantly, wagging his tail, and took a few hesitant steps. "Come on, old boy. I won't hurt you." But the dog hung back, friendly but shy.

In the pale sunlight the animal's coat was sleek and glossy. He looked very well tended, a healthy and happy pet. And there obviously just wasn't a vicious bone in his body. Doyle walked over to him and patted him on the neck, pulled his jowls playfully, received some affectionate licks on the hand in return. She saw Doyle lift the tag on the collar, read it, finger it thoughtfully. Then he glanced back in her direction; she thought his eyes were cold, accusing.

Doyle was glancing about him, now; Kitty sensed that he expected to see the second dog. With a leisurely air, he scouted through the shrubby trees and up the flank of the hill. At one point a tree branch knocked off his hat and the color of the red hair was almost startling. Presently he returned to the car. The dog was at his heels, still grinning, still friendly. Doyle looked in pleasantly at Kitty. "Is this about where you stopped your car, last night?"

"Just about, I guess. It's impossible to be sure."

"Yes, of course. The first thing you did was to roll down the window?"

"That's when the dog jumped."

Doyle looked down at the affable brown eyes of the yellow hound. "This dog?"

"I don't know. He didn't act like this." She met Doyle's ironic stare grimly. "Why don't you talk to the aunt, Miss Linder? She thinks that one of the dogs may be turning vicious."

"I have talked to her." He bent and picked the dog up and thrust him close to the window. "Take a good look."

"Put him on the hood," Kitty said stiffly. She waited while Doyle, with a grimace of mystification, put the big animal on the car's hood and held him balanced on the slick surface. The dog assumed an injured, bewildered attitude and tried to crawl off again into Doyle's arms. Kitty raised herself close to the windshield, puckered her lips, and whistled. The dog ignored her. "It isn't the one," she said to Doyle. "It can't be."

"He does seem terrifically friendly," Doyle agreed. "I don't see the second dog. Excuse me for a minute, I'll go to the house and inquire if they've both come back."

He walked up past the garage and stopped at the door of the low white house and touched the black button on the wall. Presently Aunt Dru came out and stood on the porch to talk to him. He must have mentioned Kitty; she looked down at the car and fluttered her fingers in a wave.

Then the two of them appeared to examine the big yellow dog, which had followed at Doyle's heels. Kitty could see Aunt Dru nodding as she caressed the uplifted muzzle, so the brute must be one of theirs. And like the light that had bloomed in Linder's hand, an idea was born. Thin indeed as proof, something Doyle might not look at twice: but at home there was a single shoe to bear witness to her story.

Kitty jumped from the car and hurried up the hillside to the house.

Aunt Dru met her at the step. She had a vague, confused air, as if Doyle had been teasing her with mysteries. "Oh, Miss Quist! How awful for you to have to visit the scene of the crime over and over! I was telling this gentleman"—she motioned toward Doyle—"that it does seem as if we've all imposed on you sufficiently. With Edmund breaking your pretty lamp.... I can't imagine what got into him; he's not usually nervous. And to be dragged back up here just on account of the dogs, really ..." She made a lame gesture. "Could I make a cup of tea for you?"

"Thank you, but I'm afraid not. I came to tell Mr. Doyle something I'd remembered about that incident last night. One of the dogs got away with a shoe of mine."

During Aunt Dru's meandering remarks Doyle had been looking at her much as her nephew had, politeness thinly covering a raging impatience, until she reached the remark about Edmund. Kitty thought that Doyle filed that away carefully. It was then that he'd turned his glance on Kitty. When she told him about the dog's getting the shoe, there was no change at all, no sharpening of attention. Was he still cross-filing that remark about Edmund's breaking the lamp?

"I thought perhaps your men had found the shoe," she went on, "during the search this morning. It's a detail which confirms my story."

He shook his head. "We didn't find any shoes, Miss Quist. Sorry."

"I have the one shoe in my closet. Won't that be proof of a sort?"

He seemed to debate the point inwardly. Aunt Dru waited, wide-eyed, as though the decision held a great suspense for her. She's such an odd little old lady, Kitty thought; so round and soft, like a pigeon, and eager to be friendly, and especially most anxious to smooth over with small courtesies the irritations created by people like her nephew and Doyle.

When Doyle spoke, it was to Aunt Dru. "If the other dog shows up, Miss Linder, will you telephone me at once?" He gave her a card.

She fumbled with a lace ruffle at the bosom of her dress. "But I don't know them apart! Only Edmund can tell one from the other!"

He explained patiently: "If you see two of them, call me."

"Well, I'll telephone you," Aunt Dru decided, "if I see the two dogs here."

"Thank you." He led Kitty down off the porch. "I'll go and look at your one shoe if you like." He flashed a smile at her, sidewise; but the glance was wise, probing.

"You upset her," Kitty said coldly.

"Not intentionally. Tell me about Edmund breaking your lamp."

He'd been quick to seize it, Kitty saw; and she wondered if she was beginning to be able to read him, just a little. An enigmatic man. A cynic, amused by the foibles of humanity. Well, let him be amused by Edmund Linder. "Aunt Dru surmised that there had been a trap set for Sunny Walling, that Sunny suspected it and sent me as a decoy." She watched Doyle's face, thinking to catch his reaction, but he was ready for her; the careful mask remained a blank. "Edmund didn't like it. He flung out a hand in protest, I think. The lamp went over."

She led the way into the apartment, down the hall, into her bedroom. He could see, if he would, the signs of the morning's hurried departure. Nothing here was staged, false, or arranged. It was the room of someone who worked for a living, who didn't have much time for housework except on week-ends, and whose clothes represented too much value in relation to the pay-check to be thrown away to convince a detective.

She opened the closet and pointed to the shoe-rack in the wall.

Doyle looked with interest at the neat array, the sport Oxfords, the extra pair of low-heeled working shoes, the beach clogs, the old gray pumps she intended to give to the Salvation Army, the white sandals left from last summer, the neat red galoshes. He raised his eyebrows gently. "Where is the extra shoe, Miss Quist?"

Kitty felt paralyzed. On the lowest rung of the rack hung the blue satin dancing shoes she'd worn last night. Both of them. Together.

CHAPTER EIGHT

He must have caught her strained, incredulous sense of shock. He straightened, regarding her levelly. "Isn't it here, as you thought?"

"N-no." Kitty couldn't have said just why she lied; behind the panic was a simple wish to spar for time.

"Could your roommate, Miss Lake, have removed it?"

"I must have tossed it somewhere, after I came in. After all, I'd hardly hang it up as usual, would I, without its mate?" She began to stumble around the room, looking under things. Doyle remained by the closet. There was a sharp line between the red eyebrows. He turned his hat in his hands. "Do you see it on the floor? It's a … a pale green slipper with Rhinestones set in the heel," Kitty told him.

He gave her a look she couldn't analyze, didn't like. "What dress were you wearing?"

"The—the white one. Pull it out."

He pulled the closet door fully open. Kitty's limited social whirl required only two evening dresses. The white one was the more expensive. It had come from a good shop in Beverly Hills. It was of thin, paperweight taffeta, with a tight strapless bodice and a full skirt pulled into a bunch of folds around the hips which gave almost the effect of a bustle. Kitty didn't wear it much; it was really too spectacular for all but the biggest parties. The dark blue, the dress which matched the satin pumps, was her favorite and much more useful. Its quiet color and simple lines lent themselves to many different groups of accessories. Last night she'd worn a border of white artificial flowers in the low square neck; they were still pinned there and she saw them shake as Doyle pulled out the white dress to look it over.

"Don't know a lot about dresses," he explained. "This looks costly."

"It was," she admitted ruefully, "and I was a fool to invest so much money in it. I don't wear it a lot. Too fancy." At the same time she wondered, with another flare of panic, if Doyle had already gathered the fact somewhere that she had worn the blue. Looking past him, and knowing what she knew, she had the impression that the blue dress shrieked aloud that it had been out in the rain, had been put away not quite dried. There were gross wrinkles all around the hem.

Doyle looked from the glittering white dress to her, and she imagined that he was trying to figure out how she looked in it.

"With light green pumps, hmmm?"

His glance flustered her. She stammered, "When I'm quite rich, I invest in some of those small greenish orchids. The effect is positively staggering."

His next remark was a strange one. "Did you ever have a hankering to be an actress?"

"Yes. Do you think it's an actressy dress?"

"I don't know. I think when you have it on, it would be hard to think of you as a University secretary."

Heat rushed into her head, pounded between her ears. "What do you mean by that? That I'm what Sunny Walling was? That I'm covering a lot of sex shenanigans with an innocuous job? You can forget it. My life is just as drab, just as work-ridden, and just as sexless as you can imagine." She went on staring into his eyes, pouring fury at him.

He hung the white dress in the closet. There was a hint of tiredness about him, as though he suddenly missed the sleep he hadn't had early this morning. "You don't understand me."

"I think I do."

He went out then, mercifully. Kitty felt that she must have turned pale at this parting crack—since it had rushed into her mind at once, on seeing the two shoes together in the closet, that Ardis was the only person with the opportunity to return the missing pump.

She had no doubt about what she had done last night. She remembered precisely coming in, shedding the damp blue dress, hanging it up, spreading the slip and other garments on a chair, putting the single blue pump into the closet rack; it was all burned into her mind, unforgettable. In her nightgown she had gone to the bathroom to set her hair; it was there Ardis had found her.

Where had Ardis found that missing shoe?

Again her rushing thoughts turned to that single track that funneled up to the question: Who was on the telephone in the middle of the night?

Two questions. No answers.

She hurried frantically to Ardis's bedroom and rummaged among her belongings, seeking some hint that Ardis had been out of the house and in last night's storm. She was there when she caught a faint sound from the kitchen. For an instant there was a tug of fear. Then she turned away from Ardis's closet, crossed the room and the hall, opened the kitchen door.

Ardis was at the sink fixing an untidy sandwich and pouring a glass of milk. Kitty had never seen her so haggard, so dull of eye, so shaky. Even in the worst days following the breakup with young Burns, she hadn't been like this. It was as if in some horrible traceless way she'd been unmercifully beaten. She poured the milk as if the carton weighed a hundred pounds, as if only by great effort could she keep the stream poised above the glass. She didn't look around. "Hello, Kitty." Her voice was husky and low.

"My God! Ardis! Where have you been?" Kitty ran to her, pulling her around by the shoulders. "You're sick, you ought to be in bed. And the police are looking for you, to talk to you about Sunny's death."

"I know. I waited for the red-headed man to leave."

"You'll have to see him, Ardis!"

"Not ... not right now." She set the carton down with a bump, as if she had misjudged the distance. She began to drink milk. She poured part of it down the front of her coat.

Kitty stepped back. She had become suddenly aware of something. An odor. There was a peculiar miasma surrounding Ardis.

It was a smell of dust, of earth.

From a dry throat, Kitty said, "You've been digging."

Ardis shook her head as she set down the glass of milk. She looked at the sandwich, meat and lettuce jammed rakishly between two chunks of bread. "I'm going to be sick. Help ... help me, Kit."

Five minutes later Kitty held Ardis and the two of them staggered out of the bathroom and into Ardis's bedroom. Ardis was feverish; her skin was taut and dry, her lips cracked. When she reached the bed, she fell on it and flattened there, not even seeming to breathe. Kitty pulled off shoes and hose, removed the earth-smelling coat, the dress, the under-things, and brought the big flannel gown with its pattern of cabbage roses.

While Kitty tucked covers over her, Ardis whispered, "Sorry. Awful mess in the bathroom." Her hands moved weakly. "Get—somebody. A cleaning woman."

"To hell with a cleaning woman," Kitty said in anger. "We have enough snoops coming and going as it is. Look, Ardis. Just open your eyes long enough to answer one question. Wake up. Hey!"

The black lashes opened slowly and unwillingly. The hollow eyes were deep.

Kitty bent over her. "Who called on the telephone last night after I'd gone to bed? No, don't try to go to sleep. I won't leave, I won't let you alone until you tell me. Ardis! Answer!"

Ardis sighed. Her eyes stared off at the corner of the ceiling, and they were weary, with no fight left. "It was Sunny Walling."

"What did she want?"

Ardis shook her head again. "I won't ever tell you, Kitty. It doesn't concern you, or anybody else. It's something that belongs to me alone."

"You went to meet her, didn't you? You went out in that storm, up the hill to Du Moyne Avenue. How? You don't have a car, you don't even drive well—did Sunny meet you somewhere, pick you up?"

There were answers here, under the stubborn exhaustion of Ardis's closed face; there was the secret of the disappearance of Sunny's car and the fur stole, the return of the blue pump in Kitty's closet. She shook Ardis again, but there was no response. Ardis was either genuinely past knowing or caring what Kitty did to rouse her, or her determination was such that the effort was useless.

Kitty stormed out of the room. She took some of her anger out in scrubbing the tile floor in the bath, in clearing up the spilled milk and the drying sandwich in the kitchen.

Kitty made a pot of coffee, strong coffee, and drank two cups. But anger and fright were having their natural reaction. She felt the way Ardis looked: half dead, aware only of buzzing nerves.

It might help to lie down for a little while. She could think then. In the quiet of her room she might figure out a few answers—in spite of Dena, who had ideas about blackmail; in spite of Edmund Linder, who lied about the viciousness of his dogs; and in spite of Ardis, who had some secret hell itself couldn't pry out of her.

Kitty stretched out on the bed under a comforter. It was not as easy to relax as she had thought. The ideas that flittered through her mind were disorganized, fragmentary.

Start with Sunny, she commanded herself. Sunny wasn't a nice person, and everybody knew it. Why didn't they just cut her dead, leave her out of things? What possessed Maud, for instance, to go on inviting Sunny to her parties, when Sunny's reputation as a man-trap made her the candidate most likely to come to a bad end?

Maud's attitude toward Sunny had a funny indulgence behind it, Kitty thought. A secret amusement. Was Maud so sure of Hal that it tickled her to have Sunny running rough-shod over the other women?

I must ask Maud about it, in a tactful way, Kitty told herself.

And you'd better find out from Ardis about the history of your shoe. Had Doyle been fooled? Did he suspect that the two blue pumps hanging together in the shoe-rack were positive evidence that Ardis had been up there on the hill at the scene of Sunny's death?

And why did Ardis's coat contain that musty smell like leafmold, or earth?

I've got one answer, anyway, Kitty told herself; I know what it was that would take Ardis out to meet Sunny Walling. Anytime. Doyle said there were letters from young Burns in Sunny's things. Just the promise of one of those letters, the final thoughts of the boy who was dead, would have taken Ardis into hell itself.

She opened her eyes on the darkened room. For a minute she thought that this must be morning, the first breaking of the gray light; and she wondered at the stale tiredness that nagged at her as she rose on an elbow to look at the clock. Then she remembered falling into bed in the afternoon. This wasn't dawn. It was the end of twilight.

She pushed back her hair. She shouldn't have let go, have slept so long. Ardis needed someone to look after her.

Then she heard again the sound that must have wakened her, since she sensed at once that she had heard it before. A padding noise with a kind of after-scratch. A dog. There was a dog in the hall.

The reactions of terror are immediate and instinctive. Kitty was at the bedroom door, soundlessly, turning the key in the lock. There was no memory of rational thought, of realization, or even knowledge of such movements as must have occurred, getting out of bed, approaching the door, seizing the key.

She leaned against the door-jamb to listen.

The padding noise went past, hesitated, came back. There was a sniffing at the keyhole, a faint whine. Under these sounds Kitty thought she caught other movement, heavier, more cautious. Her eyes froze on the door-knob. If it moved, she would scream. In this agony, this paralysis of terror, she could feel a raw screech building in her throat, her lungs. In a moment the knob would turn, and something would explode inside her—insanity, perhaps. She could feel herself tottering on some edge of madness.

When you screamed, they leaped for your throat. That's what had happened to Sunny.... Sunny—sprawled, torn....

She hung there, trembling on some invisible line between sense and frenzy, and something happened which changed everything.

Abruptly, it was only twilight in a familiar room, and she'd slept too long so that she was fuzzy-headed, and someone wanted to see her.

For there had been a small rap on the door and a woman's familiar voice had asked, "Are you there, Miss Quist?"

Aunt Dru. Small, round, apologetic—these qualities dwelt in her voice and were transmitted through the panel in the vibrations of her anxious, precise tone. "Yes," Kitty managed from a cottony throat, "I'm here. I'll be right out." She hurried to the dressing table, smoothed her hair, looked at her own face as if seeing it for the first time. She seemed quite ordinary now, but what had she looked like as she clung to the door-jamb? Didn't such hideous fright leave any more mark than this?

Aunt Dru was in the living room. A lamp was on. A dog was sitting under its light. He seemed a duplicate of the one she and Doyle had seen in the road today, shy and friendly, full of dignity in spite of the grin. Aunt Dru said, "I hope you'll forgive me walking in. Your door was ajar. For a minute I thought something might be wrong."

"Don't apologize. I see you brought a dog. Are there two of them now?" It was Kitty's idea that Aunt Dru had brought the dog, now that he'd shown up, with the mistaken notion that Doyle was permanently in Kitty's company. But Aunt Dru was shaking her head.

"There's still just the one dog. This one. Edmund says it's Saladin. So it's Saki who is lost. I came about dinner." In her round face was the beginning of an excitement like a kid's, planning a party. "It was Charles' idea in the beginning. To have you tonight, you see. He asked Edmund a lot of questions about you, and said you sounded nice—much too nice to go on thinking of us as a trio of ogres guarded by man-eating beasts."

Aunt Dru twinkled a little; perhaps she sensed Kitty's dilemma. "So I've come to take you to our house. Do you mind?"

"No ... no. It's very kind of you. But—I'd better check up on my friend. She's been home today, ill."

"Oh. I'm so sorry."

"I'll see how she is, then I'll be right back." Kitty hurried down the hall. If Ardis was even still abed, she promised herself, it would be an excuse not to go to the Linder place. Why should I go and sit opposite that man, and have to meet his eyes? It was with almost a feeling of outrage that Kitty awoke to the scene her mind had painted—Edmund across from her, his face bitter and aloof ... and Aunt Dru and the other brother, Charles, mere shadows at the fringe of vision. He made me mad, she told herself; that's why I can't forget him. That's the one reason.

She opened Ardis's door and snapped on the light. The bed was made, the room straightened. Ardis wasn't in it.

She'd gone again.

Kitty went back to the living room, feeling lost. Aunt Dru said quickly, "Is something wrong? Is she quite ill?"

"She's gone out." Kitty rubbed her temples. The sudden awakening, the panic, had left her with a muzzy feeling. "I'm not sure what I ought to do."

"If she felt well enough to go out, she mustn't be too ill," Aunt Dru pointed out. "Why not leave a message, tell her where you're going, and that if she needs you, to telephone our house?"

It was neat and logical. As if to add a further argument, the big yellow dog stood up, walked over to Kitty, looked into her face, then licked her hand, a single sloppy kiss expressing final friendship. Kitty couldn't help what she did then: she knelt by the big dog and rubbed his ears. "I've absolved you of any blame," she said. "You aren't the beast of last night. You couldn't be."

He unrolled a tongue about two feet long and caressed her chin. In the depths of his eyes was approval, liking, confidence.

Kitty went to her room again to change clothes. As she dressed, from the corner of her eyes she could see the blue pumps. She thought of Doyle. She'd lied to him at every possible opportunity, trying to lead him away from Ardis. What would he say if he knew of this excursion to have dinner with the Linders?

She had a hunch that he would say she was a fool.

CHAPTER NINE

They were on the stairs, Aunt Dru's dumpling shape round in the dim light from the lower door, the big dog making a craggy shadow on the wall, when Kitty heard the telephone ringing in the apartment. "I'd better answer it. Wait for me, I'll only be a minute." In her mind was the idea that it must be Ardis. Ardis was in such deep torment, such trouble, and with such need of help that Kitty felt the breaking point, the admission of helplessness, would come at any time. She ran back to the apartment, to the telephone in the hall. But it wasn't Ardis. It was Dena Frayne.

Dena sounded jovial. "Are you home? I thought I might drop in."

"I'm just leaving. I have a dinner engagement."

"Well.... Don't let me interfere. It wasn't important, anyhow."

"I'm sorry, Dena." Kitty was also puzzled. Dena had always been direct in her approach, and usually it was easy to see that her sociability had a sense of business behind it. "I'll probably be home fairly early, though, if that would be any use to you."

"I *said* it wasn't important," Dena insisted, still being jolly. "I just wanted to celebrate, mildly, with a bottle of champagne. I have a job now, you see. Do you think I'll make a nice receptionist? It'll be a change from acting, anyway. Easier on the feet, I guess."

"Who gave you the job?" In her worry over Dena's possible risk, Kitty forgot how much older the actress was than herself, and how many years Dena had been looking after her own affairs without help or supervision. But she had roused Dena's annoyance now. The next remarks were crisp, formal.

"Didn't you talk to Hal DeGraffen about me this morning? Didn't you suggest that he might keep an eye out for something for me?"

Kitty recalled her lunch with Hal. "Why ... why yes, I did."

"The receptionist is leaving, and Hal spoke to Mr. Baron about me, and they're going to give me a chance. I went and had a look, quiet-like, at the girl I'm supposed to replace. I can see there'll have to be some changes made in the old personality. God, she's like an icicle. But I've played a lot of parts, I can manage this one. One thing I wanted to ask you—because of your being a secretary—was whether I ought to tone down the hair a bit. It's natural, but I could use a rinse." The original jollity, the subsequent annoyance, had vanished in an eagerness almost like a child's. Kitty was stirred; she felt sorry for the anxious, aging woman who seemed to see a new career opening before her.

"There isn't any reason you couldn't be a good receptionist," she said thoughtfully. "Don't use any artificial color on your hair—if it's naturally red, leave it alone. Wear it very simply. I think you'd look very professional if you'd pull it back into a chignon." All at once Kitty grasped the way Dena could look if she put her will to it: chic, with the fundamentally good planes of her face revealed by a simple coiffure, her figure slimmed by a plain dark dress, her expressive hands free of the garish nail-polish and the nails filed to somewhat less than their talon's length. "I—I have a few ideas if you'd want to talk them over."

"I'd love to!"

"Give me a ring at around eleven. I'll be home by then."

"I'll be seeing you! And ... Kitty ... thanks a million. You don't know what this means to me!"

Still Kitty was nagged by that sense of worry. "Of course you're welcome. I'm glad this break came when it did. I was a little bit afraid you might go ahead with that other thing."

The answer was quick, almost querulous. "What the devil do you mean?"

"I thought you had some idea of putting the pressure on someone over Sunny's murder."

"Oh, Kitty, that's absurd!" Dena laughed into the telephone.

"I suppose it was," Kitty said, letting Dena think she had been convinced. "But I would like to know—who gave Sunny the mink stole?"

"Maybe I'll tell you, tonight. As of now, I'm off to the store for a bottle of champagne. Ho, ho! Champagne for Dena!" She began to hum *It's Only a Paper Moon*, and Kitty imagined her feet doing a quick little step on the floor of the shabby apartment.

"Call me at eleven!" Kitty commanded, the odd sense of worry stronger than ever. She hung up the telephone and went down to join Aunt Dru. She shouldn't have thrown a shadow on Dena's jubilance. At last there was a break for her, a chance to fit into a new job.

During the trip to the house Kitty found out a few things about the Linders' background. Aunt Dru was the unmarried sister of the Father of Edmund and Charles. Their mother had died when they were quite small, and she had assumed the management of the house for her brother. Previously, she had taught school and done library work, without, Kitty gathered, much formal preparation, so that her jobs, as standards went up, were successively less important and less well paid. Probably she had escaped from some out-of-the-way village, and from a miserable situation, into the freedom of her brother's home. She spoke feelingly of her pleasure at being the boys' foster-mother, and of various problems which she had met and solved in their upbringing.

Around 1944, the father had died and the two sons had been in the Army. Aunt Dru said that she had been utterly lost. She spoke of this time briefly, and with distaste, as if it represented much unhappiness to her. There had been a succession of governess jobs, probably not much more than baby-sitting for working mothers. When Edmund and Charles had come back from war, she'd set up a home for them. Then Edmund had got into trouble—Aunt Diu didn't specify, but Kitty knew what it must have been: the beating of the Army officer whom Edmund blamed for a bad command—and for a while Aunt Dru and Charles had lived by themselves. It was at this time that they had bought the house off Du Moyne Avenue. When Edmund had come back from his "trouble" (Aunt Dru never mentioned the word *prison*), they'd had some difficulty getting him to move back with them.

"If we'd have let him, he'd have ended up quite badly," Aunt Dru concluded worriedly. "A lone wolf, morose, sullen. Edmund has that possibility in his temperament. Of course I've loved him since he was a toddler, and all of his many fine points outweigh his faults. But I wasn't blind to what he might be. I made Charles keep after him until he gave up his room—a dreadful place, almost on skid row—and come back with us. Things have been going evenly ... until this."

Aunt Dru parked in the driveway, led the way up to the house. The dog walked by Kitty's side with a grave air of introducing her to the place. At the porch he stopped, looked back at the road, seeming to search for something, and whined deep in his throat.

The door opened. The man who looked out at them must be Charles Linder. He was of a slighter build than Edmund, though still of better-than-average size; there was a certain fineness, slimness, of jaw and wrist that contrasted with his brother's; and on seeing him Kitty remembered at once that he was an author, had written a successful book. There was something professorish, bookish, about him. He was smoking a pipe. He smiled at Kitty, and she felt a surge of liking for him: the smile was so genuine, warm, and unreserved. He held out a hand. "Welcome to the ogre's castle," he said.

"It's a very nice castle," said Kitty, going in to admire the front room. The place had an air of informal comfort, and there was lacking any sign of the meticulous tidiness, the doilies and the what-nots, that she would have expected of Aunt Dru. The room was big; the windows looked out at the little lane, the shrubby trees, the hills green under their new grass. The furniture was good: big, solid, and mannish; and Kitty thought to herself that Aunt Dru had let Charles furnish this room to his own taste. She looked around for Edmund, but he wasn't in sight.

"We ogres have put away our fangs and claws," Charles advised her, "since we don't serve live young ladies for dinner except on Sundays. Won't you choose a chair and sit down?"

Kitty picked out a big leather chair and sank into it. Aunt Dru made an excuse of having to peep into the oven, and left them. There was a moment of silence; not awkward—from a chair opposite, Charles Linder was openly studying her, and his odd greenish eyes seemed full of interest and pleasure. "I can't believe you were lost in the storm in our little lane," he said finally. "Do you mind telling me about it?"

"It all began with a party. I wasn't having a good time, all at once, and I decided go home. A girl I knew told me about a shortcut. Du Moyne Avenue."

He tapped the pipe out into an ash tray. His face was turned from Kitty. "This is the girl, I understand, who is dead."

"Yes." Kitty went on with the narrative, familiar now; she found herself using phrases she had recited to Doyle, to Dena, to Hal DeGraffen. When she came to the interlude with the dogs, Charles appeared to take on new intentness, to examine every word. When she had finished, he waited for a moment or so as if expecting something more. Finally he asked, "She followed immediately, according to these other people, and yet you didn't see any sign of her?"

"No, nothing." There were at least two things Kitty had left out: the glow of a car's lights from the hill behind her, and the telephone call Ardis had received from Sunny long after Kitty had been home in bed. "There really isn't any proof that she did come here at once."

"But isn't that the popular theory?" he wondered. "Isn't she supposed to have followed you to set you right on the turn-off, and met up with the dogs, still hungry after having only a taste of your foot, and been all but gobbled down to make a canine dinner?"

It was meant to sound light and amusing; but in Kitty's memory was the sight of Sunny, under the blanket, in the cold, still light of a cloudy sky; and sudden revulsion shook her. Charles Linder saw it instantly.

"I'm sorry if I sounded callous. I never met the girl. The crime is horrible. I—I don't see how I can talk about it at all unless I regard it as a kind of puzzle, a game." He put down the pipe and sat there looking rebuffed and confused. Aunt Dru made a welcome interruption, bearing a tray with cocktails. Four cocktails.

She looked around the room. "Hasn't Edmund come in?"

"Still slicking down his hair for Miss Quist's benefit." Charles brought Kitty a glass, bent for a moment above her chair. There was a queer stiffness in his position. It occurred to Kitty that though there was no definite limp, he walked somehow as if he were crippled. She looked up at him, receiving again that impression of warmth, openness, a proffered friendship. "Let's drink to new acquaintance." He lifted his own glass toward Kitty.

There was general talk for a while. It was Aunt Dru who brought the conversation back to Sunny Walling. "Do you think we could figure out a solution to the girl's death, if we tried?"

"My dear aunt," said Charles, "if we found a solution, we should have to do something about it. And that might be quite sad."

It seemed to Kitty that their eyes met for an instant; that, without any change of expression, some thought was exchanged between them.

Charles went on, "I am very curious about the behavior of the dogs as Miss Quist related it. Could someone have drugged Saki and Saladin so that they were temporarily vicious and irresponsible?"

"If so, the drug wore off with remarkable speed, as soon as your brother appeared."

Charles began to refill the pipe, turning from her toward the tobacco humidor on the table beside his chair. Aunt Dru's eyes were bright, her cheeks pink. Kitty thought that she was feeling the drink a little.

"I'll tell you what it was then," Charles said with an air of discovery. "There were *three* dogs. Our two, Saki and Saladin—and a ringer.

When Edmund appeared, the strange dog slunk off to join his master, who was, naturally, lurking about to reclaim him after he'd done killing Miss Walling." Charles got out of his chair to reach the lighter on the table. He remained standing. In all of his movements, Kitty was becoming aware, there was a hint of stiffness, of caution. She wondered if he had been injured in the war. It seemed to her now that as he stood by the coffee table, lighting the pipe, he was, in addition, in some obscure way, testing his balance, his control.

He went on, "That's the best theory to date. Had you thought of the possibility of there being three dogs out there, Miss Quist? Could you swear that there were *not* three?" He waited, his eyes half amused behind the filmy smoke.

Kitty said slowly, "No, I couldn't say definitely that there were just two dogs—I saw two together at one time. When your brother appeared and flashed a light at them, there were only two. But that doesn't cross out the possibility that there could have been another."

"You see? When you think about it, almost anything could have happened."

Kitty *did* see: in a way much more subtle than Edmund's, he was destroying her story. There was no blunt attack, no sharp denial; there was just one silly theory after another, each more colorful and imaginative than the last. And at the end she would have to admit that it was all very ridiculous, and that the dogs, if they'd been doing anything resembling what she said they had, were just playfully teasing. In spite of her irritation, she had to smile wryly; Charles was so obviously displaying his talent for fiction.

She saw that Aunt Dru was looking at something behind her and to her right; she turned, and there was Edmund in a doorway. He nodded to her, came forward to take the drink waiting for him. The deep-set eyes seemed tired, the square face tough as stone. A sudden frost seemed to have fallen on the room.

If Charles felt the change in mood that Edmund had brought, he gave no indication. He said to his brother, "We were theorizing about this grim affair of Miss Walling."

Edmund looked at Kitty. "Were you?"

"There are so many possibilities to explore. I'm going to draw up a chart. The scientific approach. Utilizing all the material Miss Quist has given us, plus what we know of Saki and Saladin. What you know, rather—the mutts were always so much more loyal to you."

"I think that point has been brought up before," Edmund said evenly.

Charles shrugged it off. "Well, it's true. Then, we'll have to take into consideration the weather, the amount of time Miss Quist thinks may have elapsed between the first attack and the moment you showed up, and the dark. The dark and the rain could have concealed anything—or anyone."

Edmund said, "I didn't think you wrote mysteries, Chuck."

"Charles could! He could write them if he wanted to!" Aunt Dru cried, obviously admiring, and Kitty thought suddenly that she was beginning to get a hint. Aunt Dru had a favorite—Charles. Charles, who'd never been in trouble, who was friendly and warm, and who didn't want to go off to live alone, whose ways were normal and likable. He was Aunt Dru's pet. And then Kitty thought of the natural outcome of this situation. If Aunt Dru had always preferred Charles, Edmund couldn't help but know it. And this would account for many things. It might explain the violent temper, for a child's reaction to lack of love is jealousy and hatred; and the patterns of childhood guide the ways of the adult. Most obviously, it would explain Edmund's wanting to live away from these two.

The dinner went off nicely. Aunt Dru was a good cook. There was onion soup, a casserole of little meat balls and noodles in a spicy sauce, a big salad, hot cornbread, a pudding rich with rum. The coffee was splendid.

After the meal, Charles played the piano. He wasn't brilliant, Kitty saw, but he had fun with music and he somehow communicated that fun to his listeners.

At ten-thirty, Kitty said she'd better be going home. Aunt Dru got up as if to go for her coat, but Edmund told her to sit still. He'd take Kitty home. For a little while, Kitty thought he was doing it out of friendliness; but the trip down the hill to Hollywood was a silent one. She had plenty of time to think. The idea came that what Charles had said about there being a third dog wasn't such a fantastic impossibility after all.

There could have been a third dog, one closely resembling the Linder dogs, and its being there could have had something to do with the car which had followed her to the top of the ridge.

CHAPTER TEN

When she arrived at the apartment she looked first into Ardis's room. It was unchanged. In her own bedroom, she stripped off her clothes, donned a gown, got into bed.

She clicked out the little lamp beside the bed, and said to the dark; "I never want to spend another day like this one." Then, in the street below, she heard a car start.

Could Edmund Linder have waited all this while? And if so, why? To see if she had any visitors? I'd be flattering myself, she thought, if I believed he waited to see if I got safely to bed.

The sound of the car dwindled off into the night, and there was silence. Kitty slept, deeply, dreamlessly. She had forgotten about Dena, about Dena's intended call.

She awoke to find the room full of gray light. The cloudy sky outside showed the pink stripes of dawn. She sat up, shivering with the cold, the damp, of the morning. The clock began to buzz; she reached out to switch off the alarm. This was a workday. Its beginning was routine, set in a pattern that was calm and familiar. She got out of bed, put on a terry-cloth robe, and went out into the hall.

She turned on the floor furnace, then continued on into the bathroom. When she had washed, she went to the kitchen. She ran water into the percolator, spooned coffee into the metal basket, assembled the pot over a burner on the stove. Then she laid out silverware and put sugar, cream, salt and pepper, and butter on the small table in the kitchen nook.

She rattled the dishes unnecessarily, and listened for some answering sound from Ardis's room.

There was no warning, no sound of the door opening, no step in the hall. All at once Ardis was there in the doorway, leaning against the frame. She had on all her clothes, and it was obvious that she had slept in them. One side of her face was crusted with a gummy mixture like mud, or blood. Her hair was a tangle.

After a moment she straightened up, crossed the room to the breakfast nook, sat down heavily, holding her head in her hands.

Kitty went over to the nook and sat down, facing Ardis across the table. "Can't you tell me about it?"

Ardis looked up slowly. Her eyes were reddened, the lids swollen, not from crying, Kitty sensed, but from exhaustion. "Maybe I'd better. I think the police will be here pretty soon. I'd like you to know my side of it—first." She spread her hands on the table and stared down at them; the nails were broken, dirty, and the flesh was marked with scratches. "They saw me with Sunny's car last night. They'll identify me."

"*With Sunny's car!*"

"That's what I've been doing.... If I could have figured out a place to leave it—but every time I thought I had it safely put away, something would turn up to make me afraid. At first, it was the garage in San Fernando. I was sure no one would find it there. But after I'd rented the garage, and paid the woman she asked if she hadn't seen me in an office somewhere. A flower shop. It wouldn't have been long until she recalled Weidmann's. She must have been a customer of theirs. I couldn't turn around and take the car and leave—I'd made up such a careful story. I had to come home and wait until night and go out there with another story about a sudden change of plans."

Kitty tried to understand what Ardis was talking about.

"Then I took the car up to Mulholland Drive and tried to find a place to let it go off the road, where it wouldn't be found soon. But it was dark by then. I couldn't judge how much of a drop there was, or whether shrubbery would offer any concealment. I finally came down Laurel Canyon to Hollywood. That's when a police car took out after me."

Ardis leaned toward her, eyes haunted and full of fear. "Were you ever chased like that, Kit? It's nightmare. I cut corners, ran over lawns, bounced off curbs, and I never could lose them. The only thing that saved me was a fluke, an accident—I turned into what I thought was an alley entrance. It was a private driveway, a big one. I tore through and found myself in a big courtyard. I rammed a fence before I could stop. I got out of the car and crawled through some shrubbery, and waited for the police to come, and search the car, and finally find me."

"This was someone's home? Didn't they hear you?"

"No. The place must have been vacant. There were no lights, and no one was roused by the noise I made. After a long while, when I was cold and stiff with crouching on the earth, I decided the police weren't going to find me after all. I crawled out and got into the car, turned around in the courtyard, and left. It taught me one lesson. I didn't get on the main boulevards after that."

"Go back to the beginning," Kitty begged. "Start with Sunny's telephone call, night before last. What did she want of you?"

"It was all a lie." A spasm of fury crossed Ardis's face. "She said there'd been a message—a final note—from ..." Ardis couldn't go on. Her clenched hands writhed and shook. Kitty knew what she meant; Sunny had pretended to offer a message from the Burns boy, and to Ardis there was always the thin hope that someday, in some mysterious manner, a final word would come proving that at the end he had returned her love.

The doorbell buzzed. It didn't seem to make any impression upon Ardis, but Kitty sat in electrified fright.

This was the end for Ardis. The police had come for her. Kitty stood up, urged by a confused idea of getting a coat on Ardis, getting her out the back door. But the bell had been replaced by pounding.

She went with dragging steps to the front door, opened it, looked in stupid surprise at Maud DeGraffen. Maud stalked in with her long-legged walk. She looked crisp and alert, her suit neat, gloves and bag and hat all carefully matched, the gray coil of her hair shining. "Where is Ardis?"

"In the kitchen."

Maud didn't waste any time. "Get her clothes."

"She's dressed."

Maud shot her a quick look, walked into the kitchen, bent over Ardis.

"Oh, heavens. This won't do. Bring a wash-cloth and a bowl of ice, Kit. And coffee, if she hasn't had any." Maud tried to get a hand under Ardis's chin. She withdrew her fingers and looked with distaste at the tear-stains on the lavender suede glove. "Does she know the police are after her?"

At the refrigerator, getting ice-cubes, Kitty said, "Yes, she knows."

"They came to our house, asking if we'd mind if they looked through to see if she was there. Of course we let them. Then the thought hit me they won't expect her there, now. I can't understand how I managed to beat them here, though, unless they're watching the place. They may nab us when we walk out. But we'll take that chance." She had Ardis up now, and was working on her with the ice-cubes. Ardis made weak protests, but seemed too disorganized to resist. Maud bent close, spoke as she would have to a retarded child. "I'm taking you to my house. Do you understand?"

"It won't do any good," Ardis muttered.

"Well, you can't face them like this. They'll have you clapped into a cell quicker than you think." Maud looked at Kitty. "Bring her coat and a hat. Something she hasn't worn recently. No, better—bring her something of yours."

Maud was so definitely in charge, so determined, that Kitty obeyed without question.

On her feet, dressed in Kitty's things, her face repaired by cosmetics from Maud's handbag, Ardis didn't look too bad. She went with Maud, holding Maud's hand. Anger and fear had drained away; she looked hollow with tiredness, indifferent, stunned.

They went down the stairs to the street, and Kitty rushed to the window. On the sidewalk, Maud didn't hesitate. She led the way down the block where her car was parked. She put Ardis in and went around to the driver's seat, and the car pulled away. And not until that moment did Kitty stop to wonder, with a touch of uneasiness, just why Maud had done this.

Of all the people she knew, Kitty thought, Maud was the one most apt to regard the situation with a cool, self-interested eye. She was not a sentimental woman. Even her attitude toward Hal, her husband, was more rakish mockery than wifely love. She was fond of her friends, but never in her wildest conjectures could Kitty imagine Maud's doing a favor that might injure herself.

Later, she stood at the door and checked the contents of her bag—pen and pencil, cosmetics, keys, handkerchief. She opened the door with the bag still not snapped. In sudden fear, before she realized that it was Doyle standing there, she dropped the bag and its contents clattered across the floor.

"Sorry if I startled you. I was just going to ring." He began to assemble the scattered stuff. She stood aside, hating herself for this lack of control, this easiness at terror. It was as if she'd expected some sort of horror on the landing, she told herself; she'd been ready to jump. He offered her the bag. "I imagine this affair of Miss Walling's murder has been some strain for you. Considering the involvement of your friend, and other factors."

She wouldn't let herself be led into conversation with him. "I'm sorry that I haven't time to talk. I have to go to work."

"I thought I might drive you out to the University, if you'd let me. And we could cover a few points on the way. I'd like to inquire about Miss Lake."

"She isn't here."

He smiled a little, wryly. Under the red eyebrows his gaze was wise, a trifle tired, cynical. "I had guessed that. Do you mind riding in my car?"

"I don't mind the ride. It's the official doubt and disbelief I resent," she stated.

"I don't disbelieve you." He was following her down the stairs. "In fact, I may as well tell you now—we're convinced that the dog did what you said he did."

"From the very beginning," Kitty said evenly, "you have acted as if I were a liar or an idiot, or both. Furthermore, in any inquiry, you pretend total ignorance, whereas really you are already in possession of all the facts and the repetition is gone through in hopes of catching somebody in a lie."

He drove down to Sunset, turned right in the direction of the University. The early work-bound traffic was fast and thick, most of it going in the opposite direction, toward downtown Los Angeles. "No, you're putting a false construction on it. I'm not pretending ignorance. I'm keeping an open mind, so far as possible. Everyone has a right to tell his story in his own way, the first time, and a detective is a fool who doesn't listen and who doesn't realize that what he is hearing may be the truth no matter how badly it conflicts with what he's already heard."

Kitty said slowly, "If you believe me in what I said about the dog's behavior, then you believe that Edmund Linder is lying."

"Not necessarily." Doyle shrugged inside his loose, somewhat shabby overcoat. "He may be optimistic, unwilling to face facts. Few dog owners want to believe their pets are vicious."

Kitty saw an opening now, a way to distract Doyle in what she felt was his aim of quizzing her about Ardis. "A fantastic idea occurred to me. Do you suppose there might have been a *third* dog? One which didn't belong to the Linders?"

Usually she got some reaction out of him, but now he was deadpan;

he reminded her of those minutes yesterday when he'd first listened to her story, not moving a muscle to betray foreknowledge. "Tell me, was the idea really yours?"

She evaded this. "Is it so impossible, this theory of a third dog?"

He let out something like a sigh. "No, not impossible. A little unlikely. A lot more clever than the usual. Your theory evolves into something like this: Miss Walling has an enemy. He wants to murder her, and to conceal the murder by making it look as if she'd been attacked by Linder's dogs. He finds a hound which is a duplicate of Linder's, trains it to attack women alone, sets him to guard in Linder's lane. Meanwhile arranging a rendezvous with Miss Walling."

"Yes, I see all of that is necessary."

"The thing which is slipshod and open to error is the timing. How's your theoretical murderer going to make sure that at the right moment Miss Walling—and only Miss Walling—will be in the lane for the dog to attack?"

"That wouldn't be too difficult."

"And he'd have to be there, too, waiting. He couldn't just leave the dog and trust to luck, and come back perhaps to find a half dozen corpses, none of them that of Miss Walling. This would mean that he couldn't establish an alibi elsewhere."

"He may not need an alibi elsewhere. He may be someone you'd never find trace of among Sunny's acquaintances and friends. Mr. X. Like the man who gave Sunny that mink stole—faceless, a blank."

He took his eyes off the traffic for a moment. "Wouldn't you like to make a guess as to who gave her the fur wrap?"

"No." Kitty shrugged. "I haven't the least idea."

He didn't say anything else. Presently the University buildings rose ahead, mellow brick in the midst of rolling green lawns.

At the last moment, getting out of Doyle's car, she thought that he had a look of expectation. He had believed that she would tell him something of Ardis's adventures, perhaps. Then it occurred to Kitty to wonder why he'd timed his arrival as he had, and why he hadn't come earlier, when Ardis was at home. Under her dislike, Kitty felt a cold respect for his mind. He wasn't stupid. If he had wanted Ardis, he'd have come for her. What was his purpose in leaving her at large?

"Goodbye, Miss Quist."

"Thank you for the ride."

CHAPTER ELEVEN

Kitty plunged into the day's work gratefully. There were charts to make up, reports to file, some dictation to take.

"Is it too warm in here for you?" Professor Galem wondered, glancing up at her. He was at the other desk, on the opposite side of the office.

"No, not at all."

"You look sort of"—the mild little man sought for a word—"well, pink. Flushed."

"I was thinking about something else, I guess. About the murder of the girl I knew."

He appeared interested. "Tell me about it."

Perhaps it was because she knew he'd expect a clean-cut, logical account, but in this retelling all the stumbling blocks stood out like headlamps. Professor Galem seemed to follow her words closely, weighing, evaluating; and when she was finished, he asked two questions.

"Did you notice any car behind you *before* you reached the top of the hill?"

"Not that I can remember."

"Has this woman, this Dena Frayne, telephoned you since yesterday?"

"No."

"I think I would try to get in touch with her if I were you." He nodded toward the telephone on the corner of Kitty's desk. "Now, at once."

She dialed Dena's number, but there was no answer.

She and Professor Galem had no further conversation about the case until late in the day, when it was almost time to go home. Then he asked about her friendship with the DeGraffens. Had it preceded her acquaintance with Arnold?

"Oh, yes, by several weeks. I met Hal and Maud when I first came to Hollywood, when I was first trying to break in as a radio actress."

"Did Hal DeGraffen offer any help in regard to your ambitions?"

Kitty remembered the hopes she'd had, the desperate hints she'd laid at Hal's feet. "No. He appeared not to understand how much I needed and wanted a job."

Professor Galem began stuffing papers into a brief case. "Perhaps time has mellowed him, since you say that he is sympathetic toward the difficulties of Miss Frayne."

"Dena's known them so much longer than I. For years and years."

"Yes, that too might account for the difference."

The scientific mind, Kitty thought, always spotting the inconsistencies. She had the greatest liking and respect for Professor Galem, but at times his queer insight disturbed her. Take the matter of my pink face, she told herself. He knew that the office wasn't too warm. He was poking into my brain, the way he pokes into those thinking-machines of his. He likes to see my wheels turn over. She glanced over at him to find his eyes on her, wise and watchful.

"I'm not much good as a detective," she offered.

"You are trying to protect a friend. Forgive me for saying so—but perhaps not wisely. Miss Lake may be in danger."

"She's with Maud and Hal. They'll protect her."

He snapped the case shut, went to the hat-stand, put on a gray felt, and nodded to her from the door. "I'd check up anyway."

"Of course."

He went out, closing the door. Kitty began to put stuff away into the drawers of her desk. She let the typewriter down into its hole, swept the last discard off into the wastebasket. Why had Professor Galem seemed to find interest in the DeGraffens? Of all the people in the case, they were the ones most above suspicion. The host and hostess can't disappear from a party without notice being taken of it. And the time element didn't enter in particularly either, since the DeGraffens' parties always lasted until dawn. Some die-hards were there, she would swear, for breakfast.

How late had Dena stayed?

That was something she hadn't thought to ask, and yet it could be important. Dena's desperation had made her sharp, observant.

Kitty decided to go to Dena's apartment now, before going home.

She took the bus to midtown Hollywood and walked north on Vine to the tangle of narrow hillside streets and Dena's address.

She was not far from Dena's front entry when she recognized Hal De-Graffen. He was at the edge of the steps, facing the street, his face full of a worried indecision. He looked at Kitty for several seconds without seeming to recognize her. Then he came to himself with a start. "Oh, hello. I've been trying to locate Dena. She doesn't answer the telephone or the doorbell. Where do you think she might be?"

"Perhaps buying clothes, or taking some beauty treatments. She's terrifically enthused over the job you got her, Hal."

"She didn't show up for her appointment to talk to the boss." Under the obvious worry, Hal showed other signs of distress; he had, Kitty thought, a vaguely down-at-heels air in spite of the good, expensive suit, the handsome tie, and other signs of money. He had forgotten something; Kitty decided it must be an afternoon shave. He had a thick beard and probably freshened himself around five o'clock with an electric razor, like many a man whose dinner appearance was important. And his shoes were dusty. "She rather put me on a spot with Baron. I can't put in a good word for people and then have them just not show up."

"I'm sure only something very important could have kept her from see-ing Baron." Kitty was worried now. She recalled Dena's fresh enthusi-asm of last night and then something more. The champagne. Had Dena gone off on a tear, and had to spend today repairing the ravages of a hangover? "Perhaps she telephoned, and the message wasn't relayed to you."

"No, I asked tonight when I left the office. She didn't come in and she didn't phone, and Baron made a nasty crack about it. He thinks his time's so damned valuable." Hal's face was suddenly bitter and vindic-tive. Kitty remembered the gossip she'd heard about Hal's boss. A slave driver.

"Surely if she'd been able to, she would have telephoned."

"You'd think so. But hell, what are we standing here worrying about? If she doesn't give a damn, why should we?" He came down the steps and took Kitty's elbow. "Come on, Kit, and I'll drive you home."

"No, wait. She could be ill. She could be in there suffering from some kind of attack. Her heart. Or migraine. We ought to investigate." Kitty began to urge Hal back toward the door.

He exploded with rage. "Dammit, the woman's made a fool of me, put me in bad with Baron, and him waiting for a chance to nail my hide to the door! I'm through with her! She's all washed up as far as I'm con-cerned!" His voice crackled in Kitty's ear. She realized that Hal hadn't come here to find out what was wrong with Dena. He'd come to vent his fury on her for making him the butt of Baron's dangerous anger.

"No, don't judge her yet!" Kitty ran up to the front door, tried to peer in through the tiny, dusty square of glass set high in the panel. She could make out a bit of Dena's front room. The couch. It seemed to her that there was a humped, unmoving heap on it. Kitty pounded on the door. The heap didn't stir. "Hal! I've got to get in!"

Grumbling, he came and tried to see what Kitty saw. "Can't make out anything but a bunch of clothes. Something she took off and threw down, probably, as she headed for bed."

They tried the front door and the small door at the side of the house that apparently led into Dena's kitchenette. Finally Kitty discovered a window whose screen was unlatched, whose pane rose with a push.

Hal helped her to climb in, still with that air of grudging unwilling-ness, of distrust toward Dena.

The kitchenette was narrow and ill-lit. A tiny sink was piled high with soiled dishes, over which a couple of flies buzzed. A clock sat on the refrigerator; its ticking seemed loud in the stuffy quiet. Kitty went on into the front room. The blinds weren't up very high and the room was full of shadow. But a few steps showed her that Hal's guess was right;

the stuff on the couch was a pile of clothing. Almost smothered under it was an open suitcase. On the floor sat a row of shoes.

Dena had been packing. Kitty remembered her previous impression, that Dena felt herself only temporarily marooned in such a place while she waited for the break that was sure to come. Had Dena been so confident of her success at Hal's agency that she'd already begun preparations to move to a better apartment? It seemed illogical. And yet, the champagne might account for a rosier view than the facts warranted. And the packing had been abandoned, Kitty thought, as if a more cautious attitude had at last prevailed. She went into the bedroom, half expecting Hal's prophecy to be true. But there was no stricken figure on the bed. The apartment smelled close, shut-in, but there was no odor of liquor.

She heard a step behind her. Hal appeared in the bedroom door. "Whew! Needs air in here. No sign of Dena. Let's go."

The room showed a great disorder. The bedding was pulled awry, the blankets stripped down over the foot of the bed so that only the sheet remained to cover the mattress. All the bottles and jars of cosmetics on the old-fashioned dresser had been swept into a huddle. Some old press-notices, clipped from newspapers, were scattered on the floor, as if pulled recently from the walls or around the mirror. Everything spoke of haste, turbulence, and departure.

The notion to move must have hit Dena like a bomb.

Kitty glanced towards the closet, whose partially open door showed another wadded heap of garments. "Her clothes will be ruined, crushed together like that. Look at them—on the floor." In concern for Dena's few good things, Kitty started for the closet. Behind her Hal made a sound she was to try to analyze later: a muffled protest, or warning—she couldn't figure out which. She pulled the closet door wide and stared in at the heap of stuff. The room, the world, spun like a top. She heard herself scream. Hal had jerked her away from the closet door. She found herself clinging to a bed-post, the scream dying in her dry throat, her legs trembling.

Hal was looking into the closet. "Good God!"

"Touch her," Kitty begged. "See if there's a chance that she—"

"Like *that?*" Hal said hoarsely. "There isn't a hope."

With a tremendous tightening of her will Kitty stilled the shaking in her body, let go of the bed-post, walked to the closet again, and bent to touch the stained, outstretched hand. Its warmth was a shock. Kitty jerked away in spite of her effort at control, as though she'd touched a snake. She forced herself to look calmly at Dena's face, disfigured as it was by blood and bruises. The eyes were puffed shut. The throat seemed chewed to a pulp, macerated. Kitty shuddered.

Then she turned, running, and made for the phone in the front room. There it sat, squat, black—the thing that Dena must have pinched pennies to keep and that she had hoped might ring with news of a job. Now it might well be the means of saving her life. Kitty lifted the phone out of its cradle.

Hal reached from behind to snatch it from her hand.

She turned swiftly, stunned by his sudden act. His face was working, the eyes wild as if with fear or rage. "What are you going to do, Kit? Who were you going to phone?"

"The police. They'll send an ambulance."

He took a handkerchief from his pocket and wiped the phone thoroughly. "Let's leave this place. You can telephone from a drugstore, anonymously. You don't want them to know we were here."

"Why not?" Kitty made a grab for the telephone. She and Hal struggled together until he forced her off-balance against the arm of the couch. She put out a hand to save herself from falling. Hal had backed away, the phone still clutched against his chest and still swathed in the handkerchief.

"Kitty—all right. You can call the cops. Only, promise ... promise you won't say I was here too. Please, Kit. It's my career. It's ruin, destitution, disaster, for me and Maud. All I've worked for—Baron will throw me out. He'll accuse me of all sorts of things. Murder, maybe."

The chattering voice full of fear did not seem to belong to Hal at all. It was like a voice from a phonograph record, a little scratchy, a little off-key, and reciting something so ingrained in the mind that it was like something spoken in a play.

"No one will accuse you of anything, Hal. You came in with me. It was natural for you to be curious, to be worried. You'd given Dena a good chance to reorganize her life, to get out of a rut. Naturally you'd wonder why she didn't show up."

He was shaking his head, the wild light dying in his eyes. "You don't understand, Kit. Don't drag me into this. If you do, it's"—his voice broke in a husky noise like a sob—"it's the end for me. For Maud, too. The end of our home, our life together, the fun we've had. The funny kind of trust Maud puts in me. Yes, that most of all."

Kitty reached for the telephone. "I can't lie to the police about this, Hal. For one thing, they'll find your fingerprints all over the place. Wiping the phone won't help. Try to be reasonable!"

All at once he shook his head, dropped the phone. It clattered on the floor. Hal disappeared into the kitchen; Kitty heard the door open, his steps dying in the distance.

She called the police, then went back to sit in the dismal bedroom. There seemed no possible chance of life in the broken thing in the closet, to judge by appearance. And yet the warm hand spoke of a flicker remaining.

How long had Dena lain here, dying? Since last night? Since before the time that she was supposed to call, at eleven? It didn't seem logical, and yet, under the deterioration, the blowziness, the tippling, Dena had had a constitution like an ox. You could sense that, Kitty thought. The woman wouldn't give up, go under, under the blows of ill luck. She was a fighter. And the stout heart that had kept her in there battling against the indifference, the cynicism, of Hollywood still pumped away inside the broken body, undismayed.

She might even live, to identify her attacker.

There would be danger to someone if she survived. Uneasily, Kitty waited and listened for the coming of the police.

Doyle rubbed his red hair back out of his eyes. He looked bitterly tired, Kitty thought, as if the day had consisted of a long, exasperating wild-goose chase.

They were in the police car, parked in front of Dena's place. Dena was in an ambulance on the way to the hospital. The apartment, brightly lit, had technical experts working in it. In the thin blue dusk, the old houses looked neat, almost pretty; and Kitty thought, you could almost recreate that long-ago Hollywood, as naïve, as pretentious, as the stucco facades.

Doyle said, "Tell it slowly and carefully, please. Try not to leave out any detail that might be significant. Try to bore me." He settled down and put his head on the cushion, pushing his hat over his eyes, folded his hands on his stomach, and prepared to listen.

Kitty remembered that last despairing look Hal had given her, before he had bolted out of the house. Could she get away with a lie?

"I was worried because Dena hadn't called as she had promised. I came here after work. A window in the kitchen wasn't hard to open. I crawled in."

"Wait a minute. Did that window look as if someone else might have used it the same way, recently?"

"I don't know. The screen wasn't latched."

"Go on."

"I saw the signs of hurried packing in the living room. Then I—I got the idea Dena might have celebrated the new job too thoroughly. Hal DeGraffen thought he might get her on as receptionist at Waddell Brothers."

The end of Doyle's nose twitched. "Yes, I'd heard that elsewhere."

"I expected to find Dena prostrate on the bed, sleeping off a hangover perhaps. At first I didn't realize that the thing on the floor of the closet wasn't just a mass of clothes. When I touched her hand—"

Doyle covered a yawn. "Uhh, let's go back to the beginning. When you arrived here, did you see any sign of another visitor?"

The tone didn't warn her, though it should have. And she should have remembered Doyle's immemorial preparation for his quizzes: advance information. But all of Hal's begging, stumbling words seemed to run like an echo through her head. She told the lie, for Hal. "No. There wasn't anybody."

"Okay. Go on."

She told the rest, and had a queer feeling that he wasn't listening. He was still back there with that *No*, figuring it out.

CHAPTER TWELVE

Kitty sat up in bed, shivering, aware that the doorbell was ringing. She looked at the clock. It was ten minutes before the alarm was supposed to go off, before the swift workaday routine began: breakfast and a shower and the quick, careful dressing, the ride to the University, the office, the slow rise of the typewriter from its hidey-hole in the desk.... Her thoughts skittered through this familiar path, while a sixth sense warned that the doorbell's ringing meant an interruption of all this, a change, a delay.

She got out of bed, put on a robe, and went to the front door. She saw there the last person she had expected. Aunt Dru, round and woolly in a big knitted stole, peered in at Kitty. She had a newspaper in her hands. An old-fashioned beaver cloche was pushed down over her gray curls. "Did I wake you?"

"No, I was up," Kitty lied politely. "Come inside." She shut the door behind Aunt Dru, then ran to light the heater.

When she came back, Aunt Dru had the papers spread out on the coffee table. "As soon as I saw the headlines on the paper the boy leaves at our house, I came here. I bought others on the way. They all say that you found this woman, this Miss Frayne."

Kitty's memory jumped to the previous evening. "Yes, that's right."

"It's dreadful." Aunt Dru looked pinched and scared, Kitty thought. "And there's a kind of hint here that the terrible attack on Miss Frayne had something to do with that other—the thing in our lane."

"I guess that's the official theory."

"Were they ... alike in some way?"

Kitty shuddered at the memory of poor Dena's torn throat. Aunt Dru must have seen the involuntary creeping of Kitty's flesh. She asked: "Did you see Miss Frayne—up close?"

"Yes."

"And she ... she looked like —"

"As if a beast had been at her," Kitty said in a stifled voice.

Aunt Dru seemed to huddle and shrink inside the woolly wrap. "Do you know if Miss Frayne is still alive?"

"I'll find out." Kitty went to the telephone and called the emergency hospital, and learned that during the night Dena had been transferred. Kitty felt that this was a good sign. There must be some chance that Dena would survive. She called the second hospital, but here there was no information for her. The nurse who answered was cool and guarded, and all at once Kitty realized that the police would have a watch over Dena, and that any news concerning her condition would have to be obtained through official channels. So she tried to reach Doyle at headquarters, only to be told that he wasn't on duty until eight-thirty. They refused to give her his home telephone number.

She returned to Aunt Dru.

"What did they tell you?"

"Nothing of importance."

Aunt Dru thought about it. "The police will be guarding her, won't they? If she doesn't die, she'll be able to tell who attacked her?"

"Yes, that seems logical." Kitty was a little puzzled now by Aunt Dru's visit. Was it simply a quest for information?

"Wouldn't you think the murderer would be afraid?"

"Yes, of course."

"And that he'd make some new attempt to kill this woman?"

"He wouldn't be able to get past the police guards," Kitty pointed out.

"I wish I could see her." Aunt Dru's eyes darted about the room. Her manner seemed hesitant, evasive. Like a rabbit, Kitty thought, sticking its head out of a hole, ready to jump back at the least hint of danger.

"I doubt if the police would allow that."

Aunt Dru swallowed. "I—I might *know* something."

"If you know anything about the case, other than what you've told, you'd better go at once to the police with it. Dena Frayne knew something. I think she tried to use it for blackmail." But Kitty's inner thoughts jeered at the advice. She was telling Aunt Dru to be honest with the police, while she herself was guilty of all kinds of lying.

Then she realized that what she had said must have shocked the little old lady. Aunt Dru was quite pale. "Why do you say this—about blackmail?"

"It's just based on an impression I got while I talked to Dena."

"What was it she knew?"

"She didn't tell me. She hinted around about a gift Sunny had received.

Something some man had given her. Then Dena clammed up, pretended I wasn't to notice what she had said. It wasn't a very good act, but Dena was doing her own dialogue and that could account for the poor quality."

"You sound sort of bitter," Aunt Dru said wonderingly.

"It was so stupid of her to fool around like that."

"Yes, I suppose it was." Aunt Dru's manner was vague and thoughtful. She began gathering up the papers. "I won't keep you any longer. I'll run along now. Just one thing—Edmund may be coming to see you. Please don't tell him I was here."

Kitty was reminded of Hal, of how desperate he was that no one would know he was at Dena's place. "I won't mention your visit." What did the little old lady have up her sleeve? Most of their conversation had concerned the possibility of someone's getting in to murder Dena at the hospital. A funny subject for Aunt Dru to be worried over.

Aunt Dru was rather puzzling, Kitty decided as she closed the door behind the dumpy, old-fashioned figure.

At first the little old lady had seemed completely dominated and overshadowed by her nephews, lost without them, according to her own story, during their wartime absences, her life wrapped up in making a home for them.

But perhaps there was more to the picture than that.

Perhaps Aunt Dru was the power behind the scene. Some women got a certain satisfaction out of running men, ordering their lives, influencing their thoughts and actions. Even causing them to do things that they shouldn't—Kitty was remembering that it had been a remark by Aunt Dru which had caused Edmund to fling out, breaking the lamp.

That remark, Kitty recalled, had concerned the idea that Sunny might have sent Kitty as a decoy, to test the danger of the trap set by the murderer. Why should it have upset Edmund so much?

Under the whole incident had run the question of whether Charles Linder had been acquainted with Sunny Walling.

Hal DeGraffen had said that he believed Sunny Walling had been mixed up in the deal to make a radio series out of Charles Linder's book. Who else might know something about it? Sunny had been far from being an intellectual type, so it hadn't been the writing end of the deal in which she might have been involved. Had the plans for the program reached the point of casting? Had Sunny been promised a part? Dena might know; Kitty mentally kicked herself for not having asked. Then she thought of Maud DeGraffen.

Maud had dabbled in much of Hal's business, had overheard a million scraps relating to new shows, to casting, to contracts. Yes, Maud might know whether Sunny had actually played a part in the fiasco over the book.

Besides, it was time to check up on Ardis.

The telephone began to ring as she walked toward it. She lifted the instrument and Maud's voice crackled in her ear; as if, Kitty thought, the very wish had produced it. Maud said, "I've got to see you at once."

"I'm due at the job," Kitty reminded. "I haven't much time."

"We must talk. The police have been to the house and taken Ardis. I'm not home. I'm a couple of blocks from your place, a café. The one with the neon coffeepot. You know."

"I'll be down," Kitty said, remembering that the café was opposite the bus-stop.

"I'm in a rear booth." Maud hung up abruptly.

There wouldn't be time for breakfast, if she and Maud were to have much of a conversation. Kitty decided she'd settle for a cup of coffee at the café. She bathed and dressed quickly, let herself out of the apartment, locked the door.

She saw Maud in the rear booth. Maud's appearance was a shock—this was the first time Kitty had ever seen the woman when she was not immaculately groomed and in command of herself. Maud's hair was pulled back helter-skelter into an unbecoming and untidy knot. She was without makeup. She had on tan shoes and carried a black purse. The top button of her blouse was in the wrong buttonhole, so that the neckline was pulled askew. On Maud these details stood out like red danger-signals. She was crushing out a cigarette with a hand that trembled. "Kitty—what did you tell the police?"

"About Ardis? Nothing, of course."

"Not about Ardis. About Hal." Maud waited while the waitress came over, took Kitty's order, and went away again. "About this mess with Dena."

Kitty scarcely knew what to answer. She had thought that Hal intended to deceive Maud about his presence at Dena's place.

"Speak up," Maud commanded curtly. "I know he was there. He went all to pieces this morning. If the police had waited five minutes longer, he'd have fallen into their hands like a rotten apple." Her tone grew savage. "He thought he'd fooled me. What a stupid idiot he is!"

Suddenly Kitty felt sorry for Hal. "I think he meant well from the beginning. He wanted to help Dena. But she put him on the spot with Baron, not showing up."

Maud shot her a quick look, as if surprised. After a moment she asked, "Did you tell the police anything about Hal in connection with this second attack?"

"Only that Dena was grateful for his getting her the job."

"They suspect something." Maud looked with empty distaste at the cup of coffee the waitress set in front of her. "They searched the house."

"Is that when they found Ardis?"

"No. Ardis simply walked out and gave herself up, as soon as Doyle arrived. She hasn't any more nerve than a mouse, actually. She couldn't stand the waiting, the fear, any longer. She'd rather just get it over with."

"I have to talk to Doyle," Kitty wailed, starting to rise. "I've got to make him understand —"

"Sit down." Maud pushed at her. "My God, if she didn't kill Sunny, they'll know it in time. Meanwhile, the rest of us get a breathing space. Look, I'll tell you what I want you to do. I want you to tell the police that although Dena was grateful to Hal for trying to get her the job with Waddell Brothers, she had decided not to take it. She had something better in the offing. Or so you thought."

"But Dena will tell them differently, when she's able to!"

"She may never be able to," Maud said cryptically.

"Won't it look strange, my suddenly remembering this information?"

"It might. Will you take that chance, Kit? For Hal and me?"

Kitty was reminded of Hal's frantic begging that she forget to mention his presence at Dena's apartment. He and Maud were now together in trying to cancel any evidence of his contact with the broken-down actress, and to put over the idea that Dena had even refused the offer of the job. All at once Kitty remembered something Professor Galem had said, a hint of curiosity about Hal's sudden urge to help Dena.

Kitty asked sharply, "Tell me, Maud—why did Hal try to get Dena the job at Waddell's?"

Maud's mouth twisted wryly. "Oh, a bad conscience, I guess. You know how obvious she was in working on people's sympathies."

"No, there must have been more than that. He'd turned her down on a part in his show. He could have worked her into it if he'd wanted to, a minor part somewhere."

Kitty saw rage flare in Maud's eyes. Then some movement near the door of the café drew Maud's glance, and she froze. She was as still as if she'd seen a ghost.

Kitty continued: "I hadn't thought, until now, that Hal's motive could have been anything except a real desire to help somebody on the rocks, as Dena surely was—"

"Shut up!" Maud hissed between clenched teeth.

Someone stopped at their table. Kitty turned, looked up. Doyle had his hat in his hand. His red hair was slicked down neatly. His eyes looked tired and wise. He said, "Good morning, Mrs. DeGraffen. Miss Quist. I'm sorry to interrupt, but business of this sort doesn't wait. Miss Quist, I'll have to ask you to come back to your apartment."

Kitty rose quickly, not missing the meaningful stare Maud bent on her, half-warning, half-hope.

"I'll try to see that you get to work on time," Doyle went on. "This concerns Miss Lake."

"Kitty," Maud cried, "I'll phone you after a while, at the University."

Kitty nodded. Her thoughts were busy with frantic plans for misleading Doyle in regard to Ardis. Ardis was so defenseless. Sunny had struck her where she lived, taking the man she loved, leaving her in torment that must have had its moments of almost insane hatred. There was motive there for murder. Doyle must be deceived, somehow.

They were on the sidewalk now. Doyle touched her elbow, turning her toward the apartment building two blocks away. "I talked to your boss on the phone, asking him to excuse us if we were a little late. He sounds like a nice guy."

"He is nice," Kitty said, her thoughts busy elsewhere.

"He had some very interesting ideas."

Kitty nodded, only half-hearing. She was wondering what his opening gambit concerning Ardis would be. Did he intend to try to use her to pin the murder on her friend?

"I wish you had been honest with us," Doyle went on, regretfully. "The truth doesn't hurt innocent people; it protects them. Of course, you were hampered in regard to Ardis Lake. She hadn't confided fully in you."

Kitty looked at him quickly. "Do you mean that Professor Galem told you—"

"No, no. I got it from Miss Lake herself. She had some idea of protecting herself by trying to hide, and of saving you trouble by keeping secrets. Whereas, in a way, your two stories corroborate each other, and might have given us a better lead if we'd had them both sooner."

Kitty remembered the point on which he had seemed to doubt. "You mean—she told you something about the dogs?"

"Dog," he corrected. "Just one. She saw it standing beside Sunny Walling's body, up there on Linders' road."

Kitty listened carefully, searching for a hint of disbelief in his tone. Had Ardis convinced him? "Then it's true, the thing Miss Linder somehow guessed. There was a trap set there. Sunny sent me on ahead. But I wasn't killed. She was."

"There was someone with the dog," Doyle said quietly. "Miss Lake claims not to be able to identify this person. It was just a shape, a dark form with a pale blotch for a face, standing off in the rain."

Again Kitty listened for a hint of doubt. It was not like Doyle to accept such a story without reservation.

"I am checking up on certain details," he went on, "which might help confirm her story. For one thing, she says she brought your shoe back. Remember—the one you said the dog took?"

They went up the stairs to the apartment, and Doyle followed her in. In her bedroom, he took the blue pumps off the rack and examined them. And now even Kitty could see, distinct in the satin, the marks of savage teeth.

CHAPTER THIRTEEN

Doyle set the two shoes carefully aside. He glanced at the array of clothes in the closet. "You didn't wear that white dress, either, did you?"

"No. The blue one. If you'll look you can see the marks left by the wetting it got."

"I'm not much of a detective," he muttered. "I take it you guessed that the shoe had been put back by Miss Lake, and you thought you were protecting her by lying."

"That's right," Kitty admitted stiffly.

"I'd like to see Miss Lake's room, now."

He carried the two blue pumps, following her as she led the way into Ardis's bedroom. Again he went to the closet. After a moment's search he pulled out the coat, the dirty, earth-smelling coat Ardis had worn two nights before. "This might give us something." He rolled the coat into a bundle, then began to look at shoes.

"Won't you tell me what Ardis's story is?"

He glanced up and back at her. "She claims that there was a telephone call, a voice which identified itself as that of Sunny Walling. At the time she didn't question the identification. Now she isn't sure. The voice told her to come to a rendezvous at the top of the grade on Du Moyne Avenue. She demurred. Then I gather that something was said about the young soldier, Burns, some offer made to show a letter from him, written just before he died. She's very reticent on this point, won't give out much information. She says, however, that she did go to keep the appointment. She took a cab, according to instructions, as far as the forty-five hundred block, then got out, dismissed the taxi, and walked."

Doyle's voice was dry, commonplace, without emotion. But Kitty's mind painted a picture of Ardis, alone in the buffeting dark, her face stung with rain, her hair blowing, walking up the hill in the hope of finding out, at last, whether young Burns had loved her again before he died.

"She claims that she saw the lights of Miss Walling's car through the rain, and walked in that direction. When she came even with the car, she could see ahead, past your stalled car, into the lane. Miss Walling lay there, the dog sitting near. She also caught a glimpse of someone, a dim figure she couldn't identify. The dog frightened her by rising and growling. She turned to run."

"That must have been a moment of sheer horror."

Doyle nodded. "I judge it was. She slipped and fell, stumbling down among the trees. She waited, expecting the dog to attack. When nothing happened after a moment or so, she pulled herself together, stood up, and tried to walk. She'd twisted her ankle, though, and it was temporarily useless and very painful. So she got into Miss Walling's car, backed it out of the lane, and drove away. Most of the time since, she says, has been spent in a desperate effort to get rid of the car without being involved in its disposal."

Even Kitty saw the thinness of the story. It seemed to be built upon just such facts as the police already had. The identity of the person off in the rainy dark was conveniently obscured. The story gave the police nothing new, no new track to start on.

"How did she find my shoe?"

"It was in the car."

"I might say that there *was* a telephone call. The ringing of the phone awakened me, sometime after I'd gone to bed."

"Any idea of what time it might have been?"

"No, I'm sorry. There might have been quite a lapse of time, or again—almost none."

"That last is a good guess. The autopsy has proved that Miss Walling didn't live over an hour after leaving the DeGraffen party."

"How do you know that?"

"Stomach contents. We know what she ate at the party."

"What about her mink wrap?"

He went back to examining Ardis's shoes. "We haven't found that yet."

"But you know who gave it to her."

He raised his reddish eyebrows at her. "Don't you?"

"Dena was going to tell me—or rather, she was teasing me with a half-promise to tell."

She saw the interest flicker behind his eyes. He stood up, faced her. "This is very interesting. You might have mentioned it before. Just what was it she said about the mink wrap?"

"She hinted that she knew who had given it to Sunny. Then when I tried to make an open question of it, she clammed up. I had a funny idea that she intended to use it to her own advantage. Dena has been looking for a break for a long while now."

Doyle's eyes were thoughtful. "That means that the information applied to someone who'd be able to help, probably professionally. DeGraffen was getting her a job. Didn't that coincidence strike you?"

Kitty remembered the story Maud had begged her to tell—that Dena had decided to turn down the chance to be Waddell's receptionist. But the lie stuck in her throat. She had a feeling that Doyle wouldn't be taken in. "I thought about it, just this morning. There's something else I've been wanting to ask. How is Dena? Will she live?"

"She's a fighter. They're giving her a fifty-fifty chance."

"Has she told you anything yet?"

He shook his head, cutting off further questions about Dena. Kitty realized that the police would be very wary about admitting information—or lack of it—until they were ready to act. As Aunt Dru had surmised, there must be a great deal of suspense in one guilty mind.

"You're guarding Dena carefully, of course," Kitty said, "since she's in danger until she can tell you who tried to kill her."

He was wrapping a second pair of shoes, Ardis's muddied ones, into the soiled coat, along with the other pair belonging to Kitty. "Don't worry on that score." He took Kitty's elbow. "I'll get you to work now, before you ask so many questions you know more than I do."

She found Professor Galem bursting with questions and theories.

He made her tell him in detail about finding Dena. She omitted any mention of Hal DeGraffen, but there must have been some awkwardness in her story, for he pounced with an interruption. "You were all alone, except for the injured woman?"

"Yes. Why should you think not?"

He pulled at his lip. His thick gray eyebrows went up, then down. He rubbed a hand over the close-cut, curly gray hair, making it stand a little further on end. "No reason. Just a hunch. You could have been requested to forget the presence of a third person. Am I embarrassing you? You're turning pink."

"With guilt," she admitted. "There was someone there. I lied to the police about it, too."

"Oh, dear." Professor Galem looked distressed. "That's not good. This Doyle fellow seems quite decent. You shouldn't be afraid of him."

"The person who was there was terrified of being mixed up in the affair. He said it meant professional ruin."

Professor Galem thought about it for a little while, a somewhat sleepy expression on his face. "DeGraffen. That's the one, isn't it? Notoriety wouldn't hurt these other two, especially. They're independent, being in business for themselves. I'm talking about the Linder brothers, of course."

"My mind keeps coming back to one striking fact," Kitty said. "It was *their* dog which was involved."

"You *think* it was their dog," Professor Galem corrected. "But the theory propounded by Charles Linder, that there was a third animal, isn't as stupid or farfetched as you seem to think."

In anger at herself, she plunged into the day's work.

After what seemed a short time, she looked up to find Professor Galem putting on his hat. "It's lunch time, you know," he reminded, "though I expect you might have overlooked it. Very busy, you are, and if I were a psychologist instead of a dabbler in physics, I'd say you had something on your mind. Or someone." His look was keen, though humorous, and Kitty had to control the urge to stammer excuses. He went on: "There is someone in the hall. I think he's waiting for you. A nice-looking young man."

Kitty remembered in a flash Aunt Dru's warning that Edmund might come to see her. She ran dismayed hands over her hair, tugged at her clothes, then rushed for the cubbyhole where the wash-basin and mirror permitted repairs. Professor Galem—the beast—snickered.

After five minutes, she went out into the hall. Charles Linder was leaning on the opposite wall in a manner that suggested he had wasted some time there. He straightened, came forward to meet her. "Hello. Might I, in my ogreish way, entice you to lunch? I'm waylaying you, you see, in the most accepted villainous manner. But the truth was, I caught several glimpses of Mr. Poodle-Cut in there, and I was afraid to snatch his secretary openly."

Kitty was smiling. He had an easy, graceful air. "I have an hour. How much ogreing can you do in that time?"

"You'd be surprised. Where do you eat in this temple of learning?"

"There's the faculty cafeteria."

"Sounds dreadful. It just struck me. No martinis."

"We couldn't have liquor on the campus. What would the regents say?"

He shook his head. "If you'll hike as far as the parking lot, I'll take you to more broad-minded spots."

They drove down to the Village, found a café. Charles Linder ordered cocktails as a preamble. "Have to get it right. The first step is always to ply 'em with liquor." Under his light tone Kitty sensed a more serious purpose. He turned at once to what must be on his mind. "I heard on a newscast about an hour ago that the police are holding your friend Miss Lake in the murder of the Walling woman."

"That's right," Kitty said. "She isn't guilty, though."

"What are they holding her for?"

"I suppose, until they can check her story."

"You're sure she's in the clear?"

Kitty's heart contracted with nervous fear, and she realized at the same time that she was putting a strange trust in Doyle, believing that he would be incapable of pinning Sunny's murder on Ardis. "She wouldn't have done the horrible thing that ... happened in your lane."

His gaze was studying, shrewd. "I notice you don't deny motive."

"Sunny Walling did a very cruel thing to Ardis. But months have passed since then. The police must realize that a motive based on jealousy and anger diminishes with time."

"Don't you think that depends on the personalities involved?"

"Ardis isn't a brooding type, nor does she magnify wrongs in a neurotic manner. She tried to forget young Burns, the man Sunny took from her."

"The all-powerful Sunny," he mused, tapping the table. "She sounds like something out of fiction. As a matter of fact, I had a character like her in that book I wrote. A femme fatale. Only I made my character slightly ridiculous. An old maid at heart, slightly bewildered by the wolfish response she roused in the male population."

Kitty said cautiously, "I was talking to Hal DeGraffen, and he mentioned that his agency handled the radio deal on your book."

"Mishandled is the word," Charles said with a touch of grimness. "I never saw such a bunch of knot-heads. They were so busy working in their stock radio personalities, the idiot comic who says *du-u-uh ... du-u-uh* and the other creeps, they finally lost all track of my yarn. I finally threw in the sponge. Of course it smelled, and of course the front office decided not to put it on, to look for something fresher. But now you mention DeGraffen—didn't I see his name mentioned in connection with the attack on this radio actress, this Miss Frayne? Something ... he was getting her a job ... or—"

"Yes, he was trying to help Dena out."

"As I remember him, not the good Samaritan type."

"I suppose he felt guilty—he'd turned her down on a part in a new television show. This job was to have been the receptionist at Waddell Brothers."

"I can't imagine that." He caught Kitty's surprised glance, and went on. "I met Miss Frayne somewhere or other during the time I expected my book to be made into a show. I had a lot of radio friends then, sudden and temporary. Anyway, as I remember Miss Frayne"—he smiled widely —"she was not what I would call the receptionist type."

"I think she might have made out. She is adaptable."

It seemed to Kitty that his glance sharpened. "Do the police expect her to live?"

"I guess she has an even chance."

He was thinking this over when the waitress returned. For the next few minutes they were busy ordering lunch.

"Did you ever meet Sunny Walling?" Kitty asked, when the waitress had gone.

His glance fixed on her. "I may have. I met hordes of people when I was on the agency merry-go-round. You've lived in Hollywood a while, I understand. You know how it is."

"Yes, I know."

His voice seemed to grow quieter. "Has my aunt been to see you?"

Kitty remembered, it was Edmund whom Aunt Dru didn't wish to know of her visit. "Yes, early this morning. She's upset over this second attack."

Charles was frowning. "I can't figure out what she's trying to do. Did she talk about Edmund to you?"

"She seemed more interested in Dena's condition. She thought the murderer might get into the hospital to strike again."

"She'd know better than that," he decided. "Perhaps she was just curious and wanted a firsthand account of finding the body. Aunt Dru puzzles me a lot. For instance, she's not doing Edmund any good with the police. It seems she let drop the fact that Edmund alone knew the dogs well enough to tell them apart. That interested the cops remarkably."

Kitty recalled that Aunt Dru had also mentioned, in front of Doyle, the incident of the broken lamp. It seemed that in some strange way she felt impelled to call attention to the small, puzzling items in Edmund's behavior—things which might in time be incriminating. Kitty felt baffled. Aunt Dru was a peculiar little old lady indeed.

The rest of the lunch passed without incident, until they rose to leave. There was a moment of awkwardness as Charles tried to leave the booth.

His right leg seemed to twist, to buckle. He caught at the booth wall to steady himself. "Damned cork leg of mine," he grinned ruefully.

It explained the stiffness, the uncertainty, she had sensed in his walk and manner of holding himself.

"A little memento of Saipan and a lieutenant who misread his orders," Charles said, standing erect. "I don't mind terribly. Don't go grieving over me."

Kitty wasn't struck with grief, exactly. She was remembering what Hal DeGraffen had told her, the reason that Edmund Linder had gone to prison. He'd beaten up an officer who was inept, whose stupidity had cost the lives of his men. "Were ... were you and your brother together during the war?"

He shot her a swift glance. Perhaps he wondered how much she had heard; or perhaps her face betrayed something. "Oh, very. Edmund always had the weird idea I needed looking after—a thoroughly boring attitude, I can tell you. We had some battles over it, and his feelings were hurt, and he didn't live with us for a while. All settled now. Don't worry."

He was offering an explanation for the interlude Aunt Dru had mentioned, when Edmund had got out of prison and had wanted to be alone. What a queer trio they were, Kitty thought, as she walked with Charles out into the street. Their relations among themselves seemed full of con-

flict, a struggle of wills. In one direction was everything smooth—Aunt
Dru's obvious admiration and affection for Charles, the favorite.

Charles returned Kitty to her office. "If I'm out this way again tomorrow, will you do a repeat on this?"

"Of course."

"Not still scared of the ogre?"

"Not a bit."

At her desk again, she allowed herself to puzzle over his motive in seeing her. It could be, she thought wryly, that he really likes me and I'm
being unnecessarily cynical about him. Or perhaps he's keeping track,
through me and other people, or what's happening in regard to Sunny's
murder—for reasons of his own. Her interest in the question was not
allowed to linger long. The phone rang; it was Doyle, wanting her to
come at once to the hospital.

He didn't say so, but Kitty got the impression that Dena wasn't doing
well. And Dena had something to tell. She wanted to tell it to Kitty.
There was an edge of urgency in Doyle's voice.

Panic thudded through Kitty as she put on her wraps. Dena had put
up such a good fight. All in such a short time, opportunity had seemed
to open up for her, then horrible savagery had struck her down.

Professor Galem came in as Kitty started for the door. He listened to
her explanation. "Look, we'll close up shop here for today. I'll drive you
downtown. Save time in more ways than one; I won't have to wait for
the news of what's happening."

He put his hat back upon the poodle haircut and they went out together.

CHAPTER FOURTEEN

The hospital was quiet, the corridor shadowy and empty except for a
door at the end where a uniformed policeman sat uncomfortably in a
straight white chair. Doyle guided Kitty toward this door, took her in after a brief nod to the officer. The room was dim. A nurse stood beside the
bed. The one spot of color was the coppery glow of Dena's hair spread
out on the pillow. Her face was gray, her voice a husky whisper. "Hello,
Kitty." Her jaw and throat was wrapped with bandages, and there was
another white swathe across her forehead. "I look like hell, and it isn't
early in the morning either."

Doyle's glance at Dena was exasperated, and Kitty guessed that
there had been some conflict here. He had wanted Dena to talk fully. She
had asked instead for Kitty.

"Sit down," Doyle said to Kitty. He jerked his head at the nurse and she went out of the room.

"You, too, copper," Dena whispered.

His glance jumped from Dena to Kitty, linking them in feminine wiliness and bullheadedness. "What a pair you are." Then he, too, stalked out of the room.

"He amuses me," Dena said, in her strained, husky voice. "So damned transparent. He makes me think of a guy I almost married once. A damned movie writer. Always suspicious."

Kitty touched Dena's hand gently. "Perhaps you shouldn't talk a lot."

Dena raised her eyebrows. "What's the matter? Have they got you believing that boloney, that I've practically got a toe inside St. Peter's gate? Nuts. You know, Kitty, I'm too tough to die. Here, raise me a little. Wind that hoot-nannie at the foot of the bed. Go on!"

Kitty thought guiltily that if Dena had been supposed to sit up, the nurse would have attended to it. She hesitated. Then, under Dena's urging, she obeyed. The head of the bed rose and Dena nodded in satisfaction. She went on talking. "They almost had me convinced, too, until I suddenly saw through what they were trying to do. They thought if I believed I was dying I'd spill everything I knew."

Kitty was appalled. "But you should, Dena! They should be told who did this terrible thing to you."

"If I knew, I'd tell them," Dena rasped. "Hell, I don't remember a thing beyond about the fifth drink. I was celebrating. Celebrating the job. And that brings us to the errand I've got for you. I want you to tell that bitch that the job better be ready for me when I walk out of the hospital."

Kitty sat dumfounded. She thought for an instant that Dena must be referring to the receptionist at Waddell's. Then she realized that there must be some other meaning behind the remark. "Who?"

"That damned DeGraffen woman, of course," Dena snapped, as though the truth must be obvious. "You tell her old Dena's still perking and that there hasn't a damned thing happened to my memory."

Anger swept through Kitty at the woman's foolish avarice. "What do you mean about Maud? I'm not running any errand until I know the facts."

Dena's stare was belligerent. "That woman's your friend, isn't she? You'd like to keep her out of trouble."

"I thought she was more your friend than mine," Kitty said coolly. "I have liked Hal and Maud, ever since I met them. But we're not exactly bosom pals. And I wouldn't conceal something from the police to protect her."

"Wouldn't you? I have a strange hazy memory of Hal DeGraffen being with you, staring at me in that closet. A very fugitive impression, of course. But interesting. A little interlude of light in a long stretch of darkness. You can tell me I was wrong, but I won't believe you."

Kitty refused to be swayed or be drawn into an argument. "You're going to tell me what you've got on Maud, or no dice."

"You didn't tell the cops about Hal DeGraffen."

"I mean it, Dena."

All at once Dena threw secrecy to the winds. "Oh, hell, I haven't the pep to fight over it. At the party the other night, Maud went out with Sunny—all the way out. She didn't come back. I think she followed Sunny. A long time later I saw her sneak in through the side door of the bar. Guess what she was carrying over her arm?"

There was only one possible answer. "The mink stole."

"Give that lady the sixty-four dollars," Dena jeered weakly.

"But how stupid! Why should Maud deliberately incriminate herself like that?"

"Because that stole has been a stone in her craw for a long, long time, baby." Dena was grinning, a strange caricature of a smile on her damaged face. "Don't you really know the story of that damned mink?"

"No."

"Maud's a little nuts on the subject. Hal gave it to Sunny. She was playing around with young Burns then, and he got scared that the affair might be serious."

"Hal—and *Sunny?*"

"Poor child," said Dena pityingly. "Really, I hate to tell you all this dirt. You're going to find out what all these people are actually like. And they aren't nice. Not the DeGraffens."

"But ... but Maud made it a point to have Sunny around, to invite her—" In Kitty's disbelieving mind rose the memory of Maud's amused smile, her attitude of wry condonement.

"Maud's a gal who would never let you know you'd got inside her guard. She wouldn't cut Sunny, or even give her a chilly glance, if it killed her. But the mink stole, and Sunny's flaunting it, must finally have gotten her down."

Fragments of memory rushed through Kitty's mind. There was the thing Maud had said about Sunny's mink wrap: given by a producer who must remain anonymous because he had a wife. Jeering at herself, really. And then the cynical tolerance Maud had displayed toward Sunny's many conquests.... "But you're implying, then, that Maud killed Sunny!"

"Sunny was due. She was overdue."

In the distaste she felt over Dena's cold attitude, Kitty was reminded of what Ardis had said when she'd learned of Sunny's death: *And high time, too.*

Dena went on in the weak, whispering voice. "I've never known another woman so thoroughly a slut that she could match Sunny Walling. I think she must have been fundamentally sick, somehow, either something wrong with her glands or in her noggin."

Kitty thought, in a kind of mental hysteria: I came in here feeling sorry for poor Dena because she was dying. And all she wants is the pressure kept on her blackmail plot. She's as full of plans and energy as a bear in a honey-tree.

"I won't keep a secret like this," Kitty said. "The police have Ardis; probably they're trying to pin Sunny's murder on her. If they knew what Maud had done, they'd let Ardis go."

"You let out a peep, and I'll play dead dog," Dena affirmed. "I'll tell them you came here with a crackbrained idea to help out your little friend Miss Lake, and tried to force me to put it over."

Kitty's temper was growing waspish. "And then what will you use as an excuse for wanting to see me?"

Dena shrugged. "I'll say I was warning you about somebody else."

"Who?"

Suddenly Dena's eyes were veiled and secretive. "Maud's not the only one hiding dirty linen, Kitty." Dena's hands withdrew, hid themselves under the edge of the coverlet as though some involuntary movement might give away some secret.

"What are you talking about now?"

Dena pinched her mouth Shut. "If you're worried about your little friend, why not suggest to Doyle that he search a bit for that stole? Like in the DeGraffen house?"

"You know he won't find it," Kitty surmised, remembering that Maud had said that the police had made a search that morning.

"No, they won't find it, but it'll keep Maud in a co-operative mood. Have you seen her today, by the way?"

"Yes. She wanted me to tell the police that you'd decided to turn down the job at Waddell's. She was very insistent, in fact."

Dena's eyes twinkled between gray, puffy lids. "Well, well—she must be worried!"

"Dena, you're a scoundrel. Hal pretended to me that Maud didn't know about his getting you a job. What did you do? Go to him, ask him to protect Maud by giving you a job?"

Dena nodded. "I knew he'd run to her with it before long. He's always yapping about women, how dumb they are. I figured long ago it was a defense mechanism. He clings to Maud, actually, like a kid to a mother's apron strings. And he cuddled up to Sunny like the stupidest juvenile."

"Nevertheless, I can't go to Maud with this nonsense," Kitty said in exasperation. "If she murdered Sunny, what's to prevent her getting annoyed with me and disposing of me in the same way?"

"You'll be all right. Do it for poor old Dena. I've needed a break for a long, long time. And don't make up your mind definitely about Maud's guilt. As I said, there are other people who had knives sharpened for that Walling bitch." Dena's gray pallor seemed to increase. "I'm tired now, Kitty. You'll have to run along and let poor grandma get her snooze in. Don't forget what I told you to do." Dena's eyes drifted shut. Her face looked putty-colored, lifeless.

As in response to some psychic summons, the nurse stuck her head in at the door. When she saw the lifted bed, she let out a squawk of dismay. She ran in and began to wind the little handle, letting Dena sink flat again. All the time she was telling Kitty what she thought of visitors who meddled with her patients.

Kitty went out into the hall. Doyle wasn't in sight. Professor Galem was talking to the uniformed cop, pumping him probably in regard to any interesting experiences he'd had lately. The Professor's mind was as quick, as omnivorous, as any of his thinking-machines at the University.

Walking to the car, Kitty told him of Dena's request.

"Are you going to do it?" he asked, looking at her sidewise.

"I don't know."

"You'll do it," he decided, "because you want to know what Mrs. De-Graffen will say when you spring it on her."

Kitty wondered to herself if she ought to quit and look for another job. Professor Galem was getting to know her too well for comfort.

"I wonder why Lieutenant Doyle didn't wait to try to pump me?"

"He said something about a date with a Dictaphone," Professor Galem said with dry humor, opening the car door.

Kitty was stunned, then angry with herself for not guessing sooner that Doyle, before giving up so easily to Dena's request for privacy, would have seen to it that he had a listening-post. It was useless to go to Maud's. The police would be on their way there now; they'd take the place apart with tweezers, if necessary, to get that mink wrap. Then Kitty thought of Hal. He might still be in his office, still unaware of what was closing in on him and his wife. "You can drop me at Sunset and Vine," she told the Professor.

"Need any help?" he wondered hopefully.

She knew his interest was based on curiosity. "I'll telephone you and tell you if anything exciting pops."

There was another receptionist at Waddell Brothers' desk—an older woman with metallic gray hair, fuchsia lipstick, an unnaturally pointed bosom inside a gray cashmere dress. "What may I do for you, Miss?"

The look had studied her, weighed her as nothing, in the flash of an instant. The woman had an air of long experience, and Kitty wondered if she was a permanent replacement for the blonde. Dena's chances did-n't look too good.

"I'd like to see Mr. DeGraffen."

"He's over at NBC," said the gray-headed woman, implying that this was the natural habitat of an advertising man. "Would you like to wait?"

"I'll try to catch him." Kitty hurried out, went down the block to the massive green building which housed the broadcasting company. She went over to the lobby desk. "It's very important that I contact Mr. De-Graffen, of Waddell Brothers. He's in the building." She tried to look like an executive's secretary panicked by the thought of losing a big account through missing her boss.

The bored girl behind the grill, importuned all day by ticket-seekers, autograph-hunters, and hick writers with ideas for new radio pro-grams, all but yawned in Kitty's face. She turned to a page standing nearby. "Ted, do you know a Mr. DeGraffen?"

"Sure. He's with Mr. Wix."

"He's in conference with our Mr. Wix," the girl said kindly to Kitty.

"I've *got* to see him!" Kitty pounded on the rim of the counter with her fist. The girl watched the movement as if from a great distance, or from within a vast core of indifference.

"You could get into Mr. Wix's office if you had an appointment," she sug-gested.

Kitty's urge for acting a part deserted her suddenly. She leaned to-wards the receptionist and was on the point of saying "To hell with Mr. Wix!" when the page spoke up.

"There's Mr. DeGraffen now."

Kitty looked around, then walked over to Hal, who had just come down the steps from the upper floor and had paused with an air of uncertainty. When he recognized Kitty, his expression was not exactly one of wel-come. He managed a smile, but it was weak. "Hello, there, Kit."

"Hal, I must talk to you."

He licked his lips. "Not here."

It seemed to Kitty that the lobby of NBC, with people hurrying about them, was about as private as one would wish. Anyone who stopped to listen would stand out like Martin and Lewis doing a routine in the mid-dle of the lobby floor. But she saw Hal's air of jumpy fear, of nervous ha-rassment. Either Mr. Wix had been exceptionally stormy, or Hal's pri-vate life was deteriorating. He was definitely less well groomed, his eyes haunted, lines of pessimism and defeat graven into his face.

They headed for the Brown Derby as if wolves were after them, and Hal stopped at the bar for a quick one before going into the dining room with Kitty. He summoned a waiter. "We'll have a couple of old-fash-ioneds. Make mine a double. Yours, too, Kitty?"

Kitty declined the double whisky. "You don't seem curious about what I have to say, Hal."

He looked at her with his haunted stare. "Sorry. Didn't mean to seem rude. I've got a lot on my mind these days. Old Baron is riding us with a bull-whip. He's had an efficiency man in the offices, as if there weren't hell enough already. He's trying to run an advertising agency like a canning factory—and you can't do it. Too much depends on personal push, individual effort. And personality. That's the core of the advertising business. The human element." All at once Hal seemed to run out of words. The look of defeat increased. "It's about Maud, isn't it? She came to see you this morning." He grabbed the old-fashioned as the waiter set it down.

"No, this is about Dena."

"She's dead?" He set down the drink abruptly. Kitty couldn't tell if his look was one of hope or not. She thought he was fundamentally a kindly man. Right now he was not his normal self.

"Very much the opposite. She sent a message. She wants the job at Baron's kept open for her."

"Good God, I haven't a prayer! If Dena had showed up this morning, had an interview, made a good impression—well, there would have been a chance. As it was, the other receptionist had to leave sooner than she'd expected—some family emergency—and Baron got hold of a woman he'd known before. She's as cold as a steel knife, and just as businesslike. Maybe you saw her."

"I saw her. Dena isn't interested in excuses, Hal."

He shot her a look from under a frown. "You sound as if you know quite a bit about this."

"I know that it concerns Maud's having Sunny Walling's mink wrap right after Sunny was murdered."

He turned pale, then red. His lower lip puckered. "You listen to me, Kit. Dena's way off the beam. It was *I* who followed Sunny from our house that night, not Maud. I won't have Maud taking the heat off me that way, no, not even if it means old Baron kicking me bodily out into Sunset Boulevard!" He rubbed his hands distractedly through his thinning hair. "Why in God's name didn't I get out of this racket years ago! Maud and me—we've been on a merry-go-round. I was trying to protect her, she was trying to protect me. I was stalling Dena with the job. Maud brought Ardis home to pump her, to make sure she hadn't seen me up there where Sunny died."

"Then you were the one Ardis must have caught a glimpse of in the rain!"

"I guess so. I saw some girl up there, didn't get a close look at her. The cops tipped us off, coming looking for her at our house. Maud put two and two together. I was still trying to keep Dena's little blackmail a secret. This morning I—I let it slip."

"You took Sunny's mink wrap. Did you kill her, Hal?"

"Will you believe me if I say I didn't?" He shook his head. "Whatever possessed me to take it, anyway? I must have been crazy. It seemed to me that it made a link between me and Sunny, something the cops could get their teeth into—I didn't have sense enough to know that its being gone would make even more of a mess..." He groaned dismally into his hands.

The waiter was stealing glances their way. Kitty got the impression that Hal's edge-of-disaster appearance had attracted the notice of others than herself. She said, "Let's go, Hal. Let's walk a while."

He followed her with a shambling, loose-jointed gait. On the sidewalk, though, he spoke with sudden energy. "Just get one thing straight. It was the dog. I was there, I saw it. The dog's the guilty one."

CHAPTER FIFTEEN

"Why didn't you just tell the police that, at the very beginning?" Kitty demanded with some heat.

He stared doggedly out into the traffic. "I keep trying to explain, if you'd just listen—I can't afford to be mixed up in this mess over Sunny. You don't know old Baron. He's a bear. He's been married to one viperish old woman for almost thirty years, and he hates the idea of ... of anybody playing around, having fun. Sin. He's always harping on sin. He'll sit down and plan an ad campaign with nothing but practically naked girls in it, and at the same time he's writing letters to the vice squad about moral conditions in Hollywood. Oh, God, Kit—I'm cracking up. I've got to go home and take a pill and go to bed."

He did look hollow-eyed, despairing. Kitty felt the familiar rise of pity. "The police will be at your house now, Hal. They had a tip-off about the stole."

"Dena ... Dena—she—" His face turned almost purple with rage.

"Dena didn't tell the police anything," Kitty said.

"Then you —"

Kitty shook her head. "You and Maud can't blame anyone but yourselves for a blunder, Hal. If the dog is the only guilty one, and you knew it, you had no business creating a mystery."

He grated his teeth, his lips drawn back like an animal's. "Dammit, don't be dense. The damned dog had been put there, hadn't he? Somebody had sicked him on Sunny. Who's to prove it wasn't me?"

"I was there earlier," she reminded him, "and only a miracle saved me from that brute."

He shook his head. "Have the cops admitted that it was the dog?"

Kitty remembered Doyle's queer evasiveness on the question. "No, not exactly."

"Then you can bet your boots there's more to it than that. A drug, maybe. It could have been slipped into Sunny's drinks at our house. She had plenty of people around who wouldn't mind slipping her a dose of knockout drops if they thought she'd wind up in Linder's road with one of his bloodhounds."

"But there's a matter of time," Kitty objected. "Sunny was supposed to follow me almost immediately. Yet a long while elapsed before Ardis stumbled on her body up there in front of the Linder house. I had time to go home, pin up my hair, get into bed and fall asleep, even to sleep awhile, before the telephone call came which summoned Ardis to that rendezvous with a corpse. And then Ardis had to dress, to get a cab, to drive part of the way to the top of the ridge, and to walk the rest of it. All this happened between the time Sunny was supposed to have left the party and the time Ardis found her dead." She took Hal's arm, forced him to walk with her, though he seemed to cringe away. "What did Sunny do after she left your house? You followed her. Tell me."

He evaded the question. "Some dope takes longer to act than others."

"I don't think Sunny was given knockout drops at your house. Neither do you. I think she might have been knocked out by a blow or possibly strangled, then the dog set to maul and finish her off. The dog was there, I know from a very unpleasant experience, and he was bent on murderous business. But what took Sunny up there to meet him—so long after she'd have thought I'd be there? You know. Come on, Hal."

He rubbed his forehead with a shaking hand. "I can't talk standing here in the street. I've got to sit down, to relax. I need another drink."

Kitty was struck with an inspiration. "Come up to my place. I've got a bottle in the cupboard. I'll mix you a drink."

He looked at her as if befuddled. "You will?"

"Sure I've had plenty of drinks at your house. Let me serve you one for a change."

She could see that the idea of rest, of reprieve, appealed to him. On her part she was more determined than ever now to get out of Hal the truth about Sunny's actions preceding the murder. There must be some detail in the story which would clear Ardis once and for all.

She and Hal sneaked into the agency parking lot like a pair of thieves. Hal assured her that Baron's spies were everywhere, that Baron himself might easily be looking out of a rear window at the agency this moment, and that he would not be above calling Hal in for an accounting of work accomplished as of this hour—Kitty thought to herself that Hal was almost psychotic on the subject of Baron. He seemed obsessed by the man.

Hal drove his Cadillac out through the alley and headed for Kitty's place. Occasionally he mumbled indistinguishable remarks to himself. He seemed sunk in some abyss of wretchedness and confusion. The drinks he had had appeared to have dulled the fright that Kitty had originally sensed in him.

In her apartment, he fell on the couch and sat hunched, blankfaced, his hands clenched in his lap. Kitty went to the kitchen, set out two glasses. He seemed well on the way to getting drunk and wanting to get drunk, and it wouldn't do any good to water his drinks. She made his stiff, hers light, and took them into the living room. She had been gone at the most five minutes. But now Hal looked entirely different.

He was sitting erect, his face gray, his eyes staring. One arm was raised in a blocking, defensive attitude.

"What's wrong, Hal?" She set the small tray on the coffee table.

The words he said struck her with a jolt of astonishment. "The dog," he muttered. "I saw the dog. There in the doorway." He pointed. His hand was steady. His eyes didn't waver.

Kitty looked where he pointed because his attitude of fear and surprise was so convincing. The door was shut, of course, exactly as she had shut it on coming in. In the kitchen she had heard no sound to indicate that the door had opened. Most of the time—not always—the latch squeaked a little when the knob was turned. There hadn't been any squeak. The kitchen, such a short distance down the hall, with the door open, was well within earshot. She said, puzzled, "I don't see a thing, Hal."

He turned his eyes to her, and again she got the impression that he was haunted, that some inner torment had taken over. It occurred to her that Hal must be seeing things. The drinking could have started earlier, might have been going on all afternoon. The dog was a hallucination.

Hal licked his lips. "You didn't hear the dog? You didn't hear him growl?"

"No."

His hands fell into his lap. He waited as if listening, his eyes fixed and still, his body tense. "Don't open the door, Kit," he whispered.

In spite of her conviction that he was seeing illusions, Kitty felt a chill of terror creep up her spine. It was difficult not to believe in the dog, the vicious beast waiting on the landing on the other side of the door. Then she recalled her previous fright and its solution, and she wondered if Aunt Dru might be out there with Saladin. Perhaps the door had drifted open and Aunt Dru, seeing Hal, had thought Kitty was entertaining a man; it was the sort of thing that would logically embarrass

the little old lady. Perhaps Aunt Dru had stolen down again. Kitty went
to the window to look down. The sidewalk was empty except for a very
small girl in a blue pinafore, riding a kiddy-car. Kitty went over to the
door then, reached for the knob. But Hal cried, "Don't! For God's sake,
don't!"

She hesitated, restrained by the hoarse fear in his voice.

"Listen!" His haunted eyes burned in his gray face. A shudder ran over
him, shaking his arms, his hands, his big frame.

The room was silent.

All at once Hal reached for one of the drinks on the table. "I don't feel
good," he muttered. He downed about half of the stiff mixture.

Kitty forgot about the dog. It had been a figment of Hal's imagination.
She went over to sit beside him on the couch.

He looked at her queerly. "You really didn't hear the door open?"

"No, Hal, I didn't."

"Nor the growl."

"No."

"What do you think it was?"

She thought about it for a few moments. "I think it was something left
over from that horror in Linders' lane, a trick of the mind reliving its
fright."

"You saw that dog up there, didn't you? That morning when you
came to see me—when was it?"

"Just two days ago," Kitty supplied.

"—and I sat there big-eyed listening to your yarn about the dog, did-
n't you get any hint I'd seen him too? Didn't I really give that away?"

"No. I didn't dream you'd been up there, too."

"I keep thinking people can ... can sort of read my mind," Hal stammered. "Like Maud. I had to tell her all at once about Dena's proposition; I thought in some subtle way she already knew. Only she didn't.
And she flew at me like a witch. I tried to tell her that in a way I'd been
protecting her, too. She was the one who met me outside, saw me with
the stole, trying to stick it into some shrubbery, and she took it inside—
where Dena saw her."

He downed the rest of the drink, sank back into the cushions, sat there
inert as if discouraged.

"Dena seemed sure that it was Maud who had followed Sunny," Kitty
said, wondering if Hal was lying.

He shook his head. "Dena made a mistake. I didn't try to set her right.
I just let her think I was protecting Maud."

"You haven't said why you followed Sunny, Hal."

He didn't answer at once. He seemed to be turning something over in
his mind, some puzzle. Or perhaps some lie. It was finally with an air

of unwillingness that he said, "Sunny had a deal on the fire. I don't know what it was. I don't know if it concerned one of the Linders. Sunny was a very mercenary baby, so I guess money figured in it somewhere. It had something to do with that lane up there, the turn-off from Du Moyne. She'd been there before. I caught her leaving there one day, one evening about twilight, and she was dressed up in the damnedest garb I'd ever seen outside a museum. Like a mummy. I almost didn't recognize her."

Kitty couldn't make sense of it. She wondered if Hal had fished up this wild red herring to get her curiosity away from Maud. Was he really that loyal to his wife, in spite of the admitted affair with Sunny? She remembered the attitude he and Maud had held toward each other and their marriage—a jeering tolerance, more poking-fun than love. Perhaps they were like that because they were sophisticated people, too worldly wise for the common type of matrimony. Or perhaps they thought it was what their world, their friends, expected of them. It could have been a mask for genuine affection. Or it could cover boredom, loss of interest—even hatred.

"What do you think she could have been doing?" Hal demanded.

Kitty wondered if he was testing her, probing for doubt in her mind. "It sounds very strange."

"Sunny wasn't deep," he said. "She was even a little transparent."

"I can't imagine your getting mixed up with her," Kitty told him.

His face crumpled with self-pity. "I'm getting old, Kit. I get into a kind of panic, sometimes. Sunny made me feel—oh, there's no use trying to explain it to a woman."

"Don't underestimate women, always, Hal." Her mind added: *Don't underestimate Maud, either; she had a perfect reason for murdering Sunny.* But how could she bring in the dog? Was the dog, as Charles Linder had half-gibingly said, a ringer, a stranger?

"There's much more I want to know—" she began, but he shook his head.

"Run the errand first."

"Then you'll talk about Sunny, about what she did the night of her murder?"

He nodded. He looked shrunken and tired. "Before you go, bring the bottle, Kit. Leave it on the table."

She did as he asked, then grabbed her coat and started for the door. He'd already downed a quick one straight; he hissed at her sharply, and looking back, she thought how very much drunker he seemed. "Not that door," he whispered.

"You think the dog's still out here?" she demanded, her hand reaching for the knob.

"Well, the cops might have an eye on that front entry," he evaded.

She tried not to show her concern over Hal's persistent delusion, which he had tried to cover weakly by mention of the police. "Very well, I'll go out the back," she said, humoring him.

"When you see Maud ..." He broke off. "I guess you'll know what to say. Don't let her take the blame for me. Tip the cops if you have to, then give me a ring so I can start running."

"There's no need to run," Kitty said with irritation. "Why not tell them your story? They've already heard from me about the dog. It shouldn't be too hard to convince them you're telling the truth."

His glance sneaked back toward the door. "No, no," he replied, dropping his voice to a whisper. "I can handle this. I'll clear things up first."

Kitty went out through the kitchen, the rear stairs. Hal had left the keys in his Cadillac; she used it to drive up Du Moyne, over the hill— she passed the Linders' short street and saw the house, peaceful and well kept and mellow in the late afternoon sun. Over in the valley on the other side of the ridge she turned into Hal's street, parked by his big gate, went in to ring the doorbell.

Doyle came to the door, trying, Kitty thought, to suppress a smirk. His eyes had the familiar look of having seen too much for his young life. He cocked a red eyebrow at her. "Oh, Miss Quist. Been expecting you— sooner, though. You made a detour from the hospital here."

"I don't care anything about that stole. It doesn't prove murder," she said. "I'd like to talk to Mrs. DeGraffen if she's here, and if you give your permission."

His eyes grew distant. "You'll want to talk in private again, I suppose, hmm?"

"Minus a Dictaphone, if you please."

"Mrs. DeGraffen isn't here. Lots of fugitive people these days. We have a warrant for her, so I think you'd better answer truthfully when I ask— do you know where she is?"

"No, I don't."

"Quite a coincidence, but we have a warrant for Mr. DeGraffen, too, and we'd like very much to see him. Certain parts of his story interest us."

For some reason, Kitty thought of Sylvia somebody, the girl with the pouting mouth, and she had a hunch Doyle had put the girl through the hoops and discovered that Hal hadn't been with her when he was supposed to have been.

Doyle's glance held a warning. No more lies. Kitty had a sudden hint of fear for this pleasant young red-headed detective who had a genius for digging up bits of information and making traps for liars out of them.

"Do you know where Mr. DeGraffen might be keeping himself?"

"Have you tried his agency?" Kitty stuttered.

"They said he was gone. A young lady had come looking for him." There was a stony set to Doyle's jaw, and his voice was grating.

Kitty's mind ran in a circle. Hal's story should be told to the police. It was, in some respects, corroboration for her own. Hal's fear of the imaginary dog was an indication that he was not himself, a hint that instructions given now might best be disregarded. It was really to Hal's best interest for him to contact the police. "He's at my apartment."

"He sent you scouting?" Doyle asked.

"He was worried about Mrs. DeGraffen."

"I suppose he's going to take the blame for bringing Miss Walling's mink stole to the house?"

"Yes." Kitty saw that to Doyle it was just another lie, another subterfuge; and she wondered if he ever saw people in a murder case as human and frightened and acting under the extreme of desperation.

"Let's go talk to him." Doyle came out and took her arm and led her back to Hal's Cadillac. "I'll follow you in the official car. Wait for me on the sidewalk, will you—out of sight of your windows."

"You're afraid I'll warn him?" Kitty's lip curled.

"Give me credit for one act of charity today," Doyle said patiently. "I spoke to your Professor Galem about the Dictaphone, so you wouldn't come tearing out here and blunder into a police net. Do me a favor in return. Don't try to tip off Hal DeGraffen that I'm coming."

He walked away and got into his own car. Kitty started the Cadillac. She drove the way she had come.

As she crested the hill, she glanced at the Linder house. Aunt Dru was on the porch, in an apron, shaking a small rug from the banister. The big yellow dog stood beside her.

The scene was peaceful, domestic, even a little old-fashioned. Few women shook out rugs any more. They preferred the easier way of the vacuum cleaner. Yes, Kitty thought—the scene was an odd one for the luxurious home.

She drove down into the city, parked down the street from her flat, waited there for Doyle. When he came up, he gave her a tentative half-smile, but she ignored it. She led the way, walking a little stiff-legged, feeling a little ridiculous, too, because now Doyle didn't seem like a cop. He trotted beside her with the friendly wistfulness of a pup.

They went up the stairs. Doyle cautioned her with a look, then reached for the knob. He threw open the door. For an instant he remained here, blocking Kitty's view. Then he turned as if to shove her backward. But in turning he revealed what was in the room.

Hal still sat on the couch, but he didn't look the same. He hung drunkenly against the arm of the couch, his head thrown back. Before he had died, he had tried to fight off ... something. His clothes were torn, soaked with blood. There was no way to describe his face and throat.

Kitty started back down the stairs—headfirst. Doyle's grabbing her was like part of a dream; his shout was an echo of the roaring in her skull.

CHAPTER SIXTEEN

She came out of it all at once and sat up, wide awake, on the bed. A woman she recognized as the neighbor in the downstairs flat rose from a chair and went to the door. She beckoned to someone, down the hall in the direction of the living room. Then she came back to Kitty. "Do you feel ill?"

"No, I'm all right." Kitty tried to orient herself. Judging by the look of the dying afternoon, it was only a short while since she and Doyle had come up the stairs. There was no disorder here. She had on all her clothes and she'd been lying on the bedspread. She got the impression that Doyle had dumped her here (cursing, probably, at the delay) and then gone on about his business. She rubbed hair back from her face. Her shoulder ached as she moved her arm, and she remembered Doyle's clutch at her as she had started to fall, and the painful wrench as he had jerked her back from the tunnel of the stairs.

Sounds penetrated—she heard crying noises, a woman's crying, and then Maud's voice, almost unrecognizable, babbling in a high, hysterical shriek.

She got up, frightened, driven by the need to know; and though the neighbor woman stood up and said something about waiting for Doyle, Kitty pushed past her. She hesitated at her doorway, then braced herself and went on. She glanced in at the open door of the kitchen. Maud was in there with a policewoman, a neatly uniformed lady cop. The policewoman was trying to get Maud to drink a cup of black coffee. But Maud stared at the world through the lacing of her shaking fingers, and what she said had neither sense nor coherence. She looked at Kitty without out a sign of recognition.

Doyle was beside Kitty all at once. There was no hint of the smirk, and his face seemed old enough to match his eyes. "Go back to your bedroom."

Things pounded through her head, things like this being her apartment and how dare he order her around in a voice he might use for a park bum. She opened her mouth to say something, but he merely grabbed her and shoved her back into the bedroom and came in after her. He looked at the neighbor woman, a dismissing look. "Thank you very much for staying with Miss Quist."

"You're quite welcome." The woman scurried out as if something about Doyle had scared her.

"Now," he said in a voice like a sigh. "Let's hear it. Let's hear it real straight and clear for once. I don't know why you lied for DeGraffen, saying he wasn't with you when you found Miss Frayne. But that used up your quota, Miss Quist—I want the bare facts, no embellishments, no omissions."

She sat down on the bed to get out of range of hitting him while she gained control. He was a loathsome man.

"I can't figure out whether you lie for fun, or for practice, or if you're possibly stupid enough to lie for these people because they ask you to."

He sat down beside her, well within striking range. Kitty clenched her fists. Then she winced; her shoulder had hurt her.

"What's the matter?" he asked.

"You almost tore my arm off," she gritted at him.

"Sorry. You were swan-diving downstairs. I may have saved your neck."

"Thank you," she spat.

"I'll have the police doctor look at you when he's through with DeGraffen," Doyle offered.

"I'll get my own doctor."

He began to light a cigarette. He sat slumped, as if he was tired all at once. "Okay. Any way you say. When did you meet DeGraffen this afternoon? And why?"

She told him, flatly, as he had asked, without embellishment. "I thought you'd be at the house and have Maud and there wouldn't be any way I could put pressure on her, using the information Dena had given me. I remembered Hal, then. He might not have heard about you and your Dictaphone. I found him at NBC, and we went to the Brown Derby and then came here. He was tight. He had something on his mind which he didn't explain to me. He just wanted to get drunk. At one time during his stay here he thought that he saw the dog, the Linders' dog, at the door. I think it must have been a hallucination. Finally he asked me to go to check up on Maud, and I went."

"Why are you so sure that it was a hallucination?" Doyle wondered.

"There wasn't any evidence, just his imagining it."

"You looked out onto the front landing?"

Kitty started to say yes, thoughtlessly, and then recalled how Hal had stopped her each time she had put a hand on the doorknob. "No. He seemed so uneasy, I humored him."

"You don't know, then, whether the dog was there or not."

"What are you trying to make me say?" she flared. "That the dog was there and I knew it and I deliberately left Hal here alone so he could be murdered?"

"What did he think this mysterious dog looked like?" Doyle asked, ignoring what she had just said.

"He said it was the dog in Linders' lane, the dog that killed Sunny."

"He told you about being up there?"

With deadly patience, Kitty related to him the few facts which Hal had
admitted: that he had followed Sunny when she left the party, that he
had been present when Ardis had discovered the body in the rain. "He
wouldn't tell me what I really wanted to know, the events in between.
He wouldn't account for the lost time."

Doyle didn't get excited over the lost time. "This queer business today—did he say the dog lunged at him? Did he hear it growl?"

"He said it growled."

"And who was with it? Who was standing on the landing beside the
dog?"

She stared at him blankly. "Why ... no one. He didn't mention any person."

"That isn't logical."

"I can't help it. He didn't say anything about a person there."

"Perhaps the idea hadn't occurred to you," Doyle said smoothly, "that
the dog must have been brought by someone."

She felt color flame in her face. "Do you think I made this all up? That
it's a concoction to cover some actions of mine?"

"It's hard to know, Miss Quist, just what is true and what is false in
any story you tell." He stood up from the bed and went out of the room.
Kitty heard the front door open in the other room, the murmur of voices.
He was asking some expert or other to decide if there had been a dog
on the landing. He didn't come back afterward, and his absence was
somehow an indication that he thought Kitty had lied to him.

There was no sound from Maud now. Either they had calmed her, or
she had been taken away. Kitty sat in the bedroom, alone, her thoughts
whirling. Every once in a while, involuntarily, her mind returned to that
glimpse she'd had of Hal, dead, and shock rose again like a black wave.

In a painful ticking off of facts, in an effort to keep that black fright
out of her mind, she began to think through the events of that day, the
people she'd seen. Starting with Aunt Dru, out and abroad at such an
early hour, full of the queer hints about Dena being in danger, another
hint that she herself might "know" something. A touch of fear, too. And
Kitty's queer impression that Aunt Dru might wield more power in her
nephews' lives than had at first seemed probable.

Then Maud, and her demand for a lie that would protect Hal. Poor Hal,
who wouldn't need help, now, ever again.

Doyle had interrupted their conversation in the coffee shop, wanting to check Ardis's story ... or pretending that he did. He had left her then with an enigmatic remark: one of the people she knew was a murderer.

Why not Kitty herself? She'd had a motive to hate Sunny Walling. Had Doyle decided that it wasn't strong enough? Or did he have hopes of lulling her into betraying herself?

She thought of the lunch with Charles, the revelation that the motive for Edmund's attack on the Army officer must have had something to do with his brother's injuries. A strange man, Edmund, with moods she could only guess at. Kitty rubbed her temples tiredly. Edmund, according to Aunt Dru, was the only one who knew the brutes apart, knew Saki from Saladin. The knowledge hinted at familiarity, control. If it had been Edmund on the landing—if Hal's vision of the dog hadn't been just nightmare—would Hal have decided he could manage Edmund? Would this explain Hal's remark about handling things his own way? What had Hal really thought of Edmund Linder? What was it he had called him? *A wild man....*

Confusion boiled in Kitty's mind. She jerked her thoughts along, to the interview at the hospital with Dena. Hal wasn't going to help Dena now. Would Dena somehow land on her feet anyway; did she have other strings to her bow? Kitty remembered Dena's cryptic remark, that other people besides Hal had dirty linen to wash in secret so far as Sunny was concerned. Could it be that there was someone whose name had never entered the case, to whom Sunny was a danger and a scourge, whose fear or rage had exploded into violence?

What had Doyle thought of the cryptic suggestion?

Probably he intended to question Dena thoroughly when she was out of danger.

From the hospital, Kitty had gone to find Hal. She remembered his air of fright, of nervous worry, of being on the edge of some precipice of danger. She had thought that his fear was of Baron, and the embarrassment of being involved with the police; but it was obvious now that he was aware of some real menace. At the end, fortified with the false courage of alcohol, he'd elected to face it alone.

Was there a clue in the day's events? Had some hidden meaning escaped her? Had some scrap been dropped which would fit into the rest of the pieces to make a picture of the murderer? She tried to force herself to concentrate. Unwillingly, her thoughts returned to Aunt Dru, the funny little old spinster, worrying over her nephews like a hen with two chicks.

Anger at herself washed through Kitty's mind. Why try to pretend that anything about Aunt Dru amused her? When the truth, though bitter, was so simple? Aunt Dru was afraid, and her fear was a contagion to Kitty—the terrified conviction that Edmund had done something horrible.

All the details of the two murders added up to a violent and brutal killer. And the most violent, the most unpredictable, among those in the affair ... was Edmund Linder.

I don't care, Kitty told herself. He isn't anything to me. She found that she was beating the counterpane with her fist.

She got up from the bed and went to the door. She could see down the hall, to where Doyle stood with his back toward her in the living room. Hal's body had been removed. The couch was covered with a clean sheet. Maud sat on a small chair nearby, hunched over, her face drawn and exhausted, her posture and movements those of an old woman. She was speaking to Doyle; her words reached Kitty plainly.

"Of course my husband had enemies. Who hasn't, if they're in a position of any importance in Hollywood? Frustrated actors and actresses—he brushed them off every day. And writers, trying to force him to show an interest in their ideas ..." She spread her hands in an abrupt, angry move. "Do you have any conception of the pressure a man like Hal is under, day after day? The agency hounds him to produce accounts. The sponsors howl for fresh, original shows, new faces, better talent, more selling power—on less money. And the small fry go on dogging him endlessly for the chance, the one chance each of them is sure is all he needs." She searched Doyle with a bitter, tearful glance. "If you ever get the idea you've got it tough ...just remember my husband." She bent over to sob brokenly.

Doyle said patiently, "I've been around, I know what you mean. But I want something special, somebody with a definite grudge, an enemy who hated him enough to kill him."

"Put Baron through the hoops!" Maud's teeth ground together.

"Mrs. DeGraffen—" Doyle's tone was conciliatory. But what he meant to say was interrupted—the telephone rang, in its niche in the hall, not more than a foot or two from where Kitty stood.

She reached for it. A man's voice grated in her ear. "Miss Quist? This is the garage. Your car's ready for you. I'm working late tonight, be here until about nine, if you want to pick it up."

Doyle was watching her. Kitty said, "Thank you." The man on the other end of the line hung up. She said into the dead phone, "Yes, thank you, but I'm not in the market for insurance just now." Then she replaced the phone in its niche and went back into the bedroom.

Kitty realized that she was dreadfully hungry. There was no way she could prepare a meal, eat it here, even if she'd wanted to. The cupboard was bare. I'll slip out, she told herself. I can get the car, go somewhere for a decent meal, come back here later. Doyle won't like it; but to hell with Doyle. Slipping into her coat and taking her purse from a chair, she bit her lip in anger. She looked into the hall again. Doyle was out of sight, but he must still be close to Maud; she was speaking to him.

Her words chimed in Kitty's head like the sound of bells. "If you're looking for a real suspect, I'll give you Lin Linder—Edmund's his real name. He owns those dogs. He warned Sunny Walling to stay away from his brother months ago, and I don't think she obeyed."

Doyle's tone was sharp, full of interest. "They've both denied knowing Miss Walling." He moved into Kitty's line of vision, but not looking her way.

"I can't prove anything," Maud went on. "It was an impression I had, that Sunny didn't think much of Lin, didn't mean to stay away from Charles. I don't know how Lin knew the sort of girl she was—whether he'd had any personal experience with her or not. But one more thing is a fact—Lin had a quarrel with Hal, too, over his brother. He thought Hal had ruined the chances for a radio show based on his brother's book."

Kitty had crossed the hall, slipped into the kitchen. It was nearing twilight, now, and the room looked gray and stark. She shivered under the coat. They were putting a noose around Edmund's throat, in there.

I ought to be glad, she thought. It means that Ardis will be free of any hint of guilt. They'll let her go, and she can begin to forget the cruel things, the flowers young Burns sent to Sunny, the days she waited alone, the letter that never came.

Kitty stole through the rear door, began the descent of the stairs. In her thoughts, under the ought-to-be-glad feeling about Ardis, was another emotion entirely. It was no use fooling herself, either, where she intended to go. She couldn't choke down a bite of dinner. As fast as her car could take her, she'd go to the Linder house.

When she had paid for the repair to the car and driven off and swung into Du Moyne Avenue, she was aware of a kind of release. Doyle was going to be more than furious, she knew; this was one stunt he'd never forgive. But there were things she had to know, questions she had to have answered. She didn't want those answers second-hand from the police. She had to know, at last, from Edmund himself, just whether he could have committed murder because of his brother.

The Linder house seemed closed and quiet. Kitty left her car and walked up the path to the door. She rang the bell, then waited. It seemed a long time until she heard movement inside. The door swung in and Aunt Dru peeped out at her. For an instant her face remained cold, blank, as though Kitty had interrupted some train of thought whose end she must pursue. Then she brightened, drew open the door with a show of politeness. "Miss Quist, do come in. Excuse my appearance. I've been cleaning house."

Her head was tied up in cloth, her hands covered with mittens. As Kitty stepped in, she was aware of an odor of floor polish, a faint breath of dust. She turned to Aunt Dru, who was now watching her expectantly.

"I wanted to see Edmund."

"Oh, too bad, he isn't here. Could he call you when he comes in?"

Kitty had noted the lack of an invitation to stay; she pretended to ignore it. "I'll have to wait for him. It's important. There's been another death, a second murder."

The room was shadowy. Aunt Dru moved to turn on a lamp. "How ... how horrible. Do you mean that Miss Frayne is dead?"

"No, this wasn't Dena. It was Hal DeGraffen. Edmund knows him."

"I know him too," Aunt Dru said quickly. "A big gray-haired man, very distinguished-looking, had something to do with an advertising agency...." All at once she put her hand over her mouth. "He's the one who—"

"—who handled the radio show when the agency was interested in your nephew's book," Kitty finished for her.

Aunt Dru tottered as if from a blow. Kitty sprang to help, but Aunt Dru waved her back. She fell into a chair. After a moment she asked, "Why did you come to see Edmund about this?"

"I think he ought to know what's being said about him."

Aunt Dru licked her lips. "It's quite ridiculous to think that he had anything to do with this affair."

"'This affair,'" Kitty quoted grimly, "had its beginning in the murder of Sunny Walling in the street before your house. Your nephews denied knowing Sunny, and the DeGraffens apparently co-operated by not telling what they knew, either. But now Hal is dead and Maud De-Graffen isn't keeping the secret any longer. She's just told the police that Charles knew Sunny and that Edmund disapproved, and that Edmund warned Sunny to stay away."

Aunt Dru was shaking her head frantically. "Edmund wouldn't ... wouldn't—"

"*What* wouldn't I —" said a man's voice. Kitty jerked about to face the inner door. Edmund stood there. He had on the raincoat Kitty remembered from that other night. His head was bare. A few drops sparkled on the coat and on his thick, light-colored hair.

Aunt Dru began to babble out what Kitty had just told her. Edmund didn't seem to pay much attention. He was watching Aunt Dru, not listening to her. Suddenly he crossed the floor with long strides, bent over her as she sat hunched on the chair, began to pull at the mittens.

She resisted fiercely. All at once he gave up and turned his attention to the cloth around her head. He tugged, and the wrapping came away.

Above the right temple, the hair was streaked and matted, thick with blood. Aunt Dru put up a hand swiftly as if to conceal the stain. As she did so, Edmund caught her wrist, jerked off the mitten. The hand, too, was bloody. Deep scratches and welts marked the flesh.

"You killed the dog. How long ago?" Edmund said in a low voice.

She didn't answer. Like a broken doll she toppled forward into his arms.

CHAPTER SEVENTEEN

Edmund carried his aunt into a darkened bedroom. Kitty threw back the covers; he laid the little old lady in her bed, drew up the blankets, then walked away to stand motionless by a window. It was almost night outside, and the rain had begun again. Kitty could see the drops dimly, coursing down the pane. The room was silent except for Aunt Dru's broken breathing. She asked, "Shouldn't you do something for your aunt?"

"Try some brandy," he threw over his shoulder. "The cabinet in the dining room—the right-hand door...." He hadn't turned. He went on looking at the dark.

Kitty was baffled by what she sensed in him: hostility, even hatred. Was it directed toward her, or Aunt Dru? She brought the brandy, tried to get Aunt Dru to lift her head. There was a weak mutter of protest; a hand waved her away.

Suddenly she found Edmund beside her. He said, "Stay here until I come back. Listen to anything she says."

It was a command. He walked out of the room without waiting for an answer. Kitty crouched on a chair, listening. The rain made whispering sounds at the windows, but she thought that she caught the creak of the big overhead garage door. She waited for the purr of a car, but none came. Far away, it seemed she could hear a clanking noise, as if a tool had struck cement, or had fallen against another tool. Kitty hurried to the window. The view was all but obscured by the dark, the falling rain. But she made out the row of little trees, and a hint of empty hills against the sky. And something else. Something that moved.

Suddenly she heard Aunt Dru's voice, a whisper in the darkness behind her. "What's he doing?"

"I don't know."

"Do you think the police will come here?"

"Soon," Kitty said. "I'd bet on it."

"They'll be coming for Edmund?" Was there a hint of malice, of victory, in Aunt Dru's tone? Or was she really concerned, fearful for her violent and unpredictable nephew?

"They'll want very much to know why you lied about knowing Sunny

Walling."

Aunt Dru was whispering in her ear. "I have to go and scrub myself. Don't stay here. The police will accuse you, too, of doing something wrong. Go with Edmund. See that he doesn't come back here."

Kitty asked heatedly, scornfully: "Do you think he can outrun the police?"

"I—I'll delay them," the little old lady promised. She faded from the room like a ghost.

Kitty said to her vanishing form, "It will seem like an admission of guilt, if he runs away." There was no reply. Kitty remembered those other incidents; at each of their meetings, Aunt Dru had managed to bring out some fact about Edmund which indicated temper, violence, little things that had needed explaining, that pointed to his possible guilt. Now she wanted him to run, to avoid the police. "You don't like him, the way you do Charles," Kitty accused. There was no indication that Aunt Dru had heard. A door closed softly down the hall.

Kitty ran out into the rain. Clouds had closed in the sky, shutting off the thin remains of daylight. She stumbled on the porch steps, almost went headlong. She flung herself toward the wall of the house. Her hand came down on rough wet fur.

She choked down the scream; the dog stood there sturdily, letting her regain her balance by leaning on him. Timidly, she put her other hand on his head. There was no move, no lunge. She said, "Saladin?" A faint whine acknowledged the name. Then she caught a hint of restlessness. He wanted her to move on.

Together they went down to the road, through the little shrubby trees that glistened dimly, silvered by the rain.

She could hear footsteps ahead on the slope of the hill, and the dog seemed to want to hurry now. She clutched at his collar and he dragged her with him. The slope of the ground lifted; there were stones here and there, and rough places where earth had been pushed and piled. Rain beat in her face. She was getting wet. Once she had to stop to catch her breath; the dog circled her worriedly, whined once, then stood looking off into the dark. Ahead there was a sudden wink of light that burned for an instant, then went out.

She stopped near the crest of the ridge, sensing rather than seeing the figure that stood there. She caught a clank of steel on stone, then the grating of a spade in earth. Edmund's wet raincoat glistened; she saw that he had paused, was looking toward her, his face a blur in the dark.

The dog whined. Edmund said, "Keep him there."

She clung to the dog's collar, but he was too strong, too big. He pulled loose. She heard his sudden, heartbroken howl, then Edmund's voice, low, comforting. She stood in the rain, feeling shut-off and alone.

All at once Edmund spoke again. "Why did you follow me?"

"Your aunt asked me to. She wants you to keep away from the police, to avoid being captured."

He waited a minute as if thinking. "And what do you want?"

"I —" In Kitty's mind the words spaced themselves: *I want to go with you.* Her mouth wouldn't get them out; somewhere, shutting them off, was her pride, and the memory of Ardis, too, perhaps, poor Ardis whose humble love and whose patience had, at the end, brought her nothing. I'm not that kind of woman—the thought flashed through Kitty's mind. I can't give over; I'm not a dog to run at his heels.

He took a couple of steps toward her. She could see the movement of his eyes under the heavy brows. "Look." He switched on the flashlight, turned its beam downward. A dog lay spread out on the stony earth. Saladin's eyes beseeched help for his fallen brother; he whined and pawed at Edmund.

"Is this the dog who jumped you that night?"

Kitty flinched; the dog was bloody, its dead eyes filmed, its neck twisted inside the leather collar. "I don't know. It looks just like Saladin. Is it your other dog?"

"Yes, it's Saki. If you could identify it, for sure, one question would be answered."

She bent down, lifted one of the dog's feet. She remembered the paws, the big muddy pad on the windshield only a few inches from her face. Which foot? The right one, she thought. She searched for some identifying mark, something to stir her memory. There was nothing.

Was Saki the dog which had attacked her car, which had leaped for her when she opened her door, which had ripped off her shoe?

"Why did your aunt kill him?"

"Perhaps she thought that she was covering someone's crime. Mine, for instance." He waited as if, half-jeering, he expected her protest.

"Perhaps she was defending herself," Kitty said. "The dog must have been used, just a little while ago, to help murder Hal DeGraffen. A dog like that—you couldn't depend on him not to attack a friend." But her thoughts rushed on: Aunt Dru had acted peculiarly for someone whose motive was self-defense. She'd tried to conceal evidence of what she had done. Kitty must have interrupted the cleaning-up process, or else Aunt Dru had already donned the dust-cap and gloves to mislead someone else. Charles, possibly? All at once Kitty recalled the view of Aunt Dru on the porch, shaking out a rug, as she and Doyle had driven past on the way to the apartment. A big dog had been with Aunt Dru on the porch; obviously it must have been Saladin. There had not been time for a dog to have been brought from the apartment after Hal's murder.

Or had there?

In the half-dark, she sensed Edmund's attitude of stunned attention. "What did you say about DeGraffen?"

"He was murdered. That's what I came here to tell you—that, and what Maud has told the police, that you and Charles both knew Sunny Walling, that you'd warned her to stay away from your brother."

After a while, in a monotone, as though speaking to himself, he asked, "What am I supposed to do with this information?" Without waiting for her answer, he continued, "Did you expect me to run?"

"Your aunt wants you to leave."

"Yes, I'd guessed that she might." He began to dig again, fast, fiercely. "She'll have to wait until I finish this."

"If the dog is the one used in the murders," Kitty protested, "you should leave it for the police. It will look very strange for you to have buried it."

"Does it look strange to you?"

She wouldn't face what reason told her, that this was the act of a guilty man. "There are tests they can make. They'll find out once and for all if your dog was the one used by the murderer."

"Saki never hurt anyone," he said roughly.

"Then where—where did the other dog come from?"

"That's what I mean to find out." He paused. "If you want to help, we could use your car. Go back to the house and drive it on over the hill. I'll meet you there." Then he added, "Take Saladin with you. Leave him in the house with Aunt Dru."

Aunt Dru was seated in the living room. She had on a terrycloth robe. Her damp hair was wrapped in a towel. A generous dusting of powder partially concealed the welts and scratches on her hands. She said disapprovingly, "You shouldn't have come back here." Her glance was cold, bitter.

"Edmund sent me back." Kitty released the dog's collar. "He wanted you to have Saladin."

A twinge crossed the older woman's face. "Is he going away with you?"

"Yes." Kitty went back to the door, turned there. "How can you show your preference so obviously? How can you give so much love to Charles and so little to Edmund? How can you send him out to run like a hare before the police, taking a chance of being shot down as a murderer, without a trial or any chance to speak for himself? How can you be such a failure at the task your brother left you ... the job of acting as a mother to his sons?"

Aunt Dru had grown pale as Kitty spoke.

"I can understand Edmund's moodiness, his violence," Kitty flung out. "All his life he's seen your preference for Charles. He's been the unwanted one, the misfit. You and Charles were a closed corporation. I don't blame Edmund for not wanting to live here with you. I'm surprised that he ever let you talk him into coming back."

Aunt Dru's chin was quivering. The hunched shoulders seemed to bend under the lash of Kitty's words. "You don't understand —" Aunt Dru quavered. "You're quite wrong about it all."

"How can I be wrong? Look what you've done to him. To top it all off, you just finished killing one of the few things he loved—his dog."

Aunt Dru shook her head helplessly, as if bewildered by Kitty's angry words. "You yourself know that the dog was vicious—"

"Edmund says that Saki never harmed anyone."

The chimes of the doorbell cut across Kitty's words. Kitty jerked around, thinking of escape, thinking of the errand Edmund had asked of her. She thought briefly of running, of trying to reach the car to drive over the hill, to wait as he had told her to do. But it was too late. She saw the finger Aunt Dru put to her lips. All she could do now was to keep silent. The only thing that could help Edmund was for the police to be kept in ignorance of what he was doing and where he was.

Doyle didn't come in for a moment after the door was opened. The dark made a frame for him. When his eyes met Kitty's, she felt with a shock their bitter, impersonal animosity. He was sizing her up as an enemy. Then his glance swept past and settled on Aunt Dru. He took a step backward. He took the arm of the person standing beside him in the shadow, pushed her forward. It was Maud DeGraffen.

"I see that you've been outside recently, Miss Quist."

Kitty ran her hands guiltily over her wet hair, the damp collar of her coat.

"Where is he?" Doyle asked with ominous gentleness.

His question hung in the air, unanswered. Maud walked to a chair, fell upon it as though her legs could no longer support her, sat there with an expression of dull hurt on her face. Perhaps she was thinking of the empty years she'd spent with Hal, goading him on to success, denying him the wish to seek sanctuary in the mountains, to get off the treadmill of his distasteful job. Perhaps she was wondering whether the change would have meant that the Sunny Wallings of this world would no longer have found him attractive, useful. She said with sudden venom, "I'm not your tool here, Mr. Doyle. I won't be a goad to make these people say what you want them to say."

"We'll get to that in good time," Doyle promised, his gaze still on Kitty. "Where were you?" he asked her directly.

It was a chance, the last chance, perhaps, to put herself right with him again. Kitty's throat grew tight.

Her own silence was frightening to her. It seemed to her that Edmund's guilt was no longer to be denied. He had defended the dog, Saki, because he knew better than to believe in the animal's viciousness. Aunt Dru was trying, in a perverse way and in spite of her dislike, to keep him away from the police. These two knew the truth.

Kitty even realized the background of Edmund's violence. Aunt Dru had always favored Charles, had drummed into Edmund from their childhood that Charles was the more perfect and superior being. Some backwash of this old training had caused Edmund to beat up the Army officer responsible for his brother's mutilation, for Aunt Dru's horrified grief over it. Probably Aunt Dru had voiced disapproval of Sunny Walling, too, and again Edmund had been caught up in the old unending and frustrating effort to win his aunt's love and liking. Defend Charles—that had been the pattern. Its source could have come from but one direction, Aunt Dru.

Doyle's voice cut across her abstraction like a knife. "You haven't answered my question, Miss Quist."

She sensed the threat, now. He could put her in jail for obstructing justice, for concealing the whereabouts of a suspect in a murder case. An idea suddenly occurred to her. "I don't know where Edmund Linder is now. He was up on the hill, burying his dog." The words hit Doyle like bombshell. She saw the sudden disbelief, almost shock, flash across his face. She looked down at her folded hands. Edmund would have seen the police car. He wouldn't be up on that hill, awaiting capture like a sitting duck. "You can find the dog's body if you'll look. It's my understanding that the animal attacked Miss Dru Linder and that she killed it in defending herself."

"*No!*" Aunt Dru stood up, shaking in agitation.

Doyle turned to her with the deceptive air of patience. "You don't agree with Miss Quist's statement?"

She looked from one to another, from Kitty to Maud, to Doyle, to the two men who had come in following Doyle and who stood like anonymous shadows on either side of the closed front door. "What I mean is ... my nephew helped me to kill the dog," she stammered in a high, weak voice. "I didn't do it alone. I couldn't have." Her voice ran down and she stood there like a child who has been scolded for telling lies. She licked her pale lips. "It's true, quite true."

"Which nephew? Edmund, I suppose?"

Kitty, too, had expected this last weak lie, this sure putting of a rope around Edmund's neck, a pitiful and transparent attempt to mislead the police. But Aunt Dru shook her head. "No. Charles."

"And where is Charles now?" Doyle asked gently.

"I don't know. He had to go out on an errand to do with the store."

Doyle gave a glance at the other men. They turned and went out. The hill would be searched, Kitty knew. The bloodhounds of the law would be at Edmund's heels. And someone else would check to see where Charles had gone. On the surface, Kitty thought, it seemed that Aunt Dru was a bewildered, frightened little old lady. Yet her two nephews were on the run and she sat here, smug and safe.

Kitty's mind returned to that scene she'd glimpsed from Du Moyne Avenue. Suppose there had been time, with desperate hurry, for the murderer to return here from the apartment—by all stretch of speed, wouldn't they just about make it to the porch? The sound of cars would be a flash-warning; there would be the possibility that the cars were coming here. And so what more clever course of action would there be than to seize a rug put out to air, to shake it with housewifely thoroughness? The casual viewer would think, of course, that the rug had just been brought from inside the house.

Was it possible?

With beating heart, Kitty regarded the little old lady on the other side of the room. Aunt Dru could have murdered Sunny Walling—who would have made two of her—with the help of a dog as big as Saladin or Saki. She could have killed Sunny because the voluptuous, immoral girl was untying, at last, the apron strings that had bound Charles so firmly all these years.

Dena's hope had been of blackmail, and this presented a problem. How could Dena have expected to get anything out of Aunt Dru?

As if in answer to this problem, Doyle asked: "Miss Linder, I'd like to get a little background to your situation here. For instance, I'd like to know who owns this house?"

Aunt Dru looked up at him. "I do."

"You paid for building it? It isn't mortgaged?"

"I paid every cent in cash," Aunt Dru said proudly. "Thirty thousand dollars. I wanted a home for my nephews."

Kitty wondered dazedly where she'd ever got the idea that Aunt Dru was poor.

CHAPTER EIGHTEEN

Doyle didn't look surprised. This information wasn't new to him. He'd checked up, elsewhere, with his usual thoroughness. "You and your nephew Charles first occupied the house together?"

"Yes. But I'd built it ... well, mostly ... for Edmund. He was always the lonely, difficult one. I didn't want him living by himself, friendless."

How adroit she is, Kitty thought to herself. She's reminding Doyle, very gently and subtly, of Edmund's career of violence. The bad one who never minded well, whom people avoided, who was the world's enemy ...

"You have other property, too?" Doyle purred.

"Not real estate." For the first time, Aunt Dru's air of innocent frankness faltered. "Do you really want to know all about *me?*"

Doyle interrupted this excursion. "Are you worth as much as a hundred thousand dollars, Miss Linder?"

Her eyes got big. "Oh, no!"

"Fifty thousand?"

"A ... a little better than that, I suppose."

"Might I estimate roughly—seventy-five?"

Her face was pink now. She looked at Maud and Kitty as if resenting their presence. In another moment she'd demand that Doyle conduct the interview in private. Then she appeared to check her rising temper. "You may."

"Well, is the balance of your wealth, outside this house, in cash?"

Her mouth was pinched with disapproval of his nosiness. "Some of it. I'm not just sure how much."

Doyle walked over to a low table, used the cigarette lighter there to get a cigarette going. "You know a woman named Dena Frayne? She contacted you after the murder of Miss Walling?"

Aunt Dru went slack, like an old-fashioned doll which has been punctured and is losing its sawdust. Or like a balloon with a slow leak. Her face crumpled with fear.

"You paid Miss Frayne the sum of five thousand dollars," Doyle went on. "What for?"

"So—so that she wouldn't tell you that we knew Miss Walling. I mean, that my nephews knew her." Aunt Dru's voice seemed to come up from the bottom of a well; it was hollow, drowning.

"Just for that?" Doyle's gaze was boring into her.

"Just —" she couldn't manage the rest of the words.

"How did you give it to her? Cash? A check?" All of Doyle's words, since his first mention of Dena, had had the harsh impact of bullets; and now, indeed, Aunt Dru looked around as if someone were shooting at her and she had nowhere to go. "Come, Miss Linder. You know what form that bribe took. Let's have it."

"A check."

"Has the check been cashed?"

"I don't know. I haven't called the bank yet."

"Perhaps there isn't any need to call the bank. Perhaps you are sure now that the check will never be cashed."

Aunt Dru, flustered and dismayed, was somehow like a kitten badgered by a mean bulldog. "I—I don't understand you. Miss Frayne can tell you, since she's talking so freely, that I paid her the check at her apartment. It was understood that the check would be cashed the next morning. This morning, that is."

"Only," Doyle pointed out, "Miss Frayne happened not to be in any shape to cash a check."

"That wasn't my fault." Aunt Dru tried to meet Doyle's drilling gaze, and faltered. Either he had frightened her too much, or she was lying.

He now turned to Maud, bringing her into the conversation. "Did you know of Miss Frayne's blackmail scheme upon Miss Linder?"

"Of course I didn't," Maud threw out. "Dena was riding Hal over that mink stole. She made him think that she was positive one of us was guilty of killing Sunny. She didn't let us know of her other suspicions. It might have weakened her hold on us."

"The hold you mention—" Doyle was walking around now, as if examining the room, its casual masculine furnishings. "There was more to it than merely the stole. Isn't that true?"

"I told you before—I won't help you trap these people."

Aunt Dru threw her a grateful glance, straightening a little as if encouraged. But her optimism was short-lived. Doyle went on: "Actually, since I have the story from Miss Frayne, I don't need your help. Once she found that her conversation in the hospital with Miss Quist had been overheard, and that the job with Mr. DeGraffen's firm was gone up the flue with his death, she was more than co-operative. Vindictive might be the word."

Maud spat out: "I wouldn't believe that woman on a stack of Bibles! She's mercenary, utterly conscienceless, without honor or decency!"

"Oh, I don't know," Doyle argued. "She's interested mainly in self-preservation, it's true, but these Hollywood characters get that way. This town is a little bit cut-throat, to put it mildly. Take Miss Frayne—she saw you bring in the mink stole which your husband is supposed to have picked up beside Miss Walling's body. But Miss Frayne didn't just see something. She heard something."

Maud licked her lips nervously. "Whatever she heard—she misunderstood."

"Possibly," Doyle agreed.

"My husband didn't see the actual murder," Maud went on, emphasizing each word. "He didn't know who the murderer was. His position there at the scene of the crime seemed like a set-up, a deliberate trap. A trap that Sunny herself had set, though he couldn't figure out how it was managed."

"Miss Frayne believed that she overheard a confession of murder, that your husband admitted killing Miss Walling."

"She was mistaken." Maud snapped her mouth shut. Her eyes glittered with repressed anger.

Her anger made no impression on Doyle. He went on speaking; to Aunt Dru, now, and in a manner that was almost friendly, confiding. He might have been asking the little old lady to help him with a knotty problem. "Miss Frayne tells us that she overheard Mr. DeGraffen tell his wife that he had followed Sunny Walling as she drove away in this direction, and that Miss Walling had stopped her car just before getting to the top of the ridge, had waited until the coast was clear—that is, probably, until Edmund Linder had driven Miss Quist away in his car—and that Miss Walling had then walked down the lane in front of this house and talked to someone there, someone Mr. DeGraffen was not able to identify."

Aunt Dru's color was chalky; her eyes seemed about to pop out of her head. She was still as a mouse in the corner of the couch.

"Was it you?" Doyle demanded.

Aunt Dru seemed to consider what she should say; not choosing words, Kitty guessed, but wondering what sort of yarn would sit best with the detective.

"Well, it's not important," Doyle went on, "since Miss Walling wasn't murdered at this time. She returned to her car, and with Mr. DeGraffen still following and observing, she went to a boarding kennel on the outskirts of San Fernando and there picked up a dog."

Aunt Dru's breath made a whistling sound between her teeth.

"Now we get to the interesting part." Doyle dominated the room as an actor on a stage. Kitty felt mesmerized. So much of what he was relating seemed impossible, fantastic. "Miss Walling returned here to your lane, the dog with her in the car. Then—it is Miss Frayne's impression that Mr. DeGraffen considered himself the cause of her death, though she was not sure just why."

"She's lying," Maud said shrilly. Her accustomed poise and coolness had flown. She was witch-like, shrewish. "Hal went over and over the incidents that followed. Sunny parked her car, took the strange dog, and got out. She spoke a few words into the dark, as if expecting somebody to be there. Then she whistled softly. In that moment"—Maud paused; her voice had risen to a squeak and her eyes were suddenly full of fear—"all hell broke loose. Sunny screamed. The dog—a dog, I mean—leaped upon her. She went down. The only thing that Hal blamed himself for was not going to save her. He said he thought at first it was some sort of game, a ruse—after all, she had brought the dog here. Afterward he was not sure that the dog which jumped her was the same dog—but this was an afterthought. It seemed as if Sunny must be putting on some kind of act. Actually, Hal was embarrassed, and afraid someone attracted by the ruckus would discover him spying from the shrubbery. So he walked away ... temporarily."

"Miss Walling didn't die of the injuries inflicted by the dog. She may have, in time. But actually she was murdered by some heavy weight, probably a stone, striking her at the base of the brain."

Maud wet her lips. "Hal didn't know anything about that. He came back when things seemed quieted down. There were two cars there, the one Kitty had abandoned because it was broken down and Sunny's, parked beside it. Sunny's car had its lights on. He caught some kind of movement, some shadowy thing withdrawing, he thought. Then he came into view of the road in front of the headlights, and saw Sunny. She was dead. Hal panicked, almost died himself, he told me, of heart failure. He grabbed the stole and turned to leave. At that moment he heard somebody running up the lane. It was Ardis Lake. She was only there a few moments. The dog frightened her off. She drove away in Sunny's convertible."

"And your husband?"

"He came home. To me." There was a well of bitterness under the words.

Doyle walked around the room some more. "How much noise and excitement was there, during the dog's attack on Miss Walling?"

"There must have been a lot. Hal seemed convinced it should have been heard for miles."

Doyle's wise, ironic stare drifted over to Aunt Dru. Kitty remembered the little old lady's insistence that she had heard nothing of what had happened that night. She had even expressed regret at her ability to sleep so soundly that she had missed it all. Doyle said to Aunt Dru, "Any comment, Miss Linder?"

She saw a red herring and dragged it in. "What mystifies me, Lieutenant, is the fact that Miss Walling brought the vicious dog with her. And yet Miss Quist had said that it was already here, that it attacked her when her car broke down."

"We don't know which dog was vicious," he said quietly. Then he turned and walked over to the front door, opened it, was gone for a couple of minutes. There was a dead, uncomfortable silence in the room between the three women. Doyle returned. Two men carried something between them on a piece of canvas. They laid it on the floor and Kitty saw that it was Saki, the dead dog on the hill. Then a third officer appeared in the doorway. Beside him stalked a huge yellow brute, a duplicate of the one on the floor.

Saladin had been lying in front of the couch beside Aunt Dru's feet. Now he rose, his hackles standing, a growl rumbling in his chest.

Doyle looked at Aunt Dru and said, "Which of these two—the dead one, the one on the leash—is the mate to your dog there?"

She quivered and shut her eyes.

"We're going to have the truth sooner or later," Doyle went on. His tone had taken on the quality of a steel file. "For one thing, we're pretty sure now that all three of you in this house knew what was going on in the road. You and your nephew Charles would have been awakened by the noise, if you were sleeping; and your nephew Edmund, having just barely returned from taking Miss Quist home, could scarcely have yet been in bed."

"You're taking her word...." Aunt Dru pointed to Maud DeGraffen. "And it's all just hearsay, just a story her husband is supposed to have told—"

"Oh, we've been busy checking," Doyle put in brusquely. "For instance, we found the kennel where Miss Walling had been boarding her dog. The dog showed up there sometime during the night, was on hand next morning with sore footpads, muddy coat, and an injured ear. This is him." He motioned, and the big yellow brute was brought forward by the officer holding the leash.

Saladin growled again, half crouched, his eyes fierce, unblinking.

Kitty realized that Doyle had tricked Maud into telling her story by seeming to accuse Hal. A moment's thought would have shown Maud that he didn't think Hal had had anything to do with Sunny's murder. But Doyle had led her into a trap.

Now he went back to Aunt Dru, cornering her, badgering her. "Why don't you tell the truth about that night? Why don't you admit that you knew Miss Walling was being murdered? You might have been frightened by the noise, have been too scared to go out to see what was going on—" He was coaxing now, letting in a little ray of light. "That might have been logical. You could have called to your nephews—"

"I did, but—" It had seemed to pop out. Then Aunt Dru looked sick.

"They didn't answer? Either of them?"

"I—I didn't call very loud."

Suddenly Aunt Dru cried wildly, "You mustn't shoot him!"

"Why do you think we intend to shoot him?" Doyle inquired, with gentle reasonableness.

She stuttered: "Y-you've made up your mind that Edmund is the murderer!"

Doyle regarded her with curiosity. "Isn't it a pretty good theory? Edmund is gone, hiding. He was trying to bury the dog—its body is evidence of the most crucial sort. There was some sort of trickery involving these two brutes, the dead one and the one belonging to Miss Walling. Your nephew was attempting to confuse us by removing one of the dogs. Perhaps, instead of Charles, it was actually Edmund who helped you kill the brute."

Kitty was moved to protest. "No, I'm sure that it wasn't. He came in while I was here, noticed the injuries to his aunt's hands and to her head, and surmised that she had killed the dog."

Doyle's flash of interest was not well concealed. "Do you mind showing me these injuries, Miss Linder?"

She shook her head and crowded back into the cushions as he walked toward her.

Doyle's voice had dropped, grown quiet, soothing. "He came in and took a look at you, and decided the dog must be dead? Then he must have known its vicious nature. He must have been expecting an attack, another attack like those he'd arranged on Miss Walling, Miss Frayne, and DeGraffen. It's not a bad method at all, clever in fact—the dog gets the victim down and keeps him busy while the murderer gets in the necessary blow. Since the dog evidently attacked you, Miss Linder, it could almost be supposed —"

Aunt Dru screamed: "*No!* No, it wasn't! He wouldn't!"

Kitty suddenly felt cynical over the little old lady's emotional outbursts. She kept feeding Edmund to them in little pieces, then when they suddenly went whole-hog on the evidence, she tried to back up, to retract. She was like a child playing a game, Kitty thought. Only, Kitty added to herself with bitterness, Aunt Dru was playing with a life. Edmund's life.

Why should I care, Kitty demanded of herself. So—she's sewed him up. He lied to me. He told me Saki couldn't have hurt anyone, and I believed him. Only, Saki had to be the one. The other dog, the one that Sunny had brought here for some strange hocus-pocus, had been back at the kennels next morning, sore-footed from the trip. And then Dena was torn and almost killed, and Hal was murdered ... and the dog involved had to be Edmund's dog. The one he knew so well that he could tell it from Saladin, its twin.

Charles had speculated that there had been three dogs. Perhaps he knew much more than Edmund guessed he did.

Aunt Dru had speculated, too—she'd wondered if someone had set a trap for Sunny, if Kitty hadn't been the decoy, testing it out. *A trap.... A trap—*

Something buzzed around in Kitty's head; she felt as though in the next moment some pattern would be revealed, some lost piece of the puzzle would fall into place. If a trap had been set, if Kitty had been the decoy, it didn't necessarily follow that Sunny—

She opened her mouth to speak, and then realized that no one was looking her way, that the attention of everyone in the room was upon Aunt Dru, still quivering and crying in the corner of the couch. They were all silent, almost breathless, listening to the incredible words as she spilled them out.

"—and it's true, I'm confessing now in front of all of you." The little old lady brushed tears off her cheeks; she sat a little straighter, as if to face once and for all the shame, the guilt, she had coming to her. "I murdered Sunny Walling. Now you can cart me off to jail."

CHAPTER NINETEEN

Doyle bent over the cringing little old woman, barking words at her, the line of his body cruel, his face sharp and hawk-like. In that instant Kitty wondered briefly how she'd ever been deceived by him, had thought him too decent for the cynical, worldly pose he'd assumed. He was just a cop after all.

"Why did you kill her?"

"She was a bad influence. She was a wicked woman," Aunt Dru stammered.

"Oh, come on. What did she do to you?"

Aunt Dru's eyes skittered around the room. "Well ... she—she was trying to get money out of me. She was threatening me for money."

"Threatening you? What about?"

He was going too fast for Aunt Dru. She was getting confused. "If I'd put up some money, Sunny would see that the radio show ... I mean, the interest in Charles's book for a radio show ... would be revived. She'd killed it, you see, with DeGraffen. She'd made him think there was a love affair between her and Charles, and he'd sidetracked the program."

"Wait a minute. You still haven't told me why you killed her."

"I just did. Because of what she did to Charles. He'd been ill, and getting that book on the radio meant a terrible lot to him just then —"

"What did she do to you?" Doyle almost bellowed, making her flinch.

"She was going to break up our home here," Aunt Dru whimpered.

"I'll be damned," Doyle muttered.

"I—I don't want to be all alone and lonely, a friendless old woman," Aunt Dru wept.

"I guess you could kill over a thing like that," he ground out. "If you're nuts enough. If you're pushed hard enough, and somebody says just the right words. I wouldn't know. I wouldn't murder to hold anybody." For some reason at that instant his glance strayed in Kitty's direction. "What about Dena Frayne?"

"As you suspected." Aunt Dru bobbed her towel-wrapped head almost eagerly. "I'd had to pay her for her silence, but I didn't intend that she should cash that check, ever."

"You've got the check now?"

"I burned it," she said quickly.

"What did the Frayne woman have on you?"

For an instant Aunt Dru sat there with her mouth agape, like a child who has forgotten his recitation. "You mean, what was she blackmailing me for? Why, she—she'd heard Sunny Walling bragging about what she was going to do to me, and she put two and two together and figured I'd done the murder."

"She figured you murdered Sunny because Sunny was blackmailing you, so she blackmailed you, too. Isn't that taking a chance, a long chance?"

Aunt Dru said carefully, "She knew Sunny intended to break up our home here."

"Oh, yes, I keep forgetting," Doyle snapped. "You were afraid you'd be lonesome without Charles."

"Yes." Aunt Dru tucked in an end of the towel on her head.

"How about DeGraffen?"

For an instant Aunt Dru was haggard, meeting Maud's gaze from across the room. Then the little old woman stiffened again. "I thought he'd seen me, the night of Dena Frayne's murder."

"How do you know she didn't see you?"

"I waited until she'd gone to bed and was asleep," Aunt Dru said firmly.

"Tell me about it," said Doyle in his new low, quiet voice.

"Just ... just as I said. She'd gone to sleep, and I crept in." Aunt Dru was looking him in the eye now, not very firmly; and her face was full of a false courage, bravado. "She was lying there. The light was dim. I ... I hit her."

"You had the dog there, too," he reminded.

"Yes. The dog." Aunt Dru looked from Saladin to the dead Saki, to the big yellow stranger pulling at the leash. "He ... he helped subdue her."

"Tell me a few details, how she was lying—things like that." Aunt Dru rubbed her head worriedly. "Well, I had a hatchet."

"You hit her with a hatchet? With the blade or with the hammer?"

"To tell the truth, my memory isn't clear. The horror of it all—when I kill people, I just go blank, sort of."

"You're not sure whether you hit Miss Frayne with the hatchet?"

"No. Nor Mr. DeGraffen, either. I may have just let the dog do it." She was perspiring now, a cold sweat that stood out on her plump face. Her eyes were begging for release.

"Is there a hatchet missing here at your house, Miss Linder?"

"Yes, it's gone. I don't remember where I hid it."

"I see." Doyle walked away thoughtfully, stood silent, then turned swiftly. "Get into your clothes, please. I'll take you down to headquarters now."

Aunt Dru flashed him a grateful, brimming look, then fled from the room as if pursued by demons.

Doyle spoke to Kitty: "Will you help her get dressed? She acts a little off her rocker. I wouldn't want her to hurt herself. And give a yell, will you, if she starts to take off out a window? It's raining out. I don't like my suspects to get wet."

Kitty obeyed, glad to get away. Doyle had lost all use for her. She had put herself beyond the pale. And Maud breathed grief and fury.

Kitty found Aunt Dru in a bedroom. There was a four-poster with a canopy, lots of dotted swiss, pink silk ribbon, ruffles. A dressing table with a billowing flounce held a mirror that reflected the room. A chaise was upholstered in pink plaid taffeta. Aunt Dru was at the closet, taking out a gray wool dress. She looked over her shoulder, startled, as Kitty came in. Then she dropped the dress on a chair and ran to clutch Kitty's cold hands. "Promise you'll stay, you'll wait here for Edmund and tell him what happened. Tell him I confessed. There's no need for him to be afraid any more. I've made a mistake and I'm paying for it."

"I'll tell him," Kitty said gently.

Aunt Dru searched her anxiously. "You believe me, don't you? I convinced them all—didn't I?"

"You did one of two things," Kitty said. "Either you confessed your real guilt in so stupid a way that no one could possibly credit it, or else you decided to protect somebody else."

Aunt Dru looked as if she might cry.

Kitty said, "Aunt Dru, who gets your money when you're gone?"

"We won't talk about that now," Aunt Dru replied. "Money isn't important in the face of death, or hatred, or evil. I—I've come to realize that. I shouldn't have killed Miss Walling, for instance, over the blackmail. It wasn't worth that."

"You didn't kill her because of the blackmail," Kitty reminded, "but because you were afraid she'd take Charles away."

"Yes, thank you for reminding me," said Aunt Dru in a slightly absentminded way, putting on a gray toque, smoothing her still-damp hair over her ears. "You remember, too, to get it straight when you tell Edmund."

Aunt Dru donned the woolly shawl and picked up her purse, and they went back to the other room.

Everyone was gone now but Doyle. The dead dog and the one from the kennels had been removed. Doyle nodded approvingly at Aunt Dru, then glanced at Kitty. "I noticed your car outside. You're leaving now, I take it?"

"Yes, of course."

He stood there for a moment as if uncertain. Then suddenly he stuck out his hand. "Good-by, then."

She clasped his fingers. "Good-by, Lieutenant."

Her use of the official title brought a smouldering light to his eyes. The red brows twitched; she thought he would say something further, but he turned instead, opened the door, ushered them out. Saladin still sat on the floor by the couch; he watched their going with a faint, uneasy whine in his throat.

Kitty got into her car and followed Doyle down Du Moyne for several blocks. Then she began to lag, and when his tail-light had disappeared around a bend, she swung to the curb, backed, and went back the way she had come. The door was not locked. She went into the big, quiet, empty room, where the dog rose with a question in his eyes, then wagged his tail.

"Good boy," she said. She wondered then at Aunt Dru's insistence that she keep Saladin with her. She remembered that Edmund had sent her back to bring the dog to his aunt. They seemed to take especial care of the big animal, as though he represented some quality of watchfulness, of safety, which must be rewarded. Just then Saladin came and put his chin on the couch beside Kitty. She stroked his head. He *is* a nice dog, she thought, and nothing like the vicious hound that first night in the lane.

The bad dog who had chewed at her toes had been Saki. Edmund's arrival had calmed the beast, or frightened him, into being decent. Then afterward—the unexplained zany hocus-pocus, Sunny bringing a third dog. The third dog had been meant to play some part in a scheme, that was sure. But what sort of scheme could it have been?

She puzzled over it in the big, silent room, with the only sound a faint swish of rain at the windows.

What was it Hal DeGraffen had told her in their last talk? That Sunny had had a deal on?

Ghost words in Hal's voice echoed in her mind. *Sunny was a very mercenary baby, so I guess money figured in it somewhere. It had something to do with that lane up there, the turn-off from Du Moyne. She'd been there before. I caught her leaving there one day about twilight....*

Kitty thought of the lonely, deserted lane, the little trees blue with dusk, the sharp ridges to north and south cutting off the sky. And Sunny, as Hal had so strangely described her: *dressed up in the damnedest garb I'd ever seen outside a museum. Like a mummy. I almost didn't recognize her.*

What had it meant? *A museum. A mummy.* Hal couldn't have meant the words literally; Sunny couldn't have been wrapped exactly as an Egyptian mummy, it would be too freakish, too absurd; and Hal would have thought, not of a scheme afoot, but of the need for a psychiatrist.

The word museum suggested something very old-fashioned, and mummy could have meant simply the presence of a great many additional clothes. Wrap Sunny Walling up in a lot of old-fashioned garments, and what would she look like? Kitty tried to imagine the scene.

The dog hadn't been with her in her car, or Hal would have mentioned it. So the scheme, whatever it was, which involved all the padding of old-fashioned garments, had had something to do with Saki. Saki was the key, the pivot.

Kitty was startled by the sound of a footfall from somewhere in the recesses of the house. She turned so that she faced the door to the hall that led to the bedrooms. No one appeared, but after several minutes she caught other sounds, and she guessed their direction to be the kitchen. In another couple of minutes Charles Linder walked into the room. He had on an overcoat, with a hat under his arm. In each hand he carried a steaming cup.

"I made us drinks, hot ones. With rum. Like rum?" he asked pleasantly. He let his hat drop from under his arm to a chair, then crossed to where Kitty sat. "Don't think I'm psychic. I peeped in here a little while ago. You were just coming in. I guessed you might be wanting to wait for Edmund." He put the drink into her hand.

She looked at him, noticing as she had at their first meeting the air of bookish whimsy, of abstraction, as though he found the world quaintly amusing, and life a game with a great many funny moments. "They've arrested your aunt," she told him.

"Aunt Dru? How ridiculous. But you can't mean—for murder."

"She confessed."

"Here?" He looked around the room as if astounded that it had held such a scene. "But of course the detective didn't take her seriously. He couldn't have."

"He's taken her to police headquarters."

Charles sat down, sampled his drink slowly, then stood up again to shed the heavy coat. Kitty recalled that she had heard no car come into the road below, and Charles's coat was wet with raindrops. He'd been walking. As if sensing her train of thought, he said ruefully, "I guess I should have been here. It might have helped straighten things out."

"So much happened, all at once. It was hard to keep it all straight, and I'm not sure you could have helped. You see, the police found out that Sunny Walling knew both you and your brother. And other odd things— for instance, that the night she was killed, she brought a third dog here, a duplicate of your dogs. She'd been keeping him at a kennel."

Charles shook his head as if baffled. "That sounds obscure enough to keep them puzzling for a while. Tell me, how well are we supposed to have known Miss Walling? Intimately?"

"Your aunt confessed that her motive for murdering Sunny was to keep her from breaking up the home here by taking you away."

He made a wry mouth. "Oh, dear. Did the police believe that?"

"There was something else, a detail that didn't seem to fit—something about Sunny demanding cash to see that interest was revived in your book as a radio possibility." Watching Charles's rueful surprise, Kitty corrected herself. The foolish detail fitted in one way: it stacked up with Hal's surmise that Sunny must have been involved in a scheme to get money. Suppose Sunny *had* approached Aunt Dru with that proposition, and Aunt Dru had been willing to pay? Without letting Charles know, of course—no writer wants to think his material is so poor that its financial backing must come from relatives. Kitty asked, then: "What about this—could Sunny really have gotten Hal DeGraffen's agency interested again in the program idea? Did she have that much influence?"

"I've denied knowing her, so technically I ought to say, in answer, that I have no idea," Charles said. "But it was a poor lie to begin with. So I'll admit—I haven't any idea what she could have done with Hal. I thought she was friends with both of them. I didn't know she had any hooks in the guy. If she did, and if he was holding still for it, I guess she might have worked a deal on it. Only it's silly to think that Aunt Dru would put up a dime to see the radio program put over. I was never my aunt's favorite."

He smiled, mildly regretful, as if at a fault he could never quite correct.

"Of course you are," Kitty protested. "It's very obvious."

He was shaking his head. "No, no. You know little of psychology if you take the surface for the truth. Aunt Dru leaned over backward to be fair, because of a terrific sense of guilt—she felt morally obligated to love Edmund and me equally. Only she couldn't. Edmund was always terribly earnest, honest, and yet with an explosive streak that got him into trouble. Surely you haven't forgotten the parable of the prodigal son? The parent—or the parent-substitute—can't resist loving the black sheep."

"She concealed that love, that preference, very well then," Kitty said. "She kept reminding the police of little things about Edmund that they should be interested in." Charles murmured some sort of disagreement to this, but Kitty failed to catch it; her thoughts were taken up suddenly with the memory of Aunt Dru's remark, the idea which had caused Edmund to lash out, to break the lamp in startled confusion. Aunt Dru had thought that there might have been a trap. And again the word ran through Kitty's mind, teasing, frightening.... *A trap*. A trap for whom? Not for Kitty, whose arrival had been an accident. And not ... no, not for Sunny. Sunny had had some scheme, some net spread of her own. The trap had been Sunny's making. And it had gone awry.

"What big eyes you have, Gra'ma," Charles murmured, "and what big, big thoughts are mirrored in them. Just what bolt of lightning has struck your pretty noggin? Tell Uncle Charlie." He was leaning toward her, his face half gay, mocking.

"It seems there must have been something prepared that night, some kind of plot going," she began slowly, "and though I stumbled in upon it, and later Sunny was its victim—it must not have been planned that way at all. When you stop and think, Sunny's death didn't benefit any-one. A lot of people—women, mostly—despised and hated her, but not, I think, bad enough for murder. Whereas, a profit motive—"

She had caught Charles's attention now, definitely. He was sitting quite still.

Kitty went on: "I'd thought until tonight that your aunt was poor. She spoke of the jobs she'd held. But I see now that she's just a cautious, sav-ing, perhaps even stingy little old lady. Or perhaps stingy is a mean word, and I don't intend to be critical. Aunt Dru has money, and if the plot was to be worked against her, it would have a good motive behind it."

"Yes, it would." His voice was a trifle husky. His face had changed a little, grown a little tight, Kitty thought, as though some inner tension had shown through.

"Only, I don't know where Aunt Dru's money would go if anything hap-pened to her. I asked her, but she wouldn't tell me. Do you know?"

He was looking with mock distaste into his drink. "I think this rum has a remarkably poor flavor. I'll mix something new. As for Aunt Dru's money, as I said before, Edmund is her favorite. I imagine she's left it to him."

He got up, claimed Kitty's drink from the table beside her, went off into the kitchen.

But Kitty's logic didn't falter. If someone had been after Aunt Dru's lit-tle fortune—the thirty-thousand dollar home, the seventy-five thousand in cash and securities—it hadn't been Edmund. Not with Sunny. Not plotting and sneaking, covering his actions with a pretense of loyalty and love. Edmund's temper was explosive; he reacted to pressure with violence. He was not the kind of man to plan, to wait, to snare his vic-tim when least expected.

She heard Charles's returning footsteps and in panic stood up. He came and was framed in the doorway, and looked at her across the room. "Oh here—not going? You haven't seen Edmund."

She tried to speak, to get out something coherent. His eyes on hers were light and clear, and yet—at the core—still, watchful. He said, "Sit down again. Drink this."

He knew, and she sensed that he knew. He had somehow read in her face that fearful conviction which illuminated her mind.

CHAPTER TWENTY

She looked down into the glass, the clear green liquid. "You can't let them keep Aunt Dru down there; you must go and make them let her out. Your aunt has done all that she can, even to giving up herself, but it won't help you in the end." Kitty found that, once she managed to start speaking to him, the words came easily. "Your brother and your aunt have protected you, letting guilt fall on themselves. Now you must set them free. Once and for all."

He waited with his own glass poised, in a way that took for granted that they would momentarily drink together. When Kitty didn't drink, he spoke. "You must have had more of the rum than I'd guessed."

She shook her head. "It's all quite clear now. I believe what you said about Aunt Dru, that Edmund was actually the favorite. She is the overly conscientious type and she would see in you defects which she considered of her own making. Defects of coldness and self-interest which she might think she should have seen and rooted out while you were still a child."

"This amateur psychiatry bores me," Charles said.

"Why did you kill Sunny?"

He frowned. It was as if a crack showed in the smooth armor, the unchanging amused sophistication. "Since you insist—drink your drink and I'll tell you."

She looked down again into the clear green glass. There was no odor but the faint dry one of gin, no greasy surface, no hint of grains in the bottom of the drink. She lifted it toward her lips. The cuff of her coat hid the lower part of her face. When she lowered the glass she made a wry mouth.

"Too dry?" he asked solicitously. She set the glass on the table and his eyes studied it.

"It's all right. What about Sunny?"

He smiled a little, as if to himself. "As you may have known—Sunny was quite money-conscious. Mercenary. She liked being loaded with cash, and since she had acquired a rather odd idea that I intended to marry her, she thought it would be nice if I were loaded, too."

Kitty thought, he used her. He played upon her unscrupulous greed.

"The method of disposing of Aunt Dru was Sunny's inspiration. There had been several small incidents which indicated that one of the dogs, Saki, was becoming vicious. I think he may have been sick, perhaps, but anyway he was rapidly becoming bad. Sunny thought we could work out a little plan in which Saki would play the leading part. There would also be some indication that under Saki's attack, Aunt Dru had fallen and struck her head on one of the rough stones in the lane. We had a few rehearsals—" He broke off. He motioned toward Kitty's glass. "Why don't you finish that?"

Again Kitty lifted the glass to her lips. Again she set down the drink with less of the green liquid left in it. "You might be interested to know that Hal DeGraffen saw Sunny driving off one evening, dressed, I suppose, in some of Aunt Dru's clothing."

"Yes, the idea was that she would tease the dog, hurt him, and escape. We were sure that since she was wearing Aunt Dru's garments, he would connect these attacks with her; we even let him get a scarf and tear it to bits, to fix the personal odor in his mind. Somehow, though, it didn't work. When Sunny came that night, bringing the other mutt, which was to take the place of Saki afterward—we couldn't have the police experimenting with him, finding out somehow that he'd been trained to attack my aunt—well, as I said, when Sunny arrived, old Saki went for her. There wasn't a thing I could do. Aunt Dru was supposed to go out to a meeting of some music society or other, some such thing, and she hadn't gone—but I thought we might get her out into the lane on some excuse. There wasn't a chance. The dog tore into Sunny. I'm not much good at a situation like that, you see, having the stiff leg on top of a deep sense of caution. I was snapping my fingers, trying to get the damned dog off her, and then she must have realized what a mauling she was getting, that she'd probably be scarred from it, and she began to mouth threats at me. She was going to tell everybody what I'd done and what the plot had been."

"That's why you killed her with the stone," Kitty said.

"There wasn't anything else to do." He shrugged. "Look, drink the last of that and I'll drive you somewhere. In your car. Up on Mulholland, perhaps, and we can watch the lights of the city."

There was a hint of grogginess in the way Kitty now lifted the glass. She held the glass high, poured the liquor out of it. Her sleeve cuff brushed her face as she took the glass away. He said, "Your chin's wet. Do you want a napkin?"

"I'm ... fine."

"Feeling okay?"

"Go on about Sunny," she commanded.

"What else is there to tell?"

"DeGraffen said that the noise of Sunny's murder, the attack by the dog, must have been audible in here."

"He's crazy. The rain kept it down. Besides, there wasn't a lot of noise. If he was there, spying, and knew what was happening, it might have seemed quite noticeable to him. But someone in here, not aware of what was happening—unnh, unnh."

Kitty saw that Charles was impatient now; he wanted the interview over, wanted her out in her car to be driven away.

"What about Dena Frayne?"

He moved forward in his chair as if to rise. "She was getting money out of Aunt Dru to keep her mouth shut about Sunny's knowing me. Dena was a snoop. And she guessed a lot more than she told—I was afraid that sometime she'd let drop the fact that it might have been my aunt who was really supposed to die in that road down there. I couldn't have that. Nor could I depend on DeGraffen to keep his mouth shut. He'd been spying, following Sunny; he knew too much. He was on the verge of running to the police, too. I had to act fast there."

"Were you really out on that landing when I was in the room with Hal?"

Charles grinned with a wolfish humor. "You'll never know how close you came—" Suddenly he broke off. His eyes were fixed on a point past Kitty's shoulder. She turned. Edmund had come into the room.

"Go on," Edmund said. "I seem to have gotten here in the middle of it. Explain things. You killed DeGraffen because he was going to tell the police something about—what?"

"Go to hell," Charles said thickly. "I don't have to do any explaining to you."

Edmund crossed the room, reached for his brother. Charles put up a hand in a gesture that seemed weak, ineffectual, and then when Edmund was close enough, jabbed two stiffened fingers at Edmund's eyes. But Edmund jerked his head aside, then pulled his brother to his feet. "Talk."

"Your aunt confessed to murdering Sunny Walling and Hal DeGraffen," Kitty said. "The police have her at headquarters."

Edmund's glance swung around, as if he realized her presence there for the first time. Then he saw the glass. "What did he give you to drink?"

Charles's arm moved swiftly; he brought his elbow up in a sharp jerk that was adroit, vicious, aimed for Edmund's chin. But Edmund seemed almost to expect such tactics. He slammed Charles down into the chair again, ran to Kitty. "What have you drunk?"

She pulled her coat aside, revealing the front of her dress, dark and wet. "Nothing. He mixed a drink, but I didn't drink it."

She was never to know why this particular detail, this last frustration, so enraged the other man. Charles came at her like a tiger, leaping straight from the chair like an animal, his body convulsed in the springing movement, his face tightened in a mask of fury. It seemed to Kitty that the moment lasted an eternity; she all but felt in her flesh the impact, the ghost of his hands clawing at her. His maniac's face blew toward her like a balloon-mask in a gale. She tried to scream. Then there was the sound of a smashing blow, and Charles rolled and crumpled on the floor.

Kitty found that she was standing, that there were arms around her. She looked up, expecting to meet Edmund's eyes. But this was Doyle.

Time fled away, and she felt weak and sick. She tried to find Edmund in the dizzying mist. He wasn't far. She saw his cold, set face, the eyes deep-set under the heavy brows, full of thought, remote.

Doyle said carefully, "You'd better sit down until I can attend to Charles." With the air of moving a doll, he put Kitty back upon the couch.

She went up the stairs to her apartment slowly, each foot leaden, the thin carpet harsh under her shoes, the banister splintery. Such a cheap place, she thought; Ardis and I aren't anything here, and when you aren't anybody in Hollywood, you're really at the bottom, much more than you are in other towns. I wonder why I stayed? When it became clear that I wouldn't make the grade as an actress, when I didn't have the courage or the gall or the stripped self-interest to promote myself somehow, I shouldn't have tried to console myself with a job at the University. Being a University secretary isn't anything in a town where everybody else is busy fighting his way up in radio, television, or the movies.

She opened the door and for a minute she was surprised at how warm the room looked, how home-like and full of light. Ardis came out of the kitchen with an apron on. She said, "Good Lord, Kit, you're a ghost. Come sit down. I'll mix a drink. What on earth have you got on your clothes?"

Kitty looked down at the wet things. "A drink. I've got to save it for the police. They took Charles Linder. He did it all." She dragged on past Ardis to her own bedroom, opened the closet to take out a bathrobe, then began to shed her clothes on the floor. Ardis clucked around. She began to tell Kitty about various things that had happened to her since they'd last seen each other. The words ran through Kitty's mind without meaning, except that now and then Doyle's name popped up like a red signal.

She looked into the closet where the white gown glowed, the taffeta full of soft light, and she remembered that Doyle had wanted to see her in it. She took it down and looked it over. He'd be coming for the clothes in a little while, but she had time to bathe and comb her hair and powder her nose.

"What happened to Edmund Linder?" Ardis wondered, picking up the wet garments as Kitty stepped out of them. "Did he bring you home?"

"No."

Ardis shot her a quick, curious glance.

"I don't know how to explain it to you," Kitty said. "All at once I didn't want into the corporation. Charles may have done the killing, but there was knowledge there, guilty knowledge, or Aunt Dru wouldn't have confessed to murder, and Edmund wouldn't have been burying the dog that had turned vicious. They were all in it together. I don't mean equally guilty, but something more subtle...." She stood thoughtful, her eyes on the white gown. "I said I couldn't explain."

"I think I understand," Ardis said warmly.

"Even though Aunt Dru was supposed to be the victim ..." Kitty bit her lip. "Even though the dog got loose from wherever Charles had kept it and attacked her, and she had to defend herself by killing it, in the end— there was just silence. A conspiracy of silence. Charles mustn't be given away to the police. And so it was as if the sickness was somehow a part of all of them—"

Ardis was rolling up the clothing. "Have you time to eat? I guess you'll want a shower first. I've got chops cooking, two lamb chops. What do you want to do?"

All at once Kitty's spirits had lifted. It wasn't bad to be little people, even in Hollywood, when you had friends and a warm home and a job with somebody like Professor Galem. Or even a detective on your trail like Doyle. Kitty said, "I'll shower, then eat."

"You ought to go to bed after that," Ardis worried.

But Kitty wasn't listening. She had taken the white gown from the closet and gone over to the mirror. She put it up in front of herself. The effect wasn't too good. Witch-locks hung about her face, and she was too pale, and there was a fine-drawn look of pain in the flesh around the eyes.

Ardis's voice took on a kind of squeak, as if she thought Kitty might be a little mad. "What are you thinking of?"

If Doyle came in and found her waiting for him with that dress on— there wouldn't be any question. He'd know.

"I'm thinking of a red-headed man," Kitty admitted to the mirror.

THE END

Dolores Hitchens Bibliography
(1907-1973)

Novels:

As by Dolores Hitchens

Jim Sader mysteries
Sleep with Strangers (1955)
Sleep with Slander (1960)

Standalone books:
Stairway to an Empty Room
(1951)
Nets to Catch the Wind (1952;
reprinted as Widows Won't
Wait, 1954)
Terror Lurks in Darkness (1953)
Beat Back the Tide (1954;
abridged as The Fatal Flirt,
1954)
Fool's Gold (1958)
The Watcher (1959)
Footsteps in the Night (1961)
The Abductor (1962)
The Bank with the Bamboo Door
(1965)
The Man Who Cried All the Way
Home (1966)
Postscript to Nightmare (1967;
UK as Cabin of Fear, 1968)
A Collection of Strangers (1969;
UK as Collection of Strangers,
1970)
The Baxter Letters (1971)
In a House Unknown (1973)

As by Bert and Dolores Hitchens

F.O.B. Murder (1955)
One-Way Ticket (1956)
End of the Line (1957)

The Man Who Followed Women
(1959)
The Grudge (1963)

As by D. B. Olsen

Rachel Murdock mysteries
Cat Saw Murder (1939)
Alarm of Black Cat (1942)
Catspaw for Murder (1943;
reprinted as Cat's Claw, 1943)
The Cat Wears a Noose (1944)
Cats Don't Smile (1945)
Cats Don't Need Coffins (1946)
Cats Have Tall Shadows (1948)
The Cat Wears a Mask (1949)
Death Wears Cat's Eyes (1950)
Cat and Capricorn (1951)
The Cat Walk (1953)
Death Walks on Cat Feet (1956)

Prof. A. Pennyfeather mysteries
Shroud for the Bride (1945;
reprinted as Bring the Bride a
Shroud, 1945)
Gallows for the Groom (1947)
Devious Design (1948)
Something About Midnight
(1950)
Love Me in Death (1951)
Enrollment Cancelled (1952;
reprinted as Dead Babes in the
Wood, 1954)

Lt. Stephen Mayhew mysteries
The Clue in the Clay (1938)
Death Cuts a Silhouette (1939)

As by Dolan Birkley

Blue Geranium (1944)
The Unloved (1965)

As by Noel Burke

Shivering Bough (1942)

Short Stories/Magazine Novels:

Stairway to an Empty Room
(*Collier's*, Mar 31, Apr 7, Apr
14, Apr 21, Apr 28 1951)
Strip for Murder (*Mercury
Mystery Magazine*, Oct 1958)
The Watcher (*Cosmopolitan*,
May 1959)
Footsteps in the Dark
(*Cosmopolitan*, Feb 1961)
Abductor! Abductor! Abductor!
(*Cosmopolitan*, July 1961)

The Unloved (*Redbook,* Oct
1965)
If You See This Woman (*Ellery
Queen's Mystery Magazine,* Jan
1966)
Postscript to Nightmare
(*Cosmopolitan*, June 1967)
A Collection of Strangers
(*Redbook*, Sept 1969)
The Baxter Letters (*Star Weekly*,
June 26 1971)
Blueprint for Murder (*Ellery
Queen's Mystery Magazine*, Aug
1973)

Plays:

A Cookie for Henry: one-act play
for six women (1941, as Dolores
Birk Hitchens)

Made in the USA
Columbia, SC
22 December 2019